PRINT

THE

LEGEND

Also by Craig McDonald

Head Games
Toros and Torsos
Art in the Blood
Rogue Males

PRINT
THE
LEGEND

Craig McDonald

Minotaur Books
A Thomas Dunne Book
New York

A THOMAS DUNNE BOOK FOR MINOTAUR BOOKS.
An imprint of St. Martin's Publishing Group.

PRINT THE LEGEND. Copyright © 2010 by Craig McDonald. All rights reserved. Printed in the United States of America. For information, address St. Martin's Press, 175 Fifth Avenue, New York, N.Y. 10010.

www.thomasdunnebooks.com
www.minotaurbooks.com

Book design by Phil Mazzone

Library of Congress Cataloging-in-Publication Data

McDonald, Craig, 1962–
    Print the legend / Craig McDonald.—1st ed.
        p. cm.
    "A Thomas Dunne book."
    ISBN 978-0-312-55437-8
    1. Authors—Fiction.   2. Manuscripts—Fiction.   3. Conspiracy—Fiction.
    4. Hemingway, Ernest, 1899–1961—Fiction.   I. Title.
    PS3613.C38698P75 2010
    813'.6—dc22

                                                    2009039936

First Edition: February 2010

10   9   8   7   6   5   4   3   2   1

This novel is dedicated to
Betty and James McDonald

and once again,
for Debbie McDonald

There are never any . . . successful suicides.

—ERNEST HEMINGWAY

PRINT
THE
LEGEND

July 2, 1961

He rose with the sun as he had every morning since childhood.

It was Sunday, and the old man was alone in the house with his wife, Mary.

George, his ex-boxer pal, was in the cinder-block guest quarters next door. He trusted his damaged memory on that much.

The old man shrugged on his "Emperor's robe," which draped his wasted frame like a red circus tent. He hardly recognized his own face in the bathroom mirror—his wispy, white, flyaway hair was going every which way, and his smile back at himself was something terrible to behold. Passionate brown eyes each of four wives praised as his best feature were now as empty and dead as those of the trophy heads gathering dust at his abandoned Cuban Finca.

He reached for his toothbrush with a trembling hand, then thought better of it: Perhaps the funk of morning mouth would mask the taste of the oiled barrels of the shotgun.

Mary had locked his guns away from him in the storeroom. She left the key to their hiding place resting on the ledge over the kitchen sink. He had seen the key there last night—as she had perhaps intended . . . left the key just sitting there on their first night back from the Mayo Clinic. The old man's rattled brain kept wondering at Mary's reason for hiding the key in plain sight.

A taunt, or invitation?

A characteristic half-assed kindness?

He snorted at the mystery of his last wife's motive for making what he was about to do possible, and, grimacing, tiptoed down the stairs to the storeroom.

The old man selected a silver-inlaid, 12–gauge double-barreled Boss bought years before at Abercrombie & Fitch. He broke open his carefully cared-for shotgun and cradled it in the crook of his left arm. He pulled open a drawer and selected a box of shells. The old man's hands trembled so badly he couldn't draw any from the container. Disgusted, he emptied the shells into the drawer and scooped a handful in a fast reach for his robe's puckering pocket. Two cartridges—more than enough to do the job—fell true; the rest pinged as they hit the floor and rolled to the four corners.

The self-declared "former writer" would normally be deep into his morning's composition at this early hour, but that was in another country, the old man thought bitterly, and his muse was at last dead.

He trudged back up the stairs, lugging the big English-made gun. He thought of his father, making a similar last climb up a flight of stairs, intent upon effecting a bloody escape from his own intolerable half-life. He now had the answer to the question he had posed so many years before, in a story inspired by his father: "Is dying hard, Daddy?"

He knew now how easy it could be, denied your desires and the things you are driven, for better or worse, to do.

He crossed the living room to the foyer directly under Mary's bedroom, pausing to stare out the window at the cloudless sky and rising July sun glistening on the ripples where the rocks lay thickest on the bed of the Wood River from which two deer now drank.

Gnats sported in the rapid's spray in easy reach of the trout that gorged on them.

Chipmunks darted through the dew-kissed grass, unaware of the old man's stalking cats.

Bald buzzards wheeled on the rising vapors.

It would be a good morning for others to hunt or hike or go fishing.

As he turned, he was startled by a reflection in the mirror on the wall—thought he saw a familiar, hated face peering through the window. He whispered distractedly, "Creedy? Creedy, is that you?" He turned but there was no one at the window. He shook his head: What did it matter if he *was* out there? He was so tired of looking over his shoulder. *So tired . . .*

Seppuku by shotgun: If he could wait nineteen days, he could celebrate his sixty-second birthday.

The old man's trembling hand rooted the pocket of his robe for the first shotgun shell. His heart beat faster. Robbed of his own words, he resorted to those of another to whom he had once been improbably compared. He muttered the favorite quote over and over to himself:

A man can die but once. . . . he that dies this year is quit for the next.

August 1961

Fidel Castro stood behind the Finca Vigía, Hemingway's Cuban "Lookout Farm," watching the Widow Hemingway fussing over the boxes, stuffed with her husband's papers and manuscripts, that she had traded the house and nearly all of its possessions to "liberate."

The young Irish woman with the widow had started a fire below the tennis court, and some of the papers—just selected letters and old magazines, Mrs. Hemingway insisted—were being burned.

What a strange little woman this widow was.

Castro tried to reconcile Mary Hemingway with the sense of the man and writer he had gotten from reading *For Whom the Bell Tolls*—one of the books that had actually guided him in the guerilla warfare he had so successfully waged against Batista—and, much later, with the old but boisterous man he'd met at Hemingway's fishing tournament.

Mary Hemingway struck Castro as a bizarre, poorly chosen woman for the great Papa.

Sensing motion behind him, Castro turned. Smiling at the foreigner, Castro fired up a fresh cigar. He gestured with his cigar at the little blond woman bustling around, supervising the loading of the precious boxes; directing the burning of her husband's papers. "I suppose you have plans for those containers, too, eh, comrade?"

The man, this "Creedy," smiled and said, "In time, certainly, *Jefe*. Papa loved your country very much. It's important his readers see some of his writings in those boxes, so they, too, can see how much Papa loved Cuba.

Particularly how much he thought of you, *Jefe*." Inside, Creedy was cursing himself. If he'd only gotten here *sooner*—gotten first access to all these manuscripts squirreled away in various Cuban safe-deposit boxes.

Castro grinned and hefted the ornate shotgun Mary had given him. He said, "She is nice, *si*?"

Creedy didn't really know guns—not his weapons of choice. Winking, Creedy accepted a cigar. He leaned in for a light from one of Castro's lice-ridden stooges. It grated to have to be deferential to this son of a rich plantation owner now playing the role of revolutionary, but Creedy managed a short, "It's swell, *Jefe*."

Standing on the tarmac of the Miami Airport, Creedy wiped fresh sweat from his forehead. Like Cuba, south Florida was sweltering. Creedy cursed and waved his men away.

Airports were a vexed fixture in his life: More gambits and schemes had been saved by a hasty flight out of some theater of operation or blown to pieces on tarmacs, runways, and concourses than he cared to count. Seemed he was forever checking mirrors and over his shoulder every time he crossed a frontier, his stomach in knots; always waiting for some ticket taker to say, "So sorry, Mr. Creedy, but there seems to be a problem. . . ."

And how many running from him had Creedy managed to ensnare at passport desks and ticket counters? Dozens, at least. There'd be dozens more, he was sure.

This time, the system was working against Creedy, threatening to slide this gambit over into his airports-of-the-world loss tally.

Creedy had hoped to get some time alone with the Hemingway manuscript boxes when they reached Miami, but the indomitable little widow was standing guard over them like some goddamn bottle-blond sentry, ordering around airport staff and staying constantly in sight of the precious containers as they were loaded in the plane's cargo hold.

Mary might have unwittingly beaten him in Cuba, and beaten him in Miami, but if that toad Hoover back in D.C. went for Creedy's pitch, he figured he'd yet carry the day. After all, what was this boozy widow really, when ranged against a man of his talents and dark imagination?

The Topping House was bound in the season's first mountain snow.

In the storeroom of the Idaho house where Papa had found the shotgun that killed him, Mary stared at the boxes and shopping bags full of priceless manuscripts arrayed around her.

She fingered the key to the storeroom, now worn on a chain around her neck where it would always be safe. Mary looked around at the small room—its locks fortified at a time when she was still trying to keep her suicidal husband from his guns.

It was a good and safe place.

Mary turned her attention back to the manuscripts, thinking of the enormous job and responsibility before her. Knuckling down to the grand task, the thought made her smile—she'd been preparing for this for *years*.

BOOK ONE

To Have and Have Not

(Idaho, 1965)

God knows people who are paid to have attitudes toward things, professional critics, make me sick; camp following eunuchs of literature. They won't even whore. They're all virtuous and sterile. And how well meaning and high-minded. But they're all camp followers.

—ERNEST HEMINGWAY

1. HANNAH

"The house where he died. Call it the scene of the crime."

The scholar and his pregnant, newlywed Scottish wife walked along the berm, spooking some crows pecking at the bloated carcass of a black dog killed crossing U.S. Highway 75.

The scavengers scattered in a flurry of wings and reeling shadows and high-pitched shrieks, beaks dangling remnants of rotting flesh and pelt matted with dried blood. The big blue-black crows came to roost on a wire, cawing and flapping their wings at the academic and his bride peering at the house.

Richard Paulson pointed at the brown house with the three green garage doors. The home that was once known as the Topping House was surrounded by pines, and fronted one bare, cloud-shadowed hill and another dense with pine trees.

"It's attractive," Hannah Paulson said, her voice a husky burr. She pushed her sunglasses back on her head. "Seems right for him. Rugged and handsome; built from the materials at hand."

Richard shook his head at his wife's assessment. "From here it looks good enough, sure. By all accounts, it's something else up close."

Hem's house, which looked like alpine wood construction, was actually fabricated from poured concrete, stained brown and molded to resemble timber. They were the same construction techniques used at the Sun Valley Lodge, where the Paulsons had had lunch. One of Hem's sons, Gregory, bitterly described the concrete house as a fortification fit for the paranoid man Greg's father had allegedly been at the end.

Hem's last wife, Mary, declared the house "depressing" shortly before she and Hem moved in during an October day in 1959.

"They say Mary will be moving soon," Richard said. "Mary's lived here on and off since the day he died. Aaron says she may move to New York. Word is she's mostly drunk these days. She talks of leaving the property to the Nature Conservancy. The home and fourteen acres of surrounding ground would be declared a preserve in Papa's name if Mary did that."

Hannah stroked her blond hair behind her ears and wrinkled her nose. "How can Mary stand to live there after . . . ? To have to step over the spot where he blew his brains out every time she passes through that entryway? It's unthinkable."

"For you, sure. You're using yourself as a yardstick for Mary. The two of you are nothing alike."

Richard squeezed his wife's hand, the two small diamonds in Hannah's wedding band and ring—the fourth pair of bands he had bought in his life—digging into his palm in a freshly unfamiliar way. "I just can't believe anybody before me hasn't seen it the way it must have been," Richard said. "I can't believe it took me so long to see it truly."

"And how exactly was it, Richard? You've been cagey about all of this. What's your scheme? Ready at last to share?"

Richard fingered the vial in his pocket—the mysterious drug given him by *that man.* He hated to throw in with their lot. Every scrap of his spirit and intellect rebelled against it. Still, in the service of a righteous cause . . .

This time, at least, Richard was on the side of the angels. He was sure of that. The ends, he comforted himself again, more than justified these dark means.

He said, "The famous suicide is nothing but a myth, Hannah. I know it. I think the old bitch killed her husband. I think Mary murdered poor sick Papa. Blew the ailing son of a bitch away with his own shotgun."

EXCERPT FROM THE FOURTH ANNUAL SUN VALLEY
HEMINGWAY CONFERENCE PROGRAM

Keynote Speaker: Hector Mason Lassiter (1900–)
Biography: Noted screenwriter and crime novelist Hector Lassiter,

popularly regarded as "the man who lives what he writes and writes what he lives," is by most measures also now recognized as "the last man standing of the Lost Generation."

As a novelist, Hector Lassiter represents a kind of vanishing breed of martial men skilled in American letters—an author of the sort typified by Ernest Hemingway. It is Mr. Lassiter's long and storied association with Hemingway that uniquely qualifies him to keynote our fourth annual Hemingway conference here among the Sawtooth Mountains.

Hector Lassiter and Hemingway met while serving as ambulance drivers along the Italian front. Hemingway soon followed Lassiter to Paris, where the expatriate fiction writers honed their mutually iconic, distinctive, much lauded, and laconic prose styles.

Later, Papa followed Lassiter to Key West, where they weathered the Great Depression, writing, fishing, and allegedly rescuing Cuban refugees between novels, nonfiction books, and screenplays.

They also shared the early days of the Spanish Civil War, and both men ran afoul of military authorities during the Second World War for allegedly stepping outside their proscribed roles as war correspondents and actually organizing their own guerilla units—

———

Asking a working writer what he thinks about critics is like asking a lamp-post what it feels about dogs.

—CHRISTOPHER HAMPTON

2.   HECTOR

"Just five minutes, Mr. Lassiter. That's all I'm asking."

"All of you want just five minutes," Hector said.

She frowned. "All of us?"

"You're not the first, sweetie." Hector sipped his Glenmorangie and ground out the stub of his cigarette. "How many of you 'academics' would you say are here in Sun Valley for this Hemingway conference?"

She shrugged. "Maybe two hundred?"

"And now I think I've been approached by every single one of them," Hector said. "What's your name, honey?"

"Rebecca. Rebecca Stewart."

Rebecca was twenty-three, maybe twenty-four. Her blond hair was piled high in a beehive that looked like it could stop a bullet. Her blue eyes didn't quite track. "At first I thought maybe you were that actor. You know—William Holden? Then I looked again and checked against the photo in the conference booklet. That's how I recognized you." She smiled, flirting a little: "Hector Lassiter—the last of the great *Black Mask* writers. The 'last man standing of the Lost Generation.' The handsome novelist, screenwriter, and adventurer. The 'man who lives what he writes and writes what he lives.' You're almost as famous as Papa, Mr. Lassiter."

Hector managed a smile; that last dug at him in myriad ways. "Lucky me. You're by far the prettiest Hemingway egghead to intrude on my writing, Becky. As it is, however, I'm not granting interviews. Not even to a pretty young woman like yourself."

A pout: "But you're the only one left who really knew Papa, all the way back to the old days, to Paris and Italy. They say you're the only one Mrs. Hemingway is seeing." Her off-kilter eyes grew wide. "You're the keynote speaker!"

In the old days, Hector was indeed popularly called "the man who lives what he writes and writes what he lives." That was a collar Anthony Boucher had hung on Hector in the early 1930s that stuck and chafed because it hit far too close to home.

Hector couldn't deny he viewed the stuff of his life as grist for his fiction—a tendency that had only deepened and grown more complex with time. That made covering old ground and recalling memories not just tedious for Hector, but potentially damaging to his work—exposing too much of the skeletal structure underpinning his fictional output.

And Hector liked to stay fresh: Vapid and harebrained as much of their talk was, he was much more interested in listening to these so-called scholars and young intellectuals. He was more interested in tapping *them* for his fiction than mining his own memories to support their ephemeral scholarship.

Hector shook loose another Pall Mall. He hesitated, his Zippo spitting blue flame. "That's right, honey," he said. "I agreed to talk *at* all of you at once, not *with* each of you, one on one. Though you'd certainly be the one if I inclined that way. But I don't. Sorry, honey."

"But Mr. Lassiter, you were there."

"Tell you what, Becky: Come to my 'keynote speech.' I'll try my best to make it feel like you were there, too. All of you."

Hector gathered up the papers set before him and put them back in their file folder. He stared at the folder: this sleeve of paper that had come to dominate his thoughts these past several days, plowing down everything in its path like a rolling boulder.

The manuscript inside was the real reason he'd come to Idaho.

A few weeks ago, a rather breathless rare bookseller had contacted Hector. He said he'd come across an old manuscript of Hector's dating back to the early 1920s. The bookseller was eager for more information on his amazing find—hungry for more "about the holograph's antecedents" so he could stick some damned collector for those extra precious dollars.

As the bookseller described the short story, Hector had gone cold all over. He remembered the piece well enough.

He had also long ago reconciled himself to its loss.

Hector had given the handwritten draft along with several other precious writings to Hemingway to read, ages ago, in Paris. The folder had gotten mixed up with Hem's own manuscripts—packed by Hem's first wife, Hadley—and then lost forever when the suitcase with Hem's writings inside was left briefly unattended by Hadley in the Gare de Lyon rail station in 1922.

The loss of Ernest's manuscripts had driven a wedge between Hem and Hadley that had doomed their marriage. Years later, Hadley was still apologizing to Hector for the theft of his works along with her husband's.

When the short story that couldn't possibly exist suddenly turned up a few weeks ago—passing from one greasy hand to another on the underground market—Hector was left reeling.

At first he wondered if Hem had lied about the suitcase's loss so long ago. Hem always had a tendency to embellish, embroider . . . to tell outrageous stories on himself and others. In the old days, Hector had forgiven these tendencies in Hem where he might not have in another. After all,

Hem was a fellow fiction writer, and that often made the lines between the world and the page . . . blurry. Hector had also read much of Ernest's allegedly stolen output: it wasn't top-shelf Hemingway by any stretch. But the myth of having all that prose stolen? Well, it was a nice, tragic element in a young author's biography. Something sexy for the publicists and eventual biographers. A thing to bolster an author's long game.

Still, in the end, Hector couldn't believe Hem would go *that* far.

Then Hector began to wonder if Hadley Hemingway was the liar.

He tracked Hadley down to her home in wooded, mountainous Chocorua, New Hampshire, where she now lived with her second husband—a retired journalist turned poet. Hector spent half an hour on the phone with "Hash," as he affectionately called her during the old days in Paris. The ex–first Mrs. Hemingway had convinced Hector the suitcase had been stolen from her, just as she'd said so many decades before. She even cried again, the hurt now every bit as lacerating to her as it had been back then.

Hadley apologized to Hector, over and over, for losing his works forty-three years earlier. Hector hung up after repeatedly forgiving her; hating himself for opening the wounds.

If Hem and Hadley hadn't lied, then some third party was involved, and the prospect existed that Hector's other lost works—and Hem's—were maybe yet recoverable.

Hector's attempts to trace the manuscript through the rare bookseller had stalled out—the transaction had been handled through cutouts. That, too, was strange.

Still, there *had* to be a way. . . .

Shaking his head, Hector looked at Becky, the Hemingway professor. Here was a so-called Hemingway expert, yet she could bring nothing useful to the table in terms of helping him with his current Papa-centered problem.

He smiled to himself: If he granted her access to even a fraction of his current thoughts, he'd probably send poor Becky into a Hemingway professor's version of an apoplexy. He drained his drink. Hector closed his notebook and capped his pen. He patted the back of the young academic's hand. "You should forget this stuff about studying and writing about dead writers' writing, Becky. I know Hem looms large—largest of us all,

I reckon—but stop chasing ghosts. Stop fretting over the writings of others. Go and write your own novel."

"Becky" looked aghast: "Oh no, I couldn't do that."

Hector smiled, his brow furrowed. "Why the hell not?"

"Haven't you heard, Mr. Lassiter? The novel is dead."

A literary movement consists of five or six people who live in the same town and hate each other cordially.

—George Moore

CREEDY—Paris, France, 1922

Donovan Creedy sat in his chair with his hands thrust deep into the pockets of his overcoat, his gaunt face shadowed by the brim of his homburg. He ground his teeth, watching the boisterous American writers at the table next to the flickering brazier. All them had supposedly come to Paris to write and experience life in ways that America was too rigid to let them attempt back home. Yet, for their kind, it was really just a long drunken party . . . time wasted laughing and drinking too much. Dissolute dilettantes, all of them.

Across the table, the girl was saying something to Creedy. He had realized early in life that if one had ambitions in a situation, there were few things better than to control the attention of an attractive woman. The all-purpose prop. So he turned, awarding her the eye contact that would serve to indicate he was listening attentively to the latter half of whatever thought she was struggling to frame in her heavily accented, sometimes uncertain English.

"The nineteenth-century version of the novel is dead."

Wanting to keep studying the men at the table, Creedy felt his anger rise and he turned fully toward the woman.

"More Hemingway crap." Under his breath, he said again, "Hemingway." Watching the men at the table out of the corner of his eye, wanting to direct his comments at them—and the more so because it scared him to do it—he said to the woman, "I'm so sick of hearing about how he's going to be the one to reinvent our language. I'm sick of all this tripe about Hemingway being an undiscovered genius and Paris's best-kept secret." Creedy lifted his hat and ran his palm back across his slicked-back, blue-black hair and pulled the brim low again.

Simone, a struggling poet with a pretty, kind face—a young woman who in the relative poverty of post–World War I Paris had been trailing puppyishly after Creedy since Thanksgiving, drawn to him by his nice clothes, slender, tall body, aristocratic, aquiline features, and penetrating dark eyes—shrugged and said, "Everyone says it is so, Don—that Hem's a genius. They say it's only a matter of time for him. I've read a few of Ernest's small pieces and poems in the little magazines. There is something there, I think. He's a modernist. Hem's ideas about writing, and particularly about concision, are . . . interesting. Perhaps valid."

Creedy shook his head. He had selected this girl because of her affinity and propensity for just such sentiments, but he was beginning to think it was too much—the price too damned high. Should he cut her off completely, get rid of her somehow without running the risk that she would still be around, talking him down to the others of this perverse social set? He said, "And look at Pound there with that crazy hair of his and cheap suit. The so-called great poet. Actually giving time to these fools. When do they find the time to write between drinking and hanging around cafés? And Christ's sake—Hem's shabby suit jackets worn over old sweatshirts . . . Fucking Hemingway looks like some kind of anarchist. He needs a haircut." Creedy chewed his lip and said, "At least Pound has the right notion about the damned Jew menace."

Simone thought then that Donovan Creedy must have forgotten her last name. Maybe he thought it was German. She sipped her brandy and rested her head on her hand. "Have you ever talked to Hem?"

Creedy had. Once.

Hemingway had been with more of the Left Bank's alleged up-and-comers that night last summer. Among them was the rather well-dressed, good-looking and tall man now sitting between Hemingway and Ezra Pound. They had all rebuffed him that sultry night—Hemingway making harsh jokes at Creedy's expense in just the two or three minutes he'd stood in their scornful presence.

They'd all been drunk, of course. The good-looking man had been with some pretty tart. Drunken degenerates, that's what they were, these modernist American writers.

Creedy sipped his wine and shook his head. "No," he said, "I've never tried to talk to Hemingway. I don't need to do that to recognize him for the poseur and braggart he is."

He held some wine in his mouth, letting it numb his tongue and front teeth. Creedy said finally, "The man with Hemingway—the one with the dark hair and blue eyes . . . the leather jacket and brown fedora. Who is he, exactly?"

"Hector Lassiter," Simone said. "Another star-in-the-making, to hear Gertrude tell it. Texan. He's often in her salon, and one of her darlings." She looked around the café, then, sotto voce, Simone said, "Despite their pledge to work only to elevate and invigorate American letters, they say Hector secretly writes crime stories for the pulp magazines back in the States. That's where he gets his money for the clothes and fine restaurants. He supposedly writes for something called *Black Mask*. Isn't that wild?"

Thinking to perhaps make Donovan jealous, Simone said, "Hector's actually quite charming and a fine writer. The women of the Quarter all love him."

Creedy ground his teeth, staring at Hemingway and this other one called Lassiter.

Days later, Creedy sat in the back of the café, dressed in a crisply pressed black suit and tie, writing furiously in his notebook while other expatriate writers and poets—slovenly, sloppy drunk—danced and joked and frittered away precious time, abusing their livers.

Rummy rubbish—that's what Creedy thought of them. And so many Jews from back home crowding the Left Bank; dominating the little magazines that wouldn't accept his work. It lately seemed the whole Paris literary scene was run by the Jews. Creedy thought of Gertrude Stein and the single night she'd allowed him to stand in her vaunted presence. Squatting in her throne, leaning forward so her fat arms rested on her thick thighs, Stein had looked at him with her dark Jew eyes and said, "We've read your story you left for us, Mr. Creedy."

Eager, eyes shining: The moment seemed to drag on for an eternity.

He briefly faltered, unable to meet Stein's penetrating, unblinking gaze. Glancing away, he wondered whether she could see something inside him—something about himself he'd not have this crowd know about him. Creedy didn't really love their work—hell, Stein's stuff was nonsensical and childlike—but he'd heard positive attention from them, from *her*, would almost certainly get him published. In preparation for meeting Stein, he'd read an essay on the moderns by Edmund Wilson, and he struggled to remember some of the piece's points to parrot back at Stein.

Creedy figured if he was already in their presence, he might as well espouse their beliefs . . . talk to them in the sorry shibboleths of their own literary language. But the article had bored him, and Creedy had begun to skim. Now, when he needed the stuff to drawn on, his memory failed him and he drew a blank. He felt his own sweat at his armpits and collar. As Stein stared at him, the voluminous sentence he'd hoped to dazzle them with reduced itself to a single choked word. Creedy said, "And?"

Stein had raised a hand, annoyed he had interrupted her in midpronouncement. She said, "People ask for criticism, but they only want praise. So, I will say nothing, Mr. Creedy, and you may take that any way you choose." As he stood there, trying to think of something to say that would cut deeply into Stein and her crowd of sycophants, she turned her attention to that other, *Lassiter*.

Many weeks had passed since that confrontation. Many pages of his notebooks had been filled with new prose, yet Stein's few words haunted him.

Now a shadow fell across Creedy's notebook, shaking him free of his bitter memory of Gertrude Stein's slight. Creedy looked up: It was a tallish man, dressed in black and about fifty. An American, judging by the cut of his suit.

Not waiting to be asked to sit down, the stranger pulled out a chair and threw his black overcoat across its back. He settled in and lit a cigarette with a match he struck off a polished thumbnail. He said, "Donovan Creedy: I have an opportunity for you. A rare privilege."

The man didn't look like a writer. He also didn't look like any of the publishers of little magazines crowding the Left Bank. Another writer had recently told Creedy of some "publisher" who was charging authors fees to publish their work in low-run "vanity press" formats. Maybe this man was one of those. Creedy turned his head on its side, said, "Who the hell are you?"

"Let's just say I was in that café, sitting behind you a few nights ago when you were talking to your pretty French friend. I heard what you said about Hemingway. About Pound. I think we can help one another."

"Who are you?"

"My name is Wilson Kurtz. I work for an organization back home. A man in our organization—a man named Hoover—is concerned about what effect much of the poetry, painting, and writing being done here by American expatriates, and increasingly finding its way back home, might have on the moral condition of our country—particularly on our youth."

Creedy was inclined to agree, but warily said, "This Hoover—he's some kind of preacher? This organization some kind of church?" If so, Creedy had no patience for the man and prepared to dismiss him. Creedy had dispensed with God as a child, before his family came to America—too many unanswered prayers and myriad wishes not granted; pleas for vengeance against despised rivals ignored. You made your own luck; exacted your own revenge. The world belonged to self-possessed, self-made men.

Kurtz blew smoke in Creedy's face and, smiling, said, "Hardly that. Mr. Hoover was originally in charge of the Enemy Aliens Registration Section. He recently joined the Bureau of Investigation as deputy head. Mr. Hoover's a brilliant, visionary man. He's a comer. And he's fiercely committed to seeing all this bohemian loose living and degeneracy does not find its way back home via 'art' produced in this filthy Gomorrah."

Creedy gave the man another hard look, trying to decide if he was authentic. Maybe Hemingway and Lassiter were having him on—had set this man up as another of their ceaseless barroom pranks. "I'm not sure I understand," Creedy said.

"You will. Unlike the lazy dreamers who populate these cafés, we don't talk. We act. We have a first task for you—a kind of test. And I think, by the way, it's something you're going to savor. This Hemingway—we've been watching him for a time. Particularly the fact that he's a journalist, and publishing romanticized articles about all this dreck"—Kurtz waved his hand as if to indicate and indict the entire Left Bank—"makes him doubly dangerous."

Kurtz handed Creedy a cigarette—custom-made from the looks of the distinctive three gold bands at one end—and lit him up with another thumbnail-struck match. The expensive, exotic tobacco gave Creedy a head rush.

"I've come into possession of some secret knowledge," Kurtz said. "Knowledge that lends itself to the performance of a certain type of task. For a certain kind of man."

The stranger leaned in confidentially. "In a few hours, Mrs. Hadley Hemingway is going to board a night train at Gare de Lyon station. She'll be carrying a valise filled with her husband's extant fiction. If you could fit it into your schedule to be on that train and perform a certain duty, for now, let's just say that Mr. Hoover would be very grateful."

Kurtz sat back and blew smoke rings at the ceiling. "It's a lucky thing, you know, having Mr. Hoover grateful to you, I mean."

One learns little more about a man from his feats of literary memory than from the feats of his alimentary canal.

—FRANK MOORE COLBY

3.   THE SCHOLAR

Hannah looked up from her notebook at the rather rustic, macho mountain restaurant in which they were eating. In her short story, she was writing about Scotland—the village of Glencoe. Hemingway always said it was necessary to be away from a place to *really* write about it.

So where would Hannah go in order to write about Idaho? Maybe some café in Paris? The romance of that setting for a writing session certainly appealed to her . . . the culture . . . the fine wines. The wine . . .

Hannah watched Richard savoring *his* wine.

She had been one of Richard Paulson's best students—he'd told her that, and Hannah didn't think he was just paying lip service to the fact.

For whatever reason, Richard had focused attention on Hannah. Maybe at first it had been her Scots accent—those juicy *r*'s everyone called adorable. Either way, from that point on, Hannah hadn't just attended Richard's lectures, she'd been privy to the research upon which they were constructed.

As a lecturer, Richard was partial to audiovisual support. Sitting in the dark next to everyone else, one of forty or fifty invisible faces watching with rapt attention, Hannah had studied Richard's face in the light of the small lamp set above his lectern as he delivered lectures he had tested on Hannah earlier, making his points as images of Hemingway and his wives and various houses flickered on the screen at the professor's back.

And now, here she was, actually in Hemingway's Idaho, in his favorite restaurant and perhaps sitting in a chair Papa had sat in many times himself. Living in a slide, so to speak.

As a child, an avid reader, Hannah had believed books just existed somehow . . . came into the world whole. When she'd learned they were written by men and women, little Hannah envisioned some exotic or special race of storytellers.

Exposure to Richard, and academia in general, had demystified much of that—reduced her sense of wonder and left her feeling a bit bitter for the wisdom.

She remembered the night it started: that invitation by Richard for a coffee that had stretched into a bottle of wine; a romance and marriage. And somewhere along the way, she had crossed some other line and lost even more wonder for the writing life. At least as it was embodied by Richard. He made the literary world seem somehow smaller, less romantic.

Hannah considered her husband across the table. He was browsing over the Hemingway conference program. He had his pen out and was making occasional notes across the faces of the other scholars depicted there, writing things like "asshole" or "faker."

Maybe, in the end, professors were really just hucksters. You might pick up some wisdom from them here and there, but they literally extracted a fee for their lessons, all the while warping writers' words and works through their own tunnel-vision prisms that could be scaled down to enticing course-catalog listings or monograph titles. Many writers hated critics and academics, and now Hannah understood all that a little better. Critics, it now seemed to Hannah, too often looked at everything but the passion inherent in a good piece of writing; those critics intellectualized it all and sucked it dry of life.

But for all the "academic" things Hannah now knew about Hemingway and his works, Papa still loomed large, and although she knew no room in which he once sat could make her a better writer or grant her a wonderful opening line, the thought that Papa might have drawn inspiration from these very surroundings excited Hannah to the possibility it might do the same for her.

She realized, then, that she had stopped writing some time ago. Hannah closed the blue notebook containing the short story she had struggled all morning to shape, and sipped her ice water. She contemplated the restaurant's cathedral ceiling from their corner table. The ceiling was pitched like most of the roofs in town—sharply slanted to shed the snows that made the Sun Valley portion of the Sawtooth Mountains a skiers' destination from the day of its Papa-assisted launch in the mid-1930s.

Richard topped off his glass of wine though it was still two-thirds full.

"Looks more like a church than a club," Hannah said, frowning as Richard freshened his drink. "So this is where the self-condemned man ate his last meal?"

Hannah stared back at a thin, tall man in a blue blazer who had been stealing glances at their table for the past hour.

Richard chewed his porterhouse steak, oblivious to Hannah's growing preoccupation with the stranger on the other side of the restaurant—a man who, she was increasingly certain, was watching them.

Richard shook his head. "'Self-condemned?'" He sighed. "I told you how I think it was." He poured himself more red wine, the house cabernet, from the carafe at his elbow. "But, yeah, he ate here with Mary at that small table in the southwest corner there, his table, on July first. The night before the shooting."

"What did Papa eat?"

His fork hung in the air. Richard scowled and sat back, his brow furrowed. "Jesus Christ. You know: I don't know. Nobody has ever gotten around to reporting that so far as I know."

Well, *at last*! She'd found something in Hem's biography that had eluded the academics with all their digging and amateur psychoanalysis. Hannah would never deign to compare herself to Hemingway, but wouldn't it take another fiction writer to find it?

Richard pulled his hand away and scratched the back of his neck. "Gotta think one of us has gotten round to looking into that. Just because I don't know it, doesn't mean someone else doesn't."

It was a remarkable statement, coming from Prof. Richard Paulson—the twice-awarded Hemingway scholar.

Hannah stirred her food with her fork. She was afraid that Richard's rare instant of self-effacement was fired by wine. She said: "Oh, aye, rob me of my discovery." Then she shook her head. "No, I'm first to this, Richard. It's too obvious a question to have ever occurred to the scholars."

Richard shrugged and smiled.

Hannah smiled back and squeezed his hand. "Could be a fine doctoral thesis: 'From Aperitif to After-Dinner Mint—Papa's Last Meal as a Paradigm for *Une Génération Perdue*.' That'd do as a working title, eh?" Hannah deepened her voice: "The condemned man made a hearty meal of ..."

Richard half-smiled, raising his glass and trying to steer conversation back to his own track. "May have something there. Work Papa's dinner order up into some trippy Marxist diatribe and stir in some *Waste Land* imagery, and we might peddle the thing to Barbara and that other menopausal bitch at Northeastern."

He winked and nodded at someone passing behind Hannah. She turned, but only caught sight of the person's back: short, fat, crammed into a too-small black suit. Stringy hair just touched hunched and dandruff-dusted shoulders. Richard had already turned his back to the stranger.

Hannah said, "Who was she?"

"He," Richard corrected. "Berle—another academic." Richard shrugged. "But more academic than most. Pathetic, really—never has contributed a thing of worth to Hemingway scholarship."

Now Richard raised the nearly depleted carafe, holding it at a slight angle over Hannah's unused goblet. "Sure you won't have a little, sweetheart? Finish it off?"

"I'm certain, Richard." Hannah bit her lip. Dear God, how could he put that question to her when she was so adamant about not drinking while pregnant? Then she remembered, and shivered a little: It wasn't the first time he'd tried to entice her into a drink in her present condition.

Lamenting it was "no fun"—even "dangerous to drink alone," Richard had tried to get Hannah to drink with him in "celebration" the night she'd told him she was pregnant. He'd said something about the liquor helping to keep the baby's birth weight down in case she "wasn't big enough down there."

She'd made a joke about that assertion reminding her of his hero—of Papa's strange obsession with recording his wives' monthly cycles in a journal; even resorting in correspondence to having his publisher mediate frictions spinning out of his third wife's secretive gynecological issues—her resulting barren condition first confided to Hem's publisher rather than to Ernest himself.

When Richard didn't put away the wine, the joke had turned to a remark about him aping Hemingway—even in this odd way—and she soon enough saw Richard found no humor in her gentle barb.

Hannah stared at her plate, stirring the food around there some more, not hungry at all.

She wondered if maybe he was kidding this time, but the carafe was still there in his hand, hanging above her empty glass. "Seriously," she said, "I don't want any. Maybe you should take it easy, too."

In the early days of their romance, Richard had been courtly, charming . . . reasonably fit. In the past few months, he'd put on nearly as many pounds as Hannah, edging into a build that recalled circa-1950s Hemingway—this formidable drinker's gut that strained his shirt buttons.

And where had Richard found that white, Hemingwayesque guayabera shirt he was wearing now? Apart from being inappropriate garb for the region and the restaurant, it was also months out of season. Richard used to be more in the tweedy academic mold—English herringbone jackets with leather patches at the elbows and a necktie. Now Richard was sporting the very Hemingway-inspired slovenly togs he had once mocked other Papa scholars for affecting.

Looking away from the carafe hefted in Richard's hand, Hannah stirred her food around more with her fork. Then there was Richard's increasingly surly demeanor. Pressed, he would probably cite Hemingway there, too, but it was something else, drawn from some set of deep-seated problems all Richard's own. And it *was* getting worse, wasn't it? Hannah remembered it starting almost from the night he'd learned he'd be a father again. But it seemed to be growing more acidic as they drew closer to Idaho and Richard's long-planned rendezvous with Mary Hemingway.

Richard smiled and emptied the dregs into his own glass. "'Every man should eat and drink, and enjoy the good of all his labor.'"

Hannah said, "That from something of Papa's?"

"The Bible. At least I think so." Richard stared up at the ceiling. "I wonder what Hem did order that last night?" As he said it, Richard caught himself trying to sip from an empty glass.

Hannah halfheartedly smiled, reluctantly following his lead. "May actually bear research, eh? Little something for your fall quarter class to impress the next undergraduate you seduce, make pregnant, marry, and neglect?"

Across the room, the party seated at the Hemingway table got up to leave. Hannah noticed Richard was no longer paying attention to her; instead, Richard's gaze was locked on the vacated seats. He had both his arms in the air, waving down their waitress. As the woman approached, he pointed to Papa's favored table and said, "There's a draft here. Can we move to that one?"

Palms pressed to the wooden surface of the table, Richard looked as if he might mystically summon up some lingering essence of Papa through the veneer. His wedding band glowed in the low light. Hannah remembered the night Richard first tried to escalate their relationship—to move them from teacher and student to lovers. Hannah had pointed to the ring on his finger, said simply, "But you're married."

Richard had held up his hand, considering the ring there. "For me, this is number three. Hem had four wives. So maybe I should keep my options open."

Hannah was left to shake her head at that now: It cast her in the role of last wife, with all the attendant, bloody baggage. She looked around some more, then caught that stranger with the widow's peak stealing looks back at them.

"That man over there in the sports jacket—no, don't look," Hannah said. "He's been watching us for the last hour. Not in an idle way."

Richard's eyes narrowed, then he rolled them. "I saw that guy come in," he said, waving a hand. "With that cheap jacket and those shiny slacks, he's got to be another scholar. Some professor from some cornfield college in the Midwest. Probably hoping trailing around behind me he might overhear something—pick up some scrap he can use to inform his own so-called scholarship. Probably hanging on my every word, the sorry bastard. Probably figures my crumbs will get him his tenure."

Richard toyed with his empty goblet. "I mean, look at it from his perspective, Hannah: Here he is, in earshot of the man who wrote what's regarded as the finest treatment of Hem's Paris apprenticeship, and he's here with me in situ where our greatest writer's life ended. Not inconceivable there are several like that guy, dogging my heels, hoping to rob me blind."

Hannah rubbed her temples: The man was seedy, a bit slovenly, but not in the careless, eccentric way of an academic. He just looked, well, *sleazy*. Menacing.

She glanced at Richard and saw how closely he was looking at her now. She braced for it:

Richard said, "On the other hand, it could all be in your head. Maybe we should have gotten another opinion. Maybe there is still something you could take until the baby is born."

Hannah bit her lip. She knew well enough what Richard thought was "in her head." But he was wrong. The man was watching them, with intent. Just because she suffered from an impulse to always brace for betrayal or violations of trust didn't mean she couldn't sense a real threat.

"It's not like that." She stole a glance at the man in the dark jacket. His cheeks were wind-burned; high forehead. His thinning dark hair was slicked back from his widow's peak. He wore bifocals. He *might* be an academic. But something was a bit off. Maybe it was because he wasn't scribbling away in a notebook between bites like all the other academics back in the lodge's lounge. Maybe it was the fact his face wasn't buried in a Hemingway novel, or a scholarly study about Papa, as he wolfed down his food.

There was no way, to Hannah's mind, that the stranger was just a typical local, either: not in those cheap, careworn dress slacks and those scuffed, wingtip shoes.

Not a sportsman.

Not a shopkeeper.

"It's not like that at all." Hannah thought it, but didn't say it—a quote from a philosophy professor that had resonated all too strongly for Hannah: Even paranoids have real enemies.

Writing, I think, is not apart from living. Writing is a kind of double living. The writer experiences everything twice. Once in reality and once in that mirror which waits always before or behind.

—CATHERINE DRINKER BOWEN

4.   THE LONG GAME

Hector racked the receiver and slipped out of the phone booth. Mary Hemingway had invited Hector up to the house for cocktails with the single academic with whom she'd agreed to meet—some scholar purportedly interested in writing Mary's biography.

Taking up his stool at the bar, Hector shook his head: Hem was not yet five years dead, and they were already writing books about his poorly chosen women.

Hem's homes in Cuba and Key West had already been made into museums.

Hector stared into the mirror behind the bar and sipped his whiskey, shaking his head again.

Hem would have hated it all. He was always focused on his career, on his legacy. Always talking about writing for the "long game"—the career that would extend far past his lifetime. But that attention had all been focused on the writing itself, on the stories and the novels.

And the notion that sweating tourists would pay money to stare at the bed where he made unsatisfactory, infrequent love to his second wife; at the pool in which he rarely, if ever, swam, and at the desk where he sat in the Key West morning heat, writing? All of that would have angered and unhinged Hem if he'd ever thought to consider the sorry prospects.

It was just a matter of time, Hector figured, until the Topping House, like its predecessors, would be opened to the public; guided tours given of the place where Hem had died. Gawkers stepping over the spot where Hem had fallen, his head blown to pulp.

Or perhaps not.

Maybe Mary would surprise Hector: She had once or twice before.

As Rebecca the Hemingway teacher had said, the crime novelist and Hem had gone back to their days as ambulance drivers in Italy. Hector had known, or at least met, all four Mrs. Hemingways. In Paris, and in Spain, he'd stood by Hadley Hemingway as she watched Pauline undermine her marriage to Hem.

Later, when Hem had settled in Key West—partly at Hector's urging— he'd gotten to know Pauline, the second Mrs. Hemingway, though Hector had never really become fond of her.

Then, in the tumult of the Spanish Civil War, Hector had encountered the soon-to-be-third Mrs. Hemingway, Martha Gellhorn—the only one of Hem's women whom Hector truly loathed.

In 1959, after twenty-two years of estrangement, Hector had gone to Cuba to patch things up with Hem. There he had met Papa's last wife, Mary Welsh, journalist turned hausfrau and professional Mrs. Hemingway.

Hem was already in the throes of a quickening physical and mental decline by then.

During his few days at the Finca, Hector had been hectored into reading several of Hem's works in progress—two novels and Hem's Paris memoir, recently published as *A Moveable Feast*. Hector had also spent a couple of mornings getting to know Mary. As far back as 1959, Mary had been anticipating widowhood, already formulating strategies for dealing with Papa's presumptive posthuma. That hadn't endeared Mary to Hector.

On the morning that Hem died, Mary had called Hector: Papa's oldest surviving friend deserved to have the news of his friend's death broken to him by the widow, Mary had insisted.

It had been a very strange phone call.

Mary was admittedly under remarkable stress, but it went deeper than that, and in ways Hector couldn't yet fathom or characterize. It left him wondering about the full circumstances of Hem's death. Sometimes, when Hem's memory ambushed him at odd moments, Hector would wonder if Ernest's death was indeed a suicide, or something more sinister. Particularly since in Cuba, in 1959, Mary had been chomping at the bit to become Hem's literary executrix.

Nagged by those occasional suspicions, Hector had elected to stay in touch with Mary during the four years since Hem's death. Then, quite abruptly, a few weeks ago, about the same time that bookseller alerted him to the sudden surfacing of his own long-lost manuscript, Mary had invited Hector to Idaho to assist in, or at least to provide some input into, the editing of the next of Hem's unfinished works to be published—a long novel Mary was thinking of titling *Islands in the Stream*. She also mentioned something about her own memoir.

Hector leapt at the opportunity: He didn't much care for *Islands*—he'd read the manuscript in Cuba and had found it bloated, unfocused, and too reminiscent of *To Have and Have Not*. And he wasn't crazy about tampering with another writer's works—particularly not Hem's. But there seemed to be some sinister confluence swirling around all things Hemingway now.

Apart from Hector's recently surfaced short story, word had reached Hector from the academic world that *other* Hemingway posthumous works tied to Hector were lately being whispered about, including a "lost" or cut chapter of *A Moveable Feast* that actually focused on Hector.

Even more worrying in terms of Hector's own long game—his own encroaching posthumous career—was the possibility, as indicated by marginalia on the typescript of the lost chapter from *Feast*, that an entire manuscript of a novel, a roman à clef based on Hector's decidedly picaresque life, might exist.

The novel, according to the friendly academic who'd heard about it and who then had confided to Hector, had been composed in the final, crazed months leading up to Hem's disastrous treatment at the Mayo Clinic.

Hem knew where too many of Hector's "bodies were buried," to coin a phrase. Hem knew too well all of the skeletons in Hector's closet, to resort to another cliché.

And in the last few years of his life, Hem had been frequently deluded, the membrane between fantasy and reality all but annihilated.

Hector hated to imagine what such a manuscript might contain about him, and what it might mean for Hector's own long game—for his own legacy, humble as that might be. If it was to be at all.

So Hector had accepted Mary's invitation.

He'd do what he could to help her clean up *Islands*.

He'd try to get a firmer handle on Hem's last days. Maybe learn more about what really happened that terrible morning in July 1961 . . . set his own mind to rest that Hem's death hadn't been something other than suicide.

Hector would try to figure out how that long-lost story of his had come to light, and whether Mary might know something about all that.

And he would look for that lost chapter of *A Moveable Feast*—look for that rumored posthumous manuscript centered on Hector.

And if he found them, he'd destroy them.

Hector felt quite justified about all that: His life (that sorry affair) was Hector's own to write about, and Hector's alone.

He looked at his drink; looked back in the mirror. Across the lounge, a young, dark-haired man was sitting alone with a notebook and pen. He wore the usual suit and tie; had the usual haircut. Hector made a sour face. He signed the check, scribbling down his room number as he sighed and rose.

After a moment's wrestling with it, Hector wandered over to the youngish man. "Calling it a night, Andy. You should turn in, too. I might make it an early morning—you never know. What do you say, son? Up for a little fly-fishing *mañana*?"

The young man didn't look up. He just sat there, acting engrossed in reading whatever he'd written in his notebook. His cheeks and ears began to redden.

For about seven months, Hector and his youngish, perpetual

shadow—Andrew Langley—had shared similar one-sided exchanges. Hector snorted softly and shook his head. *Goddamn FBI . . . Goddamn J. Edgar.* He said, "Night, kiddo. Be sure to write I did something real interesting so the Director will feel he's getting his money's worth from you."

Hector was turning to leave when he glimpsed the name written there in Andy's notepad—the name that set his heart beating faster:

Donovan Creedy.

The individual is handicapped by coming face to face with a Conspiracy so monstrous he cannot believe it exists.

—J. Edgar Hoover

CREEDY—Greenwich Village, 1934

Donovan Creedy hated the Village with its bohemians and Reds and homosexuals: fey or even mincing men who dared hold hands in public on the side streets.

Everywhere he looked, scruffy painters and leftist novelists freighted their canvases and books with dogma and propaganda . . . writing in coffeehouses; looking just as unkempt and slovenly as all those expatriates back in Paris a decade before them.

Creedy saw writing as a craft and a calling. He wrote in jacket and tie, sitting in a stiff-backed chair, and committed to writing no fewer than three thousand words at each sacred sitting.

Writing was a trade for those with passion, dedication, and above all, discipline. That's how it was supposed to be. A meritocracy.

He checked the address in his notebook again and surveyed the numbers stenciled above the brownstones' doors. Creedy found the address, and squinted at the mailbox in the soft summer rain: THE BLACK ROOK PRESS. *Hm . . .*

He buzzed the bell and was admitted by a dumpy woman with mousebrown hair and pale skin. She was dressed in a badly pilled sweater, threadbare dress, and several seasons' out-of-style shoes. She said her name was Esther.

As he sat in the waiting area, leafing through some of Black Rook's other publications, Creedy realized he'd never heard of any of the novels. He turned a book edgewise and checked the spine: the Black Rook logo was new to him. Amateurish. He was fairly certain he'd never seen any of the independent publisher's titles in a single bookstore, not even a public library.

Creedy sighed and thought about leaving. Just then, the woman put down the book she was reading—Hemingway's *Winner Take Nothing*— and checked her watch. "Mr. Sapperstein will see you now."

She led him back through a warren of dingy offices and corridors. Creedy thought he smelled the stench of decomposition, then saw the dead and swollen mouse rotting in a trap—its skull flattened by the metal spring bar.

Esther led him to the end of the hallway and opened a door, said, "Mr. Donovan Creedy for you, Mr. Sapperstein."

A short, portly, bald man rose and spread his arms, waddling around his battered desk. His suit jacket was off and his sleeves rolled up. Sapperstein had his office window open, and an oscillating fan drifted left and right across his desk—the papers there weighted with staplers, unwashed coffee mugs, and other odds and ends to keep it all from blowing away.

Frowning at the dark sweat stains under the publisher's arms, Creedy quickly thrust out a hand for a damp shake.

Creedy rubbed his now slick palm down on the fabric of the chair he was offered and sat down across from his prospective publisher. Creedy had already just about determined to walk away from this publishing "opportunity."

He could tell already the Black Rook Press wasn't going to be his ticket to success as a novelist—not the horse that would carry him to the kind of financial writing success that would at last let him shake free of intelligence work.

"Let me say up front, Donnie—I can call you Donnie, can't I?" Not waiting for an answer, Maurice Sapperstein said, "I *looove Cold Black Rain*. That intelligence stuff in there strikes me as very convincing. The novel is near perfect. Just some tweaks here and there. All that anti-Semitic stuff, for instance. We need to lose that. Also, we need some romance in there for the skirts who really buy the books now. So I had this notion: this partner of your hero—you know, Artemis Stryker's sidekick, Bill Foster? I really think—just thinkin' out loud here—Bill needs to be a dame. I've even got a name. We'll call her Constance Faith, a beautiful Jewess who..."

Creedy sat in his apartment in front of his typewriter, staring at the publishing contract. His feet hurt from the long walk back from the Village; he felt like kicking off his shoes, doffing his jacket, and loosening his tie. Instead, he sighed, set out the handwritten notes given him by Sapperstein, then scrolled in some paper. Looking down at the notes, at the scrawls that passed for the hack editor's comments, Creedy thought of a controller he'd once had in Berlin . . . an obsequious little man who later was rumored to be a mole and then abruptly "disappeared." Creedy shook his head and began to revise his novel to the notes.

He abhorred the notion of incorporating Sapperstein's suggestions . . . of twisting his work to conform to the man's dubious notions. But it was the literary way: The relationship of author and editor was sacred. And some writing-editing teams passed into canon history. Now, with a contract in hand, Creedy was officially and meaningfully a part of that sacred literary tradition. He was to be a published author, and authors, the professional ones, submitted to editing.

Creedy could *adjust. Adapt.* His parents had told him stories about the ones back home who were too weak, or too proud, to thwart fate. They died in flames, bullets . . . worse. His parents remembered for him the ones literally starved under the Romanovs, the ones who hadn't resorted to cannibalism as their village sank into starvation that last hard winter before they fled for America.

Creedy had immediately resented the fact he'd been far too young to be tested by making his own choice on that front. His parents had decided for him, and only told him much later what had saved his life, and their own.

He had a vague memory of them hovering over the body of a cousin who'd decided the *other* way. But he hadn't seen what they were doing to the half-frozen body.

Creedy hesitated, looking up at the shelves above his writing desk—burdened with stack after stack of unsold manuscripts. Sighing again, Creedy bent his head low over the typewriter and began banging the keys.

Much later, he rose and pressed palms to his back, wincing at the crack. He retrieved the old valise from the closet and began sorting through the manuscripts inside again. As he often did, Creedy returned to that particular short sketch set in Paris in the old days ... a long-ago Christmas drink shared by two friends.

The sketch was scrawled on old, yellowing pieces of paper torn from a notebook.

Several times he'd been *this close* to destroying the pieces of paper. But each time he'd cursed and then saved them from fire or the bin, hating himself for relenting ... for the envy he felt.

Jesus, if just *once* he could catch some of that voice. . . .

The cold, white expanse of blank paper shocked him back to reality.

Creedy thought more of Paris and of his beautiful, doomed Victoria, then bit his lip, seized by a notion. A *scheme*.

Maybe he could make the words there his own, after a fashion. And, hell, he could improve them in the bargain. He saw now how his gambit could serve several ends.

He took the notebook pages over to his typewriter, scrolled in a fresh sheet, and began to transcribe the words from the old, scrawled-over slips of paper.

There are four kinds of homicide: felonious, excusable, justifiable and praise-worthy.

—Ambrose Bierce

5.   CLUES

Not long after lunch—a meal Hannah had picked over but not really eaten—she'd suddenly been famished. It was always the way now—starving, then unable to touch food. Rather than run out and get something for her, Richard had instead insisted upon them both walking to the Atkinson Market—the only grocery in town, and purportedly a frequent stop for the Hemingways. Local color for his book, he'd told Hannah.

Hannah said, "How much further *is* this place? We should have taken a cab."

Ignoring her protests, Richard watched Hannah; looked at what he'd done to her. Women could be such ballbusters. But knock one up and, *heh*, you reduced them to utter dependence. Richard took nasty satisfaction in the fact his cock had done *all that* to her....

Yet...

Yet...

Richard was rather surprised she was still keeping up this brisk pace—still hanging in there. But Hannah *always* seemed to do that. It was that peasant-stock Celt heredity of hers, he guessed. But even these months without the pills, well, Richard was surprised at how her personality had presented itself. She'd sought psychiatric treatment at his urging. In the early going, when she could still take the medicines, she'd been puppyish and more pliable in terms of bending to his whims. Then she'd become pregnant, and the medications were cut off. Her personality began to change, but Richard preferred docile Hannah.

So Richard had insisted on her seeing *another* doctor—one willing to prescribe medications for Hannah during her pregnancy. Hannah had refused the second doctor's prescriptions, staying with her original doctor who had set a prohibition against drugs for Hannah.

Now that she was free of all such medications, there was an increasing impudence in Hannah—willfulness that exasperated Richard.

He'd first seen Hannah as his own Catherine Barkley—this dishy, damaged-goods Scots bedmate and perhaps doomed romantic figure. A lover straight out of *A Farewell to Arms*. But lately, Hannah was reminding Richard of some goddamned distaff version of Harry Morgan, always leading with chin and fists.

His first wife had been a kind of shrinking violet and fragile mess through her pregnancy . . . pliant, easily manipulated and cowed. Richard had expected a repeat of that experience with this young woman.

But there was something indomitable about Hannah—this dynamo drive that perplexed and increasingly unsettled Richard, pushing him farther and farther in his attempts to provoke her—to find some point at which she might finally conform to his vision of her as some quintessential Hemingway heroine—artistic . . . fragile; pretty and compliant in bed.

That's who he thought he was marrying when her pregnancy forced him to a commitment.

Well, and it had been the other, too—the desire to groom a fiction writer.

He'd seen in Hannah, if not the undeniable talent, at least the *enthusiasm* of an artist who believed herself on the cusp of great work. A bit like Papa, in the 1920s, there in the City of Lights.

Richard had felt it an opportunity and interesting experiment to guide Hannah—to shape her as a fiction writer. To—well, yes—to *police* her, after a fashion.

It wasn't enough for a writer to find a mere voice and tell a tale: It was also crucial to conform to some template and formal constructs that would allow for easier categorization and therefore clean analysis by the critical community.

That was the way for a writer to position him or herself in the canon—tacit cooperation with the literati.

"How much further is this place, Richard?"

"Not far, I think."

So far, she was still setting the pace. "Do you even know where this store is?"

"I have a pretty good idea," he said.

She said, "This thing with Mary—it's a fascinating notion. But it seems a reach."

"Don't subscribe to my theory?"

"I'm skeptical, but supportive. Given Papa's celebrity, and his calamitous departure, surely there was an inquest."

Richard nodded. He expected this one—he'd already worked the ground in his head . . . knew just how to mount his case in the face of skepticism like Hannah's.

"Look around this place," he said. "This is still the outback. Some of the streets aren't even paved. They haven't poured sidewalks in most places. And Idaho law only stipulates an inquest when there is a suspicion of foul play. The Blaine County coroner performed an autopsy, but he didn't specifically rule the death a suicide. Mary claimed Papa shot himself while cleaning his gun, yet the coroner pointedly told the press no gun-cleaning equipment was found near the body. Shouldn't Mary's lie have sparked suspicion?"

Hannah said, "Not necessarily. Mary was in denial. Papa killed himself on her watch. The coroner gave Mary her shot at launching a face-saving myth. I'd guess it was a favor for a famous local widow."

Hannah *would* take that too-facile tack. His peers—those assholes who would sit in an audience eventually, trying to pick apart his assertions—would go deeper and smarter. They'd pose the tough questions, informed by years of study. As he anticipated his fellow academics' attacks, and mused over his retorts, he said, "The coroner met with the area's prosecuting attorney at the time, and the county sheriff, and Papa's eldest son, Jack . . . and Mary."

A bit short of breath now, he continued, "A strange collection of people to decide whether or not there was any foul play involved, isn't it? Particularly since Mary was alone in the house with Hem the morning of the shooting. She had no business weighing in on whether or not there should be an inquest. Whether there was evidence of something other than a self-inflicted shot."

"What put you on this trail, Richard? What started you thinking Mary murdered Ernest? And how much further to this damned place?"

"Not far." He said, "And to the other—you're the one with the minor in journalism, Hannah. What's the reporter's rule?"

She stifled a sigh. Here they were. *Again*... Sliding into another of Richard's classroom-style, Socratic interrogations that increasingly seemed to pass for conversation between them. In the past weeks, Hannah had come to see even their bedroom exchanges were less pillow talk than recitations. Was a time that was okay: Hannah thought Richard had things to teach her. But she'd learned all his lessons, and so swiftly....

She wanted to say, "What's the first rule of good writing, Richard? Show, don't tell." Or if he insisted upon journalistic maxims, she knew a fine one for good reporters: "Don't talk; *listen*."

She really didn't want to debate with him, but simply rolling over—going along with him—only emboldened Richard to push things farther, it seemed. Besides, suicide—based on Hem's own works and his obsession with self-destruction—made sense to Hannah. It completed a tragic arc. The notion of Papa's death as nothing more than the bloody last salvo in a long-running domestic dispute lacked... romance.

Annoyed and hungry, Hannah shrugged and said, "Follow the money."

"Precisely," Richard said. "As the primary beneficiary in Hemingway's will, Mary stood to gain and gain and gain. The evil old witch stands to make a mint with Papa dead. More importantly, however, hell, Mary has effectively appropriated Papa's identity."

Hannah raised her eyebrows. *"What?"*

"Since Hem died, Mary's divulged plans to issue a bookcase-full of novels, anthologies, omnibuses, and even his letters, of which Hem expressly forbade publication. And she's going to oversee it all!"

A black sedan swung curbside, and the driver, a priest, leaned over and rolled down the passenger-side window. He smiled and said, "You should be off your feet, ma'am. How about if I give you two a lift wherever you're going? I don't mind turning around to do that. Not at all."

Hannah said, "That's so kind. We—"

Richard shook his head and waved him on. "Thanks anyway, padre. Not too much further." He wrapped his arm around Hannah's shoulders. "And she's on me all the time about getting more exercise." Richard patted his gut. The priest nodded uncertainly and rolled back up his window, sliding off the curb.

Hannah glanced back over her shoulder at the priest's distant car, stopped for a light at the intersection. That's when she saw the man following them—the man from the restaurant with the widow's peak and the cheap suit. He looked down at his feet when he saw Hannah's startled reaction. But he kept on walking down the hill behind them, his head down and his hands in his pockets.

She took Richard's arm, started to alert him to their shadow, but then hesitated. "Of course he's going our way, Hannah," Richard would likely say with exasperation if she pressed it. "I've already established he's a Hemingway scholar. Naturally he's bunked in the lodge with the rest of us."

That's how it would go, Hannah *knew* it. She looked back over her shoulder and the man again dipped his head, cigarette smoke trailing from his nostrils and bony fist.

Hannah's hopes were raised again: a turquoise and white, ragtop '57 Bel Air was pulling over to the curb. Hannah couldn't see much of the driver's face, but he seemed a stylishly dressed older man.

Before he could roll down his window, Richard waved him along, too. Hannah watched the man drive on, shaking his head.

Reconciled to having to walk the distance now with that strange man following them all the way there, to distract herself, Hannah played devil's advocate in her head: So what if Mary published Papa's scraps? The books would certainly sell like crazy.

Some of the stuff would maybe even be good, and there was undeniably still a terrible hunger for more from the man. Everybody would win, and so what? Where was the wrong in that? The same thing with the letters, which all of the scholars would slaver after when they finally saw the light of day.

If Hem truly wanted his correspondence suppressed he could have destroyed the letters himself over the years instead of assiduously archiving them; preserving even the carbons.

Papa's claims to want *all* of his letters held back or burned struck Hannah as disingenuous. Hem knew publication of his correspondence would reignite interest in his work when he was gone.

And the letters, like the posthumous manuscripts, really served to keep men like Richard in business, too. Richard certainly knew that.

Richard was still playing lecturer: "Mary lies. A shotgun blast, and Mary gains the ability to steal Hem's work and his identity. Two lucrative commodities, to say the least." The professor smiled crookedly. "In the final analysis, it could justly be said his death became her."

Hannah rolled her eyes. Clearly, the last was a key line in Richard's manuscript, perhaps even the title of a major section. Not continuing—at last pausing—Richard expected a response, and a positive one, Hannah knew, but maybe a tad recklessly, she pursued the middle ground, tentatively testing her theory: "I suppose that's a line from a draft of your manuscript."

Hannah twisted her engagement ring around and around her finger, frowning at its tightness. "But *darling*, if Mary could ape Papa's style so convincingly, why wouldn't she be writing her own stories and novels?"

"Call it testament to the strength of the original material," Richard said. "Plus, you don't need to make a line-by-line comparative study of Hem's bastardized work—I've also got a pattern of behavior. Try this on for size: Dr. José Luis Herrera Sotolongo once found Hem and Mary holding one another at bay with shotguns at the Finca."

Hannah nodded. "And?"

"Jesus, Hannah, hear me! Hem and Mary were pointing guns at one another! At the very least that smacks of self-defense on Hem's part, too." Richard raised an eyebrow. "Tell me I'm not right, Hannah."

Hannah looked again at the man walking in their trail; Richard was still oblivious to him. Hannah stepped up their pace, said, "Lord, I feel like I'm back in your class, Richard."

"So answer the question posed." Richard was huffing now; maybe finally regretting waving on those two Good Samaritans.

Hannah thought a tempered *maybe*, at best, was in order. He was so fond of the Socratic method, well, she could argue back. She came from a warring people, quick to provocation; long memories and short tempers. And Celts just weren't that squeamish about death. Her kinsmen believed drinking water from a suicide's skull could cure epilepsy.

She said, "Where I'm from, the old ones contend the corpse of a murder victim bleeds if touched by its killer."

Richard snorted: "What? So we dig Hem up—rub what's left of him 'gainst Mary to test that adage?"

Hannah chewed her lip; looked over her shoulder again. Richard was perspiring now; breathing through his mouth. She'd probably regret it— knew it would send Richard off on some new diatribe or assault on her sanity, but goddamn it, at this point, it seemed worth it.

Slowing to allow Richard to catch up to her, she turned to him and said, "That man who isn't following us is close on our heels, Richard."

Hemingway has no particular love of the FBI and would no doubt embark upon a campaign of vilification. . . . His judgment is not of the best, and if his sobriety is the same as it was some years ago, that is certainly questionable.

—J. Edgar Hoover

CREEDY—Spain, 1937

Chicote's was a tangle of smelly, lice-ridden, drunken soldiers from the front, "journalists" on more than one payroll and working girls; spies, provocateurs, unemployed bullfighters, and leftist cinema stars who'd come to get themselves some colorful press back home.

Creedy saw Spain as a sewer—better, he thought, to simply stand back and let the bastards annihilate one another. And, hell, any success in tamping down fascism in Spain only threatened the momentum of some of the promising things happening in Germany.

Hemingway and Lassiter were side by side at the bar, watching it all behind them in the dusty mirror. Creedy had dared to take up a stool at Hector Lassiter's right elbow—the only way in this raucous din to hear a sliver of what the two novelists were talking about.

Hemingway said, "If Webster's ever grows a pair and puts the phrase 'cluster fuck' in the dictionary, an engraving of this joint tonight would serve as a worthy illustration." Hemingway picked up the Zippo lighter next to Lassiter's hand, read the engraving there, said, "Lasso, one true sentence . . ."

It was an old game dating back to Paris that Hemingway and Lassiter were noted for playing: One author would start an improbable, tough-to-deliver-on sentence and the other would try to drive it home with vigor and pith. Stumbling, tipsy Hemingway repeated, "One true sentence, Lasso," then, "Just because you're buggy—"

"—doesn't mean the cockroaches aren't out to get you," Lassiter finished for him.

Creedy ground his teeth, frustrated he hadn't come up with a quick retort of his own.

"A-fucking-men to that," Hemingway said. He tapped the bar twice and pointed at their empty glasses. "Two more, Ramón, and pour 'em like you don't own them."

The waiter, strangely elegant and crisply dressed for the raucous surroundings, nodded and said, "*Si*, Papa."

"Speaking of tails, there's my latest," Hemingway said suddenly. He pointed at Creedy and grinned meanly. "How's tricks, Donovan?"

Lassiter gave Creedy a fleeting appraisal. Creedy had never been this close to Lassiter before—never fallen directly under the gaze of the crime writer's startlingly pale blue eyes. Lassiter smiled uncertainly and thrust out a big hand. "Howdy, Donovan. Have we met?" Lassiter hesitated, then said, "I didn't catch a last name. . . ."

Hemingway said, "This shit is named Donavan Creedy. One of J. Edgar's boys. And maybe something even beyond that. Spotted Donnie here in the Stork Club before I left New York. Fucking Hoover—he might as well give you Bureau boys letter jackets for the way he dresses you all, cuts your hair, and deploys you. It's no wonder the Italian mob thumbs its nose at the FBI. You can see you Bureau boys coming from next week. Put that in your next report to Hoover about me, right, Donso?"

Hemingway took a swig of his drink and then shook his head. "Lasso, can you believe Creedy here actually wants to be a novelist? Can you fucking believe that?"

Lassiter just smiled and dodged Hemingway's leading, loaded question. "The Italians? You talking about the Mafia, Hem? Haven't you heard? Organized crime is a myth. Mr. Hoover swears so himself."

Hemingway just snorted and drained the dregs of his drink. He gestured to the bartender for a refill.

Looking at Creedy more closely, Lassiter said, "You look familiar, Don."

Creedy's jaw tightened. He hated to be called anything other than Donovan.

"You already know the cocksucker, Lasso," Hemingway said, waving a thick-fingered hand. "Or, at least, you two brushed shoulders a couple of times I know of. Creedy was in Paris with us, in the early days. Well, not really *with* us, were you, Donnie? You were always around the edges, a real breath of stale air. Gertrude gave Creedy a hell of a bitching out one night, Lasso. I think you were there."

"I'm starting to remember," Lassiter said. He smiled awkwardly and slapped Creedy's arm. Creedy seethed . . . and envied Lassiter his dimples. Lassiter said, "Well, pal, any of us who walked into that lion's den that was Gertrude's salon got our ass chewed as least once. Can't count for you the tough shots Gert gave me in the early going. Let me get your next drink. . . ."

Hemingway said belligerently, "Fuck Stein. And fuck Creedy." Then, leaning in confidentially, he said, "Hey, Don! Just between us and God, what's the true gen on the Director and Clyde Tolson?"

That one had Lassiter wincing. He said, "Better lay off, Hem. No percentage in throwing rocks at the Bureau. Best drop it."

That drew this dismissive hand wave from Hemingway, who was clearly still intent upon showing himself. He said, "Hey, Creedy! I've got spies of my own. What's this business about J. Edgar not having any birth certificate on file? What's that cocksucker hiding? Is he even an American? What's Hoover hiding?"

Other drinkers were listening now. Not *good*. In the charged atmosphere of Madrid, Creedy couldn't afford to have his cover compromised.

Creedy settled up; reluctantly shook Hector Lassiter's offered hand again. He said softly to Lassiter, "You should talk to your rummy friend, Lassiter. Get him to show some restraint. Mr. Hoover has a long memory and a longer reach. This asshole is already on Mr. Hoover's to-do list. Hard to imagine Hemingway could make it worse for himself, but he just might."

Courage is grace under pressure.

—ERNEST HEMINGWAY

6.   WITH THIS RING

Hannah lay in bed, listening to the crickets and Richard's breathing. He'd been asleep at least an hour. She was still struggling to find some comfortable position that would give her some peace. The past two weeks had been particularly hard in terms of getting anything like a real night's sleep.

When the baby came, sleep would be even more impossible to achieve. She wondered when she'd find the time and stamina to write then. She wondered if Richard would actually take some time with the baby so she could have a little time to develop her own writing career in the days ahead.

At this early morning hour, life in some ways seemed so uncertain.

And her hand was throbbing. Her fingers were swollen and her wedding band and engagement ring were painfully tight on her finger—worrisomely tight.

So far, she had resisted waking Richard to ask for his help.

He'd resent being awakened, of course, but it would likely go well beyond simple irritation.

It was a strange enough problem, so he'd likely seize on it—try to elevate it to some kind of Hemingway-style moment to revel in: something that would afford Richard the opportunity to display his own dubious sense of "grace under pressure" and command presence. He'd callously martial resources—demand the lodge van be made available . . . ordering around bellhops, desk clerks, and emergency-room orderlies like he was Papa Himself reborn.

It would be mortifying for Hannah; Richard would likely *love* it.

By the time he was through, Richard would have worked it up to something on the scale of that dying writer with a gangrenous leg in *The*

Snows of Kilimanjaro: something to repeat around the English department lounge at Hannah's expense.

Still, this was getting *bad*. She held her finger up closer to her face and frowned. Her finger looked black in the soft light; the rings felt like tourniquets.

Now Hannah envisioned a worse scenario: rushed to the hospital and facing the prospect of her rings having to be cut from her finger—the bands sawed in half and twisted free from her suddenly thick digits. Richard would rage through all that—probably distract the doctor, and it would end up with Hannah's finger getting sliced to ribbons along with the rings.

She looked at the rings in the moonlight through the window: not her mother's Claddagh band which she had wanted to wear, but these other, rather homely rings that weren't at all appealing—something Richard had found in a pawnshop somewhere after seeing a similar set of bands given Martha Gellhorn by Papa.

She cursed herself: During her last doctor's visit, her obstetrician had frowned at the rings and said, "Really, it's time to take those off until after the baby's born—profound swelling isn't uncommon in the last months. You wouldn't want to lose a finger, would you?"

Maybe the doctor had been making a joke; but now it didn't seem funny. If anything, finger loss seemed a real possibility.

When Hannah had told Richard what the doctor had said, her husband had grown gloomy: "Think what rotten luck might happen to us if you do that, Hannah. It's a symbol of our union—of your commitment to me. We can't just chuck a thing like that because of inconvenience. What's it mean if you can be that cavalier about something so important to us?"

Thinking of her doctor's remark about losing a digit, Hannah realized she was now in a cold sweat. She twisted at the rings but they wouldn't budge. Her finger was throbbing, hurting at the tip with her trapped and now elevated pulse.

She sat up carefully, not wanting to wake Richard.

The thing to do was to get a bucket and visit the ice machine outside. But the door was self-locking, and Richard, slightly drunk and still dressed, had fallen asleep with the room key in his hip pocket. Sprawled on his back on the concave mattress as he was, well, there'd be no getting at that damned key.

Hannah struggled up with one arm, keeping her swollen ring finger pointed straight up, hoping gravity would pull down some of that blood and loosen the rings' grip on her finger. She grabbed the ice bucket and a copy of *The Hemingway Review*, and used the latter to bar the door from locking.

Barefoot on the cold concrete, she walked to the ice machine set up in a common breezeway facing the parking lot, her breath trailing frostily behind her.

She filled the bucket with ice and shoved her hand in, shivering at the shock that sent through her entire body. Cursing in Gaelic, she headed back to her room. Her finger was numb and yet burning there among the ice cubes.

She stutter-stepped.

There was a car parked in front of their room; in her frenzy to get ice, she'd missed it the first time she'd passed it by. Of course the car parked there was nothing in itself.

It was the man sitting inside that car at this early morning hour that scared her.

In the darkened interior of a battered green Impala, the glowing orange butt of a cigarette jittered from a dashboard ashtray to a pair of waiting lips.

In the faint orange glow, Hannah saw: dark-framed glasses and gaunt, wind-burned cheeks; a high forehead and the deep V of a black widow's peak.

She swiftly slid back into their room—trying not to give the impression of having seen him in the car; trying not to look like she was running, which was very much her impulse.

Hannah kicked *The Hemingway Review* loose and quickly closed the door, slamming home the deadbolt with her elbow.

Richard was still asleep, snoring softly now. That man out there? What the hell was he doing?

Still focused on their spy, Hannah edged into the bathroom and closed the door.

She flipped on the light, took a deep breath, then drew her finger from the ice. It seemed a little smaller, but still black.

She worked on her finger with soap and tugged and twisted at the ring.

It gave a little, but still wouldn't pass over the knuckle. She opened a jar of Vaseline and slathered that on her finger.

Slowly, painfully, she twisted the first ring loose from her finger.

The second took another minute of slow, painful twisting to free, then it was done.

Thank God.

She looked at her finger, turning from black to red now. The skin at the base was olive green—already bruising. But the pain from the swelling was better. She sat on the edge of the bathtub for a few minutes with her finger in the ice bucket, trying to take the swelling down that much faster.

She thought about the man parked outside. What did he hope to see at this hour? Well, no way he was a scholar. She was right about that.

Hannah rose and placed the bucket in the sink.

Her urge was to wake Richard and force him outside—make him confront his "fellow academic" sitting outside their room at two in the morning, staring at their door.

Instead, she wiped off the petroleum jelly, then she scooped up her rings and placed them in her makeup bag. She'd probably get grief in the morning when Richard noticed they were no longer on her hand.

But then, maybe he wouldn't notice. She sensed, sometimes, that Richard looked through her rather than at her now.

Hannah turned off the bathroom light and slipped back out into the main room. She edged to the window and pulled the shade back a crack. The man was still out there, smoking in his car and staring at the room like something might happen.

Frightening...

The light suddenly came on behind her, silhouetting Hannah in the window.

The man in the Impala sat up straighter and extinguished his cigarette. Hannah quickly closed the drape.

Richard said, "Hannah? What's wrong? Jesus, stop creeping around. I need my sleep."

"It's nothing," she said, making sure the curtain closed flush. "Turn out the light. It's nothing. I couldn't sleep. That's all."

The artist doesn't have time to listen to the critics. The ones who want to be writers read the reviews, the ones who want to write don't have the time to read reviews.

—WILLIAM FAULKNER

7.   THE THIRSTY MUSE

Hector turned up his sports jacket's collar against the needle-sting rain and, head down, trotted out to his ragtop '57 Bel Air. He turned up the heat and twisted the knob for the wipers.

He drove around downtown Ketchum, tooled around the sidestreets, wondering how Hem had settled for this outback, mountain town after the tumult of Chicago. After Paris and after all the cities of Spain . . . after Venice and Key West and Cuba. Papa always wanted to live close to water, but there wasn't even a decent lake close by. There were no buildings more than three stories tall. No cultural center, not a single downtown bookstore.

But then Hector thought of his own home in New Mexico. Hector's big, stucco hacienda sat on the sometimes muddy, sometimes dusty banks of the Rio Grande, hard up against the Mexican border.

La Mesilla was hardly the Paris of the American Southwest.

Hector squinted into the rearview mirror. The black sedan was still back there. Might be Andy, but the silhouette seemed wrong. Too tall; too gaunt. That aquiline nose in profile—it *could* be Creedy. It had been so many years since he'd last seen the bastard. If Creedy *was* lurking around, there was the possibility he might have changed so much Hector might not even recognize him. Another unsettling prospect . . .

Shrugging off a chill, Hector turned onto Sun Valley Road and began the climb up the sloped road to the lodge. He checked the phosphorescent hands of his Timex: *late*. Hector was no kid anymore: He should be in bed. He should be resting up for the trip to the Topping House to meet with Mary.

He locked up his Chevy and turned his collar up again, squinting against the rain and trotting across the parking lot to the warm paneled comfort of the lodge's lobby.

Hector held the door for a couple stepping from a cab. The woman was pretty and blond and looked eight or nine months pregnant.

A man slid out behind her. He was significantly older ... a drinker's gut; glasses and thinning, graying hair. The man took the woman's hand and placed another hand familiarly at the base of her spine. Hector arched an eyebrow: a couple. And the man—something a bit bohemian about him, a bit careless. Hector scented "scholar." He held the door for the couple and smiled at the pretty mother-to-be who smiled back, a bit uncertainly, a bit distractedly. But it was a very nice smile.

Hector recognized her then: He'd pulled over the other night to offer them a ride, but had been waved on by her companion. Louse—making his wife walk like that when she was so far gone with child. Crummy son of a bitch.

Hector followed the man and woman into the lodge and watched them get in the elevator. He heard the man say to the young woman, probably in answer to a question, "That was Hector Lassiter, the keynote speaker. He writes mysteries. Some of them are actually surprisingly good. I mean, as those things go."

Mysteries? Hector shook his head, slicked back his wet, graying-brown hair, and headed for the bar.

The lounge was cozy; low lights and a big fire crackling. Some soft music played on the sound system—"Where or When." Best of all, the coast was clear: no eggheads, academics, or scholars in sight. The bartender, recognizing Hector said, "Hey, Mr. Lassiter. What'll it be?"

Hector was working on a book partly set in Key West and in Cuba ... his own roman à clef. "I'm feeling nostalgic, Dave," Hector said. "You know how to make a mojito?"

"This is skiing country," Dave said, smiling. "That's a tropics drink. But I like to stay practiced. Yeah, I can make one of those. Have to be just one: We're shutting down soon."

"Then make me three, would you? Trying to get a little writing done.

Missed my daily word count because of all these damned *scholars* and their busybody questions. Missing the daily word count is bad luck. And I'm also humping against a deadline."

Dave winked. Dave was a fan of Hector's—they had established that early in their still young but sacred barkeep/customer relationship.

The bartender said, "You sit over there in that corner, Mr. Lassiter, where you can't be seen from the lobby. That door there is self-locking. Just let yourself out when you're finished. If you need more than the three mojitos, just leave a note for me on the spike there by the cash register and I'll see your room is billed."

Hector winked. "Dave, it's now official: You are my favorite reader."

No passion in the world is equal to the passion to alter someone else's draft.

—H. G. WELLS

8.   THE THREAT

In preparation for his meeting with Mary, Richard had finished his morning's composition and read several essays in three copies of *The Review* covering Hem's Idaho years—articles he had set aside for reading once he had reached Ketchum.

He finished up by listening to an audiotape of a BBC-produced biography of Hemingway. One of the surviving white hunters during the last, ill-fated African safari had said in reference to Hem's suicide: "He was going down a path which I think no man can follow until the end of his own life. He was dying inside—I don't think there is any doubt about that. He was suddenly a sad man. Very, very depressed."

Richard flicked off the tape recorder. He saw his wife's blue notebook. He opened it and read the short story she'd composed the day before—all the while listening to be sure the water was still running in the shower.

As always, he wasn't quite sure what to make of it. It was beautifully written—he knew good prose when he read it. And Hannah's holograph was astonishingly fluid. Apparently written in a single pass, it went on for pages without corrections, additions, or subtractions. No hesitation marks in the sense of false starts or aborted sentences.

Characterization? Story arc? Well, he could see the value in Hemingway's work well enough when it was first pointed out to him as an undergraduate, but pressed, Richard would have to confess he'd read precious little fiction other than Hemingway's in the intervening years.

And up against Papa's macho, egocentric and laconic, hyper-lean prose, Hannah's supple and sometimes relatively florid passages perplexed Richard.

He finished and replaced Hannah's notebook as he had found it just as she turned off the shower.

Richard reached in his pocket and pulled out the vial again, turning it in the light through the window. During what passed for a meeting between them—hardly more than a few whispered words in a drugstore parking lot—the man said all he had to do was put the potion in the Widow Hemingway's drink. Mary would answer any question put to her with just a little of the stuff inside her, the man said.

Richard had taken the offered vial from the man's outstretched hand like it was radioactive. Uncertain, he'd asked, "What is it, exactly?"

"We haven't given it a name yet," the man had said, smiling. "*You* might call it 'truth serum,' but there's really no such thing. But you want a particular answer? You'll get it all right. You want to know if Mary shot Papa? Give the old bitch some of that stuff and then put the question to her."

Then the man had handed Richard a fistful of hundred-dollar bills.

Hannah cracked the bathroom door to let out some of the steam; Richard quickly hid the vial.

Her back to the door, Hannah carefully slipped back on her rings. Her finger had returned to normal size and she'd decided just to watch her hands now—stay alert to signs of swelling in order to avoid a repeat of the other night's near disaster. She wanted to bring up the man hiding outside their room—force Richard to see something strange was going on around them. But this was his big day—his first meeting with Mary, a rendezvous he'd spent years preparing for.

Hannah rubbed his chin. "You're getting scruffy. Don't forget to shave again."

Richard shook his head. "Oh, that's on purpose. Decided to grow it out. I'll shave when I finish my first draft. For luck, you know?"

Hannah was dubious. She ran the back of her hand over her husband's stubble. "There's quite a bit of white in there, darling. May make you look older than your years."

Richard shrugged. Muttered, *"Eh..."*

He was also wearing his untucked Cuban shirt again... khaki slacks with brown loafers. He'd brushed his hair straight back, and it fell rather long at the collar. Faux Papa.

She saw the shot glass and bottle on the nightstand. He followed her gaze drifting to the table and said, "Girding for battle with the old bitch, and I don't want you putting your mouth all over me for doing that, right? Hem rarely faced Mary before his morning's first drink after an early bout of writing, so why should I be any different? Only way to handle this old witch is three-sheets-to-the-wind. If accounts of her drinking are remotely right, I'll still be a while catching up."

Hell, he intended to arrive at the Topping House drunk as a lord—go into this critical first meeting the well-oiled hunter and set the tone up front. Show that wicked and maybe murderous old bitch who was boss. And drunk was the only way Richard could find the edge to slip the old woman this strange potion given him by the man.

Hannah's jaw tightened. She bit her lip, thinking about possible arguments back that might point out to Richard the stupidity of going into his first meeting looking like some lush.

Richard rose and poured himself another shot of whiskey, drank it, and smacked his lips. *"That's* the stuff," he said. "Still, not sure there's enough Giant Killer in the world to prepare me to meet this goddamn woman." He watched Hannah for a reaction; expected some outraged retort.

Hannah just looked at him. Then her jaw almost dropped as he began boxing with his own shadow on the wall. After that he dropped to his knees and began a series of push-ups. After four of those—stopped at an abortive fifth dip—he struggled back up; pressed his hand to his spinning head. He poured another shot and stared at Hannah again: There were two of her now. "Aren't you going to lecture me?"

Hannah shook her head, went back into the bathroom to finish brushing out her hair. In the mirror, she saw Richard's notebook on the bed behind her. Maybe the clues to where they had gone wrong hid somewhere between the lines of all that minutia on Hemingway. Maybe its pages also traced the trajectory of their faltering relationship.

She searched her own face in the mirror. She didn't quite recognize herself—her face fuller now because of the pregnancy . . . her cheeks always a bit flushed. She looked again at the notebook on the bed.

Richard said, "I'm going to go walk around for a while. Try and pick up more of the vibe of this place. See if I can't find one or two of Papa's old watering holes the tourists haven't ruined yet."

Hannah took a deep breath and nodded. Even if he ended up in some bar, it was good Richard was going now. Hannah realized she'd increasingly begun to analyze him, systematically examining him; to pick Richard apart, just as they used to take apart characters in short stories in her undergraduate fiction-writing classes. Everybody sitting in a circle and deliberately deconstructing every facet of the man on the page.

But this man was her husband, not just some character in one of her stories.

And the sad fact was, Hannah wasn't sure Richard could sustain deep character analysis like that.

Hannah sat in a chair, biting her lip and restlessly fingering Richard's notebook.

Deep down, she knew she needed to get out while she still could get away relatively unscathed. Before she had to stand by as abused witness to Richard's seemingly inevitable self-destruction.

But run to what? To *where*? Her current situation was far from ideal, even stifling in some ways, but at least now she was part of something that touched on the literary life. Richard at least afforded a sense that words on a page, and the person who creates them, can be the most important thing in the world. Of course Richard would never put it that way—never really *see* it that way—but it was implicit in his trade.

And she was so very alone without him.

Far from home, far from family. She'd wanted to leave that Scottish village and reinvent herself . . . chase the artist's way. Hannah had found herself a man who made his living with words, a man who studied one of fiction's great wordsmiths, but this man she had married was, at bottom, another version of her father . . . controlling, alcoholic . . . probably violent.

She opened Richard's notebook, browsing over some passages here and there. She mulled over Richard's assertion that scholarship was necessary to creativity; that true artists owed a debt to their best critics. More than that—the notion that writers and critics really existed in a symbiotic relationship, writing back and forth as they reacted to each other's vision. Two sides of the same coin, in a sense.

She paused, rereading a long note Richard had written to himself in the margins—one that unsettled Hannah.

He was seemingly wrestling with the notion of abandoning the biographical form in favor of a historical novel about Papa. Richard had tried his hand at fiction as a young man—dense, strange novels that never found a readership. Was this some form of midlife crisis? A bid to try again what he had failed at as a young man? It made no sense at all— Richard had won awards for his Hemingway nonfiction. Novelizing Hemingway's life could only detract from Richard's scholarly standing.

And Richard was engaging in furious research, more than could ever be freighted by a novel. Even now, Richard was at the Ketchum Cemetery, trying to find the name of the man or men who had dug Hemingway's grave.

"We know the name of the guy who dug Faulkner's hole," Richard had said, "but who dug Hemingway's grave?"

"But surely that was Papa himself?" Hannah had chirped, smiling crookedly and sheepishly shrugging.

But Richard hadn't smiled.

Prof. Paulson left without a good-bye.

The phone rang, startling her.

"Hello?"

The voice was husky and almost feminine: "Tell your husband to drop it. Hear? Tell Richard to give up and go the fuck home."

She frowned, listening to the hard breathing on the other end of the line, her heart racing.

What in the name of God?

Hannah remembered the stranger spying on them in the restaurant, following them back to the lodge, and later, watching their room in the parking lot.

But she couldn't reconcile the face and the voice.

A woman was on the other end of the line—Hannah was nearly certain of that—but a woman with whiskey-soaked, three-pack-a-day pipes. As Hannah was deciding whether to hang up or threaten the caller with a complaint to the operator, the voice said:

"Go home, or be sent home in a box."

This is not a novel to be tossed aside lightly. It should be thrown with great force.

—Dorothy Parker

9.   THE LOST CHAPTER

"It's the pits, I know, but thanks for meeting me here," Hector said. "The lodge is lousy with your would-be peers."

"You must feel like you're in hell, Hector." Dexter Evans was a Hemingway scholar from Northwestern University. He sipped his beer and looked around the dark interior of the dank Ketchum watering hole. "None of my colleagues will ever come here," the professor said.

"Exactly," Hector said. "No *scholars* munching on scones and sipping Darjeeling tea and pontificating about the death of the novel, or the death of the author, or some goddamn thing about 'the accidental narrative,' whatever that is. They do so much talking, I'm surprised they have time to write anything themselves. I'm not much of a Frost fan, but old Bob once told me something I've liked as poets' remarks go. Bob said, 'Talking is a hydrant in the yard and writing is a faucet upstairs in the house. Opening the first takes all the pressure off the second.' Old Bob called it right, and that's for sure. But this dive, it's a place where I can write without one of your cronies asking me about Key West, or about Gellhorn and Madrid."

"It's bad?"

"It's incessant," Hector said sourly. "It's terrible. But as I've promised you, Dex—you get my Hemingway memories, and only you get 'em for publication. I mean, apart from whatever drivel I put out there in my so-called keynote speech."

"You written that speech yet, Hec?"

"Still have a couple of days to procrastinate. I'm workin' on it."

"Can't wait. Curious what you'll say."

"Me too."

"You're looking good, Hec. Better than you've looked in years."

Hector smiled. "They say stars shine brightest just before they burn out. And when was the last time we crossed paths?"

"November 1959."

"Well, 'fifty-nine was a very hard year for me. 'Fifty-eight, too. Hell, 1957 was a fucking killer."

Dexter squeezed Hector's arm. "Okay, I take it back about what I said a second ago—that younger guy over in the suit. He doesn't fit in here. Could be an academic."

"Not with the cut of that suit and his hair," Hector said. "I know him. He's my own personal FBI tail. Named Andrew Langley. We chat from time to time. Well, I talk to him. He pretends not to hear me. Not much sense of humor in young Andy, there."

Dexter swallowed hard. "FBI? Really?"

"Oh, yeah."

"You've always been apolitical, Hec. If anything, you seem to be regarded as a rock-ribbed conservative. Why would the Bureau be watching you?"

"Hell, why are they watching any of us? But the Feds are doing just that . . . spying on Steinbeck, Thomas Mann, and scores of others. Then there was that stuff in 'fifty-eight that seemed to draw me official and ongoing interest. Some things that went down in Nashville, then spread wide. A story for another time." Hector sipped his drink and said, "Listen, Dex, reason I wanted to meet with you—"

"The alleged manuscripts," Dexter said. *"Si?"*

"Si. What's the story? What's the true gen, to borrow a Hem phrase?"

"Not real clear. Carlos has been named the official biographer."

"I heard," Hector said. "He'll do an unremarkable but competent job. And I suppose that's Mary's aim in selecting him—no surprises."

"Exactly. Carlos is just getting access to the posthumous stuff. Can't quote from it, but he can characterize it. Loosely summarize it."

"Hem *really* wrote a book about me?"

"He really intended to write a book about you. Nearly as I—or nearly as Carlos—can tell, based on what he's confided to me, the manuscript, if it exists, hasn't surfaced. The working title was *All Things Toil to Weariness*."

Hector frowned. "Not enticing. And it sounds familiar. What's that from?"

"The Bible," Dexter said. "Ecclesiastes. Same book that gave Hem *The Sun Also Rises*."

"Sounds like a fucking downer."

Dexter hoisted his beer. "Mencken said, 'Character in decay is thus the theme of the great bulk of superior fiction.'"

Hector scoffed: "Wonder how that cocksucker Menck would have felt if somebody had written a novel about Mencken's character in decay. Jesus."

"Take heart, Hector. The manuscript hasn't surfaced. We only know of Hem's intent from notes left on a holograph of the chapter he wrote about you for *A Moveable Feast*."

Hector nearly spit out the swig of single malt he was in the process of swallowing. "What? Last time we talked that chapter seemed a rumor, too. It really exists?"

"I've seen it. Read it, actually."

"Christ, I need to see it, Dex. I need to read it. What's the thing say?"

"Nothing too damning ... more portentous. A teaser for the novel, you might say. Nothing to hurt your reputation. Nothing there to get you sued. As the portraits in *A Moveable Feast* go, which can be acidic, as you know, this sketch is mostly fond. You'll fare relatively well if it sees print."

Hector shook his head. "'Relatively well.' That's damning with faint praise given the knifing Hem gave Scott ... gave Dos ... gave poor Ford. I need to see this chapter on me. Hell, I'm owed a look."

"Not sure Mrs. Hemingway would agree. Mary's talking of an omnibus of uncollected, unfinished, or unprinted bits of Papa's works. Fragments and such. This would be perfect for that."

"How do I reach Carlos?"

Dexter shook his head. "He'd never give it up to you, Hector. He's under so many strictures and cautions and legal impositions regarding the official biography, he couldn't risk leaking you a copy. And he wouldn't do it under any circumstance. Too much the prig."

"Great."

"But, fortunately, I have a Photostat. I'll give it to you on the condition you'll never tell anyone you had it, and that you'll destroy it immediately after you read it."

Hector smiled meanly. "That last I can promise."

Dexter winked and slipped a folded envelope from the pocket of his suit jacket. "Here you go."

Hector snapped it up. "You're a prince among scholars," he said.

"Now who's damning with faint praise?" Dexter sipped more beer. "Read it later, yes? Somewhere where you can burn the bastard—not get all foggy with drink and maybe leave it here."

"Fat chance."

"It's pithy, like most of the sketches in *A Moveable Feast*, but not without interest," Dexter said, licking the beer froth from his lips. "Most of that interesting stuff is to be found in the margins. Those comprise Hem's notes for this novel about you that he planned. It's crazy stuff. Guess Hemingway must really have been out of his head there at the end."

"Yeah? What's the gist?"

Dexter smiled crookedly, looking dubious. "Something about you and Hem and these murders tied to surrealist painting and photography."

Hector's stomach kicked. Hector was writing that very book—only he was calling it *Toros & Torsos*. And Hector was writing the "novel" with an eye toward self-protection, obfuscation, and revenge.

"Can you believe it?" Dexter said. "I mean, conceptually, it sounds crazy as hell."

Hector chewed his lip and forced a smile. "Damned if it doesn't."

Returning to the Sun Valley Lodge, Hector drifted toward the lounge, thinking he'd get a drink and read the chapter Hem had written about him.

He stopped in his tracks. Two men were sitting at a corner table, engaged in intense discussion. One was the scholar Hector had seen the other night—the one he'd held the door for, who'd been accompanied by the pretty, pregnant blonde.

The other man was Donovan Creedy. It had been many years, but Hector recognized Creedy well enough after all.

The FBI agent hadn't spotted Hector yet. Hector covered his face with the folded manuscript and backed into the lobby.

History will be kind to me for I intend to write it.

—WINSTON CHURCHILL

10.   COMMAND PERFORMANCE

Richard was passing the front desk, returning from the cemetery and a last, preparatory meeting with the man, when the desk clerk said, "Mr. Paulson, I have a note you're to call Mrs. Hemingway immediately. She said you have the number."

Cursing, Richard began patting pockets. He certainly hoped he had the phone number on him. He didn't want to make the call in front of Hannah . . . didn't want her overhearing Mary's end of the conversation.

Even over the phone, the old bitch was typically raw and demanding. Foul-mouthed and given to giving orders. She treated Richard as though the time she was allotting him to interview her for her biography was done as some kind of favor to him . . . like he was a flunky. Mary made it all sound like a tedious imposition, but hell, she was the one who initiated the project, after all.

Well, more or less.

Richard had put out feelers for an interview with Mary for a bigger Hemingway book, but then Mary had come back at him with this counter proposal: "You can have my whole story, Dick. You, and just you, gets it. But it's *my* story you'll write. *My* life."

They had barely signed the papers for that authorized biography when the salty, boozy old bitch announced she was concomitantly working on her memoir. Two-faced old whore.

Richard unfolded the stained cocktail napkin with Mary's number written there and dialed. He expected some assistant to answer, but it was Mary at the other end, already slurring at this hour of the morning. Already at the Bloody Marys, the lush.

The thought of a morning pick-me-up made Richard wet his lips. He could go for a screwdriver—get his Vitamin C that way.

Mary said, "Today when you come up, I'm thinking I want you to bring that gal of yours along. Your wife, I mean. The pretty little blonde."

Richard scowled. Why would Mary want Hannah along? He tried to remember what he'd told Mary of Hannah. Had he ever given Mary a physical description? They'd talked a few times, both of them worse for alcohol, so maybe he had said something about Hannah's looks. Hell, he must have.

He shook his head, said, "She's pregnant. Very, very pregnant, so I don't know if she'll have the stamina to—"

"Nonsense," Mary said. "She'll be taking it easy in a chair. Besides, Hannah writes a little herself and I think it might be good to have a woman to help you with telling my side of the story. Some of the stuff only another woman will grasp. I don't trust a man, working alone, to do me justice. I see this as a partnership between you and your wife, Richard. I see Hannah as, well, as a kind of interpreter or bridge between you and me. A pathfinder for you when it comes to dealing with some of my more complex sides. I know how you Hemingway scholars are—it's all Papa Papa Papa. Jesus, I don't want to get lost in my own book."

Richard had to stifle a guffaw at that. Complex sides? The old bitch was an open book, so far as Richard was concerned. Mary was a middling journalist and camp follower who used her body to break stories during World War II. She had a middling prose style, a middling intellect, and middling college training. Hell, she came from a middling wide spot in the road.

Richard couldn't conceive of any phase of Mary's personality or aspect he couldn't easily grasp. The notion he needed Hannah riding shotgun for insight into another woman's personality was not only daft, it was fucking insulting.

Richard said, "I really think Hannah needs her bed rest now. The baby is our first priority. It's the most important thing in our world right now."

The expected words. He thought he'd delivered them with what sounded like raw passion.

"Hannah's fine, Dick. Sturdier than you think." Mary paused, then said, "I really have envisioned this as a package deal, Richard. There are other scholars with writer wives in town, you know. I could ask one of those writing couples if you don't think Hannah will go for it."

"How do you know Hannah writes? How do you know *anything* about her?"

He could hear the smile in Mary's voice: "This is *my* town, Dick. I *hear* things."

Richard kicked the bottom of the front desk, startling the clerk. Smiling through gritted teeth, Richard said, "No, it's fine. I will have Hannah there. I just want it clear—this is *my* book. I don't work in collaboration."

Mary said, "I'll be very much looking forward to meeting Hannah today. Please tell her that."

————

The writer's very attempt to portray reality often leads him to a distorted view of it.

—Gabriel García Márquez

11.   ECHOES

Hector had ordered a bottle of Rioja Alta and he sat in the parlor of Suite 206, legs stretched out on the sofa and a big fire going. He had tuned the radio to a station that played only classical music. He lit a cigarette, sipped his wine, and then carefully unfolded the copy of what was purported to be Hem's lost *A Moveable Feast* chapter and began to read. . . .

BOOK TWO

A Moveable Feast

(The Lost Chapter)

CHRISTMAS EVE AT LE SELECT MONTPARNASSE

It was another winter, the first since we had returned from Toronto, and money was even tighter than it had been the previous
year and now it was Christmas Eve and I had not yet found a gift for
my wife or for our child. Our money was mostly going for little
chunks of charcoal or sometimes for some wood and for food for
our baby. I was eating one meal a day so my wife could eat two. Because we were then very poor I had stayed away from writing in the
cafés to save money and it had been several days, perhaps even a
couple of weeks, since I had had a real drink.

I found Hector in Le Select, where we'd agreed the previous
night to meet. It was just after ten and we'd both finished our mornings' writing. It was Christmas Eve and both of us being from the
States, Christmas was still an important holiday for us. Hector was
an only child from coastal Texas, so maybe Christmas was a little
less important for him than for me. But only just a little.

I had grown up in the Midwest. There we had lived with seasons and Christmas was snow and family and a tree in the parlor.
Christmas was gift exchanges and church services and the women
of the family around the piano . . . a good fire and holiday food that
always left one feeling too full and a little sick and perhaps even a
little ashamed for having eaten too much.

I thought of the Christmases past that morning with Hector and thought I wouldn't have felt ashamed, at least not that morning, for having a too-full or at least even a full stomach.

"Lasso" was tall and slender and the one of us around the Quarter who Gertrude—whose authority on such matters one might be forgiven for doubting—insisted could have had a career in cinema with his "good looks and rich baritone" and "athletic bearing." He had a good smile and dimples and the palest blue eyes that would have been striking in a woman's face, or an actor's. But Hector was not a woman and he was not a cinema star (and some would say, not even a true or at least honest writer, though some might later call him a credible actor).

But he was then a good and loyal friend and he was celebrating a book contract and so I could kid myself he was buying the drinks in celebration that morning and not treating me. Hector was writing for the crime pulp magazines back home, and making good money. Everyone called him a crime writer but he was really a writer who wrote stories with crime and the best of his stories might have fit well in a collection of stories such as "The Killers," if I had yet written that story. Or with many of Faulkner's short stories with criminal or rather crime elements.

But Hector was publishing his stories with some regularity then, and he had recently sold the first of his first fine crime novels. He had some money and he was thinking of moving out of the Quarter and perhaps even away from Paris. He spoke of perhaps going back home and to the Florida Keys where, he insisted, the living was even cheaper than in Paris and where it was so warm, all the time, that the houses didn't have fireplaces or even radiators.

In those days, Hector seemed always to be getting to the good and interesting places before me, or at least making a convincing case that he had. But Hector was a committed bachelor and I convinced myself that gave him certain critical advantages as an explorer. I'd first met Hector in Italy. He was driving ambulances after being injured and cashiered out and he trained me and taught me the tricks of driving the old rigs with their bankrupt, metal-on-metal brakes. Later, he'd been in Paris perhaps a year, or even two years before me, and, in this other case, he would beat me to Key West, too, though it might have been better for both of us if he had not.

But that was still many years away and this particular morning we were the best of friends and it was Christmas Eve and we were sitting by the fire and drinking belly-warming, tongue-loosening rum St. James. We sat on the terrace by the brazier and it was warmer there, but it was still a very cold morning, despite the sun, and we could see our breath as we talked and even see it a little when we breathed.

We spoke a bit of our morning's work and Hector told me he would be spending the holiday with a tart he'd met a few days before and whom he was trying to reform.

The girl's name was originally Victoria. She had come from St. Louis to Paris to be a singer or dancer. But she had fallen through the layers of *bal musettes,* and then to the smaller revues in the poorest quarters, then into the Folies Bergère and finally had fallen further and now her working name was "Solange."

I'd met her once or twice and she was quite pretty with shining blue-black hair that she wore straight and long against fashion. Her eyes were blue, though not as blue as Hector's, and she had a pretty smile but she did not have dimples as Hector had. Still, she was quite pretty and one felt sad that she had come to Paris young and with dreams and had failed to meet those dreams, or even, really, to come close, and had come to debase herself as a streetwalker.

With his new money, Hector had recently moved her into his apartment, causing a small scandal with his haughty and newly religious *femme de ménage,* and so furthering his need of a new place to live.

"Vicky and me popped some corn this morning," Hector told me. "We spent the morning stringing the popcorn and after lunch we're going to go down to the Luxembourg gardens. I found a good pine tree there, like the Christmas trees from back home, and we'll string the popcorn around the tree and watch the birds eat the corn and we will drink some kirsch and sing a carol or two. You and your family should meet us there, Hem."

As if remembering then, Hector reached under the table to the empty chair next to him and fished around his overcoat's pocket. He handed me a small tissue-wrapped parcel and said, "Merry Christmas, Hem."

It was a metal flask and I could feel something sloshing inside it and was about to unscrew the lid to smell it when he said, "Pernod." He smiled and raised his rum St. James and said, *"Alla tua salute."*

I said, *"Salud!"* and we toasted one another and then he handed me two other small parcels.

"The one in the red tissue is for Bumby," he said. "Some gizmo I saw the other day." The other, he said, was for my wife. Hector was just a bit younger than me, and my wife treated Hector like a kid brother most of the time. But sometimes they would flirt with one another and I knew they were quite fond of one another and that Hector perhaps even had a kind of crush on my wife. That is, if a man like Hector could be said to have "crushes." But it was all very innocent that time, and when I had still been working as a journalist, and would sometimes be away on assignment, I knew Hector would watch out for her, and for our son, and that they were safe together and that nothing untoward would happen.

But now I could feel the contours of the gift through the tissue and I could feel the anger building in me. My wife's red hair was growing out raggedly and thick after the baby and she had lost one of her fine hair brushes in the move back from Toronto. Just that morning, as I was leaving, she had been cursing the tangles in her thick red hair.

We had been out with Hector and his reformed tart a few nights before and my wife had seen an antique silver brush in the window of a shop and had commented on it. I knew the present must be the brush that she had admired.

"I can't accept this, Lasso," I said.

"It's not for you, Hem," Hector said carefully. "Tell her it's from you. You should do that anyway. Anything else might look...improper." He gave me his best smile then, or what I knew to be what he thought was his best smile; his boyish, winning smile with dimples that could erase any slight or injury, or so he clearly thought.

Often enough he was right. And my first drinks in several weeks had left me mellow and warm.

But it still wasn't working all the way upon me yet, and sensing that, Hector said, "You two are the closest thing to family I have, Hem, and it's Christmas and that's about the giving. You'll just have to live with the receiving, you righteous son of a bitch." He pointed to the gift for our son. "I've got no brother or sisters, so I'll never have nieces or nephews, either. I'm afraid Bumby fulfills that need for me. Christ, Hem, please let me have my Christmas. Without it, I'm left to decorating trees in the gardens with fallen women. What kind of Yule is that? You can't appreciate family, truly, when you have one. When you don't, it's all you think about."

I still wasn't completely soothed or convinced, but I was then terribly fond of Hector. I didn't yet know what I would do with the gifts, and, if I took them home, what I would say about their origins, but his smile and steady blue-eyed gaze broke down the last of my resentment and jealousy and my guilt for having no money.

We toasted one another again and I tried to think of something I might have around our small apartment to give Hector as a gift.

Hector ordered us both Welsh "Rarebit" and we sipped more of our rum and I said, "What did you get Vicky for Christmas?"

Hector shook his head and then shook loose a cigarette and struck a match with his thumbnail and lit his cigarette.

He stared into the coal fire of the brazier.

Finally he sighed and said, "An abortion."

Hector sighed and bit his lip and sipped more wine. Hem's sketch of that long-gone Christmas Eve was accurate, and it *wasn't*.

Much of the distortion—perhaps intended ... *probably* intended— came in the omissions. It was tucked into the spaces between the lines. Contrary to what Hem had written, Hector had *always* gotten to the good places first. Hector's war injury had removed him from combat and sent him to Italy seven months ahead of Hem.

Hector had lured Hem to Paris and then later to Key West. He'd introduced Hem to Cuba.

The antique brush had been given to Hadley for Christmas. Hector knew from later conversations that Hem had passed the hairbrush off as his own gift.

That was fine. Hell, that's what Hector had intended, really.

It was that last paragraph that really angered Hector.

It made it sound like the aborted child had been Hector's.

Artistically, Hector could appreciate that touch: Hector recognized the effect and the contrast with Hem's own, then-happy family life that Ernest had been going for as a writer.

But for various reasons, it was reprehensibly dishonest.

Victoria had claimed to have no idea who the father of her child was. The father could have been any of a dozen of her "clients." But Vicky hadn't wanted the child and she had begged Hector to help her take care of it before they returned to the States and before she might have to see her parents again. He reluctantly complied.

The eventual procedure had gone very badly, though that wasn't apparent at first, and it eventually left Vicky infertile.

Many years later, Hector heard that her failure to produce a child had ended Vicky's fine-enough, otherwise happy marriage to a man whom, by all accounts, was otherwise a nice-enough man.

Vicky died shortly after the ensuing divorce.

Hector rubbed his temples, recalling old days in Paris with Vicky. Who *had* been the father of that child? There had been so many men in her life. She talked of them from time to time: the doomed soldiers; the rich but unhappily married men.

But there was *one* man . . .

Victoria never spoke of this man, never put a name to him, and when Hector pressed, she'd shrug and say, "You're being foolish, Hec. There's nobody."

But there *was* somebody. Hector *knew* it—some man who filled the voids Hector sensed in Victoria's biography . . . whose memory dwelt in the ellipses in her occasional tipsy reminisces. Not necessarily a lover— not anymore, at any rate—maybe not even the father of her aborted child.

But someone—some man—cast a long and perhaps even fearsome shadow over Victoria's life.

When Hector would press too hard, Victoria would take shelter in drink and solitude—sometimes ordering him out.

One night, a bit worse for drink and angry at Hector for again pressing, she'd asked him to leave. Hector had stormed out; found Hem in a downstairs café. Spurred on by drink, the two drunken authors had determined to follow equally smashed Victoria—see if she might not lead them to this mystery man who was fast becoming Hector's bête noire.

Nothing came of these nocturnal sorties. Well, not in terms of spotting this mystery man who hung in the shadows.

But later, over still more drinks, Hector and Hem more than once confided the same sense that while they were watching Victoria, someone else had been watching *them*.

Years later, when Hector's efforts to improve Victoria's prospects hadn't played out quite as he expected, he heard through channels that she was found dead in her apartment.

Her body was found in the kitchen by a custodian, who had forced his way into her place after neighbors expressed alarm over the strong scent of gas hanging heavy in the common hallway. Victoria was there in the kitchen—her head still in the oven.

Hector wasn't really surprised by her suicide—Victoria's moods always ran to the dark side. She'd never overcome the guilt regarding her accidental, sorry trade.

But some newspaper accounts sent him by a lingering mutual friend haunted Hector:

A man in Victoria's building—some nosy neighbor—insisted that he'd seen a strange man hanging around Victoria's apartment. He'd even seen the stranger leaving her place a time or two in the days just before her death.

Hector read the lost chapter again, then a third time.

Something nagged at him; worked at Hector in a deep but undefined way.

Something . . .

Damn it all: It had been so many years. And back in the day, there'd always been so many drinks. Hundreds of thousands of words had been written between then and now. . . .

Hector looked at the typeface—the margins and spacing—the document *looked* like something that could have come from Hem's typewriter. And all that marginalia about the surrealist killings—that was certainly in Hem's hand.

It vexed Hector—who, besides Hem, might have had a hand in this strange, impossible-to-exist document?

This chapter... That long-missing and now-surfaced short story of Hector's... And Creedy, here in Idaho, chatting up apparent Hemingway scholars?

Something sinister was going on in this remote mountain town, sure enough. Something directed at harming Hem's reputation, and maybe Hector's, too.

Something that made Hector go cold all over.

Widow. The word consumes itself.

—SYLVIA PLATH

12.   INVITATION

"Get dressed," Richard said, flipping on the light and tugging back the drapes, flooding the room with savage light. "She wants you to come along."

Hannah sat up in bed and ran her hand back through her tangled hair. "Huh?" she asked grouchily. "Who? Who wants me?"

"Mary. Before she and me get down to cases, she suggested we all get together socially. Just this once. I couldn't see a way around it. If nothing else, being around you might make her drop her defenses a bit. Mary'll like you. Christ, everybody always likes you."

"I feel terrible. Besides, today's my day to do my writing." Hannah rubbed her eyes with her knuckles. "You promised." Richard had. On the other hand, the chance to see Papa's house—to meet the widow and hear her side of the legendary story—the prospect privately thrilled Hannah.

"You'll feel better, and you can revise your little thing tomorrow. It's a short story—how much time can it take?"

Hannah frowned. "As a literature professor, you should be better equipped to answer that question. Or you should presume so."

He thought about it, then said, "Actually, you should bring that up to Mary. How much time your fiction writing takes—make it clear that it's your priority. Well, after the baby, of course. Oh, and since you brought it up: You need to broaden out a bit. Write about something that isn't centered around what did or didn't happen between you and your old man."

Hannah's cheeks and neck reddened. "You've been snooping. Again."

"I'm a professional, not a snoop."

"Yeah, well, Papa didn't let Edmund Wilson critique his works in progress," Hannah said. "Writers don't require academics to wet-nurse them through to final drafts. How to put this kindly? Butt out." She shook her head and sighed. "I really mean that, Richard. Don't ever ever do it again. It's like a . . . *violation.*"

"I'm sorry." Richard hesitated, then waved his hand. "Honey, you have raw talent, but you really simply must dispense with this other thing and move on. It's more than just the way everything you write about comes down to all that with your old man. Hell, you need to ignore that shit just to be whole again and find your own true voice. Forget it as fodder for your fiction. It's not translating . . . no resonance. It's self-exposure and self-confession, not literature. It's painful and uncomfortable to read."

Hannah blew blond bangs from her forehead. "Aye. Well, maybe. Anyway, the bairn's using my tailbone as a football and I feel a little sick." Hannah pressed her palm to her belly. "You know, when I'm naked and he's moving around, you can actually see the feet and arms skittering around under my skin? Sometimes you can even see the outline of an arm, or a leg. Wanna feel?"

Richard thought of the increasingly visible outline of his own liver, looking like some bloated, subcutaneous leech bent on its host's destruction: "Too creepy."

"At least let me take a shower first?"

"You've got twenty minutes."

"Not enough time."

"Twenty minutes."

They drove a new rental car from the lodge to the Topping House. Hannah looked out the window at the passing countryside... at the distant cemetery.

As she watched the passing scenery Hannah's mind returned to the strange phone call. She still hadn't thought of a way to tell Richard about it. And anyway, now was the *last* moment to think of doing that. Richard was on his way at last—finally going to meet Mary Hemingway. And, hell, Hannah was going, too. That was a dizzying development that excited Hannah very much.

She was going to actually meet and talk with Papa's last wife. Hannah combed her damp hair and grilled Richard about the widow. "What's she like *now*? I was leafing through a book of photos taken around here and she looks teensy. Too tanned. Blond in a bleachy way. Very sharp-featured."

"Starting with her tiny, predatory teeth," Richard said. "She has the teeth of a terrier, though few would know. She rarely smiles in pictures, or in person, I'm told."

Hannah shrugged. She wasn't up to another one of his impromptu lectures; wasn't up to debate. She decided to go for humor, this round... repartee: "Maybe nobody around Mary ever says anything funny."

Richard bit his lip, considering that one. Frowning deeper, he said, "Hem at first dismissed Mary as a camp follower and scavenger. She smokes like a chimney and has the foul mouth of a sailor. She drinks too much. The drinking's killing her, according to some who should know."

Hannah wanted to say, "Just like that and you've found your common ground." Instead she said, "Papa thought enough of Mary to marry her. Dubbed her his 'pocket Rubens,' aye?"

Richard nodded. "That is so. In a different mood, he also said she had the face of a Torquemada... or of a spider."

"Harsh." Hannah smiled. "Was that a black widow spider?"

"The first time Bumby met his newest stepmother, she emerged naked from the pool at the Finca."

"Bet more than the sun rose."

"That's funny, Hannah. In your joke, you stumble upon an interesting point. There have been growing retrospective rumors of lesbianism. Recently, allegations have even been made about an affair between Mary, wife number four, and Pauline, who was wife number two."

"*Hm*. Thought I read somewhere that Pauline and Hadley might have had something before Pauline stole Papa away—that the three of them were lovers."

"Dubious." Richard squeezed his wife's hand. "Which wife would you most likely have been? Which one do you identify with?"

Hannah bit her lip. Hadley was probably the most appealing, the most grounded of Hem's wives. The others were all rather messes of one sort or another. Martha, the only real writer among the four Mrs. Hemingways, had the least appealing personality to Hannah.

She said, "None of them. Given a choice, I would have been Papa's long-desired, unborn daughter. The daughter who would have absorbed from her genius daddy every trick and truth he knew about writing."

As they slowed to turn into the Topping House driveway, a green Impala swung around the back of their car and continued on up the hill. Hannah caught a glimpse of the driver: a gaunt man wearing glasses. His dark hair was slicked back from a widow's peak. His hollowed cheeks were wind-burned.

Hannah reached for Richard's arm, then hesitated: The car was already out of sight.

Like the threatening phone call she had received earlier in the morning—received alone—Hannah had only her own word to stand on. Only she could vouch that she had received the call, and only she had seen their seeming stalker in the Impala.

Hannah's word seemed insubstantial measured against Richard's stubborn memory of Hannah's mental history. She sighed and climbed up the driveway behind her husband, trying to put the phone call and their stalker out of her mind as she made her way up the hill to Hemingway's death house. Up the hill to Papa's last wife.

BOOK THREE

Death in the Afternoon

A widow is a fascinating being with the flavor of maturity, the spice of experience, the piquancy of novelty, the tang of practiced coquetry, and the halo of one man's approval.

—Helen Rowland

13.   POINT OF VIEW—Mary

Hiding in a hallway off the main room, the widow watched the scholar and his wife in the reflection of a strategically positioned mirror.

Mary had left them to cool their heels a time; she watched the professor standing there, peering with rheumy eyes at the spot where Papa had fallen dead. Richard stared at the floor and walls of the mudroom—his face ruddy, jaws tight. He stood there in his faux-Papa togs and the scrubby white beginnings of a beard, his expression impossible to read.

Hannah Paulson focused her attention on Richard—she seemed unable or disinclined to look at the infamous foyer. Mary rather liked the young woman for that.

He didn't look like much, this fucking scholar. But then Mary didn't want the man to be much—couldn't afford him to be too formidable. He'd won some awards, for what such bullshit was worth. He'd written a pretty good book about Ernest's Paris apprenticeship. But that was all.

And that was perfect, for Mary's purposes.

The negotiations with the big publishing houses in New York for her *auto*biography—the one that would score syndication deals, a motion-picture deal—those were lagging; dragging on with no resolution in sight.

Mary thought a smaller book aimed at the academic market might entice the big boys to finally play ball—to accept her vision for her own remarkable life story. The big boys wanted her to use a ghost. As if an author like herself—a journalist and now, with *Feast* under her belt, an accomplished editor, too—would *ever* bend to such a crazy-ass notion . . .

Well, she'd prove her mettle against this scholar—this "award-winning" Hemingway biographer. Let his little book whet the big boys' appetite for the blockbuster—her life in all its hard and glittering facets. The true gen as only *she* could tell it, in her own words.

Smiling, Mary nodded at her maid, signaling her at last to usher the Paulsons into the sitting room to await her arrival.

Hannah

The living room of the Topping House was awash in western decor.

Low-slung, green upholstered furniture. Floral-print wingchairs, walls paneled in oak.

The home felt slightly embalmed, but fell far short of embodying the sort of self-conscious, time-capsule shrines that Hemingway's former houses in Key West or Cuba had become.

Hannah noticed there wasn't a single photograph or portrait of Papa in sight. As Richard and Mary talked, Hannah watched the widow, trying hard to fathom what in Mary had drawn Ernest to the tiny, rather frail woman seated across from her.

It should have been hallucinatory to be sitting here with Mary Hemingway after having read so much about her—having so much trivia about the widow thrown at her by Richard these past months. But, at least so far, there was such a gulf between the legend and the reality of Mary that Hannah just found herself studying the woman, trying to detect whatever Mary had that had bound Ernest Hemingway to her for so many years.

What kept Papa with Mary through so many bitter battles? Hannah still couldn't see it.

They nibbled on small cakes Mary had had sent in from town. Hannah sipped from a glass of decaffeinated iced tea, looking at the surrounding mountains as she sat at the desk where Papa's last typewriter still rested at the ready—confronting a vista perhaps calculated by his keeper to distract a writer in decline.

Mary Hemingway settled back in her chair with a fresh gimlet mixed for her by her maid. She lit a cigarette. The chair she sat in was an oversize wingchair draped with a floral, fruit-and-vine-covered slipcover. The chair was arranged to command the room, reminding Hannah of photographs of a much larger Gertrude Stein, ponderously perched in her own half-assed throne in her salon at 27 rue de Fleurus.

No. The comparison didn't truly hold, Hannah realized, for almost lost in the depths of her overstuffed, too-large chair, Mary more resembled a midget.

And Mary had not found for herself a Toklasesque toady.

Mary was clearly alone in the bleakest sense. The more the widow talked, the more evident it was that in Mary's mind, it was Mary and Papa's ghost versus the world. The widow spent the first twenty minutes of their visit bashing first wife Hadley, then Pauline, and then Martha Gellhorn, castigating each of them for various weaknesses, character defects, or personality quirks that made them all inferior—in Mary's eyes—to herself, whom she regarded as the perfect wife for Ernest Hemingway. ("Four's the charm," Mary had said, raising her drink. "Here's to me!")

Hannah thought that Mary's busty little body, which impressed eldest Hemingway son Jack as it rose glisteningly nude from his father's Cuban pool, had grown lumpy and misshapen with premature age and the warping ravages of too many falls and badly mended bones. The life had similarly been washed out of her once-brown hair that had endured countless, many-hued bleaches and rinses at hair-infatuated, balding Papa's whimsical requests. A Cuban sun and God only knew how many acres of grain alcohol had left Mary's face deeply lined and weathered like a distressed leather couch.

Earlier, as Hannah leafed through several photo books of Mary and Ernest's time together, she was struck by the appalling speed with which Mary and her famous spouse had aged together. Or perhaps aged one another.

Fifteen too-high-mileage years.

"Papa had his darkest times, there at the end," Mary said. "The other wives never had to cope with the vile shit *I* endured. Maybe the worst was after my big fall in 'fifty-eight, when I broke my elbow. I was kind of mewling around and groaning, and Ernest lectured me all the way to the hospital, grumbling 'soldiers don't cry.' I had to remind him I was no soldier." Mary shook her head; stared into her glass.

"Still and all, I can't complain," she said. "Who can say who had it worse in his better times? Me? Martha, or Pauline? Maybe Hadley: I sometimes try to put myself in her place, that awful morning in the 1920s when she had to tell Papa about losing his manuscripts at that train station. It was the end of them, right there, although it was much later before either one really knew it. To have to tell your writer-husband you have literally lost his work? God, how horrible that must have been for her. If I had walked off and left a manuscript of Papa's unguarded—let alone allowed it to be stolen—I'd fully expect the big bastard to blow my brains out. And I would deserve no less." A sly, hard-to-read smile. "Hell, maybe I would load the fucking gun for him."

Hannah bit her lip: If *she* could have been one of Hem's women, what would she have done differently? Could she have maintained Hem's love as Hadley, Pauline, Martha, and Mary had all failed in various ways to do? Hannah certainly wanted to believe so. Perhaps as a fellow writer—not the competitive kind that Martha had been, but a supportive fellow author—perhaps Hannah could have engaged the artist *and* the lover in Hem. Perhaps, through her own passion and talent and love of sports, she might have helped Papa to integrate the various aspects of his personality that sometimes seemed so destructively set against one another. It was certainly pretty to think so.

"It must have been very exciting," Hannah said distractedly, "living with a writer of your husband's talent and stature." She almost winced as she said it; it came across as vapid.

Mary just shook her head. "Sure. There are two kinds of people, I've concluded. There are the ones who admire Papa as a personality—for the romantic, exotic way he lived his life and the verve he brought to all that. And then there are the ones like Richard here—the ones who sit in rooms and write about all that prose Papa wrote. There are the ones who savor the words, and the ones who can't stop obsessing over them." Mary lit a cigarette and said, "I'll tell you what living with a writer like that does—it demystifies writing for you, in some ways." Mary smiled at Richard. Hannah watched, trying to characterize the look in Mary's face—calculating, maybe.

Hannah smiled uncertainly. Living with Richard had changed her attitudes toward writing in some ways, after all, and not for the better. Did Mary also mean that living with Hem had made the craft of writing somehow *smaller*? Constant exposure to an academic having that effect on a fiction writer was one thing, but if proximity to Hemingway could undermine one's appreciation of literary fiction? Well, that was a terrible thought. Hannah said, "What do you mean by that?"

"Papa lived as an artist," Mary said. "Everything, every single detail and activity, was directed toward the end of writing. If you live as an artist, the art itself is just an outgrowth of the life lived. It comes as easily as anything else a person does as a simple trade. If Papa were here now, he'd spend a few minutes listening and watching you two, then he'd have all he'd need to write a sketch capturing you two in all your facets. I've seen it, and I know. Hell, I influenced him in his writing in that way, often enough. Fed Ernest material by shaping our life together in ways he could use in his books. Here, I'll show you how easy it becomes."

Winking, Mary picked up a notebook and pen from a table at her elbow and began writing.

Hannah watched the widow intently. Mary wrote in a manner reminiscent of Hannah's own compositional style—fast and viscerally, with no false starts or second thoughts. Mary attacked the page. Hannah wondered what the hell the woman could be writing with such speed and determination.

Hannah looked over at Richard. He looked very confused, even unsettled. What was happening now clearly didn't tally with any sense of Mary that Richard held. This was something new and esoteric to Richard, well outside his jaundiced view of the widow. Mary stayed at it, writing quickly—laughing here and there at something in her own composition that amused her.

The doorbell rang. Mary, beaming with her closed-mouth smile, winked and said, "That'll be Hector." She suddenly crumpled up her impromptu manuscript and tossed it at the wastepaper basket. The ball of paper missed and lay there on the floor, tantalizing Hannah. But discreetly bending to retrieve the wad of paper was something of a challenge for the pregnant young woman. Hannah looked at the paper there by Mary's chair, biting her lip.

What the bloody hell was scrawled across those pages?

Richard said, "Hector? Lassiter? The mystery writer?"

"For God's sake, don't call Lasso *that* to his *face*," Mary said.

"'Crime writer' would be much more to Hector's liking. But more and more, he's really a novelist with crime in his books. He's got the Papa illness, too, but don't tell him I said that." She winked at the professor and said, "Well, the party's starting now! Best you start mixing more drinks, Professor."

Hannah said, "What do you mean, 'illness'?"

She guessed Mary meant that this Lassiter was slipping into paranoia or dementia, but Mary said: "Hector has no distance from himself when he writes. The space between himself and his characters is almost nonexistent now. Like Papa at the end, Hector writes about writers. That so-called 'postmodern' shit like Papa was doing in *The Garden of Eden*. But Hector's okay. A big, handsome son of a bitch, too."

Hannah tried to recall the man she'd seen the other night at the lodge, but it had happened so fleetingly, and Richard had only explained to her who Hector was when he was already out of sight.

As Richard rose to follow Mary's order to mix fresh drinks, Mary leaned in closer to Hannah. She said softly, "Did Dickie mention what I said about you helping him with my book?"

Hannah was taken aback. *What in hell?* "Uh, no, he didn't."

"Well, sit tight," Mary said. "I'll bring him around. I want you on this job with him. These male Hemingway scholars, all they can think about is Papa. But you? You'll protect me, I know it. You'll look after my interests and see that bastard scholar husband of yours does right by me."

Hannah hardly knew what to say. Even if she felt inclined to give it a try, Richard would never stand for it. Hannah smiled, shrugged, and said, "I only write fiction."

Mary just smiled. "I want this. I'm in a position to get whatever I want now."

Richard

Heavy, deliberate steps on the stairs: Richard saw a long shadow on the floor and then this Hollywood-handsome, stylishly dressed older man was turning the corner; tall and tanned.

Hector Lassiter was clean shaven, and his graying dark hair was slicked back. He wore black slacks and loafers and a loose-fitting hounds-tooth sports jacket over a cream-colored shirt that was open at the collar; charisma to spare. Richard watched Hannah watching Lassiter. He thought, *Cocksucker...*

The professor shook his head: He really needed *this,* now, of all times. Christ... And now Richard was sorry he was standing. Lassiter had a couple of inches on him at least—made Richard feel tiny.

Mary struggled up and met the goddamn *mystery* writer, throwing her arms around Lassiter and then feinting a punch to his chin and delivering one to his gut. Hector seemed ready for that, and didn't react to the fairly stiff blow to his belly.

"There's my good-looking son of a bitch," Mary said. "Jesus, Lasso, you're even prettier than you were in Cuba. Looking younger. How can that be?"

Hector bent low to kiss her forehead. He looked rather angry at Mary, in Richard's estimation—now, what the hell was *that* about? Hector shrugged and said, "Enjoying the last belle époque, maybe. Before God pulls the critical cotter pin."

Jesus, Lord, if so, please pull it now, Richard thought bitterly. He fingered the vial in his coat pocket. *I don't need this man here, not* now *of all times,* he thought. *Fuck.*

Oblivious to Hector's obvious hostility toward her, the widow introduced Richard and Hannah and then punched Hector in the stomach again.

Hector put out a hand and Richard shook it. Hector's hand engulfed Richard's. The professor winced and tried to squeeze back, but Hector had the first and firmer grip. Hector said, "Your Paris book was really pretty good, pal." Hector let go and Richard flexed his throbbing hand.

Rather than take it as a compliment, Richard chose to dwell on the mystery writer's phrasing—Lassiter said it like he was *surprised* the Paris book was good.

Well, to hell with Lassiter.

Hector hesitated when he saw Hannah. He smiled warmly and squeezed her hand; Richard opened and closed his fists.

"*You* I remember," Hector said, smiling at Hannah. "You were out walking the other night and I offered you a ride, but this character waved me on." Hector jacked a thumb in Richard's direction. The professor thought he should do something to mark territory—make it clear Hannah was his woman—but he couldn't come up with a worthy gambit in time.

Hannah said, "Pleasure to meet you officially, Mr. Lassiter. It's an honor."

Hector held her hand, steadying Hannah as she eased back onto the loveseat, her other hand pressed to the cushion behind her as she sat slowly down. "Please call me Hector, darlin'."

Richard rolled his eyes and moved back behind the bar. He raised an inquiring eyebrow, and Mary smiled. "Another gimlet for me," she said. Richard smiled back, ignoring Hannah's frown. He said, "What are you drinking, Lassiter?"

Hector checked Hannah's glass and said, "Whatever Hannah's having will do."

Richard shook his head. "Don't remember the hard cases in your books drinking much decaf tea, Lassiter."

"Your confusing character for personality," Hector said. "And you can call me Hector, too, *Dick*, okay?"

Richard felt his face flush. Did the *mystery* writer with the grating Texas accent throw a little extra gravel into his pronunciation of *Dick*? Richard was pretty sure the *mystery* writer had done that. Richard glared at Hector and thought again, *Cocksucker*...

Richard tried to move around—to get his back to Hector Lassiter so he could slip the contents of the vial into Mary Hemingway's drink without Lassiter or Hannah seeing.

In his head, he was running through the questions he meant to put to Mary—circling, tightening the noose with each query he'd put to her. He'd imagined over and over increasing the pitch and probity of his interrogation as the mysterious brew given him by the man worked its magic on the old widow.

But now here was Lassiter. It *might* be prudent to back off. But there was also *the man* with the potions. The man, who had his boot to Richard's backside. Richard felt he should hold off now, with Lassiter in the mix. But the man was so adamant, and yes, the man with the potions scared Richard.

Still...

"Maybe this is a mistake," he said, looking at the vial clutched in his hand. The words were out of his mouth before he could check himself.

Lassiter said, "What was that, Dick?"

"A mistake—I . . . I forgot what you wanted," Richard said.

"Whatever Hannah's having," Lassiter said again, watching him more intently.

"Right. Sure." Richard looked again at the vial. How quickly would it take effect? Would Lassiter or the others even notice the widow was drugged? Shit, Mary was clearly quite drunk. . . .

But he didn't want to put the big questions to Mary with these two witnesses. Hannah knew his thesis, of course. But knowing Richard's suspicions and hearing Mary confirm them were very different things.

And even if he risked putting the questions to Mary in front of Lassiter, would it even work? What if Mary denied it all?

If he got his confession to Papa's murder, Lassiter, or even Hannah, might deny it happened. He could imagine Lassiter maybe trying to protect his dead friend's widow: "No, *Dick*, that's not how it was, you lying cocksucker." Lassiter would say it in that Texas baritone, and some fucking hick-town jury would eat it up.

Richard looked down and noticed something that caused him to jump slightly. He saw that as he wrestled with it all, he'd gone and done the deed—he'd emptied the dropper's contents into Mary's gimlet.

So, he was *committed*. Richard remembered now the man saying the stuff he'd been given wasn't terribly fast acting.

He looked again at the empty dropper.

Done, either way.

Thank God. Now he would just have to be careful. Get what he could get from Mary; try to get her away from Lassiter. Yes: get her alone, far from the intrusion of a pulp novelist, and go for the jugular. He'd maybe say, "You don't look well," to Mary, then hustle Lassiter and Hannah away—all the while going back over whatever he'd pulled from her to that point. Then, armed for bear, he'd return alone and tear into the drugged widow like she was an underprepared grad student defending a flawed thesis.

Richard saw there was a mirror running behind the bar above the counter. Although he'd put his back to Hector, Hannah, and Mary, Richard was facing the damned mirror. The angle made it tricky to tell, but he thought Lassiter might be watching him in the mirror's reflection.

Maybe fucking Lassiter had seen him spike Mary's drink.

But maybe *not:* The mystery writer wasn't raising an alarm yet.

No, Richard decided—Lassiter clearly *hadn't* seen him slip the mickey into Mary's gimlet.

So far, so good. . . .

Hector

Hector bit his lip, trying to decide whether to call the goddamn scholar on what he thought he'd seen—this possible poisoning of the Widow Hemingway's drink.

On the other hand, "whistleblower" had never been Hector's style. And he was still casing the room and the cast—trying to get a handle on the dynamics and subtext of this collection of characters arrayed before him. In theory, he could maybe get closer to Mary; upset her tainted cocktail, then mix Mary a drink himself. Just the fact the bastard *scholar* knew Creedy made all of this seem sinister.

But Hector was pretty sure Richard had *seen* Hector see what Richard had done. Hector figured it this way: If the stuff Richard slipped Mary was something that could really *harm* the last Mrs. Hemingway, Richard would now feel compelled to back off—maybe even spill the spiked drink himself.

Still . . .

Tough goddamn call.

Hector bit his lip and decided to wait; watch some more.

He sat down next to Hannah on the short, floral-print loveseat. Her attention seemed to be drawn to a crumpled scrap of paper on the floor. Hannah didn't quite seem the type, but Hector knew that to the typical Hemingway enthusiast, every object in the house, even a used piece of paper with a few of Papa's doodles or alcohol shopping lists, was of momentous value. Well, if the girl was some magpie, Mary deserved the loss, cavalier as she seemed to be with Hem's leavings. He hated thieves as much as the next man—hell, maybe more—but better in this circumstance to be brazen: Take the goddamn thing boldly rather than fawn and suck up and inveigle, hoping for granted scraps like the woman's egghead husband was doing.

Then again, it just looked like a crumpled-up piece of paper that had missed the wastepaper basket.

Hannah pointed at the ball of paper. "Could you get that for me, Mr. Lassiter? I dropped it, and . . ."

She nodded at her belly.

Well, what the hell? And he liked her sheepish smile. Hector smiled back, scooped up Mary's discarded manuscript, and folded it into Hannah's hand, letting the touch linger. Pretty young woman . . . some real presence there.

Richard

Mary said to Lassiter, "You married presently, Lasso?"

Lassiter shook his head. He seemed to bridle a little at Mary's use of the nickname. The pulp novelist said, "Not presently. Focusing on the career for the moment. The *long game*, you know? Vetting unpublished manuscripts. Destroying what's no good and finishing what is. Going over scraps from old days. Paris days. I don't want loose ends or castoffs of mine getting out there after I'm gone. Don't want some fool fussing over my leavings and trying to foist them on readers as my top-shelf work." Lassiter was looking hard at Mary now.

Richard was curious about the author's rather caustic, unexpected remarks—wanted to know more about what lay behind them.

Mary said, "Well, these next few days will be a pain in my ass. Have to lay low and stay shut in with all these scholars skulking around. Present company aside, academics are just sad-ass. You agree, Hector?"

Lassiter leaned back and wrapped an arm across the back of the love-seat, his arm brushing Hannah's shoulder. Richard saw. He wondered again if the mystery writer had seen him in the mirror and was daring him to a confrontation by being so flirty with Hannah. He couldn't fall prey to Lassiter's baiting him. Hell, he could withstand letting the old bastard cop a few feels of his wife in service to this greater goal. Richard suppressed a smile: He had contacts. Maybe down the road, when his book was done, he'd call up the editor of *The New York Times Book Review*. He'd offer to review one of Lassiter's mystery novels, then skewer the son of a bitch in print. Then he'd see what Lassiter had to say about academics.

The mystery novelist stretched his legs and crossed them at the ankles. Taking his time, Lassiter responded to Mary, but his pale blue eyes remained focused on Richard:

"Academics can be their own kind of problem. Poison to a writer. Worse still—more dangerous to a writer and his legacy—can be a poorly chosen literary executor. Or executrix. I reread *A Moveable Feast* recently. Have to say, it reads different to me than it did in typescript in Cuba. I mean, it was fringing brilliant there. Now? Sentimentality's crept in. Chapters out of order from what I read in 'fifty-nine. And some of that stuff in that last chapter—which wasn't even there before—hell, some of that stuff reads like someone else's writing."

Richard looked up sharply; God, there might be something in there for him—a paper, at least, for *The Review*. If only he weren't so goddamn distracted at this moment. If he could just pursue that a bit more with Lassiter.

"*That's* why you look so good," Mary said, ignoring Hector's remark. "Because you're single again, I mean. That's why you look so much better."

Lassiter just shook his head.

God, that's all he needed now—for Mary to derail and go off on some horny tangent after this famous skirt-chaser, Lassiter. Richard called from behind the bar, "Mary was telling us about her pregnancy disaster back in 'forty-six, *Hector*."

Richard knew the story well and so didn't have to listen too hard— could focus on his now-more-dangerous gambit . . . martial his tropes while Mary nattered on:

The newlywed Hemingways were traveling cross-country to Sun Valley in August of '46. Mary, a few months pregnant, began hemorrhaging internally from a tubular pregnancy.

An egg had become fertilized and lodged in Mary's fallopian tube instead of the uterus. The tube gave way and Mary began bleeding like crazy. The doctors wrote Mary off when her veins collapsed and they couldn't find a pulse or feed her plasma. They told Papa to say good-bye to Mary. Papa said that was useless since she was unconscious. It was a moment right out of *A Farewell to Arms*.

But Papa rose to the occasion; there was never a time when Hemingway was better to have by your side than when the chips were truly down.

Richard caught himself smiling as he fumbled with the ice cube trays: Papa was undeniably the best man in any crisis. Told to tell his wife farewell, Hem instead had taken charge. The chief surgeon was away on a fishing trip. Those left behind weren't up to the task. They wrote Mary off for dead. So Ernest put on a gown and mask and ordered the intern to cut for a vein. Ernest inserted the needle himself, and made sure the plasma fed correctly. Ernest milked and tipped the line to get out all the air bubbles that were blocking the plasma's flow. Papa really saved Mary while the intern just looked on like some starstruck idiot. Richard looked at Hannah: Alas, the Scot was too robust to afford Richard a chance to save *her* in faltering childbirth....

Mary said, "Five bottles of plasma, two transfusions, and a long time in an oxygen tent, but I pulled through. Papa was a hero to all the nurses afterwards! And of course he ate it up! Mostly though, Papa took it as heartening proof that once in a very very great while, in never giving up or quitting, fate can indeed be 'fucked,' as he put it. He said he never saw anybody—anybody *ever*—come closer."

Hannah said, "Sounds like he was a great man to have around in an emergency. Taking charge. Knowing just what to do to care for his woman."

Hannah *would* go there, wouldn't she? Richard cut in, "After the incident in Casper, you couldn't have children, right?" He was keenly aware that Lassiter watched him as Richard made the pulp author's and Hannah's drinks—they went untampered with, of course, but Richard's hands shook a little to be watched so intently.

Mary shook her head, scooting a small African fetish-cum-ashtray to the side of the table to prop up her feet. She winked at Hannah. "That's right. After the 'incident,' the remaining tube was 'occluded.'"

"Papa was bitterly disappointed by that," Richard called from the bar, "wasn't he?"

"It caused . . . a *rift*," Mary said. "You know, we even had a name picked out for our baby—Bridget."

"Very pretty name," Hannah said. "Goes well with the last name."

"Yes, but what a burden that last name would have been for poor little Bridget," Mary said. "Of course Bridget wasn't destined to be. She died before she was ever alive and then Ernest died before he was truly dead and now they are both just dead. As the father of three boys, Papa always wanted a daughter."

Hannah said, "Martha and Papa never had children together, did they?"

Mary turned to Hannah. "Martha lied to Ernest," the widow said. "Knowing Papa wanted a little girl as badly as he did, Martha went ahead and married Papa even though she was barren from a botched abortion. Or abortions." Richard finished preparing the drinks. God, he'd made a bit of a mess. He looked around for a towel to clean up. Between his nerves, his own buzz, and fucking Lassiter giving him the evil eye all this while . . . well, it was a miracle he'd pulled it off. He looked around for a tray or something to place the drinks on.

Hannah asked Lassiter, "Do you have children, Mr. Lassiter?"

Lassiter said, his voice thick, "Had a daughter. She died at the age of three. Heart problem."

Lassiter was standing now; striding to the bar, goddamn him!

Before Richard could react, Lassiter grabbed Mary's gimlet and his own iced tea. "I've got these, amigo." Smiling, Lassiter actually sniffed Mary's drink, said softly to Richard, "You're a hard pourer, fella."

Richard just looked up at him, trying to keep his legs from shaking . . . willing himself not to flush, but feeling his pulse in his ears.

Lassiter winked and then walked over and handed the glass to Mary. Mary smiled as Lassiter handed her the gimlet, and they briefly tapped glasses. Richard handed Lassiter the other glass of iced tea for Hannah, then quickly moved for Papa's former chair before the pulp novelist could claim it.

Lassiter sat down again alongside Hannah and clicked glasses with her. He said, "To a beautiful baby and a fast delivery."

Richard Paulson raised an eyebrow, about to take that seat next to

Mary. She held up a finger, then tipped her glass. Richard watched as Mary drained her drink at a pull and held the glass out for him. "Again?"

The stuff had been in the widow's veins for nearly half an hour. She seemed groggy, but hell, that could be all the gin. Richard kept trying to put questions to her, to lay the groundwork for his later, solo assault. But Hannah kept interrupting with busybody questions related to domestic matters that bored and annoyed Richard.

And Lassiter? He seemed to have his own strange and bitter agenda. He kept returning to the issue of Papa's unfinished manuscripts, all his queries peppered with portent and bombast.

But the stuff had a hold on Mary now—something in her eyes. And she was quicker to talk; almost manic in the speed of her answers. There was an uncensored frankness to her responses now, and she was given to sliding into monologues of intense self-exposure.

"About time someone finally got around to me," Mary said suddenly, stubbing out her cigarette. "Frankly, I don't know if Dickie here is the best one to tell my tale, but at least he appears truly interested in the gen. And he's shown insight for Papa's work. Not like so many of the others who want to warp the man and artist to suit their narrow little theses, which rhymes with feces. And it's goddamn well my turn. Lord knows that bitch Martha can write her own story about life with Papa if she ever maneuvers around her own elephantine ego to do it—which she never will. One book is already being done on Hadley, the saint, and another is coming, I hear. Pauline has had her time in the sun."

Mary glanced over her shoulder at a framed black-and-white photograph of herself with President Kennedy. "I'm the one left to carry the cross and fight all Papa's fights. Coping with the lawyers and the publishers. Seeing Scribner does right by us. Getting the last of the printable works in print. Nurturing Papa's reputation—that's Reputation with a capital R. I had to negotiate with Castro to get the last of our manuscripts out of Cuba. That cost us the Finca and the *Pilar*. And then there are the so-called scholars. Creeping Christ. All the scavengers circling, wanting to see the letters and poems. Self-gutting hyenas begging for glimpses of the unpublished manuscripts—*The Garden* and the Africa book—and the other odds and ends. Jackals sniffing for some unplumbed scrap they can parlay into tenure or some hulking-ass psychological mumbo-jumbo disguised as literary criticism. Bug-eating, cocksucking parasites."

Richard ground his teeth, thought, *Fuck you, you old whore!* And to attack his profession in front of a fucking pulp writer like Lassiter? In front of Hannah, his student? Strike that—wife. *Whatever...* Fucking unacceptable. Unforgivable. Well, he'd seen Mary up close now. He knew what he was up against. And Lassiter seemed to be dug in for a time.

He'd come back—get Mary alone and hit her with a bigger dose of the stuff. He looked at Hannah sitting there next to Lassiter, who had his arm around behind her again—looking like *they* were the couple. Hannah probably was enjoying his flirting. And probably enjoying Mary's attack on his profession as it mirrored some things Hannah had said herself recently, albeit in subtler form. Maybe, if he had extra of the drug, he'd try a little on Hannah at some point. Find out what she *really* thought about him....

It *was* a notion....

Hector

He sipped his iced tea, watching the professor over the rim of his glass and savoring the effect Mary's crazy diatribe was having on the egghead.

Though Richard was trying hard to mask it—grinning like a death's head, now—it was clear each of Mary's flippant and salty remarks was landing home like kidney punches to the academic's soul. Richard seemed on the verge of a grand tirade. And it was clear his anger encompassed not just Mary, but his pretty young wife.

It wasn't the way he looked at Hannah that made Hector think that. No, it was in the way he *didn't* look at his wife: Richard seemed to be letting it swell inside him; storing it up to launch back at his wife later, in private. Hector feared for Hannah a bit.

Hector watched Hannah watching Mary: Gal was out pretty far on the limb with this professor husband of hers. Her ears did seem to perk up at some of Mary's nastier but hard-to-deny digs. Like they maybe validated things the comely blonde also couldn't let go of. Hector had the sense that Hannah might not be in agreement so much, but also storing up . . . arming for bear for some later, private confrontation.

He hoped Hannah could hold her own. Richard Paulson was slovenly, egocentric, and clearly an alcoholic. Paulson was bitter and used up and obviously corrupt if he was tied in some way to Donovan Creedy. But he also seemed a mean drunk.

Yet Hector thought in a confrontation for the title, he might just put his money on Hannah to deliver the KO—to throw everything she had and knock the drunken Hemingway *scholar* on his ass for all day. *Maybe.*

Then Hector smiled inwardly and shook his head. Jesus, here he was again—getting distracted by a pretty face and beguiling accent. Long legs and eyes a man could lose himself in. He was here to deal with Mary, and the professor's corrupt antics aside, it was clear it was going to take Hector's full concentration—particularly with Mary in this strange, addled state.

Richard handed Mary another gimlet, then pulled the chair over closer to the widow, cozying up like some lamprey eel—clamped tightly to Mary as she thrashed around.

Richard Paulson raised an eyebrow, sitting down next to Mary. "What were you saying?"

Mary beamed at him. "I was saying I think I've found in you my own most goddamn wonderful parasite."

Richard clearly didn't like that one—not a bit.

Hannah? How did she feel to have her husband likened to a leech or a tick? Another hard call—Hector just couldn't read her expression now. He wondered if she was an academic in the purest sense? He said softly, "When you're not watching the professor here ply his trade, what do you do, sweetheart?"

Hannah said, "I write."

"Grad student? Another . . . academic?"

She smiled. "No, fiction. Short stories, mostly."

Well, well. Now Hannah interested him even more. As a rule, Hector tried to steer far clear of married women—had never really added *that* sin to his long list of vices. And Hannah's being pregnant was a double stop sign. Hector wasn't sure he was even drawn to her romantically . . . but he felt something for her building inside him. Maybe it was just the fact she was clearly badly married, and perhaps in real jeopardy from this sorry son-of-a-bitch husband who'd apparently cast his lot with Creedy.

Hector was raising his hand to comb his fingers through her long flaxen hair when he caught himself and shook his head again, ruefully.

As Richard and Mary parried, Hector sensed Hannah surreptitiously glance over at him to make sure he was watching the bickering pair. Then she reached for the crumpled piece of paper Hector had retrieved for her. She smoothed it out.

Evidently startled by the paper's contents, Hannah didn't notice as Hector read over her shoulder.

Hector arched his eyebrows. It looked like some kind of manuscript written in Mary's hand—script he recognized from Christmas cards and say-too-little letters sent in the wake of Hem's death.

And the "story" seemed to be this crazy and corrosive narrative about Hannah and Richard Paulson's marriage. *Holy Jesus*—what *was* this piece of writing?

Hector realized then that Hannah was staring up at him—that she had in fact realized he was sneaking a read. Her cheeks flushed. Hannah folded the piece of paper up and slipped it into her pocket.

Hector figured it was even odds: She was pissed at him for reading this strange document Mary had written about Hannah and her husband, or she was simply livid at the document's sampled content.

Hell, probably it was *both*.

Hector managed a smile and squeezed Hannah's hand. He said softly, so only she could hear, "You and me, kiddo, we're in a strange and lonely club here."

Mary sipped her drink and smiled, showing no teeth. "Yummy." The old widow frowned suddenly. In a confidential tone, she said, "Dick?"

Richard said, "Yes?"

"I have an important question for you, Dickie."

"Shoot," Richard said with a slight slur.

"Why are all of Papa's would-be biographers men?"

Richard could see where that was going: Mary was getting ready to raise the issue directly with Hannah—this notion that Hannah should serve as his cowriter of Mary's biography. Well, fuck that. And he'd not have that topic discussed in front of Lassiter. The thing to do, he decided, was take Hannah and go, *now*. Sooner he and Hannah left—sooner Richard got Hannah away from Lassiter's wandering eye—well, the sooner the party would break up. Then Richard could return alone to work over the widow.

Creedy

In a modest home across the street from the Topping House, Creedy sat in the window of a darkened room, wearing headphones and scanning the Hemingway place with a pair of binoculars. His hiding place glowed with lights from the various listening contraptions that lined one wall of the room. A couple of silent technicians sat before the stations, twisting knobs and checking tape.

Someone was leaving the Topping House.

Creedy narrowed his eyes: It was Richard Paulson and his pregnant wife, already packing it in. What the hell was *this*? Based on what the taps had picked up, Richard still hadn't gotten the goods.

Had Richard even dosed the widow? Judging by the sound of Mary's voice—that tell-tale manic edge—Richard had done that. But now the professor was departing, and more dumbfounding, leaving Mary in that doped state alone with Hector Lassiter. *Fuck!*

He ground his teeth, staring at the Paulsons. Creedy snorted softly. Even though he often enough used women as cover, he detested that tactic in others—men who took women into the field with them. *Fucking amateurs...*

Hector

Hector licked his lips. He watched Mary carefully. Her voice was slower, duller. Her hands were trembling and she seemed to have developed this strange tic in her left thumb. She was covered in a thin sheen of sweat. He said, "So, *Islands* is definitely the next one? Don't want to go for *The Garden of Eden*? Think I could get into *that* one."

"You read both manuscripts, such as they are, in Cuba," Mary said, slurring, looking as though it was a struggle to keep her eyes open. Her eyelids were twitching now. "Which would you truly go for—not as a writer, but as a *reader*?"

"*The Garden of Eden*," Hector said. "It's *fresh*. Hem was reaching there, moving from modernism into *post*modernism."

"And who wants to read *that* shit?" Mary wrinkled her nose. "A writer writing about a writer writing? What the fuck is that? Where's the film potential? Navel-gazing, that's what that is. Masturbatory, self-mytholigization. No thank you. At least *Islands* has some action."

Hector said, "Like I told Hem back in 'fifty-nine when I read the manuscript, it's too close to *To Have and Have Not*. Harry Morgan and old Tom Hudson's ends are too near the same, point for point. Hem was chewing his cud."

"That's why I want you to write a *new* ending," Mary said, winking.

Hector rubbed his jaw, and said, "I thought what the two of us were going to do was edit what Hem left us, not write new material. Wouldn't be anything like Hem's book if we presumed to do other. Would it?"

"We have to be realistic, Lasso," Mary said, waving a sluggish hand. "You read *A Moveable Feast* in manuscript and you said you've read the final version, too. I had to do quite a bit of work, there. That *I* could do. But *Islands* needs some machismo to bring it up to snuff. You know the milieu, Lasso. You know sports fishing. You did some rum and refugee running, according to Papa. You'll make it perfect."

She smiled. "But what I'd *really* like your help with is *my* book. My memoir. Those bastards at Papa's old house are giving me guff. Say what they've seen needs drastic editing. I'm willing to let you help me polish and smooth it out. And, with your publishing connections, I know you'll help me get a wonderful deal somewhere else."

Jesus Christ...

Hector said, "I thought Paulson was here to write your life story with you."

"That's my *biography* Richard's working on. I figure the market can really only bear a biography and a memoir about *moi*. So I'm cooperating on an authorized biography to control that, then I'll have my book with the true gen. Freeze out the other cocksuckers."

"Aha. Well, I'm a fiction writer, not a memoirist." Hector knew some critics who might argue that. Either way, he didn't want to appear to dismiss Mary's notion out of hand quite yet—not until he know more about this goddamn lost chapter. And he'd be damned to hell before he'd ever rewrite another writer, least of all Hem. Hector said, "What about other things left by Hem? There's something about the last safari, isn't there? The plane crashes?"

Mary shook her head. Her eyes closed, she said, "*The Green Hills of Africa* didn't sell in its first incarnation. Why expect the reheated version to do any better?"

Softly, Hector said, "Is the objective to enhance Ernest's reputation, or to sell books?"

"Both. But the latter, first."

"Oh."

Jesus . . . Hector saw it now, clear and terrible: Hem's entire long game was balanced on the head of a pin. Mary was mucking around with Hem's leavings. Creedy skulking around the edges toward some unknown end. This damn professor with his mysterious drugs. People inserting doctored manuscripts into Hem's cache of real leavings . . .

Hector *feared* for Hem's posthuma now.

Hector sipped wine. He decided to toe out there, just a bit. Trying to keep the anger from his voice, he said, "Heard there was more of *Feast* than you published and even more than I read. Heard Hem actually had a chapter written up on me."

"Wonderful," Mary said, smiling. "Truly wonderful portrait of you. I left it out because it was *so* fond. Didn't marry up with the tone of the book. But I have plans for it." She narrowed her eyes. "How'd you hear about it?"

Hector wasn't particularly sensitive to protecting Carlos Baker, but he did feel an obligation to shield Dexter. He said, "There are no secrets where writers and projects are concerned. You know how many letters Hem wrote; often corresponded in his cups. He mentioned it in one and that mention got mentioned and so on. I got word through channels." He watched Mary—she seemed unconcerned:

"I'll get you a copy when I get a chance," Mary said dismissively. "You'll love it." Her head dipped once, like she'd nearly dropped off.

Whatever Paulson had slipped the widow was finally firmly taking hold. Slow-acting stuff. Or perhaps the scholar had underdosed her.

Hector said, "Heard Hem was toying with a novel about me, too."

"He made notes," Mary said thickly, waving a hand again. "He never got going on it, or, if he did, I never found evidence. I've got all there is. Short of there being something in some vault, or safe-deposit box in Cuba that I know nothing about, it doesn't exist, Lasso. Sorry."

Hector believed her. He sighed: That, at least, was a load off. He said, "Too bad. Might have been good fun."

"Well, Papa was in bad shape, even in early 'fifty-nine, when you saw him." Mary offered her empty glass, and Hector rose to mix another. Out of practice in terms of serious drinking as he was, he was fairly convinced Mary might drink him under the table . . . even with whatever drug Paulson had slipped her in the mix. Hector made Mary's next gimlet a good bit milder than the last watered-down drink. Mary didn't seem to notice: She sampled it, smacked her lips, and said, "*Dee*-lish."

He lit another cigarette for her and Mary said, "After you left Cuba in 'fifty-nine, and after Spain and his birthday party, Papa went downhill fast. He became crazy as a coot. There was nothing really getting written then. Papa made plenty of notes and had grand plans, but nothing came of them."

Hector decided to risk it: "Look, Mary, I'll confess that, through channels, I've seen that lost chapter on me. It's goddamn bogus. I want to know from you how it came to be typed up, and, let's call it *augmented*."

"Bogus? Augmented?" Mary shook her head. "You've had too much to drink, clearly."

"Not at all. I knew Hem. There's stuff in there that he wouldn't write. That he didn't write. I want to know more about the provenance of this so-called lost chapter, Mary."

"You've lost me, Lasso. If you've seen a copy—a true copy, then you must have seen Papa's handwritten notes in the margins. We found it in Paris on the way back from Africa, after the plane crashes. It was among other drafts of Papa's he'd left in trunks stored in the basement of the Ritz. It obviously passed beneath Ernest's eye—he made those notes about surrealism just a couple of years before he died. Seems to me your quarrel must be with Papa. Good luck getting answers from him." Mary said suddenly, "Save money, Lasso! Stay right here tonight." Mary pulled something from under her sweater—a necklace or charm of some kind—and rubbed it between thumb and forefinger.

"Appreciate that, but the conference is covering my expenses at the Lodge," Hector said firmly. "I aim to soak those sorry longhairs for every cent I can."

"Well, that can't last long," Mary said. "Not more than a couple of days, right? This project we're undertaking, this could take many months. So…"

"We'll see," Hector said. He started looking around the room now—looking for documents, manuscripts. Given Mary's clear deterioration, he was well past the need for subtlety—Mary was clearly going down fast and hard. *We're not through with this other*, he thought. *We have a hell of a lot more to talk about regarding this matter of the lost chapter and where it came from. How it came to pass from Hem's scrawl on some slips of paper lost thirty or so years ago to a fresh document off a typewriter.*

Mary sleepily veered again: "I watched you so closely watching that girl. Studying her … especially after she told you she's a writer. What did you think of Hannah?"

"Mrs. Paulson?" Hector shrugged. "Pretty. But I didn't really get to take her measure."

"Well, mess that she is to settle for Dick, I wouldn't be surprised if she could do a better job with my biography than her so-called award-winning husband," Mary said, her eyes closed now.

He looked around the room, looked for manuscript pages. Hector had come back around to his main intent: He needed to find and destroy that original of the lost chapter.

Hem's posthuma was already becoming muddled and mauled in Mary's hands. Hector would be damned if he'd contribute to any of that with some piece of writing altered by Mary—or worse, some unknown party—being credited to Hem. There seemed to be a line of old friends, family, and hangers-on ready to feast on Hem's corpse; Hector would have no part in it.

He glanced again at Mary. Her eyes were open again, but glassy—like she didn't even see him now. She was muttering under her breath, some tune in pidgin Spanish he couldn't make out.

He drifted away from her—her glassy gaze didn't track him. Hector bit his lip, then headed upstairs to commence his search.

Creedy

Donovan Creedy hung on the dim sounds of Lassiter moving from room to room within the Topping House—passing through the rooms they'd been able to bug, anyway.

He'd heard Lassiter send the maid off at Mary's "direction" for fresh bottles of Gordon's and Dewar's—using that simple but effective subterfuge to have the place to himself for a time.

Occasionally, Creedy could see the author pass by a window. He heard doors open and close...drawers pulled open and slid shut. The crime novelist seemed to be conducting a very thorough search of the Hemingway house.

Creedy could also hear Mary making strange clicking noises with her teeth...muttering under her breath and occasionally calling out short, sharp obscenities.

Hector

In a bedroom he presumed to be Hem's, Hector found a makeshift office and a wooden shelf with slots filled with manuscript pages. Hector recognized several of those drafts. They were all Hem's...various versions of *Feast*. But nothing Hector recognized as his own.

Continuing his search of the house, Hector found a locked door that seemed to be a storeroom.

When she'd lost control of her hands, Hector had retrieved Mary's dropped cigarette from her lap before it could burn her or set her skirt on fire. As he ground it out, the key on the chain around her neck had tangled in the button of his sports jacket.

On a hunch, Hector crept back up to Mary. She was staring at her empty glass, muttering, "I'm dry, goddamn it, I'm dry!" He made another gimlet, then picked up a pair of scissors. He approached from behind her shoulder, standing behind her chair. As he let his fingers trail affectionately across the back of Mary's neck, he lifted the thin gold chain and slid it between the scissor blades. He then handed Mary the fresh drink over her shoulder. "Here you go, sweet," he said. As she took it with a trembling hand, he cut the thin chain, and then, pretending to pat her breastbone, caught the falling key. He said, "Need to get a fresh pack of smokes from my Chevy, honey. Back in a jiffy."

He was just going to have to make his remaining search a fast one.

Mary seemed focused on her booze . . . focused on the cover of a copy of *Field & Stream* on the table next to her.

Holding his breath, Hector tried the key in the storeroom lock; heard a *click* and felt the knob twist full.

Hector looked around the storeroom—more of Papa's precious shotguns and rifles in their racks . . . myriad boxes of shotgun shells and cartridges.

And more slotted shelves filled with more manuscript pages.

He left the storeroom door slightly ajar so he could hear the maid's return.

Hector slipped on his despised eyeglasses and began combing through Hem's unpublished works.

Given the urgency the moment demanded, he was surprised to feel this funny surge of affection just to see Hem's handwriting again—that downward sloping, cursive hand of Hem's that never stopped looking like a schoolboy's ciphering, even in the late 1950s when Hem was near the end, sick and struggling with those novels he couldn't finish.

Hem's holographs also pierced Hector in a very different way. Hector's first and last drafts tended to be pretty close, in sum. Somehow, for whatever reason, Hector's prose nearly always struck pay dirt on first pass.

It was clearly different for Hem—strikes and word and paragraph insertions running vertically up the borders of the page and onto the backs of some sheets. Revisions, excisions, and additions all over the place. The difference in their compositional styles was critical to Hector's search for false documents:

Hector looked for the least fretted-over pages, figuring those were most apt to be his own.

Mary

Mary realized, quite suddenly, she was on fire. She was sweating, thirsty . . . her heart racing. She narrowed her eyes: Was that dust on the coffee table there?

It *was*.

Useless hired help. Seething, Mary called for her maid. No answer. She was alone in the house. She vaguely remembered having had company, but she must have been mistaken about that. Hell, even the hired help was gone.

Goddamn her maid, anyway. Dammit!

Mary struggled up and then bustled to the kitchen for a damp rag. She'd dust the place herself! Sweep, too. "Goddamn useless hired help!"

She realized then she was talking aloud all this time. Well, so what? She was alone, anyway. Mary smiled and winked at her reflection. "Nobody around to call *us* buggy."

Wringing out the wet rag, Mary noticed some cabinet drawers cracked. Those cupboard doors were *never* left open.

"Someone's here," she said aloud to herself. Of course: They *would* be here again.

More spies.

Eyes, always watching . . . Lurkers, skulking around, inside and outside the Topping House.

Her own eyes darting, watching for shadows or figures moving past doorways, Mary made herself a fresh gimlet. A heavy pour on the gin and some missing steps in the preparation: She couldn't tell from her first sip. Mary began dusting, frantically and spottily, wiping down surfaces between sips of her gimlet and grousing out loud about her missing maid and all those spies running around her house now.

"Ah, yes, the fucking *spies*. We'd meant to do something about them, *hadn't* we?"

Papa thought they were FBI, but *he* was crazy.

Mary knew better—knew they were not Feds sneaking around her house.

No . . . *scholars—that's* what the cocksuckers were.

Rival publishers, critics, and would-be biographers, all of them angling to usurp her role as literary executor.

Hemingway hunters.

Bastards. That's who they were!

If he weren't dead, Papa would fetch a shotgun—get the drop on the maggots. Blow 'em to hell!

Well, she could do that well enough herself now. Papa had seen to that. "I know how to use a gun," she said aloud, this dark smile on her face—a rare smile that showed teeth. "I'll get my gun and I'll *kill* your asses!"

Creedy

Donovan Creedy leaned into the listening station's speaker; his heart racing to hear the widow's death threat. The bugs weren't state of the art—planted as they were before Hemingway's death—but they were good enough to hear Mary's ranting now.

Creedy wet his lips; there was no denying the drug had a tendency to provoke subjects to violence . . . sometimes to extreme irrational behavior. Early test subjects—men and women with mental capacities far exceeding that of this drunken widow—had hurled themselves from high-rise windows rather than continue taking the ride. They had beaten their heads against walls until they suffered fatal brain hemorrhages.

Standing at the window with his binoculars, Creedy cursed softly, wishing he had some kind of cameras inside the Topping House . . . some way of seeing the action.

A car turned into the driveway of the Topping House. Probably the maid, Creedy figured.

But, no, it was Richard Paulson—driving erratically, driving fast . . . slamming on the brakes and sending the rental car into a gravel-spitting stop. Creedy began pulling on his coat. Perhaps the professor had some gumption after all.

Richard

Frantic, furious, Richard sat in the car in the driveway of the concrete house, scanning his notes. He'd driven back to the lodge too fast... driven in silence, seething. Hannah's attention seemed to be split between watching Richard, watching the road for Richard, and restlessly toying with some crumpled scrap of paper she kept taking from her pocket and then putting back.

Once they'd reached the lodge, he'd hustled Hannah to their room, grabbed his sheaf of notes and a flask, and bolted back to the rental car. Wild-eyed, Richard read a few more notes to himself, trying to find the right buildup to posing the Big Question.

He realized he felt dizzy... strange. He took a slug from the flask, but that didn't seem to help anything. He felt loose-tongued... a little sleepy. And he realized his thigh was wet. Jesus, had he pissed himself?

He looked at his crotch and saw a stain over his right pant's pocket. Richard thrust his hand in his pocket and found the stopper had come loose from the vial. His eyes grew wide. The man had said to be careful with the stuff—that there was some indication it could be absorbed through the pores. Jesus, he'd dosed himself with half a bottle of the stuff, maybe!

His heart was racing and his tongue felt too big. It was hard to swallow. But he couldn't leave things as they were!

Richard took another shot of whiskey, then hustled out of the car to resume his interrogation of the widow—to get his all-important answer.

Mary

Mary moved to the upstairs gun cabinet—restocked and locked now that Papa was safely dead. Oh my! Did she actually say that last thing out loud? She was pretty sure she had. "Well... no shame in speaking the truth," she said. "Of course not."

Her heart was still racing; she was still sweating. She drained her gimlet, then mixed another. She realized she was reciting mixing steps aloud.

What *was* this oral dysentery that had suddenly seized her?

Mary took a sip of her fresh cocktail, then began to sing old songs in French and Italian—tunes and ditties she and Papa had sung together in better times. No more tipping the spies to her plans if she just kept singing: All the while, she searched for the key to the gun cabinet.

Oh, *that's* right: It was on the chain draped around her neck, *that* was it!

She patted her chest, feeling for the contour of the chain and key under her sweater. No, wait, that was the *document room key* she wore around her neck for safekeeping.

But, goddamn it, *that key* was *missing, too!*

Frantic, Mary returned to her favorite chair ... shoved her hands down the cracks between cushions—searching. *Fruitless.* She toddled upstairs—drunkenly bumping into walls—and searched her bedroom for the two vital keys.

Goddamn it! Where were they? Where was the document room key? Had she left it in the doorknob of the room?

Maybe ...

She staggered back downstairs, clutching tightly to the banister so she wouldn't fall—maybe break a hip—then wandered through the kitchen. She saw the key to the gun cabinet there on the ledge over the kitchen sink—just where it was the morning Papa used it to get at his shotguns that fateful July morning.

Mary selected a Mannlicher and slid in a couple of shells with practiced skill.

Papa had seen to it she was a crack shot.

She'd killed a lion in Africa. *Heh,* killed more than one "lion," hadn't she?

Another funny smile ...

Tiptoeing down the stairs to the storeroom where she now kept Papa's most precious manuscripts under lock and key, she saw that the door was ajar.

Damn spies. Damn scholars. Mary smiled—this time she remembered to keep her mouth shut; no more words.

They were trespassers now, and she knew the law: *Cross the threshold into my house unbidden and I can put* you down! She bit back a giggle.

She peeked through the cracked door.

The spy's back was to Mary; he hadn't heard her approach. Well, he wouldn't, would he? That was another gift from Papa—the predator's light foot . . . the stealth of the professional hunter. Of the professional *killer*.

She narrowed her eyes: It was Lassiter!

Lasso hadn't even said yes to her invitation to help her with *Islands* and her memoir! He hadn't signed contracts or confidentiality agreements. Yet here he was, rooting through THE PAPERS. So Lassiter must be up to no good—bad as all the others! *Worse!*

So, it was like that: *Fucking Judas!*

She could empty one barrel into Lassiter's head and the other into his waist—cut him in half, twice. After all, Lasso was trespassing . . . burgling her house and possessions. No Idaho jury would convict her.

Mary's finger twitched at the twin triggers. She sighted in on Hector's back as he rooted among the manuscripts.

The manuscripts . . .

Her manuscripts!

Goddamn Hector Lassiter to hell!

Damn him for meddling with her manuscripts. And what a fool Lasso was to bother with these when *she* had the best story of all to tell—one true sentence that would trump all these piles of Papa's abortive efforts. She had a sentence in her head that would be heard 'round the world.

Mary smiled as she continued to aim the shotgun at Hector Lassiter. It would be a shame to send Hem's one, true, lasting friend to his grave before Hector could hear Mary's one true sentence—the best sentence of all.

She hesitated.

The heavy front door was scraping open. Whoever it was wasn't polite enough to knock or wait to be invited before barging into her house. Or they didn't even care to conceal the fact that they, too, were there to rob her blind.

Mary bit her lip; sensed motion behind her. It was the scholar, Paulson, standing at the top of the stairs, watching Mary watching Hector.

Richard's eyes widened as she wheeled around and pointed the shotgun at his gut.

Creedy

He'd begun running down the stairs as soon as he saw Paulson head for the front door of the Topping House. He bolted onto the lawn and sprinted across the street, running up the hill to the Topping House.

Everything was going sideways now, or threatening to. One casualty could be covered. On the other hand, faking three deaths by gunshot from a deranged widow would be hard, but it might be necessary if Mary really drew down on Lassiter or Paulson.

Hell, the professor was no real threat, but Lassiter? He was known to pack a vintage Colt, and had a reputation for being pretty liberal with its use. If Mary got the ball rolling by taking down Lassiter, well, that would maybe change things.

If *that* happened, Mary might even spare herself Creedy's "suicide" treatment. Instead, he'd just give her a stiff drink from the doctored Jim Beam bottle in his pocket—filled to the brim with all it would take to make Mary sing whatever song he planted in her head, before the stuff wrecked what vestiges of sanity remained in that daffy head.

Creedy stood in the entryway of the Topping House, weighing options. He could see Richard's back—could see the scholar was trembling. Creedy decided: He backed out through the front door and scrambled around the side of the house, pressing his face to the glass of the storeroom window for a view of Lassiter. If Hector was going to die, Creedy wanted to *witness* it.

Mary

The scholar's visible terror made the widow smile: *Yes, you scholarly prick—you should fear me! That's the look I want in your eyes,* always: *fear!*

Mary lowered the gun and put a bony finger to her lips, shushing Richard.

Let's not do anything hasty, old girl, Mary told herself. *Let's first determine if Paulson and Lassiter are in league together. There'll be time later to shoot one or both, after all. Now there's all the time there is . . .*

Hector

It was slow and careful going. Hector carefully refolded each tossed-off note written in Hem's hand; carefully put each manuscript back in its allotted slot or envelope. After many minutes of searching—stopping here and there to savor a sentence or paragraph of Hem's that still displayed the old magic . . . evoking forty years of friendship, fights, and late-night deep talks over deeper drinks—Hector found the original of the lost chapter about himself. He also found a couple of other pieces of his that he'd never hoped to see again—unsigned short stories from the old days that had most certainly been in Hem's stolen suitcase . . . evidently confused by Mary for things Hem had written.

What the hell was going on?

How could Hector's own, long-ago-stolen manuscripts end up variously on the collector's market *and* in the Hemingway basement? *What the hell?*

Cursing softly, Hector kept digging. He wasn't finding everything he'd lost in Paris in 1922, but he found several pieces; some of those had notes scrawled in the margins in what looked like Mary's hand—notations to "Save this for first collection of Papa's uncollected short stories," or, more disturbingly, "Change character's name to Nick Adams for eventual Adams anthology."

Jesus Christ—he couldn't have his stuff being foisted off as Papa's juvenilia. *Jesus . . .*

At last satisfied he had everything that was his own, Hector dug a bit further, and found a much longer manuscript involving Cuban politics that, at first glance, seemed to Hector to be potentially damaging to Hem in a very different way: The manuscript made Ernest look like some flavor of swooning Fidelista—a Castro apologist.

His back to the door, Hector stuck the manuscript pages in the waist-band of his slacks at the back, hidden under the tails of his sports jacket.

Hector turned, and his stomach kicked.

Mary stood behind him, a shotgun pointed at his head. Her hands were steady; her eyes were wild. Behind her stood Paulson, his eyes at once wide and hateful.

Her voice hoarse and thick from the booze and the mystery drug, Mary said, "Ask me, goddamn you! Ask me what you both want to know. Go ahead, Lasso . . . professor—ask what you *all* want to ask me!"

Raising his hands, Hector remembered the first time he'd seen Mary—there on the tarmac of the Havana airport in 1959. He'd thought her a bit dizzy, then. Now, he wondered if long exposure to Hem—particularly in Ernest's last, crazed days—had somehow compromised Mary's tenuous sanity. Had she come to thrive on Hem's pain and mercurial temperament? His anger and his irrationality? Hector licked his lips, thought, *And if she did, does she miss it all so much now she'd tried to recapture it by actually shooting me?*

He glanced over her shoulder at Richard. Had the professor hit Mary with more of the stuff—driven her into this frenzy? Maybe. Or maybe he'd been at the stuff himself, for Richard looked as crazed as Mary—sweating furiously, and strangely flushed. Mary and Richard's pupils were the size of dimes. Richard was staring at the back of Mary's head like he might bore through her skull with his angry, horrified gaze.

Oblivious, Mary stared down the double barrels at Hector, the shotgun unwavering. Her cheeks twitched, as if some force were controlling her, trying to fight its way out, and it was pretty clearly winning.

Mary said, "You don't even have to say a word, I can see it in your eyes.

"Did I kill the old bastard? Goddamn it!

"Yes!

"Yes, I did.

"I *killed* Ernest!"

They stood there in the cramped space, Hector at the lowest level, still in Mary's sights. Mary stood on the lower step; Richard just a bit above and behind her. Mary's words echoed off the walls. Hector and Richard were still absorbing the confession.

Mary had said it with fierce pride. Hector felt weak in the knees; actually feared for himself.

The damned scholar was scribbling her crazed admission down in his notebook now, even as Mary's finger twitched against the first trigger.

It was all fucking *insane*.

Hector thought, *I'm really going to die now, just like this. Jesus Christ!*

The widow's whole body was shaking now. She pitched forward as if to force the shotgun barrels up against Hector's head before blasting him into oblivion.

For a fraction of a second, Hector wondered what the headlines would say: something about "Hemingway friend killed feet from where Papa died" . . . probably make him look like he'd died in imitation. *Fuck's sake!*

Then Mary's eyes rolled back in her head. The widow fainted.

Hector caught the shotgun before it hit the ground—before it could accidentally discharge.

The shotgun now in his hands, Hector looked up and saw the scholar staring at him, frozen in his tracks. Hector struggled against his own adrenaline—to have come so close to annihilation at Mary's hands . . . He looked again at Richard. Fucking scholar had heard *all* of it. *Now* what was Hector going to do with this goddamn scholar?

Richard was trembling. He *had* it—had the confession he'd come seeking from Mary! But my God, the way she *said* it . . . it was a darker, more operatic admission than he'd ever imagined getting from the widow. And Lassiter had heard it, too. Goddamn it!

Seeing the gun in Hector's hands, perhaps thinking the crime writer might turn it on him, Richard Paulson screamed and ran back up the steps.

Hector cursed. As the front door slammed behind the fleeing scholar, Hector examined Mary. . . . She was wide-eyed and twitching. She looked like a junkie on a very bad trip, actually foaming at the mouth. Well, things had certainly turned a dark fucking corner, now, hadn't they?

BOOK FOUR

Men at War

The great advantage of being a writer is that you can spy on people.

—GRAHAM GREENE

14.   MINION

The two men faced one another across the table. Stepping outside himself a bit, Richard saw it like this: They were both men used to being listened to. People hung on their words, and they were both information gatherers. But as a professor, Richard relied on the Socratic method of interrogation—pose a question and inspire an answer. The man across the table from him came at the craft of confrontation from a behavioral model, and the other man was, well, he was more than a bit of a thug.

Richard knew he was completely out of his element.

Cowed and beaten down, Richard flinched as Creedy leaned into him across the small pub table, his voice low and menacing: "You're *disappointing* me, Richard. You said after you got what *you* wanted—your confession from Mary to Hemingway's killing, after you got this material for your precious biography—Mary blacked out. The maid was away. You had the place, and this Lassiter, to yourself. The door to the manuscript room was unlocked. The thing to do was to beat Lassiter to that shotgun—blow him to hell, fulfill your mission in the document room, then leave them both there. Let the local police sort it out. They would have believed Mary Hemingway shot Lassiter. You'd have gotten away clean."

No, Richard thought. It wouldn't have happened like that—even if he had been capable of killing Lassiter, and he knew he wasn't. And Hannah knew Richard was headed back there to the Topping House. There'd be no explaining it satisfactorily to his wife. And hell, with his luck, some neighbor would see his return . . . or his departure.

And anyway, Richard had his admission of murder from Mary—he couldn't risk that with his own arrest, or her possible murder by this man or his helpers. And now Richard had seen that trove of papers ... stacks of Hemingway manuscripts, letters. A mother lode. He wanted to get back there, to comb through it all. To buttress Mary's stunning admission with a cache of new Papa revelations. To that end, Richard had started to create some operational latitude for himself. He'd lied to Hannah and told her he was off to Boise earlier than he actually planned to leave. Had gotten a second hotel room and stocked it with some good wine, notepads, and pens. He'd do the same to this man—tell him he was needed in Boise while he plotted his own way back into that manuscript room in the Topping House.

"There wasn't *time* for that," Richard said. "We struggled for the gun, but—"

Creedy was in his face *like that*: "That's a lie, Richard. I have the house bugged. More, I was standing behind you. Looking through windows. I heard you scream like a woman. Heard your feet pounding up those stairs as you ran in terror. I heard the door slam. Then, peering around the corner, I saw you run from the house. *Coward!*"

Creedy gave Richard a long, hard look. Creedy's lip curled. In theory, it should be easy enough for him to get into the Topping House on his own. Drug the widow, steal the key, and not rely on this drunken, yellow academic.

But procedure and protocol in such situations was always to use cutouts. Plausible deniability was the watchword. Compartmentalization a religion. It was tried and true: Find the guy who had the most to lose by going in, then push pressure points to make the cretin do just that. Then you *owned* him, all the way up and forever. All you had to do was to find the guy with a passion so desperate he'd go in with nearly no urging.

A guy like Richard Paulson.

A guy who lived far out to the margins—far outside any lifestyle that conformed to majority opinion and normative acceptance. Then, when that guy ran off a cliff or slammed into a wall with bloody consequences, well, nobody wondered too much or poked around too hard to see what pushed that guy over the edge.

Such guys were clearly crazy—loners who snapped. Something to be expected ... to shake a head over, and then file away and forget.

Yes, that was the way the game was played.

Richard said, "Are we done now? You're finished with me, now, right?"

The professor had a hopeful smile pasted on that made Creedy want to swing at him.

Instead, Creedy smiled back at him. "*No.* You see, Richard, there's no such thing as opting out once you're working for me. I don't *fire* people, and resignation isn't an option. But failure? Failure can be punished. The consequences for that can be *unthinkable.* And now I know you're capable of lying to me. So you have *much* to make up for."

Richard nodded feebly.

Creedy said, "When do you go back to the Hemingway house?"

"I *have* to go to Boise. But I'll be back in a couple of days. I'll be meeting with Mary again then. Or I would but for today . . ."

"Mary won't remember any of this, not really," Creedy said sharply. "She won't even reliably remember you or Lassiter having been there. She'll have flashes. Maybe recall bits and pieces, but she'll write those off as fragments of dreams or DTs. The ones who take that stuff always react that way."

Richard shook his head. "Lassiter will know what happened."

"Yes, he will," Creedy said. "But if Lassiter has further aims in all this, and he notices Mary has 'forgotten,' so to speak, then he'll have reason not to tell her about you or what you all experienced. Not after his own snooping around. It'll be a Mexican standoff—a tactical draw that affords both sides operational latitude. Call it a lie agreed upon." Creedy was sure of all that: He had cased every angle.

Richard said, "I don't know . . ."

"I don't care what you think or believe, or what you kid yourself that you 'know,' Richard," Creedy said. "You have no choice in any of this. You're *mine.* I'm counting on you, Richard. You *don't* want to disappoint me again."

"I understand," Richard said, feeling sick and twisted inside. He wanted to find a bottle and a remote island.

"Do you *really* understand? It's important that you really understand, Richard. Because if you fail me again, you stand to lose a hell of a lot more than mere money."

Criticism hurt me when I had failures. I thought: I'll never write another play. But I'm an alligator. Only the alligators remain. The others get out of the water.

—ARTHUR MILLER

15.   SPADE WORK

Hector sat in his corner booth in the lounge, nursing a white bull and thinking about Mary Hemingway. His mind's eye kept circling back to that crazed little woman standing on the bottom step, pointing a shotgun at his head and snarling, "I *killed* Ernest!"

He was of two minds about all of that: A part of Hector *almost* believed Mary; another part dismissed it as some drug-stoked rant... a crazed hallucination.

He'd left Mary unconscious in her bed; the maid phoning for a doctor.

What if Mary *kept* ranting on? Telling every ear in proximity she'd blown off Hem's head?

Hector felt he should probably go back to the Topping House soon to check on Mary. But she might draw down on him again, and this time, she might not blackout before pulling the twin triggers of the shotgun.

Hector took another sip of his drink and hefted the paperback he'd brought along to the bar—the single Donovan Creedy thriller he'd found in a wire rack at the local pharmacy.

The book was titled *The Khrushchev Kill*, and featured a cover illustration of a grimacing man who looked more than a little like Sean Connery. Pseudo-Sean was snarling handsomely while emptying his automatic into the face of some bald, musclebound type. Sean managed to do this despite the near-naked blonde wrapped around his torso while he was in the heat of combat. Hell, the babe was literally hanging on the James Bond manqué's gun arm. *Christ...*

Hector checked the spine—Silver Medallion Press. He knew the publisher. The fella had been after Hector for several years to blurb or write introductions for his paperback originals. Even once offered to give Hector his own imprint, affording Hector the opportunity to shape his own wing of crime and thriller writing. Hector had responded with a curt, "Fucking *no*. . . ."

He took another sip of his lackluster drink, and then Hector read the opening paragraph of Creedy's novel:

> Esther Pryl was a long tall drink of woman. She had pretty long hair, eyes as blue as cobalt vases and brother, she had a body. She sure knew how to use that body.

Hector shook his head. He caught himself reaching for his fountain pen. Instead of going at the book in the margins, Hector began to edit the thing in his head. That name, Esther Pryl, didn't work at *all*. If the woman was a dish she should be . . . oh, maybe . . . *Mitzi Bishop*. Yeah, that had some sex appeal. She'd be a redhead with pert breasts and lush hips. And there surely needed to be a comma there between "pretty" and "long." As to the rest, well, "She had blue eyes and a fetching figure" would do well enough for the readers of *this* kind of book. . . . Readers who would just want to see the hero get Mitzi out of her dress and busy putting a passionate snarl on Mitzi's face in three or four paragraphs of knowingly tossed-off soft-core pornography.

Snorting softly, Hector pitched the paperback atop an adjacent table. Let some Hemingway egghead lose himself in that sorry tome.

He squeezed the back of his neck and rolled his head. Hector had burned his copy of the lost chapter, and then hidden the stolen original in a secret compartment he'd had installed years ago in the undercarriage of his Bel Air. He'd also read the strange, long manuscript he'd stolen from the Topping House—the bizarre novel-in-progress that read as a love letter to Fidel and Che Guevara. It was meant to be interpreted as a work of Hem's, but even as a parody, it didn't come within striking distance. Hector had burned it in the fireplace in Hem's old lodge room.

Even though it was safely destroyed, Hector was desperate to learn where *that* document had come from . . . how it had gotten there, and most importantly, who the hell had written it. Having read that opening paragraph of Donovan Creedy's *Khrushchev Kill*, Hector now had some suspicions about the Castro manuscript's origins. Seemed unlikely two hack writers could be inept in so many of the same ways when it came to describing hot women.

Hector sipped his too-sweet drink, slipped off his reading glasses, and rubbed his tired eyes. As they refocused, Hector saw a dark-haired female scholar he'd been noticing around the lodge the past day or so. He narrowed his eyes; hell, she was a nice distraction from thinking about goddamn, maybe-murderous Mary Hemingway.

The scholar's black hair could have used a brushing—it didn't look careless, but uncared for. She wore it long and down, against fashion. Hector couldn't be sure, but he thought she might have a nice-enough body under her poorly chosen, ill-fitting clothes.

Hector knew his own tastes too well: he was always a goner for pretty, troubled women. "Birds with a wing down," as his fellow potboiler writer Ian Fleming had described them. The female scholar struck Hector as sad and neurotic by choice or inclination, and so not so much his type. But she might know some things about this other egghead lately preoccupying Hector's thoughts.

She was drinking something girly-looking in a Tom Collins glass.

He drained his own drink and waved his friend the bartender over to his booth.

"Hey, Mr. Lassiter."

"Hey, Dave. The woman at the bar—what's she drinkin'?"

The bartender made a face. "An apricot fizz."

Hector winced. "Well, when she hits bottom on that sucker, make her a double and then point at me, would you?"

The bartender nodded, frowning. "She's pretty in her way, Mr. Lassiter. But she's been in a few times. Some kind of teacher, I think. You know, here for the conference." The bartender shook his head. "Jesus, but the mouth on that one."

Hector winked. "What? You mean vulgar? Profane?"

"I mean never shut. Not ever."

"Ah. Well, do it anyway, okay?"

"Sure. Another white bull, Mr. Lassiter?"

"Christ no," Hector said. Dave looked relieved. "I'm writing a novel about surrealist art," Hector said. "The white bull is a prime surrealist motif. They say a surrealist invented that drink in its honor. So sampling it was kind of ... research."

"What did you think?"

Hector made a face. "It tasted like a milkshake in which the milk was turned. God never intended for tequila to be abused in that way."

"So what'll it be, Mr. Lassiter?"

"Three fingers of Talisker. Can do?"

Dave shot Hector a thumbs-up. "Want some pretzels, too?"

"Love some."

Hector broke out his old notebook and began reviewing some notes he'd made to himself back in 1947.

The sound of a cleared throat made him raise his head:

She said, "Hector Lassiter, yes?"

Hector smiled at the dark-haired academic. "That's right ... Miss ... ?"

"Patricia Stihlbourne."

"I saw you in here the other day, Patricia," Hector said. "You're a professor?"

"Louisiana State."

Hector smiled and gestured to a chair. "That where you discovered the apricot fizz?"

She shrugged. "They were out of Prunelle."

"Well, it is Idaho, after all." He slipped his notebook and pen into the breast pocket of his sports jacket.

Patricia smiled and said softly, "Don't tell any of my snooty peers, but I'm a tremendous fan of yours, Mr. Lassiter."

"Hector." He was surprised by her admission. "Really? You're a reader of mine?"

"Really," she said. "*The Land of Dread and Fear* was one of my three favorite reads last year."

She'd gotten the title right. Hector thought she might really be a reader of his work. "How'd you get onto me? So far as I can tell, I'm mostly off the *Norton Anthology*'s radar."

"You might be surprised." She sipped her extra-tall drink and said, "A couple of years ago, a precocious and percipient student of mine wrote a paper: 'Hector Lassiter and the Agony of the Postmodern Detective.' My pupil made a compelling case for you as one of the pioneers of postmodern fiction, despite your classification as a genre writer by most critics."

"Some smart kid," Hector said. "Male or female?"

"Female."

"More's the better. I need to broaden my fan base."

"Of course I already knew of you as a personality," Patricia said. "Hemingway has been my area of specialization for years, so I knew of you through your association with Ernest. But my student's paper was what made me one of your readers."

He said, "I'll confess, I was eavesdropping on you the other night in here. I was watching you, Patricia." She'd been at a table with Richard Paulson and some other academics.

She smiled, already looking a little drunk. "Why?"

"Because I have to stand up in a room in front of a couple of hundred just like you and jaw. That's a harrowing prospect for a pioneering postmodern pulp writer with a high school education."

She stirred her drink with her finger, plucked out a cherry, ate it, then put the stem in her mouth. Narrowing his eyes, Hector watched her. She smiled, then pulled the stem from her mouth with thumb and forefinger and dropped the stem on the table. She'd tied a knot in the cherry stem with her tongue. Pretty tight knot, at that.

Hector thought, *Well, well!*

"Word is you're ducking every scholar who's tried to strike up a conversation, Mr. Lassiter. But here we are." She smiled at his reaction to the stem. He bit his lip, looked up from it, and searched her eyes.

"Well, Patricia, there's conversation and there's interrogation. The latter doesn't interest me. And those others don't have your eyes and smile." *And*, he thought, *they can't do that to a cherry stem with their little pink tongues.*

"So I should be flattered we're talking now, Hector? This is a conversation to some end?"

Or someone's end, Hector thought. He shrugged. "Tell me about this Richard Paulson. I know him a little but not nearly enough. Saw you at his table the other night."

Patricia smiled. "He's got one great book about Hemingway's Paris years."

"Yeah, I read it. Wasn't terrible."

"How close did Richard come?"

Hector smiled. "Close enough, I guess. Caught the spirit of the times, anyway."

"Tell me more," she said, unclasping her purse and taking out an enameled cigarette holder.

Hector fished his old Zippo from his pocket and fired her up. She looked at the inscription:

To Hector Lassiter:
"One true sentence."
—E. H.
Key West, 1932

Patricia said, "My God, I've read about this lighter, and about the game you two played—finishing one another's sentences." She smiled. "The famous 'true sentence' challenges you and Papa set for one another: perfectly crystallized phrases that reveal an immutable truth put forth with an eye toward economy and uncluttered stylistic perfection."

Not the way Hector would have put it, but she got the gist. He said, "On the nose."

"And, wow, 1932. They built these lighters to last, didn't they?"

"Zippo offers a free repair program," Hector said. He watched her hand drift from the lighter to his fingers . . . her slender fingers stroking his. Patricia's nails were varnished red but chewed down. Hector didn't know if he would go in this direction in life, not just yet, but the opening line of a story or novel suddenly occurred to him: *When you start sleeping with women younger than your cigarette lighter, you know you've turned a sorry corner.*

He filed it to fret over later. He said, "What are Richard's politics? He kind of right-wing?"

Patricia wrinkled her nose. "Good God, no. We're nearly all Marxists, and Richard is left of me."

"I'd always heard it was so—all you longhairs being lefties, I mean."

"Then why'd you ask that?"

Hector smiled back. "Suppose I'm just trying to draw out this time with you."

She gave that the smile it deserved.

Patricia tipped her head on its side. She looked prettier to Hector now: bedroom eyes, sultry mouth, and a long neck. And Hector was suddenly aware of her leg pressed against his, moving slowly up and down.

She frowned suddenly. "What time do you have?"

Hector checked his Timex. "Ten to noon."

"Damn," Patricia said. "I have to fly—I'm moderating a panel. 'Hemingway and the Hidden Other.' Sort of considering Papa through the prism of Jung. You could come, and after . . ."

Her leg ran up and down against his again.

That felt good, but he had no patience for that panel. He said, "Got some things I have to handle over the next couple of hours. So I'm afraid I can't make it, darlin'. You here for the whole conference?"

"Yes," she said, disappointed. "You, too?"

"To the bitter end. Let's pick this up later, yes?"

Patricia smiled. "It's a date."

———————

Unless the bastards have the courage to give you unqualified praise, I say ignore them.

—John Steinbeck

16.   JACKALS

As she roamed the dark paneled halls of the lodge, Hannah's fingers trailed across the frames of the black-and-white photos of the Hollywood elite of the 1940s and '50s who made Sun Valley their winter sports mecca: candids of Ingrid Bergman and Clark Gable and Howard Hawks and sundry Olympians. Hannah lingered on glossies of the great man with his three sons and his drunken toadies and the two wives who made the annual treks to Idaho with him—Martha and, predominantly, Mary, who made the last trip, and stayed on to bury him.

Hannah—the fourth Mrs. Paulson, as she had come to think of herself since her brief visit with Widow Mary—grabbed a corner booth in the cozy, lowly lit Duchin Lounge. She positioned herself under a picture of the fortyish, paunchy Papa, sporting that "fat married look," mustached and grinning, kneeling with Gary Cooper and a forgotten other outdoorsman and two alert, black hunting dogs, all of them seemingly proud of the game birds they had killed.

"The fourth Mrs. Paulson."

Hannah still wondered how Mary knew so much about Richard's private life. And so far she couldn't bring herself to read the rest of Mary's impromptu sketch about Hannah and Richard's marriage. Just the paragraph or two she'd read in the Topping House had unnerved Hannah terribly. She quizzed Richard later. Pressed, Richard claimed he had not shared anything about his marital history with Mary in their correspondence or during phone calls leading up to the Idaho trip.

And the widow's unexpected dangling of the prospect of her helping to write Mary's biography? Well, Hannah couldn't stop thinking about that notion, even though she knew Richard would never comply.

Hannah had finally broken down and confided to Richard about seeing the man from the restaurant—the man she was sure had been spying on them, and who then followed them on foot back to the lodge—trailing their bus on its way to the Topping House the previous afternoon. Richard had dismissed Hannah's concerns, but not as callously as she had dreaded: "A little village with one big tourist attraction . . . Papa's front yard is probably the crossroads of Idaho."

As she sipped her orange juice, Hannah overheard a husky, effeminate rant:

"What the hell is Richard doing here? He's not presenting a paper, you know. Jesus, he hasn't published in *The Review* since that little piece two springs ago about that shitty unsigned poem he found scrawled on an outhouse wall when we were together in Cuba. Well, there was that little piece about double entendres in *The Sun* in last fall's number, but that was so reekingly insubstantial . . . just turning old dirt."

Another voice said, "Maybe we shouldn't talk about Cuba and what happened there. You'll just get yourself upset. Again."

Hannah glanced up from her dog-eared, tattered paperback copy of Hector Lassiter's first novel, *Rhapsody in Black*, to inspect the couple at the table next to her—a man and a woman. Hannah was mildly surprised: Based on the tenor of the voices, she'd expected to see two women. The man who had been speaking was balding, and the circumference of his skull showed through the tufted, brindle, cotton candy wisps of his badly permed hair. His glasses were black and horn-rimmed. The shoulders of his bulging blue suit jacket were peppered with dandruff. His voice was at once gruff and feminine.

The woman seated across the table from the troll lit a fresh cigarette and sipped a wine spritzer from a glass stained with pale lavender lipstick. The woman reminded Hannah of every teaching assistant she had endured during her own not-so-long-ago battery of undergraduate courses in short-story writing and critical composition. But this one was rather pretty.

The woman had long black hair, ivory skin, and penetrating blue eyes. Slanting black eyebrows evoked something feline and stray. In fact, Hannah would wager the woman had some strange, hairless, six-toed cat back home in her studio apartment—some polydactyl pussy she had pinched from Papa's Key West house—carefully picking its way among stacks of books regarding Hemingway and his take on genders and female archetypes and hated mothers. The stranger was the kind of spoiled, feline aesthete Richard would likely dismiss as a doleful, weekend "sports fuck."

"Cuba," the man said bitterly. "I'm *always* angry about that, Patricia. I'll never forget or forgive that one. Just another time Paulson dicked me. We were supposed to do that Paris book together, you know, his so-called career-making book. The one that got him tenure and the award and cost me another two years before I got *my* tenure. I helped Paulson frame-out that fucking book of 'his.' At least fifty percent of the introduction is my work. But Richard turned around and signed the contract solo. So much for gentlemen's agreements, eh? Hell, I didn't even get an acknowledgment. He stole reams of material from me, with not so much as a single footnote to my work. The bastard. I told him I was going to register a formal complaint and then he threatened me about the boy I took with me to Pamplona in 'sixty-three. Paulson still holds that affair over my fucking head. Said he'd report it to my chair if I blew the whistle on him. As if Richard hasn't fucked scores of his own female students. Then came Havana, two years ago, and the documentary deal for CBS. He fucked me again. And that was some serious money."

Hannah flinched: Could that really be true? Would Richard truly steal the work of another writer that way? And this stuff about female students?

"You keep setting yourself up for these slights, Berle," the woman said. "You should know better by now."

"What I should have done was pay some tough in San Francisco de Paula to take Richard out," the man named Berle said. "You know I could have had him put down for fifty dollars, American. Would've looked like a street robbery."

The woman arched a dark eyebrow. "Dear God, Ber, it almost sounds like you actually shopped around for an assassin."

Berle smiled to himself. "Maybe I did, Pat. Maybe I fucking did." He gestured with both pudgy hands. "Wonder what the going rate for an assassination is here in the boonies?"

Hannah was sent reeling by that one—the ugly little man sounded serious.

"Keep talking if it helps let off steam," the woman said, shaking her head.

"It doesn't, not really." He sat forward and stabbed a finger at the woman. "Did you know that that lying cocksucker Richard *loudly* called me a *maricón* who 'favors little boys' in the Floridita? I was lucky to get out of there with my fucking life."

The man sipped his gin and tonic and stuffed one short, pudgy leg up under the other. "Well, he has somehow, against all reason, secured Mary's ear. He's there now—I ran into him as he was leaving. The wicked old bitch is seeing Richard and only Richard. I don't know how he made the contact, let alone got an audience. That witch has built a wall a mile high around her to keep us all out. Hard to believe, given his last creditable work, that of all the wives, Richard would seriously consider a biography of Mary. Still, he needs a coup at this point, badly. I hear his department head is finally losing faith in him. It's been a year since his little piece on the Byron congruities had its fleeting vogue, and that was mostly European. And now Stu has all but made that subject his own. It's certain to figure in the life he is working on."

Hannah closed her eyes and rubbed her temples: In danger of losing his position at the university? That gave context to some of Richard's more portentous, disturbing recent asides . . .

"Who is ahead now, by the way? Stu or Eddie?" The woman, Patricia, had a husky voice. Hannah thought, *The things a three-pack-a-day habit will do for you.*

"Stu all the way. Although, if the rumors are true, Edward will have the best crack at being first in incorporating *The Garden* materials in his version of the life."

"I can't say I cared for his Howells book."

"I can't say I care for Howells. Who can? He's strictly for underfunded antiquarian book collectors and people who still read Arlen as literature. Anyway, Richard is *muy jornalero.*"

Hannah, who spoke little Spanish, made a mental note to look that one up at the bookstore in the lodge's shopping arcade.

The fat little man with the scalp disorder sat up suddenly. "You don't suppose that old whore is giving Richard access to *The Garden* holographs, do you? Based on Carlos and Sebastian's readings, that material is mine, by rights. Given that material, and the work I've already done on "Sea Change" and what we know of *Islands*, I can smash that crap, macho image of the big fucker's forever—and long before Pelka gets there. You don't really think Mary is permitting Richard access to *The Garden*, do you?"

"I hear Mary's out of the picture where *Eden* is concerned—way out of the picture," the cat woman said. "That's Scribners, all the way. If Mary had her way, at least as I hear it, *The Garden* would never see the light of day."

Hannah closed her eyes, listening to the woman's voice: It was similar to the voice on the phone, but not so close that Hannah could declare a match. *Yet . . .*

"Poor Richard," the fat man said. His voice sounded a bit like his companion's. "I wonder what he's up to? At least he's still trying, and I guess that's to his credit. Still rooting around for a seminal new insight."

Hannah finished her orange juice and left a handful of change to cover the bill and the tip.

"Poor poor Richard," she heard the fat man lamenting behind her. Then suddenly enthusiastic, he said, "Oh, and did you see that fat whore Barbara is here? She still doesn't get it—how magnificently impervious our guy is to the fucking 'death-of-the-author' crowd. Oh Jesus! And that book of so-called scholarly poetry she published: *Loofahs for Lepers*. What a sagging-ass suck-up to Jacques and Roland that was. And she stole the title from fucking Bud Fiske, for Christ's sake."

Hannah sighed and looked around. She saw Hector Lassiter across the lounge. He was sitting in his own corner booth with a cup of coffee and a notebook, his jacket off and his sleeves rolled up; his forearms matted with hair. Despite his age, there was something almost boyish about him. He was wearing wire-rimmed glasses—looking very much the author. He was focused entirely on his writing. There was no indication that he even knew Hannah was there. No sign he'd been eavesdropping on the professors. No hint he was even aware of where he was other than in the country of whatever story or novel he was composing.

Watching him work made Hannah feel guilty. She watched Hector a while longer, then went back to her room and to her own notebook.

Twenty minutes later, someone banged loudly on the door of her room. Hannah was stretched out on the bed, lying on her side, unable to get comfortable enough to focus on her writing. She struggled up, her hand pressed to her belly, and said, "Yes?"

"Hello," a familiar voice said. "Is Richard there?"

"No," Hannah called back, frowning. "What is it? Is something wrong?"

"I'm a friend of Richard's. I wanted to talk to him."

"He's not here."

"I'm sure you can help me," the voice said. "Can I come in?"

"No," Hannah said, edging to the door. "I'm sorry, I'm just out of the shower and not feeling very well."

"Oh, I'm so sorry to hear that. Are you Mrs. Paulson?"

"Yes," Hannah said, hesitating. "Who are you?"

"A friend—a colleague. Of Richard's, I mean."

"Yes, I know," Hannah said, trying to place the gruff, feminine voice. "But your name?"

"Richard was going to give me Mary Hemingway's phone number and we both forgot when we spoke earlier today," the voice said, ignoring Hannah's question. "If you could just give me her phone number, I'd be so grateful. I'm kind of up against a deadline I was to meet in terms of contacting her."

Hannah edged quietly to the door and peeked through the peephole: It was Berle, the fat little Hemingway scholar. His distorted smile—magnified and bent through the fisheye lens—was just this side of terrifying to Hannah. "I'm sorry," she said. "I don't know the number."

"Perhaps you could let me in to look around." He must have had his hand on the doorknob, because it twisted slowly until the bolt caught. Hannah began to panic.

"I'm sure it's in a notebook or something somewhere," Berle said. "It's very important to Richard and me. I could give you time to dress."

"I'm sorry, no," Hannah said, hearing an edge creeping into her voice, despite her effort to sound nonchalant. "In fact, Richard is with Mrs. Hemingway right now, so any 'deadline' to contact her has surely been met."

"Oh. Yes. Yes, then."

Hannah looked again through the lens. Berle was frowning and red-faced. He took a last shot: "I do have something important to pass along to Richard while he's with Mrs. Hemingway. It has bearing on their conversation. If I could—"

This time Hannah cut him off: "I'm sorry. I really have no number where he or she can be reached. If you'll give me your name, I'll tell Richard you're trying to contact him."

Through the peephole, Hannah watched as the man dipped his head sharply in anger and mouthed the word *cunt*.

"No," he said. "It will be too late then. Please, don't bother mentioning I stopped by. It's fine. Really. Thanks."

Hannah bit her lip.

She stayed by the door, then saw the handle twist again. She kicked the door, then checked the peephole and saw Berle running down the hallway. Now she was in a panic. And she was alone.

Hannah looked around the hotel room for something she might use to defend herself and her baby, all the while gasping for breath, on the verge of some terrible attack of nerves.

She saw the dog-eared paperback on the bed. She remembered what Mary Hemingway had said about the novel's author: "The man who lives what he writes and writes what he lives."

She dialed the front desk. "Is Mr. Hector Lassiter still in the lounge?"

A minute passed. The crime writer had apparently left the lounge.

Hannah said, "Could you connect me to his room, please?"

When the plot flags, bring in a man with a gun.

—RAYMOND CHANDLER

17.   SENTRY

He answered on the second ring. The girl was breathless; sounded truly scared.

Hector felt he'd made a connection with Hannah back at Hem's place, and of course they shared this kinship in the writing. And now, in danger, Hannah had turned first to him. That flattered and pleased him. At his age, being seen by a pretty young woman as a worthy protector was a heady thing.

And Hector knew how it could play out: He'd been down this road many times, after all.

A sense of being menaced had driven more than one woman his way over the years—the tension heightening emotions and sharpening the typical arc of intimacy.

Fear had often proven a potent aphrodisiac.

A part of Hector was surprised to find himself again toying with pursuing his interest in Hannah. But what *if* he played out the hand? Maybe this one would turn out better than the other times he'd waded in to help some pretty young thing. Maybe this time things wouldn't end in disaster or ruin.

And hell, in a practical, physical sense, their coming together seemed foreordained as well: Hector's room was just four doors down from the Paulsons' new room—they'd moved into the lodge-proper for the conference.

Hell, why fight what seemed to be fate?

Well, there was her goddamn husband, for one thing.

There was that other man's baby she was carrying inside her, too.

And yet...

Well, either way it went, he'd see it through. There really wasn't much choice about that: Hannah was in trouble and had come to him for protection.

Hell, given some of the past frantic cries for help—and the horrors that had resulted from so many of those—how much trouble, really, could this comely young pregnant Scot be facing in this resort full of fey intellectuals?

As he kept the phone trapped between his shoulder and ear, Hector ran a comb through his hair and tucked in the shirt that had just come back from the laundry. He said, "Just step out into the hall, honey. I'll see you here safely."

Hannah looked around as she fumbled with the lock—her hands were shaking.

The crime novelist was already there in the hallway, smiling and holding up a hand. "It's okay," Hector said. "I've scouted around; he's gone."

Hannah nodded. He was standing there calm and smiling, like it was just another chance meeting. But it wasn't. He was a successful novelist, a fairly famous one; a charismatic man's man famous for his escapades as a sports fisherman, hunter, screenwriter, and war correspondent. She didn't read many of them, but she'd seen enough screen and film gossip magazines to know some of the starlets romantically linked to Hector Lassiter.

A world apart from scholars and the aspiring literary writers she'd been surrounded by in college, Hector Lassiter was a doer, not a talker. She shook her head: Enough analysis; the fact was, from just her brief exposure to him at the Topping House, Hannah was already drawn to

Hector—could see he came by his other reputation, that of ladies' man, honestly.

As she reached his room, she was struck again by his height and the breadth of his shoulders; Hector was cast on a much different scale than Richard. And Hector had this charisma—the kind that could rob a room of its oxygen. Papa would have called it machismo—masculinity of a kind Hannah sensed was passing from the world. She wished she wasn't pregnant for the moment, that she was her former athletic self . . . like, well, like one of the women in Hector Lassiter's novels.

He stepped aside so Hannah could pass into the parlor room—his suite had two doors, the one she entered through, and a second that she presumed opened directly into the bedroom. The parlor was ringed with windows and flooded with sunlight: a television, two chairs, a long couple of couches, and a writing table; a fireplace close by the door.

Alone in his room with him now, Hannah didn't want to come off as a needy, scared little thing; some neurotic little pregnant wife running from shadows. She didn't want Hector to see her as a frightened child-woman. She couldn't stand the thought her fear might amuse a man like this novelist, who by all accounts had seen real trouble in his storied life. Yet her panicked call had brought her to his room. She had to play the hand she'd dealt herself:

"I'm so sorry to have bothered you with this," Hannah said. "It's just that with my husband away, I didn't know who else to call. It's probably nothing. . . ."

Hector almost laughed then. It was the same old dance. He suddenly felt he was playing a scene from one of the myriad B-movie potboilers whose scripts he'd doctored during the late 1940s.

Hewing to that tack, he wrapped an arm around Hannah's shoulders and led her to the French doors opening onto a private patio. He held her hand as she carefully lowered herself into a chair, her other hand cradling her belly. They both seemed reluctant to let go of one another's hands. Hannah smiled awkwardly and let go first.

Hector made sure to get downwind of Hannah, then he pulled a package of Pall Malls from his pocket. She was probably right: It probably *was* nothing—just some drunken, misogynist egghead ranting at a woman through the mutual safety of a door.

Then again, there was enough intrigue going on around the goddamn mountain town to spare. Maybe Hannah was twisted up in some of all that. Maybe it was runoff from her husband's finaglings?

Through a haze of blue smoke, he said, "So, we've got threatening phone calls. We've got scholars running down your husband in the lounge earlier. We've got strange men trying to force their way into your room. Anything else that you're not telling me?"

Hannah was surprised that Hector had noticed the scholars . . . that he had noticed her.

"I've been seeing a man from time to time—some man who is spying on us, I think. I've seen him in restaurants. Seen him following us. Following us to restaurants, stores, and the hotel. He followed us right to the foot of Mary's driveway. I pointed him out to Richard, but he dismissed it."

Hector nodded. Hell, Richard Paulson was probably so deep in his blue ruins he couldn't find Saturday morning at the end of Friday night. He said, "This man, the one watching you, following you two—he's gaunt? Red-faced? Like his face is sun- or wind-burned?"

Hannah's expression was incredulous. She was clearly surprised he'd seen the man, too. The calculated skirt-chaser in Hector sensed the hook was set pretty firmly now if he aimed to move in that direction.

Christ, stop that, he thought.

The young Scot was just a nice, knocked-up kid in a strange town, tied to a drunken and sorry excuse for a husband. A drunken son of a bitch with apparent ties to Donovan Creedy. Hector pressed on: "He has dark hair, I'm guessing. His hairline is receding and it forms a sharp widow's peak now. Wears glasses. Am I close?"

Hannah's eyes were wide; her lips trembled. She nodded, squeezing her arms to herself. "Exactly. Yes! But how . . . ?"

Here he was, balanced on the knife's edge again: torn between the urge to show off—to wow her with his knowing, deeper sense of the dark things swirling around them now—and the simple obligation to put to rest the fears of a pregnant woman who was just possibly in real jeopardy.

Hector hesitated, then said, "At your angle there at the table you can't see it, but there's a skating rink across the way there. He's down there right now with a pair of binoculars, spying on us."

Hannah couldn't suppress a shiver. At the same time, this wave of relief washed over her—a heady comfort that she hadn't been imagining it all. And there was a sense of exhilaration she worried Hector might pick up on—might see in her face.

Here on this balcony with Hector, she felt safe.

She also felt an impulsive affection for the crime writer for validating her fears.

For the first time in a very long time, Hannah felt this strange sense of happiness . . . a giddiness.

Where Richard would have dismissed all of this, Hector was fully on her side, and more, looked poised to strike out—*so* ready to *act*.

Hannah tried to look flustered . . . afraid for what might come next. She said, "And so . . ."

"And so you wait here," Hector said. "You'll be safe. I'm going to go down and *talk* to this fella, right now. Get him off your tail, pronto."

He left Hannah there on the deck and headed into the bedroom. Hard to say what he would really do next, or what kind of reaction he might get from Hannah's shadow.

Following Hector was one thing, but terrorizing a young pregnant woman?

Hector shrugged on his sports jacket, feeling around to make sure that the taped roll of nickels was secure in the pocket of his coat.

Fella didn't look like any "scholar" he'd encountered so far: Hector pulled his Colt from under his pillow, slid it into his waistband.

Hector locked the door behind him and strode down the steps and out onto the courtyard, heading toward their stalker. Looking back up at the deck above, he watched Hannah watching him. She smiled, then turned her attention to their spy.

This world is ruled by violence. But I guess that's better left unsaid.

—BOB DYLAN

18.   THE MAN WHO LIVES WHAT HE WRITES . . .

Hector kept his head down as he briskly crossed the lawn, hoping that by obscuring his face, walking with his shoulders rounded and having donned a sports coat, he would fox the man spying on them.

He sighed deeply: Here he was in the next phase of that too-familiar role—how many times in his sixty-five years had he pushed through just this same scenario (in life—never mind the printed page)?

And Jesus, still playing the good guy at sixty-five? That was manda-tory retirement age in damn near every field but writing . . . and playing Saturday matinee hero, evidently.

When Hector was about fifty yards from the man, the stranger seemed to see him and took off in the opposite direction. The way the man ran his surveillance, and promptly bolted—it didn't smack of FBI. Hell, his threads didn't even meet with Bureau dress codes.

Hector took a few quick paces, then decided he couldn't overtake the younger man across the distance. Hell, across that yardage, Hector doubted he could have caught the stranger even if he was still in his prime. Then Hector cursed and set off after the son of a bitch *anyway*, actually hurdling a low fence around the skating rink, slipping and slid-ing across the rink and dodging short-skirted skaters before jumping over the fence on the other side.

As Hector's feet hit the hard-packed dirt he nearly lost footing.

The stranger burst through a set of doors, almost knocking down some tourists on the other side. Hector followed him, weaving around more pretty young things in short skirts and tight sweaters, carrying their ice skates.

Hector crossed through the lodge vestibule and hurled himself through another set of doors on the other side of the lodge, back out into the open air, headed toward a thick stand of trees.

The stranger was half running, half falling down a slope into a glade of pines. Hector followed him down—still at least fifty or sixty yards behind and increasingly short of breath. Goddamn Pall Malls . . . goddamn age. *Jesus.*

Hector slowed down now, hobbling down the steep, wooded hill, grateful Hannah couldn't see them from this range. His current state would probably erase any vestiges of the hero worship he was picking up from her earlier.

Then he heard the click.

Hector froze.

There was another cracking sound.

Could be dry, dead tree limbs creaking in the wind . . .

Or it was maybe a rifle bolt being thrown; a cartridge being chambered.

Off there a ways something glinted in the foliage.

Lingering dew on the leaves?

Maybe sunlight reflecting on a piece of chewing gum foil that had found its way into the weave of a goddamn bird's nest?

Or had the bastard secreted a rifle here in the woods? Worse, maybe the cocksucker had a confederate—a crack-shot partner. Maybe that gleam in the trees was the sunlight bouncing off the glass of a sniper's scope. Goddamn his own imagination.

Hector had left his eyeglasses back at the lodge and everything was a blur now—every twig, leaf, and branch was just indistinct enough to be construed as a potential threat.

Hector felt a little as he figured Hannah must have felt, locked in her room and threatened through her door.

Except Hector was no Hannah.

He'd fought—formally and informally—in wars and revolutions . . . countless times been shot at with intent in exotic, dark foreign ports, yet come out on top time after time.

And now here he was at a writer's conference in Idaho, in the wooded perimeter of a world-class sporting complex on a clear and sunny day, second-guessing and being spooked by clicks and glints in the trees.

How far we've fallen, eh, old pal?

Then Hector heard it *again*.

He wasn't entirely sure, but it surely did *sound* like the clip being thrust into the butt of an automatic.

So as not to spook a shooter, Hector turned slowly—showing his back to anyone who might have him in their sights.

Feeling more like some matinee idol's comic-relief sidekick now—and lacerating himself for his burgeoning sense of impotence—Hector held up his hands in surrender to an enemy that might not even be there, then began climbing out of the ravine.

Weighing whether he'd rather think of himself as a paranoid, a punch-drunk heavyweight who didn't know when to hang up the gloves, or a coward, Hector tried to keep trees between him and a bullet in the back as he climbed back up the hill toward the lodge, and Hannah.

Hector made his way back across the grounds, head down and hands in pockets, feeling his age and disgusted with himself for having blown the chase. Hell, maybe he could use it in a novel, but only for some supporting character. The day Hector's heroes started facing such setbacks was the day it was really time to hang it up.

Jesus, was poor, sick Hem having to put up with shit like this around these parts there at his own end? If so, no wonder . . .

Hector winced a little at the ache in his knees; his Achilles' tendons hurt from negotiating that goddamn wooded slope.

Cataloging his aches and pains as he approached his suite, Hector spotted another man crouched low against the door to Hannah's room.

The man had his ear pressed to the door panel, near the knob.

Hector's stomach kicked; Jesus, could it already be the guy from the ravine—sprinted back here well ahead of Hector? Hector's palms were damp. Worse scenario—maybe he was some *other* Creedy minion. Maybe some tough young buck skilled in hand-to-hand combat who could kick Hector's aging ass.

But no.

Hector half-smiled, realizing he was wrong on both counts. This would be old good territory, after all—a standard showdown and good clean fight. Fight? Hell, a *rout*.

Even from behind, Hector recognized the man by his horrid dandruff and unkempt hair. It was the bitter egghead from the lounge downstairs—Berle.

Hector smiled and shook his head. Well, he'd blown it with the other fella, but he could sure enough handle *this* prick; get back some scraps of self-respect by solving this little dilemma for Hannah.

He drew his Colt and shoved its barrel into the fat folds of Berle's neck. He held the index finger of his other hand to his lips, then grabbed the scholar by the collar and hauled him to his feet. He led him down the hallway and out onto a communal deck overlooking the grounds. It was cool and windy, and they had the deck to themselves. Hector kept the barrel of the Peacemaker tucked up under the fat little professor's chin.

"How's tricks, Berle?"

Hector searched the man's scared face: another skulking scholar. Despite all Berle's earlier nasty words about Richard Paulson, Hector couldn't dismiss the possibility they were somehow in league; joined as academics, maybe, in this strange plot that had Richard tangled up with Creedy toward some sinister end. Startled, Berle looked down at the gun and said, "Jesus, I thought you were Richard Paulson!"

"You and Paulson working together?"

Berle was shaking, his eyes crossing as he looked down at the big Colt poking under his chins. Hector could see Berle's blood pressure mounting in his rising flush and reddening ears; the academic's knees were quaking. *Christ*—he better not faint.

"I'm an academic," Berle said, chins trembling. "Paulson's an academic. But we don't work together." He wet his lips, said, "Can you put that gun away? It scares me."

"That's what guns are for. By 'work with,' I mean, are you tied up in this thing Paulson's got going with Mary Hemingway?"

"This 'thing'? No, the son of a bitch already cut me out of one book project. I'm not part of this biography or whatever it is that old cow is giving Richard. Like I said, I *hate* the son of a bitch!"

Berle moved his head just enough to look down at Hector's gun shoved up against his throat. "This gun . . . doing this to me—what's going on here? What's going on with Richard?"

"I was hoping you could tell me," Hector said.

"Well, it must be something pretty important. . . . I mean, Richard suddenly seems to have money." Berle got a little haughty now: "I mean, he's actually picking up some tabs, here and there. Most times, Paulson's slowest to reach for his wallet when the bar bill comes due at these conferences."

"New money, eh?" Hector chewed his lip.

"Precisely. That, and this thing with Mary choosing Richard—only Richard—to meet with . . ." Berle shook his head, then, feeling the Colt's barrel digging freshly into the folds of his flesh, he swallowed hard again. "I mean, Paulson's hardly the *best* of us . . . not the most accomplished. That damned award he won for the Paris book of his—word was, the awards committee was split. Whispers were, the winning vote was cast by a judge who was suddenly awarded a grant through some obscure branch of the federal government. Ask me, the fix was in for some reason. That bastard!"

More academic bullshit: Hector felt like screaming. Then again, if there *was* truth in what this swishy scholar was saying, when did the Feds start caring who won literary awards? What branch of the federal government had sweetened the pot for this literary-award judge?

"Okay, Berle, here's another question for you: You ever hear of a fella name of Donovan Creedy?"

Berle shook his head. He looked confused again. "Never heard of him. Which university is he from?"

Hector sighed and shook his head. Berle said, "If he's a friend or associate of Paulson's he's not worth my time. I keep my distance from Paulson and anyone he's friendly with."

Hector stowed his Colt. Berle took a deep breath . . . tugged at his too-short sleeves. He said, "So we're done here!" Hector imagined the egghead really could switch it off like that—probably eager to get back to his room and sculpt some drag-on footnote to some thicket-thick essay that would be read by tens of others of scholars.

"*Nah*," Hector said. "You menaced that girl. You scared Hannah Paulson. That's going to stop *now*. Bother her again, threaten her over the phone or through locked doors—you even *look* at her—well, I'm going to lay you out flat, pal. Hell, I'll attend one of your panels and take you apart verbally in front of your silly-ass peers."

Hector leaned in close to the scholar's face, his pale blue eyes boring into Berle's muddy brown eyes. "Do you understand me?"

"I do." Berle's chin trembled again. "So *now* can I go?" Silly bastard had lived in his head so long he evidently thought it was that easy ... that there'd be no physical consequences for his reprehensible actions. Well, in this case, he was right; Hector just couldn't bring himself to swing on the sorry fool.

Hector slapped his back so hard Berle was forced to take two steps forward to recover his balance. "Sure. Show me your back now, Berle, and for Christ's sake, invest in some good shampoo, hombre—flies could make snow angels on your shoulders."

A hero is a man who does what he can.

—ROMAIN ROLLAND

19. . . . AND WRITES WHAT HE LIVES

Shivering, Hannah pulled her sweater closer around her; the man on the lawn had run away before Hector could catch him. But at least he'd seen the man, too—acknowledged his threat as Richard had not.

Hector had been headed back up to the room—disappearing under the ledge. He should have returned by now. The thought that something might have happened to Hector Lassiter made Hannah shiver again. *Dear God, what's going on in this town? This strange man following us? Scholars trying to break into our room?*

For God's sake, it was simply a literary conference ... *wasn't* it?

Hannah moved to stand up as Hector stepped out onto the deck. He held up a hand. "Don't go to the trouble."

"Is everything okay?"

Hector wanted to say, *One ran; but I did get in a few good shots at that egghead who's been giving you grief.*

But the girl had enough on her plate without hearing the scholar had circled back for another try. "I had him and lost him. Didn't get much of a look at more than his back, either. Next time I'll get him."

"I'm just glad you saw the man."

Hector nodded. Hell, their shadow wasn't even *subtle*. Unless Dick was deep in his cups, it shouldn't be much of a reach to see Hannah was right about their stalker. He said:

"You said your husband wouldn't believe you about this man watching you. Why not?"

Hannah tried to defend Richard, to at least give her husband's attitude context. She said, "Richard's very focused on his project with Mary Hemingway. Anything else he regards as a distraction, I guess."

The crime writer was still watching her, waiting for more. Hannah couldn't stop herself: "We had some rough patches early on. Richard thought I should . . . well, I've . . . I've been under psychiatric care." She couldn't meet Hector's gaze to gauge his reaction. "Because of the baby, I'm off my medications. So Richard thinks . . ." She searched for words.

Hector thought about it. He'd seen it in a few others. He decided to just put it out there; he knew he'd be giving some back to her on the other side: "He thinks you're, well, delusional, maybe . . . a little paranoid?"

"Maybe," Hannah said, trying to soften it.

"You're clearly *not* bein' paranoid, darlin'," Hector said, voice raw and his Texas accent coming through a bit stronger. "Now you have another shadow," Hector said. "Me." He winked. "I'm not letting you out of my sight from this moment on. Not till I know you're safe. Not until we know who that other stranger down there is, and what he wants."

Hector carefully pulled her up to him. He hugged Hannah, avoiding putting pressure on her belly. He kissed her forehead through her blond bangs. "C'mon, I'm starving, and we have to draw up a battle plan," he said. "You tried the Ram yet?"

"No."

"It's one of Papa's good old places here at the complex," Hector said. "I'll credit Hem this: He always knew the best places to eat and drink."

He paused by the bed, thought about it, then slipped his old revolver under the mattress. He didn't trust Berle not to maybe run to the police over that stuff with the Colt. Wouldn't do to be stopped for questioning while carrying the Peacemaker.

Hector smiled crookedly at her reaction to seeing the gun. "Best be careful about lugging that around for a time, about now, I'm thinking. Besides, for the moment at least, all your enemies have fled."

In literature the ambition of the novice is to acquire the literary language: the struggle of the adept is to get rid of it.

—George Bernard Shaw

20.   SHOP TALK

Hector walked slowly enough for Hannah to maintain a comfortable pace. She slipped her arm through his and he smiled, gently disengaging her from his arm. Hannah felt herself blush—ashamed at having been so familiar with the elder author. Hector shook his head, smiled, and kissed the top of her head. "It's not what you're thinking, honey. I'm right-handed." He offered her his left arm, and she took it.

She said, "If Berle, or this other man . . ."

"That's why you're on my left arm," Hector said. "If I should have to swing . . . Though I think Berle is safely out of the picture now." Hector smiled uncertainly. The sun disappeared a last time behind the clouds, and rain scented the wind. "Perfect timing," he said as they reached the Ram just as the rain began falling—a hard, cold rain.

Hector looked around—one man followed them to the restaurant. But he was no threat: It was Andy Langley, junior G-Man.

Well, right now Hector kind of liked having Andy around. Presumably the kid was packing a gun, and if things went crosswise, well, Hector wanted to think Andy would take his side.

Hector gave Hannah another once-over as he held the door for her. Her burr aside, there was still something palpably European about her; something in the way she moved, in the way she regarded men.

While they waited to be seated, Hector said, "Your accent . . ."

"Scottish."

"The Highlands, I'm guessing."

"That's right!" His ear for accents surprised Hannah.

"I'll hazard Glencoe," he said.

"You're amazing," Hannah said. "Kinlochleven—nearly the same as Glencoe."

"After the last war—the last big war—I was slow getting back home," Hector said. "I rambled the Highlands, and fell in love with 'em, really. Through most of the late 'forties and early 'fifties, I'd try to get back once every year or two. Go back and roam the Highlands. Fish Loch Leven and Glen Orchy. Get me a little cabin on Skye. Been a long time since I last visited. That accent of yours makes me want to go back a last time."

Last time bothered Hannah more than a little: Hector still struck Hannah as vital . . . as very much alive.

Business was slow; they were the only diners, save one particular young man who followed them in. The waitresses were on break, so the bartender was serving them.

She said, "There's another man back there in the corner table . . . the man in a black suit. He seems to be watching us."

Hector glanced over his shoulder. "You're right. Don't mind him, honey. He's *my* shadow. FBI." He caught her reaction to that, smiled, and said, "Don't look at me like that, Hannah. No worries—I haven't caught Hem's paranoia about the Bureau. They've been following me since 1958. Mostly Andy, there, of late. They really were following Hem, too. Following Tennessee Williams . . . even old Carl Sandburg. Hear Hoover is on Steinbeck, too. Norman Mailer as well. I should have warned you up front: You'll probably get your own Hoover file now, just for hanging around with me. And if you should write a novel, especially one that has any truck with young people . . . ?"

"I don't care about any of that." She looked up at him, frowning: "What did you do to justify this surveillance by the FBI?"

Should he go into it with her? Tell her about the FBI's long campaign not just against him, but nearly every other American novelist of stature? Should he tell her about Nashville, and what he'd done there to nettle Hoover? No . . . why spoil the moment? He winked: "Your mistake is to put 'justify' and 'FBI' in the same sentence."

Hector glanced out the restaurant's front window at the falling rain. There were reflections on the wet glass—looked like men with guns approaching the front of the restaurant.

Guns?

Hector narrowed his eyes—the shooting ranges were on the *other* side of the complex....

He looked again: Donovan Creedy was out there—even through the blur of the rain on the glass, he recognized the bastard. Hector's mouth was suddenly dry; his underarms wet.

Creedy was talking to two men with deer guns. Creedy pointed through the rain-streaked window. The men nodded, and Creedy passed the men some bills.

Hector swallowed hard. Well, here it was—*total war.*

The men took up seats on a bench under the restaurant's ledge, waiting.

Hector absently reached under his jacket, feeling for the reassuring hardness of his Colt '73's wooden butt. Then he remembered shoving the Peacemaker under the mattress.

Goddamn it!

The dishes had been cleared. Hector had hardly touched his food; he wondered if Hannah had noticed. The cook had, but Hector had held up a hand before the man could ask the obligatory, "Is something wrong?"

Sitting at Hem's old table in the Ram, it would be the expected thing to strap on a meal worthy of an Etruscan eating orgy; to drink an ocean of booze.

Hector had resisted alcohol since Hannah couldn't have any, and hell, she already had one problem drinker in her life. And with those men loitering out front, he needed to be sharp now. There were two of them after all, and *they* were armed. Hector cursed himself again for leaving the Colt in his room.

Now, Hector tarried over coffee ... trying to figure out some gambit that might get them out of the Ram and safely back to the lodge.

Hannah was looking at him again ... inquiringly. He figured he'd best distract her. After the scare the fat scholar threw in her, he dreaded the reaction she'd have to a couple of thugs waiting for them out front with rifles.

He kept a wary eye on the hunters sitting vigil outside, but said, "So, you said you write fiction. Published already?"

"Just recently graduated college," Hannah said. "I studied writing."

"*Studied* writing," Hector said, half-distracted. Hannah thought he said it like it was an alien concept . . . as though he was skeptical it was something that could be learned in a university.

Hector nodded, flexing his fingers under the table. He had his roll of nickels, so maybe he wouldn't break any knuckles if he got in close enough to take a shot. He said, "Novels?"

"Short stories, for now," Hannah said. "Or I'm trying, anyway. Can't imagine writing something as big as a novel."

"It's just an incremental task," Hector said, looking around the Ram. If the damned interior decorators had only opted for some more appropriate wall bric-a-brac: say, a rifle or shotgun he might be able to use to bluff those men waiting on him out front.

Hector saw the sign for the restrooms. He needed to get Hannah out of the line of fire; a trip to the ladies' room would do nicely.

He said, "Write five pages a day, every day, and in a couple of months, you'll have written a novel." He snapped his fingers, still staring out the window. One of the hunters kept tugging at his ears . . . scratching his neck. The man also had this occasional nervous tick that sent his head jerking spasmodically to one side. Hector began to wonder if that one might not be a junkie.

Hannah said, "I've been reading you at the local library. And I've been reading *about* you. They say you used to write more like thirty or forty pages a day."

"Those were in the pulp magazine days," Hector said. "I was a working writer. Had to do that. It's a pace that kills. A pace that can dry up the well."

He'd plotted his course. He said, "I'd love to see your writing, darlin'." As he said it, he reached across the table to pat the back of Hannah's hand and upset her glass of milk. "Damn, *so* clumsy of me." He frowned and righted the glass. The milk spilled over the edge of the table and onto Hannah's lap. She said, "Oh, no!"

He stood and offered a hand to help her up. "Restrooms are right down that hall," he said.

He kept hold of her arm, starting her down the hallway. He said, "You dry off and we'll get you back to the lodge. By the way, you ever hear of a man name of Donovan Creedy?"

Hannah frowned, dabbing at herself with a napkin. "No. Should I have?"

"Not at all," Hector said. He glanced back into the dining area; Andrew Langley was relishing a stack of pancakes topped with whipped cream and strawberries. The dining room was still all but empty—just Hector, the waiter, and Andy.

Hector motioned to the waiter. He nodded his head at Andy and said, "I'll take my check, and that fella's too, but let's not make a big deal out of me doing that, okay, pal?"

Andrew Langley sat staring at his pancakes, savoring the food and rustic surroundings.

He'd been following Hector Lassiter for two years now. Fact was, he felt fairly lucky to have drawn the crime novelist as an assignment. So many guys in the Bureau spent their days and nights shadowing thugs, communists, and perverts ... sundry political agitators. Surveillance of those types almost always involved a procession of fleabag hotels, dive bars, or hole-in-the-wall "safe houses."

Andy had grown up in Iowa. Before joining the Bureau, the biggest city he'd ever seen was Des Moines. But Hector Lassiter (a rough-edged guy and occasional hell-raiser, sure, but none of that found its way into Andy's reports because, hell, he *liked* the old guy, after a fashion), well, dogging Lassiter's heels had sure broadened Andy's horizons.

Hector Lassiter lived his life on a *big* canvas: exotic ports of call and only the best hotels and bars; a procession of famous faces—athletes and beautiful starlets. Andy secretly sent extra surveillance pics of the more famous of Lassiter's friends/conquests to his mother back in Fontanelle.

Fact was, Andy kept waiting for some bean counter in the Bureau's accounting department to pull the plug on it all, citing Andy's often staggering expense-report vouchers. Andy *dreaded* the day he lost his present assignment.

Sensing motion, he glanced up:

Hector was walking briskly toward him. Old guy was probably going to needle him again with some teasing backtalk: "Hey, Andy—going to play some hands with Frank and Dean; why don't you fill the fourth seat?" Yeah, something like that. *What a card.*

Andy turned back to his notes; he'd have to get a dictionary to check a couple words here; his supervisors were always on him about his poor spelling. Hell, maybe he could ask Hector the novelist for the proper spelling. Still smiling, he glanced back up just in time to see Hector's fist flying at his face.

Hector felt very bad about it: Sure, he'd picked up the tab for the kids' breakfast, but that hardly made up for what he was about to do to Andy.

The blow knocked Andy out of his chair. Though he knew the kid probably couldn't hear it, Hector mumbled, "I'm so, so sorry about this, Andy, but if I don't do this now, those men out there mean to kill me, I think."

Hector hauled the young FBI agent back up and folded him into his chair, scooting aside his pancakes and then lowering the FBI agent's head to the table; Andy looked like he was taking a nap. Hector looked out the window—the two men were still out there, laughing and checking their guns. It was still on . . .

Hector reached under Andy's jacket and took out his gun.

Turning—half-expecting the waiter to come at him with rolling pin or spatula—he saw the man was standing there with the two meal checks in his hand, his mouth open.

Hector quickly shucked some bills off his roll and said, "My girl comes out, give her a slice of pie, huh? Tell her I'll be back in a jiffy." Hector slid out the back door into the rain.

The two men were still sitting on a bench under an overhang, watching the front door—evidently waiting on Hector and Hannah to make their exit. The duo smoked and passed a flask back and forth. One looked like a drunk. The other had nervous hands and feet ... definitely some kind of addict. Local muscle, clearly—improvised hit men, or the like.

Fucking Creedy ...

Hector pointed his gun between them. They looked up sharply, their rifles balanced on their laps. The quicker of the two, the drunk, said, "Can't shoot both of us, old man. We've got the numbers on our side."

"Oh, I *might* be able to shoot you both," Hector said. "Least I'm sober and my gun is already up." A decent bluff—particularly since the knuckles of his right hand were starting to swell and stiffen from that shot he'd given Andy Langley. He said, "Guns on the ground, boys."

The men looked at one another and shrugged. It was clear this was turning into more than they'd bargained for. Hector gave them a good hard look and decided they were *both* junkies. He had them quiet and cowed for the moment, but with that junk and hooch in their veins, there was no telling how things might go crosswise, fast.

They both seemed skittish, scratching the backs of their hands. Time for another fix, from the looks of it. And from the threadbare condition of their coats and pants, money was scarce. Probably needed more scratch for their smack, and they pretty clearly were willing to do anything— including murder—to make their rolls.

Hector pulled his wallet from his pocket with his left hand and said, "Man who knocks the other man out first gets a twenty."

The words were hardly out of his mouth when the drunken hophead snarled and let fly. He dropped his taller buddy with a sloppy round-house.

Hector whistled and said, "Nasty. But you win." Hector looked at the man there on the wet pavement at his feet. Couldn't leave the bastard lying there in case some other lodgers decided to brave the rain for a drink or a dinner at the Ram while Hector was debriefing the junkie hunter left standing. He said, "Get your buddy back up on that bench *now*."

As the smaller man struggled to haul his compatriot back into a slumped position on the bench, Hector shoved Andy's gun between the juicer's eyes. "So, pal, what was the order? Scare me, or kill me?"

The man swallowed hard, said, "Follow you until the girl was out of the way ... then ..."

Kill you.

It was clear that was what the alcoholic hunter hadn't said.

Looking up at Hector, the man scrunched his neck down into the folds of his coat collar, rubbing his cheek vigorously against the lapel. The man said, "What about my twenty?"

Hector took a look around, saw there were still no witnesses. He held up the twenty-dollar bill and said, "Right here, pal. "First, there's a message I want you to pass on to that man who sent you after me." Hector smiled: When it came to routing foes, he was about to be three to one for the day . . . not a bad confidence builder. He said, "Tell him I take things like this *real* personal."

Then he swung the gun's butt between the drunken hunter's eyes.

Hector left the man slumped across his unconscious hunting partner. He fished around their pockets and found the dregs of their drugs, their hypos. He tossed those into the pines. He figured finding their rigs and next fix would keep the duo plenty busy and out of his hair.

He thought about it, and left the twenty-dollar bill there in the second man's bruised hand. Let the two argue over that when they came to.

Hector edged back around the restaurant and slid through the back door. Hannah was sitting at their table, pushing around a piece of cheesecake with her fork. She hadn't registered the commotion out front.

She smiled up at him. "I was starting to worry. . . ." Then, softly she said, "Your FBI shadow seems to be taking a nap."

Hector offered Hannah his left hand; helped her to her feet. "Yeah, I've been keeping poor Andy running hard these past few days. We'll leave him to his dreams."

The rain had subsided and they stepped out into the barest drizzle. Hannah frowned, staring at the two hunters wrapped around one another in this strange pose that almost made them look like lovers.

She whispered in his ear, "What on earth are those two up to?"

Hector shrugged. "Who can say?"

Hannah chuckled. "Sharing bodily warmth, maybe? Or, too long afield and feeling amorous?"

He offered Hannah his left arm, which she accepted. "Could be, honey," he said.

Steering her wide around the unconscious men, he kept his sore right hand in the pocket of his sports jacket, fist wrapped around the butt of Andrew Langley's gun, all the while keeping an eye out for Donovan Creedy, or more of his minions.

Thus, what is of supreme importance in war is to attack the enemy's strategy.

—Sun Tzu

21.   THE ART OF WAR

Hector walked Hannah back to his room; held her hand as she kicked off her shoes and then sat back on the bed. "Rest up a bit, darlin'," he said. "I'm going to make some calls, strategize."

"Thank you so much again, Hector," Hannah said. "If you hadn't been here . . ."

He smiled and kissed her cheek. "Thank me when I've actually done something, kid."

He checked the door locks, then moved into the parlor room. He was checked into the Hemingway suite for another few days: He'd keep the room, but Hector felt there was enough real danger now—particularly now that Creedy was evidently sending improvised assassins after him— to warrant hunkering down somewhere else for a time. It was time to think about going into bunker mode somewhere more defensible.

Hector didn't know the town well enough to think of any option better than the Topping House.

If he could only patch things up with Mary. . . .

It was clear the Widow Hemingway needed looking after, too. It made perfect tactical sense: get the pregnant lady-in-distress, the threatened widow, and Hem's papers all in one place—that imposing concrete house Hem had picked for his own fatal final scene. And hell, all those guns of

Hem's were there, too—enough to equip a good-sized guerilla unit. Then there was the matter of Mary and her dreadful admission. He needed to take a sounding on the widow . . . make sure she wasn't blurting her "confession" out to anyone in proximity.

Biting his lip, Hector checked his wallet for the number, then dialed Mary's house. He expected the maid to pick up, but Mary answered her own phone: "Hector! You've been scarce! When are you finally going to get over here so we can get to work on the books?"

That was *odd*—no threats out of the gate. No screaming at him for nosing around amidst Hem's manuscripts. He said, "Well, after the other day . . ." Hector let that one hang there, feeling a bit confused.

Mary said, "Been a long time since I got *that* drunk." He heard a smile in Mary's voice. Flirty, she said, "I woke up in my own bed and don't remember getting there. You carry me up there, you handsome ape?"

"Uh, yeah."

That smile still in her voice: "You able lug, you."

"That's me all over," Hector said. "Listen, strange stuff is going on here in Sun Valley. I'd like to take you up on that offer of staying over if you'll have me."

"I've got plenty of room," Mary said, sounding very pleased.

"Good, because I'm bringing Hannah Paulson along. Her husband is away in Boise, but maybe you know that since he's working with you, too. Given what's been going on around her, well, Mrs. Paulson needs a safe place, too."

"Sure, bring her. I like *her*. I'll expect you soon?"

"Before late afternoon, yes. If it means taking the couch, no problem, but I need to bring one more with me." Hector figured to maintain some operational latitude, he'd be needing to call in a friend, someone reliable, to have his back.

"I have a guest quarters behind the main house. They're small, but warm and quiet," Mary said. This hesitation, now: Mary asked, "This friend isn't a woman?"

Christ. It was going to be a long few days, Hector thought. And much of it was likely to be spent deflecting Mary's goddamn advances if he was reading things right, and he figured he was. *Damn it.*

"Nah," Hector said, "not a woman. More like a batman. Extra muscle."

"He can stay out back," Mary said, then, "It's really that bad—that you need some thug at your back?"

"Looking to be."

"Sounds like Cuba and 1959 all over again."

"Let's hope not *that* bad," he said. "See you soon, honey."

Hector hung up and stared at his empty glass. Not a word about her confession. No hint it had ever happened. . . .

Hector poured some whiskey and mixed in a little water from the bathroom sink.

He leaned into the bedroom and saw Hannah was already asleep. He pulled the covers up over her and closed the door between them.

Then he sat down with his black book and started calling old friends, trying to find one who was good under the gun and might be in something like his present neck of the woods.

He thought more about Mary. He'd really figured Mary might still be bedfast or fulminating after that drug Richard Paulson slipped the widow sent her into murderous, manic fits. Strange.

No one is entitled to the truth.

—E. Howard Hunt

22.   ART IN THE BLOOD

Hector had spent an hour taking Mary's measure. He'd worried about bringing Hannah into the Topping House, given its mistress's previous psychotic state.

But now Mary was her usual self. Mary's mind seemed to be a blank slate after she'd taken the first few sips of Paulson's tainted cocktail. She wrote it off as Paulson mixing too-strong drinks: Mary figured she'd simply gotten drunk and passed out. She didn't seem to have any recollection of nearly murdering Hector with a shotgun.

Mary hadn't balked at the notion of Hannah moving in. Mary was used to Hem parading a succession of young infatuations through the

Finca; through hotels in Spain and Venice. And Mary seemed to be playing to "sisterhood" with Hannah now—commiserating about wanting, dissolute husbands. Richard Paulson aside, Hector wasn't up to hearing Mary run down Hem. Hell, he was haunted by the memory of Mary looking down those twin barrels at him. . . .

So now Mary and Hannah were upstairs, in the sitting room, trading marriage war stories. Hector hoped in bringing her along he wasn't setting Hannah up for worse grief than she might find on her own. But the house was defensible, and a good base from which Hector could take the battle to the other side on his terms.

To that end, Hector had moved Ernest's old typewriter to the document room, where he sat now, facing a blank wall—no distracting vistas for Hector Lassiter. He was thinking about what to write.

He'd told the women he was behind on his daily word count; that he needed to work on his own stuff. That alibi had passed: Even though he'd brought his own portable typewriter to Idaho, Mary hadn't questioned Hector when he presumed to commandeer Papa's typewriter. Hector *had* to do that: It was critical to his evolving strategy.

But he found himself distracted by all the intrigue swirling around him—all the pressure points that might be used against him: skulking scholars, a vulnerable, pregnant woman who viewed herself as psychologically damaged . . . And Mary Hemingway, who actually *was* a bit half-wrapped, and a drunk to boot.

And Donovan Creedy.

Hector wished he knew more about Creedy. The bastard was a lousy writer, he knew that much from *The Khrushchev Kill*: leaden, hackneyed prose, and plot twists you could spot chapters out. So many fucking exclamation points!

He needed to know more about the man and his day job.

Thinking of Creedy, and of Hem, put Hector in mind of Paris in the old days.

And thinking of Hannah, a young female writer he sensed was increasingly drawn to him, irresistibly dragged Hector's mind back to *another* striking woman writer he'd met in Paris in the winter of 1924. The woman who had made Hector the writer he was, in most ways—his beloved Brinke Devlin. So many years passed, yet Brinke still stalked his dreams.

Hector had this *craaazy* notion—one Brinke would have savored as few others could. He was going to do what the malignant others only dreamed of doing. If Creedy and whatever other shadowy figures were trying to attack Hem, to attack Hector and even an innocent bystander like Hannah and do it by seeding the Hemingway papers with forgeries, then Hector was going to turn it around on Creedy.

Hector was going to write his own false Hemingway short story.

Only Hector's faux-Hemingway story would be what the others could never be, not ever, not on any of the other authors' best days at the writing table.

Hector's spurious Hemingway short story would be pitch-perfect. *Utterly convincing.* Hector would write the kind of short story Hem would have written in his halcyon days. A masterpiece. No mean feat, that.

Especially considering the short story was going to have to satisfy another, darker aim: Hidden within its convincing Hemingwayesque prose and sensibilities, it would need to contain a kind of hidden code or textual watermark. Hector's sub rosa aim was to use the story as a plant—as a *trap*.

Then, if it surfaced later in some other context as Hem's work, Hector would be poised to step forward, armed with the short's hidden rubric, and say, "Wait a minute, you lying cocksucker . . ." It would bring down the whole house of cards Creedy was trying to construct. And if one fake story had found its way into the Hemingway papers? Well, scholars and academics would then be on high alert for others—looking for other spurious pieces they could seize on . . . trying to build into tenure or the like.

It was an audacious ambition—to write a perfect Hemingway story *and* bury a hidden message in the thing. Could he accomplish both aims? He meant to try.

But now, sitting here sober and alone in one of the last rooms Hem had passed through—sitting in a room surrounded by Hem's own words, his fingers poised on the keys of Hem's last typewriter—well, it was more than a bit daunting.

Hector lit a cigarette, then reached across the desk and picked up the leather case there. The improvised valise was one of Hector's old saddlebags from his cavalry days—a souvenir from the Pershing Expedition. Following the abortive chase after Pancho Villa, Hector had turned the saddlebag into a document carrier. Hector slipped out Hannah's sheaf of stories, thinking some of her youthful writer's passion might fire his own muse. It had been a hell of a long time since Hector had written a short story; it had been all novels and script work for him since the late 1950s.

He found himself seduced by Hannah's voice, which was unique and strong, if unfocused at times. Hector finished the first of Hannah's short stories. Hector was impressed: Hannah had a clean, direct prose style and a good and instinctive ear for dialogue. In fact, she advanced her stories through dialogue in a way that strongly reminded Hector of Papa's own storytelling tactics.

But the stories Hector had read so far didn't *arc*. They read as incomplete; lacking a resolution. Hector wondered if the stories he had just read were written before or after Hannah had been forced by her pregnancy to forego her medication—whatever edge-dulling, psychiatric pharmaceuticals the sawbones had prescribed for her. The question ate at him.

Hem would have admired Hannah's stories, too, Hector thought. And Hem would have been *crazy* for Hannah. Hem would be calling the comely Scot "Daughter" and bestowing her nicknames by now.

Hem would be running Mary crazy by insisting Hannah move in with them—hell, become their constant traveling companion, just as Ernest had done with other young women nearer his own end.

But in becoming Hem's muse, Hannah's own writing would likely suffer or even be subsumed, just as happened with Pauline and her journalism.

As Hem had tried disastrously to do with Martha.

As Hem had done with Mary and her own nascent but admittedly undistinguished career in journalism.

He realized he'd stopped reading Hannah's short stories at some point and begun thinking about Hannah in a very particular way. He was thinking about her golden good looks; the haunted, candid blue eyes that seemed to hide so little, but that was a delusion—he sensed layers and layers within the young Scot . . . undertows and passions of which she was unaware. He thought of Hem's famous metaphor for his writing technique, the so-called iceberg principle, in which only an eighth of the surface is above water. Hannah struck Hector a bit like that—a vast, uncharted country to be explored by some intrepid wanderer with a poet's tongue who could send back worthy dispatches of what he found.

So, there it was: Hector *wanted* Hannah.

Equally unbidden, the whole scenario reminded him of Brinke Devlin. Brinke had been Hector's one and only lover/writer; the only fellow author in any sense in that long line of women who'd shared Hector's bed.

Hannah? Well, there was maybe symmetry in this.

Brinke had come to Hector in his wild, tyro writer days. Brinke had shaped Hector, given him focus, and pushed him in the direction of becoming a crime novelist.

Now, with many more years behind than in front of him, feeling increasingly like the crime novels he was still writing were becoming passé, well, here was Hannah: another vibrant, attractive young fiction writer— one of the new breed.

In 1958, after all that mess in Tennessee that bought him constant FBI attention, Hector had been toying with shifting direction in a profound way. Even then, "Hector Lassiter," that tiresome public commodity, was starting to feel like a straightjacket. Hector had increasingly flirted with simply walking away from it all in recent years. Maybe instead endeavor to become that writer he'd set out to be in Paris in the 1920s. But his reconciliation with Hem in early 1959, and things spiraling out of that, derailed his plans.

But now? Hell, his own persona was even *more* the albatross.

The FBI was always on his heels—fucking tiresome and claustrophobic, that.

And Hector truly sensed the reading public's interest was increasingly moving away from the kinds of books associated with his outsized, macho byline.

Becky the scholar's words echoed in his head: *The novel is dead.*

If he let himself fall for Hannah, if he took her away from this wastrel, boozing, loser husband of hers, Hector sensed he'd get a book out of it, at the very least... a very *different* novel than he might otherwise write. Hannah might be the gateway to that long-deferred self-reinvention he'd once envisioned for himself.

And Jesus, wasn't that a *terrible* thought? *Using* Hannah like that?

Hector remembered what Scott Fitzgerald said about Hem: that Ernest always needed a new wife to prime the pump of inspiration for each new novel.

Still, undeniably, Hector felt this surge of inspiration now, thinking of Hannah—thinking of bringing her into his life. She could be his muse and he could be her mentor—that would be a fair exchange, in a sense. Muse/mentor—they didn't have to be mutually exclusive ... *did* they?

Sparked by the tension driving that question, Hector began to compose his own Hemingway short story.

It was dusk. In Creedy's mind, he was now officially off the clock.

He slipped off his jacket, but still wearing his tie, still wearing his shoes, he sat down in front of his portable typewriter to commence his night's writing. These were the hours he lived for.

Typical: He was having trouble getting started. It was always like this at first. He sensed many writers—writers like Hemingway and Lassiter, say—pushed themselves to have experiences to feed their fiction. They sought out danger and intense aesthetic experiences to have something to write about. Creedy had come to believe he came at the craft from the other direction—the harder direction, which, in his mind, made him more the artist.

Creedy pushed himself to write, and in doing so found experience. Hell, he could never really use his own life and experiences for his fiction, not really. His own life was so crowded with intrigue and bombast— much of it grotesque and bizarre—that he could never really make sense of it or figure out how to use it in commercial fiction.

And other writers, like Hemingway and Lassiter, well, they were the men they were, and in Hemingway's case, all his men in his stories and novels were the same man ... that is to say, a version of Hemingway. And Lassiter? Lassiter had actually begun to use himself as a character in his own books.

But Creedy had played so many roles in his blood-and-thunder life, adopted so many guises and selectively shown calculated profiles to so many different masters, he no longer knew what his own core was—wasn't sure he owned a center. He sometimes saw himself as one of those Russian nesting dolls: Pop off Stalin's head and inside is Lenin. Creedy had to drill down deep beneath his various espionage guises to try and fasten onto a fixed point that would carry each novel.

He'd once let himself sample alcohol to try and fire his muse...

maybe gain access to his subconscious through drink the way Byron and others claimed to through drugs or absinthe.

The outcome horrified and unsettled Creedy. The resulting pages were a riot of shrill, self-contradicting voices; a cacophony of characters that so disturbed him, Creedy actually put writing aside for several months and deprived his readers their favorite author's voice.

Eventually, he struck on a different tactic. He'd regularly survey the top-sellers in his genre, then synthesize a narrative voice that combined what he perceived to be the most sellable aspects of each of the other writers' works.

If there was a certain falsity in doing that, Creedy trusted the ingenious conception behind each of his published works—his implicit genius as a writer—redeemed and elevated his resulting manuscripts.

Each novel was part of a larger conception that when available, whole, to his readership, and to the works' creator, would represent an undeniable achievement: nothing less than one of the great literary legacies of the twentieth century. A century that Creedy, as writer and spy, had helped to shape. He *made* history. In time, Creedy assured himself, his deserved position in the western canon would be secure. He was *worthy*.

His phone rang. Reluctantly, Creedy picked it up. "Report."

The young agent, rather breathless sounding, said, "Sir, all the listening devices in the Topping House have gone dead!"

Creedy racked the receiver.

Ironically, the scene Creedy had been sculpting for his new thriller was eerily similar to what was unfolding now here in Idaho: two crafty and seasoned intelligence officers angling to outscheme one another.

This stuff with Lassiter was potentially grist for Creedy's fiction.

Except Creedy had to go out now and really *live* that scene—to do Hoover's fucking bidding.

More and more these days, Creedy just wanted to stay in his chair, writing.

Creedy stared at his typewriter, realizing he was blocked.

He slammed his fist down on his desk and muttered, "Fucking Lassiter . . ."

Just get it down on paper, and then we'll see what to do with it.

—Maxwell Perkins

23.   PUPIL

Mary handed Hector his coffee. She said, "Are you sure it's the best thing, you leaving for the airport now, Lasso? You said there are things going on . . . *bad* things."

Hector nodded. "Sure, but it all seems directed at me. . . . Well, and Hannah a bit, too. You'll be fine here, I think. And I won't be too long away." He couldn't make eye contact with Mary. He kept thinking about her boasting having shot Hem. He didn't believe it anymore, or he didn't think he did, but just the thought she'd make the claim . . .

Hector slipped a copy of the document-room key from his pocket. He put the duplicate key on the shelf above the kitchen counter, just where Hem had found it that bloody morning. Hector felt like twisting the knife, just a little. But Mary didn't show any reaction if she even got Hector's implication in hiding the key in plain sight there. And putting it there would certainly make the task easier for Paulson, or Creedy, if they meant to get at the now-salted Hemingway manuscripts . . . to get at Hector's new faux-Hemingway short story, for instance.

Hector said, "Important thing is, you *don't* let that cocksucker mix your drinks anymore. Can't let Richard get you hammered like he did the other day."

"No . . ." Mary shook her head. She resented all this happening around her at Hector's instigation. He hadn't told her enough to make most of it make real sense. Yet there were bad things going on around her . . . things she didn't quite grasp yet because they were still so strange and hidden. She knew she needed an ally—*needed* Lassiter's help. But Mary hated her dependence on him.

Hector leaned in, kissed the top of her head. "Just do this, honey. Trust me, Mary—today's the day we start to turn things around on these cock-suckers."

Mary arched her eyebrows. "Who *are* these 'cocksuckers,' Lasso?"

He decided to risk it: "Various, but mostly, FBI."

Hector held Hannah's hand, steadying her as she carefully backed into Hector's blue Bel Air. They were headed to the Ketchum airport.

Rueful, Hannah said, "You'd never know as recently as a year ago I was kind of an athlete." She wished again Hector could have seen her when she was fit. It was foolish to nurse fantasies about being Hector's woman—pursuing her writing as his lover, but she had restlessly been indulging such thoughts. He was a better, truer man than Richard. An accomplished fiction writer, too. But she was still bound to Richard by law. And in her present physical state? No way Hector could be attracted to her.

"I see it in you still," Hector said. "Won't be long now until you are again."

It was raining and Hector clicked the windshield wipers up a notch. They were headed out to Hailey to pick up Hector's friend—a retired Irish cop he'd met in Europe more years ago than Hector cared to calculate.

He said, "So, you and Mary spent a lot of time talking while I was writing. Any revelations?"

"Mary's suspicious of Richard's motives," Hannah said. "She's *very* suspicious."

Hector shot her a look: "How so? What's Dick done to prompt that?"

"Seems Richard's been doing some things I wasn't aware of . . . morbid things."

Hector raised his eyebrows.

"He's been requesting coroner's reports. Talking to morticians."

He checked the rearview mirror, then bit his lip. He said, "These coroner's reports—they'd be about Hem's death?"

She nodded. "And the mortician is the one who prepared his remains for burial."

"Why is Richard doing this?"

Hannah said, "That's what Mary wants to know, too."

He reached across the seat and squeezed her hand, then put both hands back on the wheel and checked the rearview mirror again. "What does *Hannah* know about all that?"

Hannah sighed. Richard had staked everything—their life together, such as it was—on his morbid theory and what it might mean for his career. But she trusted Hector and said, "Richard has this crazy theory."

Hector said, "About Hem's death?"

"It's very important to Richard's career," Hannah said. "I can't tell you if you might—"

"What? Might tell someone else? *Never.* Now what's Richard's theory, Hannah?"

She hesitated, then said, "Richard thinks Mary might have murdered Papa."

Jesus Christ: There it was again! Christ only knew what Richard—and Creedy's—real endgame was, but it seemed predicated on the same theory that had brought Hector to Idaho—this suspicion that Hem maybe hadn't killed himself. Hector saw Mary on the stairs again, crazed look in the eyes, pointing that gun at him . . . screaming she had killed Hem. And Richard had heard it. . . .

Hector nodded. "I'd be lying if I said I haven't toyed with similar notions from time to time," he said. "Maybe it's because I write the things I write, and always expect the worst of people in certain situations. But I have wondered myself in idle times. Something about that shooting, and about Mary's behavior and the immediate aftermath, well, it's never seemed right to me. Partly why I'm here—trying to spend some time with Mary and take my own soundings. Like to put these crazy thoughts to rest."

Hannah was worried that Hector was warming to the notion of a homicide in ways that might threaten Richard's scoop. She said, "You promised."

"Yes, I did," Hector said, smiling. "I mean to keep my word. But you need to know I'm here for a number of reasons. One of those important reasons is to do what Richard's doing—nose around a bit about the death. Hem and me were best of friends for many years. If something criminal happened to him, then I owe Hem my best effort at proving that. I owe his reputation that much. I mean, if I can move him from a suicide to a homicide victim, it could make a world of difference for his long game."

She wrinkled her nose. " 'Long game'? What's *that*?"

"The posthumous stakes. The literary reputation and the legacy. The long game."

Hannah considered that. The notion of an artist taking the long view of their own career in such fashion hadn't occurred to her, but now that Hector suggested it, it appealed to her, very much. She said, "Evidently you think Mary is capable of having shot Papa."

"*Maybe*," Hector said. "I think Mary is capable of *many* things; audacious things. But murder? I dunno. I just know Mary called me the morning it happened—the morning of the shooting. It was a strange call. She was under tremendous stress. But allowing for that, it was *still* a queer call. The aftermath was strange, too. Several other people received phone calls before the local cops were alerted. The family and friends more or less cleaned up the 'crime' scene. There was no real forensic examination of the scene before that. God only knows what evidence might have been wiped out. I mean, 'evidence' if it was indeed something involving foul play."

"You sound like Richard."

Hector shrugged. "Well, Dick may be right about this one thing."

Hannah watched him a time, then said, "You keep checking the rearview mirror."

"This car behind us—it may be following us. Before you ask: It's *not* my FBI shadow."

Hannah shivered, and Hector, misunderstanding, turned the car heater on. Hannah said, "I'm actually hot. Since the baby's gotten close, I always seem too warm."

Hector nodded, turned off the heat, and cracked the wing window on his side. "Don't sweat this other—this fella who may be tailing us. We'll leave him back there once we know one way or another. If he is following us, I'll just try to get a look at the car and the plates. If I can get an identification that way, then I can deal with him in my own time. My first thought was not to lead this guy to the airport. But now I think I actually *should* do that. I think I want him to know there's more muscle on the scene."

"Okay." She sounded nervous. Hector opted for a change-up—no more scaring the girl. He winked and said, "I've read your stories, darlin'. A couple are quite wonderful and ready to be published, just as they are. I don't move in 'proper' literary circles, obviously, but I'll do what I can to help you on that front. And I'll pass the stories on to my agent if you'd like. Prepare my agent for a time when you have a novel to be shopped."

Hannah was thrilled, but she said, "And the others?"

"I think what you have in the others are the pieces of that novel you've been fretting over writing," Hector said. "I arranged them in some different sequences and found a narrative line through them. With some connective tissue—a few paragraphs you'd write here and there to bind them together—I think you've probably got the first quarter of a fine first novel." He hesitated, then said, "What's the vintage of those stories?"

"What do you mean?"

"How recently was all this stuff I've been reading written?"

"Last six months."

Hector thought about that and said, "Well, it's quite good. Stark and honest. And you can sure write, kiddo."

Hannah couldn't stop smiling; she was delighted. She said, "Mary might want me to write her biography, too. She floated the idea a few days ago. She brought it up again this morning." Hannah hesitated, then added, "She's worried that Richard isn't a *finisher.*"

Hector winced inwardly: *Goddamn that old widow.* He couldn't stand the thought of Hannah putting her own writing aside for something as sensational as a piece of ephemeral and sensationalized nonfiction— something that would be gone from bookstore shelves in a few weeks and probably never even make it to paperback.

To set aside one's true and passionate writing to be a kind of hired-gun biographer—little better than a ghost—was repugnant to Hector, and it was, he was sure, the wrong writing path for Hannah.

He said, "Even if it wasn't your husband's book you'd be hijacking, you'd never really consider doing that would, you, Hannah? You're a fiction writer—just finding your feet. The other would be at best a distraction. At worst, it might be a maybe inescapable cul-de-sac."

He looked from the road to her face. Hannah's eyes were skittish. She said, "No, of course not."

Hector, nodded. "Writers all too easily can fall off the beam, sweetheart." He looked around at the low buildings of the town they were now entering and said, "Not much of a place, is it?" Hailey was like a smaller, downscale version of old Ketchum. "Ezra Pound was born here," Hector said. "It's a long way from here, to poetry, Paris, and prison for supporting Mussolini, isn't it? But we all have to come from somewhere. Ezra's another writer who stepped wrong. Cost himself his career. Ezra's long game got away from him in the worst way."

"Did you know Ezra Pound?"

"Not like Hem, but yeah, we shared a few drinks. Shared some thoughts. He was a great poet, but a pretty sorry thinker . . . like all authors when they try to be political advocates. Ezra was also a terrible anti-Semite."

Hannah said, "Trust the art, not the artist, isn't that the saying?"

Hector reached across the seat again and squeezed her hand. He left his hand closed over hers. "That's what they say, yeah. Probably a turn of phrase coined by some despicable, rotten creative type."

She smiled, "Aye, makes sense."

Hector took his hand away, shifted down, making an abrupt left turn. The car he was focused on seemed to hesitate, Hector thought, then righted itself and continued on down the main road through Hailey. Two other cars stayed tacked to his Bel Air's tail, however. *Damn it.* Hannah said, "I couldn't see much through the rain. Not sure what kind of car that is, and the license plate? I couldn't see it."

"Me either," Hector said, angry. "Well, I'm not really sure if he was following us. But if he was, he broke it off for obvious reasons."

"Not so obvious to me," Hannah said.

Hector patted her thigh, then palmed the wheel, heading back up the road they'd come down from Ketchum. "There's only one way back to Sun Valley, sweetheart," Hector said. "He can pick us up again anywhere along that route. But he's gone for the moment, so we can go to the airport and fetch my friend."

"Tell me about this man," Hannah said. "Who is he?"

"Fella name of James Hanrahan. A cop's cop. And if you haven't gathered by the name, another Celt."

James Hanrahan was about six feet tall, and carried a few more pounds than he had the last time Hector crossed paths with the retired Cleveland detective. White-haired now, a bit tired looking, Jimmy still retained his Irish tenor—a brogue he ladled on thicker at strategic moments. Hands the size of hams. Jimmy had been fishing at the retirement cabin he'd recently bought in Montana.

Now Jimmy was stuffed into the backseat of the Bel Air and telling stories of the Great Lakes bootleg wars and Eliot Ness to Hannah, crazy tales of earlier escapades he'd shared with Hector, occasionally dropping in a few Gaelic phrases or words for Hannah's benefit.

Interrupting his own reverie, Jimmy said, "You *are* aware of the three cars following us, Hector? Not a team effort, I might add. I think you've actually got three *different* tails."

"Yeah," Hector said. "One's FBI—young fella named Langley who's my shadow. The other is probably attached to this Creedy guy I was telling you about."

Jimmy grunted, said, "And the third in the Impala?"

"Mystery man. The one that has me most wondering."

"What's the plan, then?"

"We get back to the Topping House . . . hunker down there, and I catch you up on events."

"I'm not taking your money for this, Hector. I still owe you for—"

Hector cut him off. "Jimmy, your fee is being covered by the Hemingway estate, so live it up. God knows Hem always did."

Hemingway has been accused of being of Communist sympathy, although we are advised that he has denied and does vigorously deny any Communist affiliation or sympathy.

—FBI Agent Raymond Leddy, confidential to J. Edgar Hoover

CREEDY—Cuba, 1947

Creedy had long ago succeeded in bugging Hemingway's car. Now he was following behind along the twisting, wet road, hanging on every word:

José Luis Herrera, Hem's longtime Cuban doctor, said, "Nobody we know—and all of us despise Trujillo—wanted any part of this plot for a Dominican Republic coup d'état, Papa."

Hemingway said, "I *know*. Goddamn it, I know all that."

"*Any* support was bad enough, Papa, but to write personal checks for your financial contribution to this scheme? That was *loco*. When they get their hands on those checks..."

Hemingway said, "Damn it, José, I know. I'm going to New York, just as you're urging, aren't I?"

José said: "They're holding the plane, Papa. We should just make it."

Hemingway called out louder, "A little more gas, Juan."

"In a few months," José said, "perhaps things will quiet down and you'll be able to return unmolested, Papa."

When they reached the airport, Hemingway swung out of the car, grabbed the suitcase René had hastily packed for him, and trotted across the tarmac with his slight limp.

Removing the headphones from his ears, Creedy stepped from the commandeered equipment shed and moved between Hemingway and the plane.

Yelling above the sound of the propellers, Hemingway said, "I'm in a hurry, Agent Creedy."

The FBI agent smiled meanly, gnawing on a toothpick. "Bet you are. That was a pretty crazy scheme, *Papa*, this writing a personal check to fund the overthrow of a banana republic and doing it from the shores of still another banana republic. And what you've done, you goddamn nigger-loving dabbler: Trujillo was doing good work, keeping those darkies down."

"Yeah," Hemingway said. "Killing 'em by the thousands. Him and his machete-toting death squads."

"Better to let them kill each other, I say. How drunk were you when you decided to draft that check, *Papa*? You really put your foot in it this time, *Papa*."

"I need to get on that plane, Creedy," Hemingway said. "We'll take this up another time."

"I know you need to make that plane," Creedy yelled. "That's why you suddenly have passport issues. Maybe you can catch the next plane, once these concerns over your travel documents are hashed out. I mean, if the Cuban authorities don't get here first. They will, you know."

Hemingway said, "Don't do this, Donovan. Let me go, Agent Creedy."

"Fuck you, *Papa*." Creedy smiled. "Notice you still don't have a new novel out. What's it been, ten years? My fifth comes out next month."

"Good for you, asshole. Really, Agent—please don't put me to the test now. Trust me when I say that neither of us wants me pushed that far."

"That some kind of threat, *Papa*?"

Hemingway shrugged. "Your words, Agent, not mine."

"Come on back to the terminal with me, Hemingway. We need to check that passport."

A crewman was standing in the doorway of the plane, yelling and waving for Hemingway to board . . . pointing at his watch.

"I *really* need to get on that plane now. You *really* need to let me do that."

"Fuck that." The FBI agent took Hemingway by the arm. "Let's go now."

Hemingway bit his lip, then took the agent's hand from his arm and cast it aside. "Just remember, Donovan, whatever comes of this, you pushed me to this admission. This is on your head. I'm sure the Director will see it that way, too."

"Pushed you to what?"

"I know what you Bureau boys think of me—that I'm some dissolute, left-leaning novelist who's spent too many years abroad. But I was a journalist. In some important ways, I'm still that journalist. I have skills. I've covered crime, wars, and revolution. Interviewed presidents and despots and fiends. I know how to find things out, when I really want to know them."

"What's your point, *Papa*?"

"Years ago, I told you about Hoover's missing birth certificate. Sucker suddenly surfaced when Hoover was forty-three. Well, I heard *more*. I know about Hoover's parentage now. Tell him that."

"What does that mean? What *about* his parentage?"

Hemingway smiled. "Give Hoover my message, and then if you've got balls under those seersucker pants, *you* put that question to *him*. You ask J. Edgar who his parents were, Creedy. Now, are you going to make me miss that plane? If so, I'm going to get chatty about Hoover's lineage with the world press that'll flock my way when the Cuban police hold me for that other 'banana republic.'"

Red-faced, Agent Creedy stepped aside. "Get on that damned plane, Hemingway. But you're right—you really don't know what you've just done."

Hemingway shouldered past him, mounted the boarding ladder; turned. "Don't get ideas about trying to arrange some kind of accident for me, Agent," Hemingway yelled. "Anything odd happens to me, this information will go to people even more dangerous than me. I can think of one man in particular who would really know how to use it to most devastating effect."

Hemingway gave Creedy his trademark grin, relishing the look on the G-Man's face.

He said, "I'll always remember you looking this way, Creedy."

Creedy said, "Mr. Hoover won't forget this, either, asshole."

That wiped the smile off Hemingway's face.

No artist tolerates reality.

—Nietzsche

24.   HEM'S ROOMS

Richard exploited Mary's sweet-tooth: brought her a box of chocolate-covered cherries provided by *the man* that laid the widow out flat.

Thank God for that: Despite the man's assurances Mary wouldn't remember her confession—that mess with the shotgun—Richard still felt uneasy in her presence.

And that was the *other* thing—he'd gotten Mary's confession, but since she wouldn't remember and would likely deny it all . . . well, Richard's bombshell "exclusive" was problematic. He kept thinking he was going to have drag it out of her again without the man's potions.

And that still didn't address the matter of Hector Lassiter having heard Mary's confession, too.

As Richard was checking to make sure Mary was really asleep in her chair, he heard a crash in the kitchen. He followed the sound and found Mary's Mexican maid crumpled on the floor. The woman had snuck two or three chocolates for herself. Silly bitch still had a chocolate moustache as she lay there, snoring heavily into the floor tiles.

The professor wrestled the maid into a kitchen chair; left her head resting on the table. He wiped off the chocolate stains around her mouth. Running some water to wet the rag he used to clean her up, Richard saw the key on the counter above the sink—the same place the old bitch had left the key Papa had used to get at his guns, by Mary's own account.

Richard snatched up the key, crept down to the storage room, and turned on the lights.

My God—all those shelves and pigeonholes full of letters . . . manuscripts and papers.

All of it in Papa's distinctive hand, or from his famous typewriter.

Richard began to dig through it all, finding most of it to be various working versions of *A Moveable Feast.*

But he also found a letter or two containing paragraphs here and there that revealed some new biographical insights about Hem—stuff any of his peers would give both balls to possess.

Richard shoved the letters down the front of his shirt. He followed those with a few handwritten pages of familiar passages from *Feast*. Stuff that was duplicated in other versions stored here and so probably would never be missed.

There was nothing in any of those pages for his scholarship, but it was *Hemingway's handwriting.*

And anyway, if he ever needed the money, the stuff could be sold for serious cash to well-heeled Hemingway collectors through New York rare-book dealers and auction houses.

Then Richard saw it: sitting there, glowing in a shaft of light through the storeroom window—like some heavenly beam had cast down upon it for his benefit. Richard swallowed hard: This was *a moment.* He could *feel* it.

There was a typed short story resting next to Hem's typewriter.

The title was unfamiliar to the professor. *Holy God!*

Richard sat down in the chair set before the typewriter—forgetting for the moment that Hem famously wrote and typed standing up. He lifted the sheaf of paper there. Yes, there was no doubt—this was an unknown Hemingway short story!

This was bigger than Mary's confession, in its way.

He read the story straight through—gripped by the clear, beautifully spare Hemingway prose. He savored the uncharacteristically knowing, subtle shading-in of the female character who centered the short story—a young female writer in thrall to an elder, seasoned novelist. In that, it reminded Richard a little of James's "The Lesson of the Master." He finished the story, sitting there stunned and tingling:

Accomplished . . . moving . . . it was vintage Hemingway.

Richard chewed his lip a long time. He couldn't help himself: He took the manuscript, along with a few mores pages of *Feast* and some letters, and ran up the stairs to hide them in his rental car.

When he returned, Richard locked up the storeroom and replaced the key on the counter. He retrieved the box of tainted treats and walked down to the Wood River. He tossed the box into the rippling current.

Then Richard stalked back up the hill, intent upon trying to rouse Mary. He'd say something like, "Should I call a doctor, Mary? You seem to have fainted...."

As he mulled his cover strategies, his thoughts returned to the Hemingway short story. He couldn't wait to be alone—to read the story again and study it.

Hector and Jimmy were standing along the pine-tree dense slope of a foothill above the Topping House. The sun was high overhead; a pair of snakes slithered in the high grass. Jimmy got out a fresh cigarette, and Hector lit it with his Zippo.

Hector hated running surveillance. If he was alone, he could at least have brought a notebook and done some writing, but with Jimmy along, well, that would have been rude. Jimmy, the retired cop, seemed more resigned to watching the Topping House. Although it was a staple of his former job, after about an hour of standing in the cold woods, Jimmy had said, "This is a part of the work I truly don't miss."

Hector said, "I'm a little concerned about Paulson being able to snoop around in there with Mary and her servant in the place. Unless he drugged her again, I don't see how he can—"

Jimmy passed Hector the binoculars. "Your boy's coming out again now—his arms are *full* of paper this time."

Yes, Richard had gone for it, after all. That *really* raised the question of what had happened to Mary to allow this theft. And where was Richard headed with all this stuff? Maybe back to Creedy? And all the papers he was hauling—Richard had truly gone for broke...taken much more than just Hector's plants, goddamn it. He never envisioned the scholar being *this* brazen in his theft—it was like grave robbing. Christ, he was going to have to take it all back before it fell into Creedy's hands...or the goddamn collectors' market.

Hector said, "I've got to go—gotta tail this egghead and take back what he took beyond what I intended. You get back in the house, Jimmy. Make sure he hasn't done something unpleasant to the women in there."

Jimmy shook his head. "Looks like your gambit with the faked short story might be playing out—too well, maybe, but *still*—yet it doesn't solve the other problem. By that I mean the damage the little widow is doing your friend's legacy with her 'editing.'"

"One battle at a time," Hector said. "Hell, I haven't got a single good strategy for dealing with the Mary dilemma. Not yet."

Jimmy said, "The colleen, she know about your suspicions regarding her husband?"

"Christ, no," Hector said. "I think Hannah doesn't know what her husband is up to, either. Doesn't know he's in league with the Bureau."

"*Jay-sus,*" Jimmy said, huffing as they set off down the hill toward the house and Hector's hidden Bel Air.

Hector nodded. "It's a mess, for sure."

Jimmy winked and blew smoke. "Goes without saying, but me being me, I'll say it anyway, Hector: If Hannah finds out what you're keeping from her, that you're actively conspiring against her husband . . ."

"Yeah," Hector said. "I know." He got out his car keys and jingled them. "I need you to hold down the concrete fort here, buddy."

It was 4 P.M. and there had been no phone call from Richard. Hannah had been shocked to hear Richard had returned, without giving her word, to visit Mary earlier in the day. And now he'd fled back to Boise with *still* no word. Hannah knew of no likely hotel to call to ask after him; nobody would answer the phone at the university at this hour.

Earlier, she shared a late lunch with Hector and the retired cop, Hanrahan, in the Sun Valley Lodge's restaurant—a quick bite before returning to the Topping House. There had been no cadre of academics chinning themselves on their vocabularies and gorging on bullshit, metatextual gossip.

No red-faced man with a widow's peak stalking her, or at least she didn't spot him if he was there.

Perhaps the whole rotten lot of them had stayed over in Boise.

Richard owed Hannah a phone call at the very least. But she was actually glad for the distance; savoring the time alone to soak it all up. She had seen Hector Lassiter up close and personal now. He represented a kind of model for a generation of male writers who tried to shape themselves in Hector and Hem's images ... charismatic men of action whose swagger and bluster concealed bookish, intellectual qualities such men's men couldn't quite countenance in themselves. Hannah found that endearing ... very appealing, in its way.

Richard had asked her which Hemingway wife she would have wanted to be. She still resisted the notion that she would ever have fallen into that trap Hem's other women had: drawn in by fame and then kowtowing to Hem's self-centeredness.

No, marrying Papa meant becoming a kind of satellite—eclipsed and gripped in the great man's greater gravity and outsized public persona.

Maybe it was the same to be one of Hector Lassiter's women. . . .

Mary had stopped in after Hector left. Mary said she intended to sever her relationship with Richard—his drunkenness was too great a threat to the quality of their book together. But, Mary added, perhaps if Hannah would definitely and *contractually* consent to cowrite the book with Richard, well, Mary might relent ... "Time a *woman* wrote a book about a Hemingway," Mary said.

Despite the fact Hector had cautioned her earlier, Hannah provisionally accepted. "But," she said, "you'll have to be the one to convince Richard I should help him, Mary. He'll be furious, I expect."

"Richard doesn't have the luxury of choice. It's *my* life, after all," Mary had said. "That makes it *my* book. If he balks, you'll write it, and it will be *our* book, Hannah."

Hannah was still trying to figure out how she would tell Hector she was briefly sidestepping into nonfiction writing. After all, Hector had almost snarled at her when she'd mentioned Mary's offer to have Hannah write her autobiography. Hector's visceral reaction still had Hannah second-guessing her agreement to take Mary up on her offer.

Did the strategic decision to write this book about Mary *really* represent some terrible misstep, as Hector insisted?

Before he'd left, she'd tried to broach the subject with Hector again, and the crime novelist—the former *Black Mask Magazine* pulp writer—had surprised Hannah by invoking some obscure line from William Blake: "If you, who are organized by Divine Providence for Spiritual communion. Refuse & bury your Talent in the Earth, even tho' you should want Natural Bread. Sorrow & Desperation pursues you thro' life! & after death shame & confusion of face to eternity . . . You will be calld the base Judas who betrayd his Friend!"

Hannah had furrowed her brow at that, said, "That's very . . . *daunting.*"

Hector had just smiled and winked. "Nah: They're just good words to keep a fiction writer honest."

Now Hannah picked up an old paperback crime novel by Hector, but found her mind was still racing too fast to concentrate on it.

Jimmy was downstairs with Mary. Hector had headed back to the lodge to look for someone who might be staying there, he said. When she pressed him for the identity of the person he was searching for, Hector was vague: "Just a guy from the old days. Thought I might have seen him in the lodge a few days ago. If he is here in the mix, it would explain a lot of the strange things going on here, darlin'."

She lay there for a long time, her back throbbing, unable to find a comfortable position.

Her thoughts kept returning to Hector Lassiter. Hannah struggled up and bit her lip. Set in her mind, she crept into Hector's empty room.

Hector had left his leather valise there by his own typewriter.

Wetting her lips, Hannah carefully slid a thick sheaf of manuscript pages from the leather saddlebag.

She turned the first few pages and began reading a manuscript Hector had titled *Toros & Torsos*. She was surprised to see that the story was about Hector. Hector was writing about himself in third person—using his real name and some biographical facts about himself. And Hemingway was also a character in the book.

Hannah thought perhaps it was a memoir, but as she read on, it became clear that Hector intended that the manuscript be read as a novel.

She thought of what Mary had said about living as an artist, and thought Hector must represent an extreme example. Still, the notion of blending one's life with one's work in such a way fascinated Hannah. And

Hector's prose? It transcended any notions of genre writing she'd ever indulged. She thought Hector had the chops and reach to be a literary writer if he set his mind to the task.

Hannah felt guilty about sneaking looks at Hector's draft. She stacked the pages neatly and returned them to their leather bag. She sat down with a notepad and the stacks of her own short stories in the order that Hector had arranged and then numbered them. She had some time now—before she'd have to put aside her own fiction to help craft Mary's biography.

Using Hector's portable typewriter, Hannah set about writing the "connective tissues" that Hector—her new teacher, as she'd already come to think of him—had called for to make her stories into the start of a novel.

You will recall that in my conference recently with the President, he indicated that some message had been sent to him, the President, by Hemingway through a mutual friend . . .

—J. EDGAR HOOVER

CREEDY—Africa, 1954

Agent Creedy said, trying to modulate his voice, "I'm at the hotel, yes, sir. In the bush, and flat as it is out here, it's hard to run surveillance as we think of it back home."

Donovan Creedy had been playing a double game for some time.

When Hoover found out in '51, he'd only allowed Creedy to continue his CIA affiliations and yet maintain Bureau status because Creedy's highly idiosyncratic and aggressive racial objectives coincided with his own.

And his FBI status made Creedy a valuable commodity in the eyes of his CIA handlers.

"Let's take some of these excuses and turn them into some cheerful action directed at realizing *my* desires, Agent," the Director said, fuming. "Let's do some things consistent with enforcing *my* will, Agent Creedy. I want to see you *engaged* in your efforts for me again, like the old days."

"Yes, sir. I will do that, sir." Creedy thought, *Duplicitous cocksucker.*

"The plane went down near Murchison Falls," the Director said. "It struck a telegraph line, it's believed, mangling the prop, and sending the plane crashing amid a herd of elephants. Onboard were Mr. and Mrs. Hemingway, and their pilot, a man named Marsh. There were some initial distress signals from the pilot we've successfully ordered ignored by domestic craft . . . done via channels, of course. Cutouts."

"Of course, sir."

"A passing commercial liner spotted the wreckage," the Director continued. "The liner saw no sign of survivors."

"I see, sir."

"No, you *don't.*"

Faggot cocksucker. Creedy managed, "No, I don't, sir."

"Exactly. The world is already coming to grips with the probable fact of Hemingway's death," the Director said. "We have a rare opportunity here to neutralize forever the Hemingway threat. I want you to *confirm* that death. If he isn't postmortem, then help Mr. Hemingway along. Understood?"

"Clearly." *Damn it*: He didn't have time for this; he was in a delicate final stage of an operation to kill *another* man for the Agency—one threatening to trigger an African independence movement that could easily spread wide, jeopardizing colonial interests across the continent and erasing established white rule.

Creedy had spent months planning the operation and wanted—*no*, he *needed* to be there to see it all went as *plotted*. And he *wanted* to see— wanted to see that evil black devil fall.

The Director said, "You better move then, Agent Creedy. I'm told Africa is a very big place. I'd be peeved if this didn't go to my plans. So peeved in fact, I might cease to turn a blind eye to your other, shall we say, domestic government *entanglements.* Understood?"

Creedy said tightly, "*Yes.*"

"Succeed, Agent Creedy."

The agent held tightly to the bottom of his seat and the windshield frame of the bush Jeep as his driver bounced along the rutted road. All the impacts to his spine and tailbone had Creedy convinced he'd be an inch shorter when he climbed out of the Jeep.

It had all gone to hell plenty fast enough: Creedy had reached the first crash site—nearly being trampled by elephants in the process—only to learn that the Hemingways and their pilot had walked away from the downed plane with minor injuries.

After an uneasy night camped out among all those elephants, the crash victims had waved down a passing watercraft—the actual boat used in *The African Queen*—and been taken on to Butiaba. *Only Hemingway…*

Creedy figured he'd lost his chance to "help" Hemingway along to his grave, but then reconsidered. Emboldened, and still angered to be distracted from his larger, primary objective to kill Jomo Kenyatta in his prison cell, Creedy had contacted one of his associates, a man named Stapleton, and arranged for him to disguise himself as a mechanic with an eye to "fixing" Hemingway's next aircraft.

Only Ernest Hemingway could go down in back-to-back plane crashes and not raise eyebrows, Creedy figured: It all seemed consistent with Hemingway's larger-than-life persona.

As Creedy rushed to Butiaba, the second plane carrying the Hemingways got off the ground after a bumpy takeoff, intending to fly to Entebbe. Then it abruptly nosed in and caught fire on impact. Exactly that much went to plan.

Shortly afterward, Creedy got a radio message: Hemingway had escaped the second burning plane with his life.

Agent Creedy had hurt his fist pounding on the dash when he got that news.

They reached Butiaba, and Creedy jumped out of the Jeep and hit the ground on the run, stirring up dust and drawing buzzing flies and panhandling locals. A begging black child touched his sleeve; Creedy nearly kicked the bone-thin boy to death.

Creedy shoved his hand into the pocket of his bush jacket and flipped the safety off his gun, looking for some English speaker who might direct him to the local hospital.

If he found Hemingway in a hospital room, Creedy had special chemicals and hypodermics he could administer to the author to "help him along" for goddamn Hoover.

Flustered, the agent finally put the arm on an English-speaking doctor and got the news.

Damn it to fucking everlasting hell:

He'd missed them *again*.

Hemingway was on a *third* plane now, he was told. Mr. Hemingway's injuries were bad—much worse than he was letting on, the doctor said, but Papa was expected to live.

Creedy walked out of the hospital in a daze and found a drinking hole. He ordered a bottle of Tusker beer and listened to the radio playing behind the bar—a shortwave that picked up some English-speaking news program.

The broadcast made it clear how badly he'd missed his opportunity to close the "Hemingway Affair." Papa was already before the world press, clutching a bottle of gin and a bunch of bananas, grinning and declaring, "My luck, she is running good."

According to less sentimental sources, Hemingway was holed up in his hotel room, recuperating and savoring his own erroneous obituaries.

Creedy ground his teeth.

Then:

"In other news, an apparent assassination attempt of incarcerated African independence leader Jomo Kenyatta was thwarted this morning. . . ."

Creedy went into a rage that got him thrown from the bar. He pulled himself up from the ground, brushed off the dust, and found Stapleton . . . found a plane; headed to Entebbe.

Creedy had this notion of shooting Hemingway dead in his hospital bed.

Hemingway looked bad: bandaged, burned. His eyes didn't quite track. Probably a concussion, Creedy figured. That gin Hemingway was guzzling wasn't going to help with that.

Hemingway looked up at Creedy, then shook his mangled head. "It's true what they say," Hemingway growled, voice hoarse with pain. "It's a small world after all. More's the bloody fucking pity."

Creedy's hand was wrapped around the .45 in his pocket. The grip was wet with his perspiration. His hand trembled and Creedy took his finger from the hair-trigger, afraid in his shaking rage he might accidently shoot off his own toes.

"You're a hard man to kill," Creedy said.

Hemingway gave him this strange look.

"Two plane crashes, I mean. And you survived them both. Amazing."

"My luck, she is still good."

Creedy curled his lip. "You need a new line. That one's already in all the papers."

Hemingway gestured at the stack of newspapers by his bed. "Been reading them. Bastards and their obits . . . Jesus. No man should get to read his own obituary, Creedy. The things the cocksuckers chose to dwell on . . ."

"Well, they weren't going to focus on your writing, were they? Your last novel sucked wind. *Across the River and into the Trees*: What a piece of shit."

Hemingway took another shot of whiskey. "Bad enough to be like this. I don't need to hear you work your mouth. Get out of here, Agent. Scram."

"You cost me something today," Creedy said. "Cost something important to me."

Hemingway managed a grin. "What's that, asshole?"

"I . . . I can't say." Creedy wanted to shoot the bastard, but he'd never get out of the building if he tried. And the types around here? The niggers would kill him, ugly and hard. He knew it. He thought of Hoover—fucking Director. Maybe he'd resign his post with the Bureau. Quit, and deprive Hoover the satisfaction of firing him. He said:

"Hoover remains obsessed with you. All these shots you've taken at him over the years have gotten under his skin. He's a stupid man to provoke, Hemingway. But you do it anyway. I conveyed that message to him, you know. The stuff about the birth certificate. He nearly took my head off. Despite your baiting him, I don't understand why he hates you so. Why he obsesses over you."

Hemingway shrugged, looking at another one of his own obituaries. "Maybe it's what I know."

"What was it you uncovered, Hemingway? What do you think you know about the Director and his parentage?"

Hemingway drank more gin, smacked his lips. "Back in the 1920s, there was this rumor, you know. Tongues wagging about how President Harding might have some Negro blood in him. Hoover came into the Bureau under Harding, you know. Birds of a feather? People I know found proof. Seems the Director's ancestors were slaveholders. Things got cozy around the plantation. I'm okay with it. I'm broadminded. Folks back home? Not so much. . . ."

Creedy's eyes narrowed. He bit his lip. *No . . . not that . . .*

Hemingway was still reading his own obituaries. He said, "Anyway, the Director *is* mulatto. Fancy that, eh, Donnie? America's most powerful racist, a black man. Little like learning Hitler was a Jew." Hem looked up and glanced at the door, dismissing Creedy with his unfocused eyes.

Creedy walked in a daze to the door.

To his back, Hemingway said, "I'd be real careful talking about it, Donnie. The Director's threatened his own blood, black *and* white, with the *worst* reprisals if they talk."

I regret to say that we of the FBI are powerless to act in cases of oral-genital intimacy, unless it has in some way obstructed interstate commerce.

—J. Edgar Hoover

25.   INTERROGATION

According to road signs, they were about five miles from Boise State University. Hector had stayed a couple of car lengths behind Richard since they reached more populated climes.

Hector was getting ready to further narrow the distance—position himself to grab Richard as he stepped from his rental car and retrieve all those stolen Hemingway papers—when twin black sedans overtook his Bel Air and then shot around him.

Bureau cars—Hector was sure of it.

Hector hit the brakes. He fell far back and then pulled off the road into some high grass. He slid out of his Chevy with his binoculars and watched:

The first of the black sedans overtook Richard's car, pulling in front of the professor and then hitting the brakes to slow Paulson down. The second sedan then tapped Richard's rental car's rear bumper, sending it into a spin.

Richard's car skidded sideways into a drainage culvert, landing on its side.

The impact had been more than enough to bend the frame of Paulson's car. Drunk as Hector figured Richard to be, he reasoned the professor might still survive the crash with minor injuries.

A big man in a black suit pulled out a metal rod, broke the glass in the driver's side door, and hauled Richard out through the broken window.

As they hustled Richard into the backseat of the car, Hector, staying low in the grass, made his way to Richard's twisted rental car.

There was a suitcase on the floor in the front of the car. As the Bureau boys had their backs to him, fussing with getting Richard into the trunk of the lead sedan, Hector leaned in and grabbed the suitcase. He flipped the latches and confirmed it was full of the stolen Hemingway papers. He rolled over the side of the car into the high grass to hide as the FBI agents returned to Richard's rental and began poking through it.

On hands and knees, Hector crawled back to his Bel Air with the precious suitcase.

The Bureau boys got back out of the wrecked rental, took another look around, then twisted the cap on what looked like a roadside flare and tossed it through the broken-open window of Richard's car. Hector covered his ears and opened his mouth, anticipating the fireball and shockwave from the explosion.

Through the roiling black smoke, Hector watched the FBI men leave. He gave them some distance, then began to follow in his Chevy.

The men who had snatched the professor took Hector on a little tour—out of the studied, sculpted environs of the university, through sparsely populated neighborhoods, and then onto some winding county two-lane that took them through vast tracts of empty land and on into some wooded foothills. Bastards clearly had some destination in mind, but Hector wondered what the Bureau might have in the way of a base out here in the sticks.

The sedans pulled up in front of a log-hewn meeting lodge on the outskirts of town. A sign out front said INTERNATIONAL FRATERNAL BROTHERHOOD OF THE BULL MOOSE.

Hector knew a little about the lodge: The Lions Club focused fundraising efforts on sight-saving enterprises. The Sertomans were all over hearing loss. The Bull Moose Lodge Brothers were ostensibly devoted to eradicating some dubious malady dubbed "restless leg syndrome."

A sign in front of the lodge depicted an outsized thermometer and the legend, HOW WE DOING? The thermometer reading stood at $6,200.

Seemed the Moose members were trying to raise funds for some kind of clinic to treat folks with twitchy limbs.

Hector thought, *These are truly the last of days,* then narrowed his eyes as Richard Paulson was hauled out of the back of the lead sedan. There was a black hood over the professor's head now. His hands were cuffed at his back. The men in black suits manhandled Paulson around to the back of the timber lodge house. Christ, this didn't look at all good for the goddamn egghead.

Hector slipped off his sports jacket and fished in the backseat for his black windbreaker. He pulled that on, zipped it up, and turned up the collar on his coat. He shucked his Colt from the glove compartment and shoved that down the waistband of his pants, at the back. He slid from his Chevy and followed the men behind the fraternal hall.

Donovan Creedy stood in the main meeting hall of the Bull Moose Lodge—the place they called the Rutting Room—and felt as if he was going mad.

The Boise chapter of the Bull Moose Lodge was peppered with ex-federal types . . . OSS relics and the like. The Lodge Brothers were predisposed to support the Bureau and the Agency, and had agreed to rent Creedy one of their back rooms for his "debriefing" of Richard Paulson.

But Creedy had wanted the hall to himself. He intended to put the scholar, as well as a couple of other men tied to other dark enterprises, through the ringer, perhaps.

Things might get . . . loud.

That was where they had hit this snag: seemed it was Stag Night—a quarterly bash that drunken members of the Bull Moose Order positively *lived* for—a night the boys snapped their leashes and tied it on hard: crazy costumes, lavish boozing, and grainy porn loops.

They were also entertaining a national chapter president—the so-called Magnificent Buck—and wouldn't budge at Creedy's insistence they move to an alternate venue.

"This is the *venue* of choice, and ours anyway, Agent," Chester Coleman, president of Boise's largest bank and currently installed Majestic Moose, said. "I'm happy to give you the room out back, but we ain't cutting and running from our own place, buddy. Hell's bells, I've flown in some special girls from Los Angeles." (He said Los Angeles with long e's, further setting Creedy's teeth on edge.) "I've got a spread of high-end deli food that won't keep, and beer kegs that ain't getting any colder while I stand here jawin' with you, Agent. Now, you get to your room or get out, but either way, you're not fuckin' up my party, good buddy."

The man showed Creedy his back then, sauntering over to give a mighty back slap to some fat son of a bitch in a fez adorned with felt moose antlers.

Feeling vengeful, Creedy thrust a hand into the pocket of his black trench coat and fingered one of the spare vials. *Okay, then.*

Smiling meanly, Creedy unscrewed the lid and spitefully emptied the LSD into the bowl of spiked punch.

That'd keep the uncooperative bastards busy now, wouldn't it?

Hector crept back around to the front of the lodge. Men were filtering in now, dressed in antlered fezzes and hairy brown lodge vests. Some wore robes that smacked of Klan togs—purple sheets embroidered with gold. Others wore grotesque Mardi Gras masks. Several of the Bull Moose Brothers arrived with obvious, long-in-the-tooth hookers hanging on their arms.

Deciding on a reckless course of action, Hector hoofed it back to his Chevy. He popped the trunk and rooted around—found a can of starter fluid.

He sprayed some of the ether into a rag, then put the arm on one of the Bulls as the man hauled himself out of his Olds. The man struggled a few seconds, but the ether quickly put him under. Hector helped himself to the man's fez and a black domino mask. He rooted the man's wallet for his lodge card, and then fell in behind a pack of arriving Bull Moose brothers.

Holy God: The party was swiftly descending into an orgy. The Brothers were already three sheets to the wind. They were humping women in piles of twitching bodies . . . some were engaged in fistfights. One naked man in an antlered fez was banging his head bloody against a no-longer-white wall as a stag film flickered across his bloodied body. Wincing, Hector stepped over a rutting couple and into a darkened hallway.

He followed the sound of soft cries to a locked door. Hector tried the door of an adjacent room and found that one unlocked. There was a heating return vent between the rooms, set high up on the wall. Hector doffed his fez and mask and scooted a chair closer to the vent. Through the metal slits, he could just see Richard Paulson, tied to the chair and twisting, as a man in a black suit spiked him with a hypo.

Soon, Richard was frothing at the mouth . . . wild-eyed and jerking at his bonds.

Goddamn! Well, if Hector had any lingering doubts about Creedy and Paulson's ties to one another, this certainly put those to rest. But Jesus, talk about falling-outs between conspirators; Paulson looked on the edge of some kind of seizure.

Hector wrestled with it: Let it unfold? Rush in and try and extricate Paulson from this sorry fix, despite his own disdain for the drunken egghead? Or, just sit it out and let Creedy clear the road for Hector with Hannah—let Creedy maybe widow her with this stuff he'd pumped into Dick Paulson?

Hector leaned in harder to the grill, trying to see more between the slats. Hell, those men in there were Bureau, trained in hand-to-hand combat and firearms, and they had Hector outgunned.

And Paulson? He was now a twitching madman—there'd be no guiding or steering the professor out of that room. Hell, in his present state

Richard certainly wouldn't make an effective ally for Hector in a fire-fight. And anyway, back at the Topping House, faced with that shotgun in Hector's hands, Paulson had proven himself a coward.

Richard was rocking back and forth now, spraying spittle. Yeah, no percentage in trying to extricate Paulson *now*: He was going to require carrying out at the very least.

Hector cursed under his breath; he was going to have to keep watching for the moment.

This voice, Creedy's, Hector guessed: "I appreciate the storeroom key impression, Richard. I appreciate you coming back to Boise for this little talk, Richard. But I don't believe much of what you've said to me, Richard. I want to know more about what was happening when you ran screaming from the Topping House. I want to know what Lassiter was doing there when Mary Hemingway confessed to killing her husband. I want to know much much more than you've told me so far, Richard. Because you've told me very little in the end. I want to know what you might have stolen from the document room you haven't told me about and where those materials are now. The temptation of all those Hemingway papers—I just can't think you'd leave them untouched, Richard. . . . You *know* you've been watched by us, don't you?"

There was a moment's silence. Then Creedy said, "What's the matter with him? Why isn't he responding?"

Another voice: "Drunk as he was—compromised as his system is . . . his liver, for one thing—I don't think he's *going* to respond usefully. He's just tripping, sir. Flying like a son of a bitch." A strained pause, then, "I'm afraid he *might* have a seizure."

Richard muttered, "S'true: I drink all the time. S'true. Jug of sangria wine every night through the writing of that Paris book. My so-called masterpiece. Shit. Seven nights of wine a week for a year to pull that god-damn book out of myself." Richard shook his head, giggling. His giggles turned to sobs. Then he said it: "Fuck you, *Creedy!*"

Startled, Creedy leaned in: "How do you know that name?"

Richard shrugged. "Found a paperback in the lodge lounge, Creedy—*The Khrushchev Kill*. Opened it up and there was your picture, right there in the back. Who'd have guessed you thought you could write." Richard sobbed again. *"So much booze . . ."*

Creedy shook his head. "No wonder your other fucking books read like gin-soaked nonsense. They read sloppy. Read as if improvised. Too anecdotal and drifting." Creedy got down in Richard's face. "*I* write sober, *Richard. I* write from the head. *That's* the way you write the good stuff."

Richard shrugged. "I read your *thriller*," the professor said. He said "thriller" like it was something sticky and dirty that had been forced into his mouth. "I read your *thriller*," Richard said again. "Then I found another... read it, too."

Creedy couldn't help himself: "Which other novel of mine did you read?"

"Your Spanish Civil War *thriller—Every Man's Death Diminishes Me*," Richard said. "That Hemingway character you wrote in there—what a fucking riot."

Creedy was delighted: "Well, he was supposed to be satirical, and—"

Shaking his head impatiently, slurring, Richard said, "I didn't say it was *funny, asshole*. Jesus, it was a piece of shit."

Creedy slapped Richard then, hard. He tangled his fingers in Richard's thinning hair. "What did you take from the Hemingway papers, Richard?"

Richard said, "Fucking Papa—grinning at me. Why is Hemingway grinning at me?"

Creedy scowled. "What the hell is this?"

Richard said, "Look at Hem back there, grinning at me... giving me the finger. And turtleneck sweaters? Look at all those asshole Papas in their turtleneck sweaters. Who the fuck wears a sweater in Key West in August?"

One of Creedy's minions said softly but firmly, "He's *really* tripping now, sir, like I said. Hallucinating. They usually black out about now."

Soft curses, then Creedy's voice again: "Get him out of here. Bring in the other two. We'll tackle *that* crisis instead."

"What do we do with Paulson?" Creedy cursed. The professor was washing out on all fronts. It might do better just to go in balls out... personally raid the Ketchum home and take every scrap of paper in it. Hang the theft on some scholar like Paulson, or consortium of rare-book sellers, maybe.

Creedy said, "Take him back to the university. Dump him on the front lawn. Maybe he'll die there. If nothing else, we'll further damage his reputation that way. I hope this stuff gives Paulson brain damage." It often did just that—about three times in six, in fact.

Hector stepped down off the chair and slid back down the hall. In the main meeting area, things had gotten worse: the Bull Moose Brothers were engaged in acts that would make Caligula blush. It was like Pamplona in the old days, but raised—or rather, lowered—to some new depths of carnal debauchery.

Hector cut a quick swath through all that toward the front door, intent upon following the Ford back to the university. The FBI boys were dragging Paulson right out through the main hall, oblivious to the orgy unfolding around them.

But something wasn't right. . . . There was a man, crouched down over a lodge brother, but not toward some sexual or violent end. Then it clicked for Hector: The crouching man was the Paulsons' shadow—the man with the widow's peak and red face. He was bent low over an unconscious Bull Moose, stripping the man of his fez and dark sunglasses.

Evidently, he figured to infiltrate the lodge just as Hector had.

The man saw Hector and snarled, dropping the fez and scrambling to his feet, moving for the door. Hector was still too far away to overtake him. Instead, he picked up a bottle of Tanqueray and flung it at the man's back.

The bottle hit him in the head and sent him sprawling toward the front door. With a crash, he fell through the plate glass. The stranger struggled up, clutching a hand to his gashed forehead.

Hector gave chase to the parking lot. The bleeding man was already in his green Impala, his forehead and hand slick with blood. He gunned the engine and drove straight at Hector, sending the crime writer rolling across the hood of a Buick to avoid being run over.

Hector heard more squealing tires; headlights washed over him: It was the sedan with Paulson inside.

Hector ran to his Bel Air. The stranger in the Impala's taillights had already disappeared into the darkness—too far gone to follow. But Hector knew where the car transporting Paulson was headed. He cursed and set off toward the university, giving the Chevy some gas to close the distance on the black sedan.

He thought more about the man with the widow's peak. Guy seemed like hired talent . . . a low-rent private eye, maybe. Hector made a note to himself to break out the Yellow Pages when he got back to Sun Valley . . . see if any private dicks had set up shop in the Sawtooths.

Creedy's stooges did just what their master had ordered: rolled up in front of a lecture hall, and flung his body there onto the dewy grass.

Hector waited until the agents drove off, then hauled himself out and checked Paulson's pulse. The scholar was hanging in there.

Hector dragged the professor back to his Bel Air by his heels, then wedged Richard into the passenger seat. He said, "If you piss your pants or puke in my car, I swear to God I'll kill you with my bare hands, Dick."

Back at the Bull Moose Lodge, Donovan Creedy surveyed the clot of naked, writhing bodies and said, "Call in the local law. Let's arrest them. Morals charges . . . bringing these hookers in from out of state, that might even be a trade offense, cast in the right verbiage. I'll think of other charges." Watching one copulating couple, Creedy said, "Hell, there are probably still sodomy laws on the books in this hick state."

No one, ever, wrote anything as well after even one drink as he would have done without it.

—RING LARDNER

26.   BIRDS OF PREY

"You two are having problems, aren't you, Daughter? Is it the drink?" Mary rang a bell to signal her Mexican housemaid for another cocktail before lunch with her guest. "Dickie does love the Giant Killer." Mary looked sad, then: "Does he hit you?"

"Never," Hannah said. "He's mean when he's drunk, but not physically

abusive. Just gets more critical of anyone in striking range. Always targets of opportunity. It's nothing I can't cope with."

Mary said, "Papa hit me more than once."

"Sorry to know that. Why'd you stay?" Hannah was skeptical: Papa's life had been combed over exhaustively, and Hannah couldn't remember credible reports of physical abuse against any of his wives. Psychological abuse? That was quite a different matter.

Mary said, "I was right for him."

Hannah said, "We've a saying in Scotland: 'God shapes the back for the burden.'"

The temperature had dropped double digits since dawn.

But Hannah and Mary sat out on the Topping House's deck, watching four black-winged turkey vultures glide low over the pines that ascended the mountainside. The unflapping vultures wheeled on the rising thermals, stalking something dead or dying hidden amid the densely growing evergreens—perhaps some animal wounded and lost by a thoughtless hunter, deprived what Papa termed "the gift of death."

Hannah shivered and pulled closer the Navajo patterned blanket that was twin to the one draped across Mary's hunched shoulders. Hannah tipped her head back and breathed deeply, smelling rain on the wind.

They both turned as Jimmy Hanrahan stepped back out onto the porch with them.

Jimmy handed Mary her cocktail, then passed a mug of hot chocolate to Hannah. Jimmy was sipping coffee he'd spiked with Jameson.

Hannah said, "Anyway, this morning when he called, Richard swore that he'd be back tomorrow." That was a lie—she'd had no contact with her husband. "This thing in Boise with the study center is going more slowly than planned. You know how these academics are—everybody wants to leave their mark on this center to be named for your husband; makes it treacherous to reach consensus."

Mary giggled. "Jesus Christ, do I ever know how it is. I know how all the fuckers are. They're a shitty bunch, these so-called scholars. Every last rotten one of 'em. In fact, that's our only real satisfaction now. It's been so long since they've had the man alive and moving and working to attack, that the poor damned critics and academics have turned on each other. Undercutting each other's work; pissing all over one another's dearly held interpretations and supposedly startling insights into Papa's books and stories. It's the same way with sharks and rats—wound one, and their blood drives their brothers and sisters crazy. They turn on each other and suddenly they're just a pack of wild, fucking cannibals, as likely to tear at themselves as one another. Serves the maggots right, though. And the goddamn women are the very worst. They're all blind to the art and crazy to kill the man. The clapped-up cunts are all *bulto*. Simply *bulto*."

Mary winked at Hannah. "Too bad you didn't get my little tirade about the critics down for our book. I'd love to see that in my biography. What would they say to all that?"

Hannah rubbed her arms. "You don't savage critics and expect charity. Going into print with something like that would be a little like opening a vein in a piranha pool."

Mary said, "Guess. But you're a literary writer, Hannah—you know what I mean."

Jimmy said, "Papa was a great one for taking ill-considered shots at critics. He sowed the wind and reaped the whirlwind, wouldn't you say, Mary dear?"

"Yeah, Ernest should have clammed up," Mary said, "but it's hard when they savage you. Ask Hector, if you doubt me. And Hannah, you want to write, so you'll learn the hard way."

Hannah shrugged. "Sixty percent of me agrees. The other forty percent knows serious critics and literary scholars help separate the wheat from the chaff. And as cloying, misdirected, and downright harebrained as their attentions may sometimes be, even the worst of them make some contribution toward the perpetuation of interest in a writer's work long after the artist is dead. From my perspective, they're a necessary evil." Those were actually Richard's words, not Hannah's own. Hannah had to check her tongue from straying to her cheek.

Mary snorted. " 'Serious critics.' What an oxyfuckingmoron. And wait until they have a go at something you wrote. Then we'll talk again. We'll see how charitably abstract you can be about the critics then, missy."

The vultures were moving in now, tightening their circle, each dipping one still black wing as they closed on their likely long-dead prey.

Mary handed Jimmy the pair of binoculars she had been intermittently using to survey the scavengers. Jimmy squinted through the eyeglasses at the vultures, each with their slightly angled, unmoving black wings, the undersides of whose six-foot spans were silver. The turkey vultures' heads were too small and bare and red—devoid of feathers that might be soiled and infected while rooting amidst the bloated, messy debris of stinking carcasses. Jimmy said, "What do you think they're after?"

Some motion at the periphery of his field glasses caught his eye. Jimmy tilted the binoculars low and left: There was a man down there in the fields, looking back with his own pair of binoculars. The man was tall, thin; a black suit and tie. Jimmy knew *fecking* FBI when he saw one.

Mary laughed. "Oh, some dead rabbit or stray, dead sheep. A stillborn deer, maybe. Papa used to sit out here and watch them for hours. He'd name them, too—Fenton and Edmund and Young and Carlos." Mary began gathering up her blanket. "Too cold out here." The vultures plunged below the tree line. "Let's go inside," Mary said. "I have to find that girl of mine so we can eat."

The old widow suddenly paused at the door and smiled back at Hannah. "You know, I think more and more I want *you* to write my biography *solo lobo*. To hell with Richard. You're a writer, not an amateur shrink with a book contract and an ax to grind. And you and me, Daughter, we have too much in common, God help us. I have a hunch that you can write it truly, like nobody else—especially a man, maybe especially your man—ever could."

Hannah shook her head. "All I've got is an unfinished novel that isn't publishable. Richard says it's a typical first novel: 'all bombast and self-confession.' Too much description, he said. Still, I never could cut a word of it—though it probably really badly needs it—because they're my first real words."

Hannah felt Jimmy's big hand at her back. He said, "Hannah's being self-deprecating, Mary. Hector's been reading some of her stories. He says she's quite good. And the lass is working on a new novel now, with Hector's help. She's no biographer."

Hannah shot Jimmy a look: What, had Hector enlisted the Irishman in his campaign to stop her writing this book with Mary?

The widow smiled crookedly. "And I would love to see the stories, too, then. I'm sure it's all worthier than you think, just as Hector, the old swain, says it is."

Jimmy bit his lip at "old swain." He'd known Hector long enough to know there was some truth in Mary's bitter assessment. Jimmy was forever shaking his head at Hector's young flames. Why, he remembered one colleen, back in Ohio in 1950, who—

Mary said, "And I don't need any bloody fucking biographer, anyway. I require an interpreter. Either way, you really should give me something of yours to read—a short story, perhaps. Or let me have a swipe at cutting what there is of your first novel. Maybe after, I could send it on to Charlie, you know? Get it placed with Papa's old house. Help you package it. I've got a solid résumé now in that respect. After all, I cleaned up Papa's *Feast* and the damned thing instantly entered the canon. It's a modern classic. Done pretty well for ourselves since that little bump back in summer of 'sixty-one, haven't we?"

Jimmy said, "Very well indeed. Listen, I need to get some cigarettes, Mary darling. Going to run into town . . . be right back."

Instead, Jimmy let himself out the front door and circled wide around the Topping House, staying low and behind the tree line, stealthily working his way back to where he'd seen the FBI agent.

When Jimmy finally reached the spot, the man was gone.

Jimmy was perspiring and short of breath by the time he got back to the Topping House's front door. This cloak-and-dagger bullshit was a younger man's game. He heard a car horn honk—Hector waved from his approaching Bel Air. Hector swung into the garage and climbed out of the Chevy.

He strode up to shake Jimmy's hand, said, "I just left Paulson at the lodge. Professor was out cold. Guess I better go and tell the wife her husband's back. And a hell of a lot worse for wear."

I feel sorry for people who don't drink. When they wake up in the morning, that's as good as they're going to feel all day.

—FRANK SINATRA

27. PRODIGAL

"I'm not so sure seeing Dick now is the best thing," Hector said. He pulled out a little ways to see better, then palmed the wheel and hung a right, headed toward downtown Ketchum. "He's frankly a wreck. I mean, *really* a mess."

Hannah just stared through the windshield. "Drunk, you mean."

"At least that. Maybe something else, too." Hector didn't say "drugs" because he didn't know how to put it to her in a way that wouldn't involve expanding the discussion to encompass Donovan Creedy, and all the other crazy stuff that he was, so far, sparing Hannah.

"I left him there in bed, incoherent. Dead to the world."

Hannah said thickly, "Maybe I should call a doctor."

Hector nodded, chewed his lip. Hell, couldn't hurt.

"He's killing himself with the liquor now," she said. "I don't think he can stop. Ever."

Hector took a deep breath, said, "About how I see it, too, darlin'. You should be thinking about getting away. Pronto. It's my strong instinct. Dick's circling the drain, honey. There's no good end coming."

Hannah said, "Mary's going to cut him loose." She hesitated, then said it, hedging just a bit: "Mary asked me again to write her biography. I'm going to say yes."

Hector gave her a sharp look. "That's a different kind of trouble. You *don't* jeopardize your fiction career for some goddamn whitewash about that daffy old bitch."

Christ: That came out much sharper than Hector intended. He said, "I just mean, it's a dangerous distraction. You don't want to be typed as a biographer."

"The biography will give me profile as an *author*," Hannah said. "It'll put me on the map and open doors for my first novel. Get me a much bigger push for that. More attention. I'm . . . I'm thinking of my own long game, aye?"

He reached across and squeezed her hand. "If that's so, then veering off into nonfiction is the *last* thing you want to do."

Hannah faltered: "I haven't said yet that I'd *definitely* do it. . . . I mean, I haven't signed the contracts yet."

He smiled sadly: "Then know this, Hannah: I'm going to be doing everything I can to *keep* you from doing that book with Mary. It'd be a disaster—I truly believe that."

Hannah nodded, unable to meet his sensed searching gaze.

Hannah found Richard sprawled naked on the bed, sweating booze, reeking of alcohol and something else she couldn't define. His mouth was open and he was snoring.

Hannah took a deep breath and drew herself up.

A half-empty glass of wine sat on the nightstand. Next to it was an oversized jug of cheap Beaujolais, mostly gone, that smelled of vinegar— gone sour as if the cork had been left out for a day or more. But Richard drank it.

Hannah emptied the glass and poured the dregs of the vinegarized bottle of red wine down the bathroom sink. She paused, then doubled over the sink as the baby kicked. She took another deep breath, fighting a wave of nausea. She flipped back the toilet lid in case she got sick. The bowl's basin was speckled with blood flecks. *That* did it: Hannah threw up twice and flushed the toilet. Biting her lip, she pulled out the folded-over paper filled with Mary's sketch about Hannah and Richard and finally read it through:

> She was young and pretty but always off-footing with her European-Catholic raising and her Scots' burr . . . her accent with her funny Rs that the other children teased her for. As she grew into a young woman, pretty and busty, the boys got around her accent well enough. But by then, Hannah was more drawn to her boyfriends'

fathers—to men who had been places and seen things. An aspiring writer herself, Hannah was most drawn to men who lived in their own heads. She chased aesthetic experiences—drawn to them like a nail to a magnet.

Her professor was a man who was already spent when she came to him as his student. But in those early days, listening to his lectures, his scholarship and easy ability to weave words before a classroom of fellow Hemingway aficionados enthralled Hannah and blinded her to his numerous shortcomings. Hannah admired Richard's studies of Hemingway and Anderson and Fitzgerald. Best of all, she loved his account of Papa's Paris years more than almost anything of its kind she had ever read, and she'd read it nearly all by then.

She'd saved up for the class with Richard, an overview of Hemingway's early fiction. Hannah asked Richard out as soon as she heard that his third wife had left him and that he was, more or less, fair game. Then Hannah was pregnant and Richard was offering to marry her and bring her to Sun Valley while he researched his book on Mary Hemingway's years with Papa. That was where the trouble between them truly began.

Hannah's heart pounded. It was all uncomfortably close enough to true to leave her reeling. And Jesus, she really *was* living a trite cliché, wasn't she? Hell, if Mary could catch it all with such nonchalant accuracy it must be so. She sensed a lifeline in Hector Lassiter, but then, that would be a cliché, too, wouldn't it? Leave this worm of a husband for the first masculine, seemingly worthy man to cross her path—consign her life to the first best man available . . . a kind of semicelebrity and creative writer who probably wasn't even interested in her. Not looking as she did now, and with the baggage of a baby arriving any moment.

Hannah finished reading, then felt it coming again. She threw up twice more, seeing spots after. She tore up Mary's composition, threw it in the bowl along with the rest, and flushed the toilet. She brushed her teeth, then started the shower. Fists clenched and trembling, she left the bathroom:

"Up Richard. *Get up.*"

He fought his way out of sleep. "What?"

"Get your stinking self out of bed and into the bathroom. You smell bad—like cheap aftershave masking old sweat. And you need to dry out. Get in the shower, Richard. Now."

"Tired." His voice was slurred: "'S a long, twisty drive from Boysee, ya know." Hannah put her hand over her nose and mouth—his breath stank like kerosene.

"One hundred and fifty-seven miles, Richard. I looked it up in the atlas last night while I was wondering which of those one hundred and fifty-seven miles of road you might be lying dead along. You better not have driven those one hundred and fifty-seven miles back to Boise yesterday like this. Just please tell me someone else drove."

"Someone else drove me. Ya feelin' okay? Ya seem all—"

"Angry? Could be that you infuriate me. No phone calls. *Silence.* Then you turn up days' drunk here. What do you expect, a glad-yer-back-darling pat on the head?" She wrinkled her nose and turned her head away from him. "Your breath is disgusting."

Richard Paulson dug his knuckles into his bloodshot, sleep-encrusted eyes. "You're right. I was wrong. Time just sort of flew. I know how lightly you sleep since the baby has gotten close. It was late when I got back to my room in Boise and I didn't want to call and disturb you."

Hannah pressed a hand to her belly. "You also know that since you did this to me I'm up and in the loo about a dozen times a night. There was little danger of 'disturbing' me. And what about this morning?"

"You know how you like to sleep in."

"Used to. And you could have left a message at the front desk. You could have thought to do that, if you didn't want to 'disturb' me. I certainly thought to check at the front desk, many times." She had—calling from the Topping House. "Bad things have been happening here and you were gone when I needed you most. Jesus, Richard . . ." She tugged at his arm. "Now get in the shower. I can't stand the smell or the look of you right now. You look like you should be clutching a paper bag and begging coins in downtown Detroit. You smell like something that died. Judging by all the blood you left in the toilet, your liver is dying—either that, or you've got rectal cancer. Keep this up, and you've got a date with a straightening-board."

He emerged from the bathroom half an hour later, still drunk but cleaner. While he was in the shower, Hannah had room service change the linens and bring a fresh stack of towels and a pot of coffee.

Her husband sluggishly rubbed a towel over his head. "Mary have much to say? Anything I can use?"

"She's on to your true aims, professor."

"No way. That shambling liver spot doesn't know her own twat from—"

"Shut up, Richard, please." Hannah thrust a cup of coffee into her husband's shaking hands, taunted by the java's acrid fragrance. "So much for you being sly. That little widow may be a bigger drinker than you, but Mary evidently holds her liquor better. You set off all kinds of alarms asking for death records. You're so subtle."

"Huh?"

"Somebody at the hall of records alerted her, I 'spect. Mary says all you do is pump her for information about the fatal final days, Richard."

"That's not true."

"It's her impression. Perception is reality. You, as a literature professor, should embrace that aphorism above all else, right? It's what you all do, isn't it? Remake the works of others in your own sorry image? Revise writers' canons for them every ten or twenty years when the next voguish school of criticism festers into being? Impose your contemporary spin on their decades' old works and then pat yourselves on the back for perpetuating interest? You're all so pathetic. Laundry-list critics and onanistic pilot fish."

Richard shook his finger at Hannah, his hand shaking. "Onanistic? You're an aspiring fiction writer—the most solitary, self-gratifying creation of all. Everything fashioned at whim for your own pleasure. How masturbatory is that?"

"Deliciously so. But you scholars are sicker still 'cause you like to watch and critique while we know how to pleasure ourselves."

"Take it easy, Hannah. That's enough, really. Don't put me to the test."

"Mary's right. You're all a bunch of parasites. Maggots who swarm and swamp an artist when he's dead and can't fend you off. You, and that fat little strange nance Berle, and 'Barbara,' and that scholar Patricia with the raven hair who looks like a Charles Addams wet dream."

"What?" He looked genuinely perplexed. "What the hell are you talking about?"

"I'm sick of you and of all of 'em. I'm sick of all you camp followers and scavengers. You all disgust me."

"Take it easy, Hannah. Please. I'm sorry, darling. I was awful not to call, of course. I was rotten to bring you out here, as you are now, when it is so close—your baby. I promise to take it easy on the Giant Killer."

"Take it easy? That isn't good enough. Quit. Quit now. Quit or I quit you."

"You know you don't mean that."

"I can lose you now, or lose you in a year when your liver fails or you wrap our car around a tree, Richard. Are you *trying* to drive me away? Just say so and I'll extract myself. If you've found the fifth Mrs. Paulson, tell me so. I'll pack and say congratulations for finally beating your god at his forlorn game—for going him one wife better. Hell, even in that you can't be original. Good God, Paulson, you're such a misguided crook. Aping your god won't make you understand him better. Not having four wives, nor growing and shaving off beards, nor boozing and cosseting your bent and bloated liver. And you're so wrongheaded now you only steal the surfaces and copy the mistakes. You don't fish or hunt and you don't even own a gun. That would all be dangerously like exercise."

"That's crazy talk."

"No it isn't, and if it is, fine, because you think I'm crazy anyway. I say some stranger has followed us all over Idaho, and you think I'm paranoid. I tell you Mary has tumbled to your game and now sees you as a threat, and you dismiss my insights. I tell you you're killing yourself a glass at a time, and you ignore me. And nothing I say now matters because you likely won't remember any of this when the booze is out of your blood. You sad relic. You poor rummy."

"Stop, Hannah, I mean it, damn you."

"That a threat? You probably *would* hit me in this state. You lousy drunk. You've never figured consequences. Never looked ahead. Never lived smart. Never really loved your women."

"Stop now, Hannah!"

She half-smiled at an insight—one she thought might reach him through his booze haze. "Have you ever stopped to think what you do to yourself and to all your fellow maggots if you publish this dreadful book you're planning?"

He stared back, slack-jawed. "What do you mean?"

"It's the end of you. Of all of them. Worst of all, of Hem."

Richard lost his balance and took a step back. Shaking, he turned around a chair and dropped onto it. "What the hell are you blathering about now?"

Hannah lowered herself onto the bed, grimacing at some pain in her belly. "You truly don't get it? Well, let's say for a minute you're spot on. Let's say Mary shot Papa that July morning so many years ago. Let's say you say so in print. If so, that's the end."

"In what way? What do you mean?"

"How can a man who has made his career studying another man's work lack such fundamental insight?"

Richard scowled. "I don't get you, Hannah." Startled, he blinked his eyes: for a moment, he thought Hannah had the head of a lizard. Jesus, maybe he was at last getting the DTs . . .

Hannah shook her head. "The gunshot in the foyer is the necessary capstone to the legend. It was foreshadowed in so many of Papa's stories and novels. The end of *For Whom the Bell Tolls* is a meditation on his own eventual suicide. He lived a violent life and embraced blood sports. He lived by the gun, and it was necessary that he die by it—whether by accident, as Mary initially maintained his death to be, or by suicide. Papa's death that July morning, and the ambiguity and mystery surrounding it—the lack of a note, the lack of eyewitnesses, the lack of a definitively stated cause of death—are ingredients that combine to comprise a riddle that informs his legend. Informs it in the same way that the mystery of the frozen leopard's carcass found at that unexplainable height near the summit of Kilimanjaro keys 'The Snows.'

"Don't ye see, Richard?" Hannah's eyes were wide now, beseeching. "Papa's death, as things stand now, is wonderfully, fortuitously ambiguous, and it splits and energizes his critics and scholars. In apparently shooting himself, did Papa violate his own stoic code, and was it therefore fatally symptomatic of the ultimate failure of his artistic vision? Or was the gunshot in some way triumphant—the final, forceful action of a failing man not content to live a diminished life? Was his end avoidable and therefore tragic, or was it foreordained—equivalent to the last honorable obligation of a too-long tortured samurai, as his brother insists?"

Richard Paulson kneaded his fingers. "I can't hurt him. Nothing can. Papa's reputation has survived the apparent suicide. He's more popular now than ever. He's passed into the western canon. He's immortal."

"Until the day you unleash this bête noire you're lurching toward. I swear to God, Richard, if you turn Papa into a casualty of a crazy and unworthy wife, you surely diminish him past the point of no return. You destroy Papa, and you shut your own bloody business down. This swaggering, macho man of the world can't survive characterization as a mother- and spouse-bound dependent who was ultimately murdered by his last, henpecking wife. And nothing in any of that is going to change the direction of literary criticism regarding his work. You'll simply be regarded outside your little circle of scholars as a deluded ghoul."

"There's something else," Richard Paulson said. "What about justice? That old bitch may have gotten away with murder. What about that?" For a moment, Richard almost believed his own commitment to that falsely stated goal.

"What about it? You know, Scottish law doesn't draw the line at 'guilty' and 'not guilty.' We have a third and more sublime option: 'not proven.' If it helps your mind, take it for that, Richard."

"I don't want to talk about this anymore, Hannah."

"I'm finished with it, too. On Saturday I leave. You coming?"

"I'm not finished yet."

Hannah hung her head. She decided it, just then: She was going to go find a pay phone—call Mary Hemingway and accept her offer to write the widow's biography, *without* Richard.

That trite little whimsy about characters getting out of hand; it is as old as the quills. My characters are galley slaves.

—VLADIMIR NABOKOV

28.   STALKER

Richard was taking a second shower—blasting off the last layer of liquor he had been sweating out of his system all day.

Hannah began picking up Richard's smelly clothes that Hector had presumably tossed carelessly upon the floor.

In one pocket of his jacket, Hannah found a vial filled with clear liquid. No labeling. Hannah feared her husband was now adding drug addiction to his list of demons. She hid the vial in her purse.

Hannah found Richard's wallet carelessly stuffed into another pocket of his sports coat, less the cash that he routinely carried in his breast pocket. Her hands were aching, her fingers feeling swollen. Hannah thought about it, then twisted off her rings and thrust them into Richard's wallet. She'd already made the break; this just made it seem real. She frowned. Richard rarely carried his money in his wallet; now the thing was thick with bills—hundred-dollar bills. She agonized over it a bit, then counted out three of the hundred-dollar bills and slipped them into her own pocket. Drunk as he had been, maybe Richard would just figure he didn't remember spending them.

A slip of paper fell out of Richard's shirt pocket. She scooped the paper up off the bed, unfolded it, and read what was there: Donovan Creedy, Room 36, Ketchum Motor Court.

That name, "Creedy."

Hannah remembered Hector asking her about a man with that name. Hannah slipped the paper into her breast pocket. She stepped out onto the small balcony to get some air; to try and think.

A man was standing down there with small binoculars, watching her. The stranger was tall. His slick, dark hair was scraped straight back in a

high-tempbled V. The man's dark eyes were exaggeratedly large behind
thick bifocals. His forehead was bandaged now.

Their shadow *returned*.

Hannah yelled across the distance, "Who are you?"

The stranger bolted. She watched as the stranger disappeared into the
evergreens that ringed the parking lot.

Hannah sat on the bed a long time, going over it all from every angle,
scared, desolate . . . feeling poised at the edge of another abyss. Richard
was in the shower again, his third, still trying to sober up with alternating
blasts of cold and hot water. Must be at the coffee, too, from the sound of
slurps and the click of the ceramic mug being set down, over and over, on
the toilet's water tank lid. Hannah dug some coins from her purse, and
finally went downstairs to a pay phone to call Mary Hemingway and tell
the widow they had a deal.

After she said good-bye to Mary, Hannah tapped her fingers on the
phone receiver. Well, she was fully committed now. No going back.

She pulled the three hundred-dollar bills from her pocket and looked
at them. Where had this money come from? What exactly was Richard
up to? Had he gotten hooks into Mary in some way . . . maybe blackmail-
ing her, or some other person of means?

Hannah took a deep breath and opened the Yellow Pages to the Ps.
She'd read her share of mysteries over the years, and with her recent
reading of Hector Lassiter's books, well, she had this inspiration. But
were there such things as private eyes in real life? And in places like this?
Small town that it was, Hannah found a single listing for a private investigator: a man named Harry Jordan.

She spent about twenty minutes on the phone with the man. He said
her three hundred dollars would buy a few days of his service—she need
simply send the check to his office or wire the cash into his bank account.
Hannah jotted down the account numbers as Jordan rattled it off to her.
She could hear a smile in his voice. . . . She convinced herself that maybe
he was just glad for the business.

Though it gave her butterflies, Hannah used the money stolen from Richard to cut the deal: She'd pay Jordan to *follow* Richard . . . to run surveillance on him until the three hundred dollars ran out. Wasn't it funny—using his illicit funds to discover where his illicit funds came from? Some fine web they were weaving with their secret-keeping from one another.

She'd use Harry Jordan to maybe learn some things that would give her some sense of what was *really* going on with her husband and this mysterious roll of money he suddenly was toting around. Maybe Jordan would even turn something up that would help her with the divorce proceedings, which she now saw as another inevitable terror awaiting her down the road. She might need that edge—particularly if Richard and his lawyer decided to trash her as some kind of mental.

Before she hung up, on an impulse, Hannah said, "There's another man I want to know a bit more about, too. His name is Hector Lassiter."

When she hung up the phone, Hannah swallowed hard. Having Richard followed was the right and just thing to do—she was convinced of that. But having this stranger poke around after Hector? Hannah had gone ahead and arranged for that to be done, too.

Hannah told herself it was because she was truly drawn to the elder novelist that she needed to know more about him—she had to have some assurance that this time she'd picked the right teacher, the right *man* for herself and her child.

Hector asked to be connected to the Paulsons' room. Hannah answered; said she'd meet him in the lounge.

Hector had a Shirley Temple waiting for Hannah. He ordered himself a mojito.

Hector smiled when he saw Hannah looking so fetching. But she also looked angry. Hannah told him about Richard—nothing he didn't expect there. Hannah was selective, but gloomy. He could see well enough she was left unsettled by her husband's sorry condition. Well, he'd pushed about as hard as he dared on that front.

Then Hannah confided about her returned stalker.

Hector said, "This mystery guy—he's getting much more brazen. I've *really* got to shut his business down. I'll work to try and do that today. Got some good notions about who and what this joker is. Meantime, you stay close to people. Better still, please get yourself back to Mary's place, where Jimmy can see to you. You should probably give Richard as wide a berth as you can manage from here forward. Let Dick sober up, at least." As though that might ever happen.

"He's my husband." Hannah stared at her naked fingers. Time to test it and see if Hector was there for her in the fullest sense: "How can I truly avoid him? I mean, why should I do that, in your eyes? Apart from the obvious reasons?" With time, and less bearing down upon her, she might have put that question better... a good bit more gracefully. Still, it was said, *at last*. Hector's move.

Hannah looked up from her hands; searched Hector's face.

He nodded slowly. Hector could see it—Hannah was asking him to take her on now. She wanted him to admit he wanted her.

Hesitating a moment, Hector reached across and took Hannah's hand. He ran his index finger's tip across her bare ring finger. He said, "I'm so dreadfully sorry you're having to cope with this. This should be a happy time for you now, darlin'. You should be home, resting and preparing." Hector paused, then said, "Do you want to go home, Hannah? Get back to family and friends while you wait out these last days for the little one?"

He hadn't answered her question, he knew; he could see it in her face. *Still*... he was throwing her a rope.

Hannah squeezed his hand back. "It's almost tempting. I can't stand to see Richard like this. And the idea of him dealing with Mary while he's in this condition..."

"*Right*. The old dame's not to be underestimated, even in her cups."

Hannah surprised herself: "Mary has designs on you, you know, Hector. I mean, I *sense* that's true."

Hector raised his eyebrows. "Yeah? *Jesus*. Well, that's not in the cards. Mary's not my type by many miles." He almost winced at his phrasing. Well, it *could* be taken a *couple* of ways....

"She also said you're going to help her rewrite *Islands*... even write a new ending for the novel."

"That's not going to happen either, honey. Tampering with Hem's stuff on that level—absolutely unthinkable. Especially for *this* writer. I'm focused on my own fiction. That's all."

"Thank *God*. I didn't believe Mary when she said it, but it's *good* to hear *you* say it."

"Well, you think about this other offer," Hector said. "I'll see you get home, and I'll see you're cared for through what's to come if you'll let me. Then, when I get things handled here, I'll maybe come see you and that little one, if you'll have me." She could take that a couple of ways; granted them both some latitude. "Where is home again?"

"Ann Arbor, Michigan." Well, that's where she lived with Richard.

"Now there's a place I've never been, which is increasingly rare. Need to rectify that."

Hannah smiled. It wasn't all she wanted from Hector, but it was a start. He didn't seem to rule out the notion of a life with her and her baby. She just needed to push him a bit further out on the limb—get him to say it, straight and clear.

Hannah remembered then: She pulled out the slip of paper. She said, "I found this in my husband's—in *Richard's*—wallet. It's that man you asked me about, I think. *Creedy*." Hector's startled reaction thrilled her—it made up, in a way, for having put that private eye on his tail. Or so Hannah tried to convince herself.

Arching an eyebrow, Hector reached out and took the slip of paper from Hannah's hand. He squinted at the writing there: *At fucking last*, an address!

"Who is he, Hector?"

He hesitated. "Have you talked to Richard about this?"

"No."

Of course . . . "I . . . *can't* tell you that then, darlin'. And more difficult, I urge you not to ask your husband about this man, either. With types like Creedy, just their knowing you know they exist can become a wicked problem for you."

"Unacceptable. I deserve more."

The young thing had spirit and grit—Hector had to give Hannah that. "Okay, darlin', this much: Creedy is FBI, but of the very worst stripe."

She was visibly unsettled. "How would Richard know—?"

"An important question, Hannah. But one you *really* better not put to

Richard just yet. Give me a little more time to poke around this, okay, honey? Let me try some things first. You bide your time. Can you do that for me?"

Impulsively, Hector scooted his chair around closer to hers. He took her hand again and she rubbed the back of his hand with her thumb. His body began to stir. Jesus, but he had it bad. He surprised himself by cupping a hand to her belly. He felt the baby stir inside her. She smiled at his smile. She almost told him then she had accepted Mary's offer. But this didn't seem quite the moment. She needed him to say he was hers, first. Or that she was his . . . either way.

"I'll think on it." She hesitated, then held out a vial. "I also found this in Richard's coat. Do you know what it is? Looks like some kind of medicine, but it seems strange there are no labels."

Hector looked at the vial, opened it, and examined the dropper. Sniffed the contents. It looked like the same rig Richard had used to slip something into Mary's drink. He said, "Richard's not on any medication you know of?"

"Not at all."

"Then I'll just hold on to this, if that's okay."

"I surely don't want it."

"I'm going to hang around the lodge here a bit," Hector said. "Still have the Hemingway room for a time yet. I'll stay close here until you make up your mind about getting back to Mary's or going back to Michigan. For the next few hours, you'll be able to find me through the front desk."

Hannah smiled, said, "Okay." He felt her leg press against his.

They sat there, looking into one another's eyes, still holding hands.

Heading into the lounge to look for Richard Paulson, Donovan Creedy instead spotted Hannah and Hector there at their table.

Before they could see him, Creedy turned his back to them and slipped on a pair of specially constructed sunglasses with built-in mirrors for watching people behind you.

Creedy spied on them there, holding hands and smiling at one another. He thought, *So, it's like* that *between them.*

Dick Paulson was just taking it up the ass from every direction, wasn't he?

Watching Hannah and Hector together, the way they held hands and stared into one another's eyes, Creedy's mind began turning in a new, dark direction.

Many people hear voices when no one is there. Some of them are called mad and are shut up in rooms where they stare at the walls all day. Others are called writers and they do pretty much the same thing.

—MEG CHITTENDEN

29.   TURNABOUT

Despite Hector's cautions, Hannah couldn't risk leaving Richard alone for long. She slipped down the hall to speak with her husband. It immediately flared into another argument:

"I swear to you, Richard, it was the same man. Unless, of course, you are simply trying to gaslight me. Is this mystery man doing this at your instigation?" Hannah wasn't sure why she said that—she just blurted it out. Then she realized that after her talk with Hector, she'd come to think Richard maybe really meant her harm in some way.

"Oh, Christ." Richard shook his head. "I would *never.* Jesus. I don't doubt you, darling. Really, I don't. Truth be told, I saw a guy who looked like that a couple of times in Boise. I suspect he's just an academic. Another scholar skulking around after what I'm after."

Hannah thought back. She hadn't seen the stalker since the day Richard left. There had been the car behind Hannah and Hector on the road to Hailey, but they never saw a face. Today Richard had returned, and so had their shadow.

Yes. She could accept the theory that Richard was the target of the man's surveillance. "Okay," Hannah said. "I think he *did* follow you out there. But please: I know you scholars are a cutthroat bunch, but all this skulking around and spying? I don't accept that for a second."

Richard shook three aspirin loose from the bottle. Hannah snatched them from his hand. "*No*. These won't do you any good with your insides bleeding as they are. Cope with the headache you gave yourself—more incentive to quit, aye?"

Her husband nodded feebly. "You're right. I'll tough it out." Hannah sighed: *Sure, that sounded convincing.* He stood up and walked unsteadily to the window, gazing glumly down at the grounds, searching the trees. "I agree, he's probably . . . something else. But what is he? I haven't a clue."

Hannah nodded. Of course now she had also put a spy on Richard's tail. Still, this other—their *original* watcher—she could maybe still do Richard a last favor on *that* front. Maybe she could help him solve that mystery before she exited his life.

Hannah thought about Hector, and what he might do now. "You *could* do something to make me feel better about all of this, Richard." She flipped open his suitcase and dug around for the camera he had packed with the intention of taking shots of the Topping House and other Papa landmarks that might prove useful later in the drafting of his book.

Richard Paulson kept his back to his wife, still staring out the window. "Whatever you want," he said. Hannah didn't hear much conviction there.

Hannah screwed a long lens into her battered old camera. "Take a book, a notebook, or whatever you feel like—reading or writing. Take a long walk around the grounds, maybe up Sun Valley Road to the memorial."

He turned his head aside. "Why?"

Hannah loaded the film. "Camera safari."

"Jesus pleading bleeding Christ. Who do you think you are now—Nancy fucking Drew?"

"Here's some important advice: *Indulge* me, Richard. Or lose me tonight." She stared at his back a long time, then said, "I have options, Richard. And I'm thinking hard about them."

She savored his flinch . . . then felt guilty for enjoying his reaction.

Hector sat alone in the lounge, staring at the slip of paper and vial Hannah had found among Richard Paulson's things. He slipped them back in his pocket.

Time to chase this other lead now: Time to pay a visit to Donovan Creedy.

He took another sip of his drink, then frowned at the reflection in the mirror behind the bar. He was flanked by four youngish men in matching black suits. Hector swiveled around on his bar stool, reaching for his pocket to retrieve his roll of nickels.

The four men were on him too quickly. They grabbed Hector by the arms and hauled him off the bar stool.

One of the men said harshly, "You're with us *now....*" Hector's mind immediately went to that kidnapping of Richard Paulson by the FBI storm troopers. He was swarmed by visions of hypos . . . of professional torturers and interrogators.

As other patrons looked on slack-jawed, the quartet manhandled Hector from the bar. Unable to reach his gun, or even to resist the younger, stronger men, Hector said, more frantic than he wanted to hear himself sounding, "Someone, *please* call the cops?"

The other diners and the fucking second-string bartender just looked at Hector, open-mouthed, watching him get hauled away.

Be regular and ordinary in your life, like a bourgeois, so that you may be violent and original in your work.

—GUSTAVE FLAUBERT

30.   PURSUIT

Richard Paulson set out on foot, sweating, unsteady on his feet, trudging along the roadside toward the Hemingway Memorial—a small, creekside obelisk crowned with a bust of Papa. A plaque contained words Hemingway had written in eulogy for an Idaho friend:

> *Best of all he loved the fall*
> *The leaves yellow on the cottonwoods*
> *Leaves floating on the trout streams*

And above the hills
The high blue windless skies
. . . Now he will be a part of them forever

Good words. But by all accounts from those who would best know, Hemingway *hated* fall most of all the seasons.

Hannah gave Richard a fifteen-minute head start, then headed back out to their new rental car. Though it was chilly, she cranked down the windows. She drove a short distance up Sun Valley Road and pulled onto the shoulder. A couple of gleaming black foals shouldered up to the fence, watching her. They snorted and shook out their manes, then dipped heads back to their grazing.

A man was following Richard: trailing the professor by perhaps seventy-five yards. His build, his bearing—in Hannah's estimation, the man was their shadow.

She checked the camera again, made sure the car doors were locked, and shifted gears, rolling past the man at a brisk forty mph.

Checking to see there were no cars in front or behind, she U-turned and pulled over to the right side of the road a few feet in front of the man. Hannah shot two quick pictures, then rolled her window nearly up, yelling to the man through the crack: "Now you leave us alone, or I take these and go to the police!"

The widow-peaked stranger frowned and took a quick step toward Hannah. She gunned the engine, squealing away from him. She drove four-tenths of a mile and turned around again, blasting back past the man at speed. She skidded up alongside Richard and ordered him in.

"Got it," she said proudly.

He shook his head. "Feel better for it?"

"He *is* following you again, isn't he, Richard?"

Richard shrugged weakly, then nodded. "Can't deny that now." He shivered suddenly—pointed to some ponies loping along a fence line. "Jesus, did you see all those purple monkeys riding those camels?" He shuddered again: Hannah suddenly had a dragon's head.

Hannah gave him a look and said, "*What* in God's name have you been drinking?"

Men are not suffering from the lack of good literature, good art, good theatre, good music, but from that which has made it impossible for these to become manifest. In short, they are suffering from the silent shameful conspiracy... which has bound them together as enemies of art and artists.

—HENRY MILLER

31.   DARK DESIGN

The men dragged Hector through the lodge. Hector said, "Who are you— FBI? CIA? Do you hombres actually mean to try and kill me?"

They burst through a set of doors and manhandled Hector down a narrow hallway. "Whatever Creedy's offering you, I'll—"

The men threw Hector through another door and an old man grabbed him by the arm. The old man said, "Thank *Gawd*!" He then led Hector through another door and into a large room. Dozens of Hemingway scholars sat there in chairs, staring at him.

Christ: the *goddamn speech!* He'd lost track of time. . . .

Hector managed a smile to the crowd as a scholar at the lectern facing the room said, "Ah, just a few minutes late, but here he is, our keynote speaker, Mr. Hector Mason Lassiter!"

Applause . . . some two-fingered whistles.

Hector swallowed hard. He still hadn't prepared a single note. While the academic read an introduction, Hector straightened his jacket, shot his sleeves, then put on his game face: He was just going to have to *riff.* He looked back into the wings where the four men in black suits stood. No way they were scholars or academics.

Hector searched the faces of the obvious scholars sitting before him. There was Rebecca Stewart with her blond beehive and askew eyes, right there in the front row, smiling at him. Hector winked at her, then frowned: sitting next to Becky was Donovan Creedy.

Hector's stomach kicked. He looked around the audience and saw some other men wearing too-nice suits—definitely not academics. Creedy might just be trying to unsettle Hector. Or he *might* actually intend some kind of onstage assassination bid. . . . Maybe take a shot at Hector, like Presidents James Garfield or Teddy Roosevelt. Like Chicago Mayor Anton Cermak in Miami; like JFK in Dallas. *Right*: put a bullet in Hector before a crowd, and then hang the dirty deed on some junkie scholar or the like—some brainy nut ostensibly bent on taking out "the last man standing of the Lost Generation."

It was a plausible scenario. Too fucking plausible if Creedy was the plotter.

Hector ran his fingers back through his hair and nodded to applause as he approached the lectern. There was a pitcher of water and a single glass there; a microphone set too low that Hector fiddled with—raising the mic to buy some time to think.

In his life, Hem had given one significant public speech—at a shindig to drum up support for the Spanish Civil War. Hector had been there in the back of the hall, watching. Hem had sweated through the address, looking intensely at his prepared speech, failing to cast his voice out there very loudly in the early going. At the outset, Hem was all flop-sweat and fumbles.

Hector had never given a speech in his life. He found he had butterflies now. With a hand less steady than he would have the world see, Hector poured himself a glass of water. As he filled his glass, he said, concentrating on projecting his voice, "Hem once said that at its best, writing is a *lonely* life. . . ."

Hector let his words hang there, wondering where he was headed with that.

Watching Creedy watching him, Hector raised the glass to his mouth. Creedy was smiling now.

Hector hesitated. *Of fucking course*: The cocksucker had probably laced the pitcher with some more of his poison. He looked at the glass, then back at Creedy. What would it be in there? LSD? Some other vile potion that would blow out Hector's frontal lobe; leave him some ranting, sweating, and twitching madman, fulminating in front of these goddamn academics?

Yes. That was the plan—he could see it in Creedy's face. The sons of bitches meant to spike Hector's water and turn him into a raving loon.

And when the question-and-answer session came after Hector's rantings? Well, Christ only knew what questions Creedy and his black-clad minions would put to him with that tongue-loosening poison coursing in Hector's system, and all these so-called scholars looking on.

Smiling back at Creedy, Hector emptied the contents of the glass back into the pitcher.

Trying not to distract himself by focusing on those black-clad men—distracting himself, watching them, and all the while waiting for a possible retaliatory bullet, now that he'd tossed the water—Hector instead decided to pick his audience. Hector spotted Patricia Stihlbourne and smiled at her. She'd taken some trouble with her long black hair; put on some makeup and a dress that showed off her figure. Very comely indeed. He decided Patricia would be his focal point. His good-luck charm against Creedy and Company.

He smiled sadly at her, then looked out at the crowd. The audience fell into a hushed silence as he gathered himself for a moment. Then Hector began to speak:

"What *truly* killed my friend, Ernest Hemingway? *Who* really killed Hem, and cost us more books—some of which might have equaled those first two early great novels?"

Hector shrugged. "It wasn't just a strain of depression that runs through the Hemingway family. It wasn't just Hem's failing health and his body's inability to endure and engage in the athletic endeavors that fed Hem's muse, though all of these played a role to great or lesser degree."

Hector gripped the corners of his lectern in his big hands . . . heard a firmness settling into his voice. He crossed one leg behind the other at the ankles, casually, starting to settle into a kind of serenity of certainty that he held the room in his hand and knew *just* the words and narrative line he wanted to follow—it was like writing, when the writing went very well.

Pausing for effect, searching rapt scholars' faces, Hector said, "My friend Hem was killed by an organization, at least in part. He was, in a sense, killed by a man's obsession. History, it's been said, is made at night. Historical events and watershed moments that bind us as people are too often symptomatic of deeper, darker machinations hatched by conspiring men and devious cabals with impossible-to-fathom aims. Destinies are realized or derailed by men who have bizarre but passionately held beliefs. These men, these organizations of men, often spin against the drive of the angels of their better natures, reassuring themselves that their peculiar ends justify the blackest and bloodiest of means."

Hector glanced at Creedy, who was staring back at him now, hateful, his mouth hanging open. Hector winked at Creedy, some part of him still waiting to feel that burn and then hear the lagging crack of the bullet that had already buried itself in his heart or head.

Still, Hector pressed on: "For a very long time," he said, mostly to Patricia, "there's been a war waged against our greatest writers—a campaign to silence and intimidate men and women of letters. You academics, so focused on the works of writers, have been blind to this war. Tonight, I'm going to lift the veil for you. I'm going to give you new context for Hem's final, fatal act. I'm going to tell you what the Federal Bureau of Investigation, under the direction of John Edgar Hoover, has done and continues to do: monitoring and spying on America's novelists and poets. Tapping our phones and opening our mail. Having us shadowed... People thought Hem was paranoid because he said he was being hounded by the FBI. The fact is, Hem was goddamn right."

It was a calamitous admission—his life wouldn't be worth spit after this day, he knew. The FBI would settle for nothing less than attempting to destroy Hector Lassiter.

But then Hector had some notions along those lines himself.

And his audience for this life-changing speech? It was a *crazy* mix: scholars who would spend careers trying to add his comments and allegations to the historic record, and men of secrets who'd be just as dogged in their efforts to have those same comments suppressed and stricken.

He soldiered on.

Afterward Creedy, red-faced, stalked up to Hector. Scholars were swarming around Hector, imploring him for further details, slapping his back and offering to buy him drinks.

Opening and closing his fists, his jaws tight, Creedy snarled, "You've now thrown down the last gauntlet, Lassiter. The Director will make your life a living hell." Creedy smiled meanly. "I mean, for as long as you remain alive."

Hector swallowed hard but managed a grin. He sensed Patricia hovering behind him. Hector said, "Bring it on, cocksucker. Know this—I'll give as good or better than I get, Creedy. And I swear to God, I'll see you dead long before me."

"This isn't nearly over," Creedy said.

Hector thought about the scrap of paper Hannah had shown him, and the address written there he had committed to memory. He reached over and tousled Creedy's immaculate hair. "Got that right, pal."

It was late afternoon and raining. Creedy was intent upon setting down early before his typewriter. Perhaps he'd write an *extra* couple thousand words tonight. He felt in the mood. After the Lassiter debacle he needed to do this thing he loved, this thing where he could most fully shape people and the world to his own whims ... needed to flush this dreadful day from his mind by losing himself in the words.

Creedy hesitated, his hand still on the doorknob. Hector Lassiter was sitting on the foot of his bed, his ancient Peacemaker pointed at Creedy's belly.

"Not exactly an effective weapon for a stealthy killing in a busy hotel, Lassiter."

Hector shrugged. "As you'll note from my speech, me and subtle don't often cozy up, Creedy. Not off the page, anyway. After all you've done to Hem, all you're still trying to do, I *am* sorely tempted to blow you away right now, consequences be damned."

Creedy wet his lips, staring at the big old Colt. "Where'd you get that cannon, anyway?"

"A long story unto itself. But suffice it to say, from another writer. I was just a kid. Come in, Don. Take a load off. I've already poured you a drink. We have *other* things to talk about."

The FBI agent figured Lassiter had been waiting for a good while—Creedy's ashtray contained the stubbed-out butts of half a dozen Pall Malls. Creedy eyed the cigarette butts, thinking he might yet find some use for those one day.

After he locked the door behind himself at Hector's instruction, Creedy sat down on the edge of the bureau opposite the bed.

"It's over, Creedy. I've now pointed all those academics at you regarding your harassment of Hem. They'll start digging. Find confirmation . . . fill biographies with facts about the Bureau's war against Hem. And more importantly, I've seeded Hem's papers with my own forgeries. My stuff convinced Paulson well enough he took it to be Hem's. The thing you couldn't do, I did. I wrote faux-Hemingway that *convinces*. But I've also laid traps in those plants—complex hidden codes and anagrams—things that can be used to prove their falsity."

That last was an exaggeration. Hector had intended to bury an encrypted message in his story, one claiming authorship, but using those needed letters to start each sentence to form that hidden message was too constrictive, and Hector had gotten caught up in the writing. . . . He'd instead just focused on crafting a bloody *great* short story.

Hector said, "I've beaten you on that front, Donnie. All the way, and for *keeps*. Screw around with Hem's papers now, and it'll blow up in your face, and in J. Edgar's." Hector handed the man a glass of whisky. Hector tapped his glass against Creedy's and said, "To routs and reunions . . . even the unwanted ones of the latter."

He watched Creedy sip, then smack his lips. "Top-shelf stuff," the FBI agent said.

"Some things you don't skimp on," Hector said. "I've been doing some digging on your history, Donovan. I'm thinking hard about making you my hobby, just like you made destroying Hem your project. Just want you to know, pal, I'll be watching you from now on. You look over your shoulder, *often*, and you try to stay far clear of my path, because I've made it a personal goal to see you worse than dead if you ever again try to tamper with Hem and his legacy."

Donovan sipped more whisky, said, "I don't know what you're talking about."

"I want that valise I've decided you stole back in 'twenty-two, Donovan," Hector said. "Tell me, did you do that at Hoover's direction? Does this gambit, whatever it is, extend *that* far back?"

" 'Gambit' hardly does it justice, Lassiter." Creedy stared at his drink now, frowned. He licked his lips. He looked a tad suspicious. He pressed his fingers to his lips, as if testing sensation.

Watching him, Hector went for a change-up: "This piece of Hem's you stole, this sketch about me and Hem on Christmas Eve, did *you* put that stuff in about Victoria? Did you . . . I don't know, *know* Victoria in some way? How'd you know that stuff about her and—well, call it her *procedure*?"

"I *did* add that stuff in," Creedy said. He seemed reluctant to talk, but unable to help himself. Creedy could hear a manic edge in his own voice; he despised it. "The Director wants to discredit Hemingway by planting materials in Papa's posthuma. I figured I could take advantage of that operation to slip in an item here or there that would hurt you, too."

"Why on earth would you want to do that to me, Donovan?"

Creedy's face grew dark. "Because that baby you helped her abort was mine, Lassiter. Victoria was *mine* until you stole her away from me. Then you helped her kill *my* child."

Hector was pole-armed. Donovan said, "And I don't know why I just told you that."

The FBI agent held his drink up to his nose; turned the glass in the light. He said, "You *drugged* me."

Still reeling, Hector fished the now-empty vial from his pocket, held it up where Creedy could see. "Yeah, I did," he said distractedly, still thinking of Victoria. "Dosed you with your own stuff, whatever the hell it is. Didn't know how much to use, so you got it all. Is that a *bad* thing?"

Creedy nearly came off the bed, the Colt pointed at him be damned: *Jesus*, in volume, the stuff had been known to cause irreversible brain damage. Strange visions that might be months or years manifesting themselves. The goddamn stuff was like a time bomb in your head. Creedy began spewing profanity at Hector—almost lunged at him until Hector pressed his gun to Creedy's sweat-beaded forehead.

After a time, Creedy settled down and Hector said, "Well, it hardly matters what the stuff does to you in the end as I mean to destroy you *and* Hoover now, whatever it takes. And you know, that brew hit Mary so slowly, I figured maybe a larger dose would loosen your lips faster. Seems I was right."

Donovan sneered. Unable to check himself, he said drunkenly, "That speech of yours today—pathetic. You've only glimpsed the barest tip of the iceberg. You still know nearly *nothing*. I've already destroyed you and your world, Lassiter. Going back to the 1920s, the Bureau has been infiltrating writers' groups. Putting a hand in where we could. Over the years our techniques and tactics have broadened, deepened. Become more subtle and potent. Now we're nearly in position to shape and ultimately discredit creative artists at will. Hemingway and Steinbeck and others like you might have dominated the first half of our century, but *I'll* control the second. The Hemingways and Lassiters of tomorrow are being shaped and twisted by me, and others of my kind. The Papas and Hectors of tomorrow are getting their artistic visions from LSD and mescaline we cook up in *our* labs, Lassiter. And their work is suffering, becoming fragmented … disjointed. These budding writers don't even know the truth—that *I'm* their muse."

Hector said, "You truly are insane. Even if it is so, what would you get out of it? Why would you help with all that? Such as you are, you're a writer yourself."

Creedy said thickly, "That's it, exactly! When the American novel descends into postmodern gibberish and formless prose experiments informed by deconstruction, think how my stuff with its plot and pace and clear language will be devoured by the masses. My talent will finally be recognized. *I'll* be the writer everyone reads." A sneer: "And you? You'll be more irrelevant than you're already fast becoming, Lassiter. Using yourself as your own character in your books—chasing postmodernism. Hell, you're letting yourself be influenced by all these doped-up young turks I control. So you see, clearly, I've already won."

Hector knotted his hands in Creedy's hair. Hector said, "If this is the same stuff you gave Mary, then I'm guessing you won't even remember much of this session of ours after you took that drink. But maybe you *will*, or parts of it, anyhow. So listen good: If I don't wind up killing you in the next few minutes, you son of a bitch, well, I *am* going to make you my mission now, Creedy. I'm going to stalk and hunt and haunt you into the ground, just like you did Hem."

His temper got the better of Hector then. Hector holstered his Colt and hefted his roll of nickels. He tugged a pillowcase loose and wrapped it once around his hand. Then he began beating the FBI agent until the sheets were bloody.

Creedy whimpered until he finally collapsed, unconscious. Hector tried to shake him awake—he wanted to ask about the whereabouts of his other "stolen" manuscripts . . . the whereabouts of Hem's long-lost writings. But he'd cheated himself of the opportunity. Even at age sixty-five, Hector didn't own his anger; it still too often owned him. Hell, his temper seemed to be growing *shorter* along with time.

He couldn't rouse the son of a bitch. Hector began to wonder if maybe he might not have killed Creedy. Then he decided maybe he should go ahead and do just that, fast-like.

Hector again pressed his Peacemaker to Creedy's forehead, then cursed and gently lowered the hammer and holstered his gun. He couldn't do *that* to an unconscious man. Not even *this* man.

Hector left the FBI agent on his hotel bed, breathing raggedly and drooling blood.

Hell, maybe he *had* fatally overdosed Creedy. Hector rather hoped so.

As he stood there, everything Creedy said about Hoover's long-range, insane plan to destroy authors and artists gnawed at Hector.

Crazy as it was, it gave strange, potential context to some other long-lingering mysteries that had troubled Hector's picaresque life since Paris and the 1920s.

Swarmed by Creedy's black, grandiose claims, Hector closed the hotel room door, stepping out into the harsh Idaho sunlight.

Hector saw shadows everywhere he looked. Now it was about more than his own legacy; about more even than preserving Hem's long game.

Now it was a war to save his craft; a war against an enemy Hector couldn't yet figure out how to point a gun at.

Writing a book is an adventure. To begin with it is ... an amusement. Then it becomes a mistress, and then a master, and then it becomes a tyrant.

—Winston Churchill

32.   BLOCKED

The wind pushed around their hair as Hannah drove the back roads through the Sawtooth foothills—insanely priced houses for sale ... mansions under construction.

"What's going to happen, Richard?"

"What do you mean?"

"You're a wreck. You need to get help; go into treatment for the alcohol. It's not working on any level, ya know that, aye?"

She searched Richard's eyes in stolen glances, keeping a skittish eye on the weaving, sometimes dipping and sometimes climbing road.

Richard Paulson smiled sadly and shrugged. "It's not coming like it used to. You know that description of Hemingway's about Scott Fitzgerald losing the words? He compared Scott to a butterfly who started thinking about the mechanics of flight and then could no longer fly. Like the old tale about the centipede thinking about how it walks and losing the ability. It goes like that. Technically, I know what to write. It's clean, it communicates its message. But there's no resonance. The poetry is gone. Even just the ability to turn a nice phrase here and there. Gone. Gone."

Hannah took a deep breath. From what she'd read of Richard's works, she wasn't sure "poetry" had ever been there. She said, "How long gone?"

"Don't even know anymore. Years, I guess."

"You need to write without the alcohol."

"Jesus, it's even *worse* then. The Paris book—the one you love, the one they all love? I wrote it drunk. I can only write with drink."

"You're a teacher, too. Focus on that."

"But I'm a writer in my head. It's how I think of myself, Hannah. I'm a *writer.*"

His beard was coming in so white. He looked a decade older to Hannah now. Looked older than Hector Lassiter, who had at least a couple of decades on Richard. Remembering Hector reminded her of Creedy and that vial. But it didn't seem the time to pursue any of that. Hector's cautions on that front still had her cowed. Instead, she asked:

"What are *you* going to do, Richard?"

He stared at his hands. They looked like green lizard claws now. "Keep writing."

"Writing this book?"

"Hell, yes."

They'd found their way back to the fringes of Ketchum.

She reached over and squeezed Paulson's hand. She thought of Richard's metaphors for his inability to write. "Richard, please please please, just stop *thinking* about it. Stop being that self-reflective bug," Hannah said. "Just write. Just write."

You can't study the darkness by flooding it with light.

—Edward Abbey

33.   THE END OF THE BEGINNING OF SOMETHING

Hannah found Hector in his room at the lodge.

Hector turned down the radio on Bob Dylan's "It Ain't Me, Babe" and weighed the canister of film in his bruised hand. "I hope you came here expecting a lecture, honey, because you're going to get one."

"It was a risk and it was crazy, aye," Hannah said, studying Hector's now-battered right hand. "But I was just *so* mad and frustrated. And at least now we have a picture of the man."

"You shouldn't have taken that chance," Hector said. "And now you've ratcheted things up. Despite the near-confrontations you had with him, before you did this we could all just sort of go along pretending it all wasn't happening. We could bide our time to pick the best moment to go at this. Now you've raised the stakes. It was a pretty reckless provocation. Hard to predict how this son of a bitch might react."

Hannah said, "What would *you* have done? Something just like this, I'll bet."

"That's academic, now," Hector said. God, that's the *last* thing this pretty young thing needed—some new penchant for trying to live like Hector. He was starting again to think pursuing his attraction to Hannah—or indulging hers for him—would be a disaster for both of them. Still, he couldn't quite put the thought out of his head. *Goddamn indecision carried its own warning, didn't it?* Hector shook his head. *Or maybe not . . .*

He said, "And, frankly, a lot of old *gone* friends got themselves in terrible fixes or even killed asking themselves 'What would Hector do?'" He stroked Hannah's hair behind her ear and dropped the film canister in his pocket. "Well, what I'll do now is I'll head down to Ketchum. Find someone to develop this roll of film."

"Could you use some company? I hope so."

Hector said, "What about Dick? Where's he now? Hiding in the dark and guzzling coffee in some quiet place, I hope?"

"Off to Mary's." She couldn't yet tell him the rest: that Richard was unwittingly going to Mary's to be fired by the widow. She didn't want to be alone around Richard when he returned. She also didn't want to be alone thinking about how Richard might take his dismissal. And Hector was such an enticing distraction. . . .

Hector said, "*That's* very bad strategy, too, particularly in his sorry condition." And Hector figured that meant the scholar would almost certainly return to his pregnant wife freshly drunk. And Mary—Richard might try and drug her again. But, thank God, Jimmy was there to run interference on all that.

Hector said, "You'll certainly be safer with me than here alone after that camera stunt."

Hector lifted his sports jacket from the bed, revealing his gun. He pulled out a soft brown leather holster and slid its straps over both shoulders. He holstered his old, long-barreled six-shooter—something that looked to Hannah like a gun she might see in a western.

She said, "Is that truly necessary?"

"Might well be now. Better to be safe." Hector shrugged on his big, loose-fitting sports coat.

Hannah scowled. "You often carry a gun around with you?"

"Have it close by, anyway."

"It still works? I mean, it looks like an antique."

Hector nodded. "No less deadly for that. Now let's roll downtown and get us a look at this bad customer you photographed."

Hector had slipped the man at the camera store an extra ten for a quick turnaround developing the film. It was still going to be a couple of hours before the pictures were ready, however, so Hector was treating Hannah to lunch in the Christiana. She said, "This town needs more restaurants."

"This town needs more of a lot of things," Hector said. "And those will come. I can already see the sorry signs. Another twenty years, this will be one of the West's great tourist sites. Everything about it that originally drew Hem here will be swamped or built over. I've seen it in the Keys, seen it in Paris and in the Pacific Northwest."

"You live in New Mexico now, aye?"

"Place on the Rio Grande, nearly in Mexico."

"Is it touristy?"

"Nah. I think I finally found the spot that will see me through whatever time's left me in that sense—my present home isn't going to become a tourist trap, not ever."

"Sounds like a good place to write."

"It's quiet, if that's what you mean. Solitary. Not saying I get many of them, but it's far enough away from anywhere to discourage acolytes seeking me out. Still get a few interviewers my way, but not too many wannabe writers."

Hannah sipped some soup and said, "So, you're not taking on students?"

"One at a time is all I can handle," Hector said. He relented on riding her, just a bit: "Right now, I'm committed to working with a pretty Scot."

Hannah smiled and said, "I'm taking your advice, Maestro. I'm binding those stories and fragments together into a single narrative along the lines you proposed."

"Can't wait to see what results. I know it's going to be wonderful. And please, don't call me 'Maestro' . . . just stick with Hector."

She hesitated and said, "You're the first to say it: that my writing is worthy."

"It *is*. Who else has read your stories?"

"Richard."

"He's it?"

"He's all that's read this current crop of stuff. I wrote different things for writing classes at school."

"This is the stuff that matters to you," Hector said. "I can tell—the passion comes through in the newer stuff."

"It is the kind of thing I want to write."

"And were born to."

"Not to hear Richard tell it," Hannah said. "He said it's all the same . . . too confessional."

"We all use ourselves and our lives, Hannah. Hell, the only way to justify our mistakes is to use them in our writing. You know what Papa said, 'Use the hurt.' You do that, Hannah. Don't let some academic, or a husband, dissuade you from that. It's your core material. So protect it. Don't ever deny it. This of yours I've been reading—it's all written since you became pregnant, isn't it?"

"Yes."

"Interesting."

"How so?"

Hector couldn't imagine sharing with Hannah his theory about links between her medication and the quality of her writing. But he wasn't above maybe leading her to her own epiphany on that front. He said, "Just is. Timing is *everything*."

Frowning, Hannah said, "I have to confess, the other day I read a few pages of your novel."

"It's okay," Hector said evenly. "Tables turned? Frankly, I'd maybe have done the same."

"You're going well beyond using your life. You've made yourself your own character in this novel, Hector."

"People have always accused me of doing that. So I've decided to ram the concept down their throats in this novel. They all talk about postmodernism. I'll give 'em postmodernism. And hell, Hem really kind of beat me to it with *The Green Hills of Africa*—he blurred all the lines between the novel and nonfiction, between persona and writer, in that one. He takes the concept much further in his best unpublished stuff."

"So this *Toros & Torsos*, it's mostly fiction?"

Hector shrugged. "Let others decide, that's my thinking. Maybe I'll really play with their minds: I have my own long game to think about. Maybe I'll let that sucker sit for a while. Arrange to have it published thirty or forty years down the road, and maybe under some other byline." He squeezed Hannah's hand. "Maybe something Celtic sounding."

He stirred around his food—not much appetite. He sipped some wine and said, "You thought anymore about taking me up on my offer? I think you should think hard about clearing out of here. Not just because of all this crazy stuff swirling around us, but because I think Richard is going to crash and burn, hard and soon, and I don't think you can wave him off before he slams into that sorry last wall. Sometimes a true alcoholic has to hit bottom, hard, in order to turn it around. I think Richard's headed toward that crash at the least. But in your present condition, it's too risky to have you here to try and pick up the pieces."

And there was of course the other wild card in the mix: goddamn Creedy. Hector had this vision he was suddenly warming to again—living in Europe with Hannah, both of them writing fiction together and raising that baby.

It might be a fine life, far from America and maybe even far enough from J. Edgar's reach.

"I'm still thinking about it all." Hannah couldn't look at Hector: She was angry at him for his blunt and unsolicited estimation of Richard's sorry condition and likely fate. She felt angrier still that Hector had stated again what she hadn't yet been able to bring herself to confront so nakedly—not with Hector's certainty.

Hector said, "What's on tap for tonight?"

"Dinner with some fellow academics, if Richard isn't legless by then."

Hector said, "Berle possibly going to be one of those at dinner?"

She searched his face. "Could happen." She didn't believe that, of course.

He scooted his chair closer and wrapped an arm around her shoulders. "Then invite me as your guest. Can you do that, Hannah?"

"I can, but do you really want to sit through that, Hector?"

"I think I better."

"They can be so snide, and, well . . ."

Hector smiled. "I'll finish that sentence for you: 'And you being a hack writer, Hector . . .'"

"I wasn't going to say *that*. And you're *not* that. God, not at all."

"But we both get the drift. I'm a genre writer in their eyes. You fear for me at that table."

"Well, whatever kind of writer you may be, they're never less than snide and snotty," Hannah said. "They're all so cruel-tongued. And you'll be outnumbered."

"I'll have you," Hector said, "a fellow fiction writer who'll have my back. And I think of it this way, darling: I'm not going to be at that table with all of those academics. They're going to be at that table with *me*."

It happened so fast, he didn't fight it: Hannah impulsively leaned into him. Her mouth found his. He felt her tongue pressing against his teeth. Hector wrapped an arm around her shoulder; his other hand strayed to her swollen breast. His thumb massaged her stiffening nipple through her soft cotton sweater.

He pulled away, looked around to make sure nobody was watching. He said, "That was *wrong* of me."

"*I* did it," Hannah said. "*I wanted* it. I want you in my life." She pressed her hand to her belly. "In *our* life."

"You're married."

"Not happily."

"But *married*," Hector said.

Hannah just shook her head. Marriage could be remedied easily enough; surely Hector knew that. Hell, how many wives had she read Hector had had already? Three, four? And she was already taking steps. . . .

She said suddenly, "I . . . I have told Mary I'm going to write that book about her. It won't hurt my fiction writing, I swear . . . just delay it a bit."

Hannah shuddered at the look that elicited from Hector. He said, "Oh God, honey, *no*! That's the *worst* thing you could think of doing. This is no time for an artistic failure of nerve—"

She slapped him hard, shocking herself. Hector took the blow. He pressed a finger to his lip and looked at the blood there. He said, "Darlin', please don't make this mistake with your career. This will ruin you ... mess up your whole path. Mary's nobody to get entangled with."

"I'm going to do it, Hector. I *know* this is the right thing. It's a book about a Hemingway—it will give me a head start on my fiction in a way nothing else can. I am going to do this. Better me than Richard! I can do what you're doing—protect Papa ... help protect his legacy and long game with my book."

"It's a calamitous mistake," Hector said again. His cheek still stung.

Her chin trembling, Hannah searched Hector's face, then threw her napkin across her plate and left him there, sitting alone, stared at by the other diners.

Creedy held the phone close to his face, his palm cupped over the mouthpiece lest the person in the adjacent booth overhear.

He remembered Lassiter telling him about the false, booby-trapped manuscripts he claimed to have inserted into the Hemingway papers. He remembered Lassiter handing him a drink.

Then things were ... *foggy.* A void. But Lassiter had mockingly left an empty vial on the bed next to Creedy. That told the agent *everything*: Lassiter had slipped Donovan his own dope. Creedy shuddered again, thinking of it. God only knew what Lassiter had pulled out of him with that stuff coursing through his veins. God knew what might fall out from all that ... brain damage ... burgeoning paranoia. That stuff never left your system, not really. Not *ever*.

So he had no recourse now—Creedy had to inform the Director that the Hemingway operation, at least for the moment, was sliding crosswise.

Creedy said, "Yes, I've reviewed the taps on the Hemingway phone— the recordings made before those bugs were disabled. There's no question: Somehow, this Lassiter is on to us. He's actively working to discover the provenance of the doctored documents inserted into the Hemingway papers recovered in the basement of the Ritz in 1956."

Hoover was harrowingly quiet, then said, "I'm sitting with Hector Lassiter's file now. It's prodigiously thick. This Lassiter has sometimes been of use to us. He's wily, gutsy, and worst of all, he's a chaotic idealist. In a word: unpredictable. That stuff Lassiter pulled in Nashville in 1958? Audacious. And I'm *still* furious over that. Prepare a wet team, Agent Creedy. I'm not saying we're going to cancel Lassiter, but we *might* need to."

He hesitated, then Hoover said, "Is there any indication Lassiter has come into possession of the other information Hemingway was holding against us? Perhaps he has found letters, a manuscript about . . . well, about me?"

Creedy thought, *You mean about you being a colored. That's what you* really *mean*. He said, "No, sir. None so far." Creedy thought, *Self-serving nigger prig*.

The Director said, "Then perhaps canceling Lassiter has just become more attractive a proposition. Let me think more on that. But this professor you were using? This degenerate alcoholic? He seems too dangerous to perpetuate."

"And his wife?"

"Does she know what's going on?"

"Not presently. I mean, I don't think so."

"So long as she remains in that blissful state, then Mrs. Paulson can be spared, Mr. Creedy."

Everywhere I go, I'm asked if I think the universities stifle writers. My opinion is that they don't stifle enough of them. There's many a best-seller that could have been prevented by a good teacher.

—FLANNERY O'CONNOR

34.   MISTAKES

Stretched out in the Hemingway bed, Hector smoked a cigarette, staring at the wall. Patricia was wrapped around him, warm, naked, and already asleep.

After his argument with Hannah, Hector had returned to the lodge.

Shaken as he'd been by her reaction, Hector hadn't chased after Hannah. He hadn't tried to reach her by phone and he had no intention of going up to the Paulsons' room to talk to her just yet. They both needed time for things to cool between them—to cool in several senses of the word.

Hector was bitterly disappointed in Hannah—terribly upset at her decision to undertake this misbegotten project with Mary Hemingway.

Hannah was clearly furious with him not just for doubting the rightness of her decision to cooperate in Mary's biography, but also for deflecting her advances.

Hector was certain, however, he'd made the right decision in declining her overtures.

Hannah's admission that she was going to eschew fiction writing—even "fleetingly"—for sensationalist nonfiction writing had settled it all in his mind.

The man who lives what he writes and writes what he lives.

Holy Jesus, but how he *loathed* that facile characterization of himself and his craft.

His third wife, Duff, had long ago said, "You know, Hec, one day you're going to have to choose a side of that equation. Does your life inform your writing, or does it run the other direction?"

He'd just smiled and waved his hand then. That was darling Duff—always throwing crazy riddles like that one at him. The princess of conundrums and head games . . .

But sitting there in the restaurant with Hannah, Hector assured himself he took his art more seriously than his life. He was adamant now that his art was *driving* his life, and that it had always been so.

And, that being the case, he'd be damned now if he'd take Hannah on, even if his passion and affection for the beautiful young Scot was strong. He'd have no part of an affair with Hannah—not so long as some part of him still toyed with the notion of maybe getting a novel out of the relationship.

And so, sitting in the Sun Valley Lodge lounge, still mulling his decision to walk away from Hannah, and yes, sulking a bit, he happened upon Patricia.

Tish, as he now called her, was still dressed as she had been for his speech. Dressed just for him, he could tell. Tish was *very* fetching; a beguiling distraction.

Hector didn't even mind the fact that Tish was talking to him in echoes of lines from his own novels; almost as if she were modeling herself on a Hector Lassiter–crafted femme fatale.

Hell, that made it *easier* to comply this one time. Tish's sexy game allowed Hector to treat it as the horny, one-time fling he sensed Patricia, too, knew that it would be between them.

A holiday affair . . . ships in the night.

And, frankly, Patricia seemed every bit as excited by the notion of getting naked in that famous bed as she was by the prospect of making love with Hector. Sensing that didn't hurt his ego, though . . . much. They were using one another, and it felt good. Where was the harm?

But when he was making love with Patricia, Hector found himself imagining there at the end that Tish was actually Hannah. He'd almost called out Hannah's name as he came.

That had soured things for him in several directions.

And he felt even *more* guilty lolling in bed now with this lusty, bookish looker when he should be plotting against Donovan Creedy. . . . Creedy, who must be seething and spoiling for revenge now.

Hector needed to move his ass. *Muy pronto.*

Hector ground out his cigarette and slid from under Patricia's long, bare body. She didn't stir when he left the bed. He pulled the covers over Tish and then dressed; let himself out as quietly as he could. He left a note: "Back in time for dinner."

Richard had returned from Mary's drunk again. The old bitch had fired him—taken the book away from him, despite the fact that he now had her over a barrel with her confession to killing Hem. When he played that card, Mary had just sneered and said, "What the fuck are you talking about? That's exactly the kind of crazy thing that's brought us to this point, Dickie. That's why Hannah's going to write my book. She signed the contract at the lodge an hour ago."

That last left him reeling—he still didn't believe it. Would Hannah actually steal his book from him? Christ, he had to get her back on her medications. . . .

He'd stormed out on Mary; raced back to the lodge to find Hannah.

They had started going at it in their room at the lodge—bitterly tearing into one another.

Hannah sensed how stupid it was to confront Richard in his present state. Surprising herself, she pressed ahead anyway...this enticing baritone voice with a Texas accent echoing in her head: *"But you're married..."*

Damn Hector Lassiter, anyway. Still seething at Hector, Hannah directed her rage and wrath at Richard. But then, thinking more on Hector, she said suddenly, "Why don't we talk about this in the bar, Richard." She wanted witnesses for what was to come. Let Richard see now, when it counted, she could play him the same way he'd played her in the early going—seducing her, drugging her...trying to turn her into little more than an attractive appendage.

Richard hadn't argued with that proposition of a trip to the bar, of course. He'd winked and grabbed his coat and said, "Let's do that." He'd get a few drinks in, fortify himself with the Giant Killer, then deal with this nonsense about Hannah writing *his* book.

Now they sat across a table from one another, tearing at one another in whispers...surrounded by supping scholars and tourists.

Hannah confirmed she was the one who was going to be writing Mary Hemingway's biography. Richard sneered and said, "Good fucking luck with that, Hannah." She sensed he didn't believe her.

He looked at her with this strange expression, then said, "You and your goddamn spider's head...all your fucking spider eyes."

That's what he truly saw now: A hairy brown head covered with glistening black eyes. The walls of the bar were spinning, and he kept hearing dogs barking from the lobby. Jesus, but this was the worst and most sustained drunk of his life.

Frowning at his strange stare back at her, Hannah played her trump card. Stepping into him, Hannah said, "And who exactly is Donovan Creedy to you, Richard? Hector says this Creedy is FBI and crooked, and Hector said—"

Before he could check himself, Richard swung.

Yes, *that* was it: Smash that monstrous spider's face! Cave it in!

There was a sharp smack, and then Hannah was reeling backward, sent sprawling off her chair and onto the floor, tasting blood. Diners gasped. A few men—tourists, not scholars—grabbed Richard by the arms. An elderly man helped Hannah off the floor of the lounge.

Hannah sat back in her chair, her mouth warm and wet. She held her hand to her lip, then pulled it away and saw the blood there. Irresistibly, she saw Hector, looking at his own bloody hand after she had struck the elder writer in the mouth.

"Get out of here," she snarled. "Get away from me right now or I swear to God I'll press charges against you."

Richard's chin was trembling, his eyes wide. "Darling, I'm *so* sorry," he said, pleading. The thing across the table had Hannah's face again. His poor, pretty Hannah: Her face was bleeding. Her lip was swollen. She was whimpering. He tried to stand, intending to hug her to him. Men still had him by the arms. One of them said, "I'm of a mind to take you outside and take you apart, you son of a bitch."

Hannah said, "Get out *now*, Richard. We're through!"

Richard hesitated, said, "I'll go and get some ice for your lip. I'm so sorry, Hannah. I never meant to do that. I can't bear having done this to you. Let me help you with your mouth."

She said it through gritted, bloodied teeth: "Richard, *get . . . out . . . now.*"

Uncertain, Richard shook off the men holding his arms; he backed away from the lounge, hands up in surrender. His knuckles still stung from the impact. He worried he might have broken her jaw; hell, he might well have broken his hand.

He watched as more diners gathered around Hannah—one had wrapped some ice cubes in a napkin and pressed them to her face. Richard stalked toward the front door, hearing Hannah's sobs behind him.

Hannah held a wet towel to her mouth, staring at her battered face in the hotel room mirror. The bruise was already forming on her cheekbone; her lip was fat and cut. No teeth were loose, but her jaw ached.

She tried to phone Hector, but there was no answer. She called Mary next—the only other person in Ketchum she knew and could turn to. Hannah told her everything.

"Come on back over here, and I mean right *now*," Mary ordered her. "I'll have your room ready. If the son of a bitch has the brains to figure out where you are and comes after you, we'll show 'em the business end of a .505 Gibbs—a real man-stopper. Hell, maybe that mick friend of Hector's bunked out back can put Dickie down for us."

Mary and her "girl" had met Hannah at the door. The cabbie carried Hannah's bags in and Mary tipped him generously. Mary had already warned Jimmy off—consigned him to the guest quarters out back so she and Hannah could "commiserate" and share "... girl talk. So we can eat chocolate together and cry."

Grateful to be spared all that, Jimmy had happily complied.

But now the conversation had taken a different tack: Mary had noticed Hannah wasn't wearing her rings. Hannah confided her decision to divorce Richard. Mary intuited it: that the prospect of Hector maybe waiting in the wings emboldened Hannah's impulses to shake free of her husband.

Mary handed Hannah tea laced with warm milk.

"Ye're terrific to take me back in like this. I can't thank you enough."

Mary smiled. "Nonsense. I've been down this road, long before you. First Noel, then Ernest, when he was really bad. I've gone my rounds and been left standing to hear the bell. Someday, you'll maybe do the same for another. Anyway, it's an obligation one woman always has to another. Marlene talked me back into Papa's arms before we were married, and maybe that wasn't a favor. Rest assured, I mean to see you don't return to Dickie's bed. I'll do right by you."

"You don't owe me any help." Hannah hesitated, then said, "Hector offered to drive me back to Ann Arbor before all this. Hector could see it coming."

The widow snorted. "Bet he *did* offer." Mary winked. "I like you, Hannah. And I'm serious about helping you with your writing; helping you get published. I'm also serious about you writing my story for me. If there must be a book out there about me other than my own, let it be yours. We have treaded the same path of thorns, thee and me. We've survived men plagued with similar demons."

Mary paused. "First Richard, and now Hector. I mean, you and Hec-

tor *are* getting romantic, aren't you? Bet that old crime writer loves paw-
ing on a sweet young thing like you." Mary shook her head. "I've seen
that before, haven't I? I mean, the used-up writer and his fresh-faced
muse. *Jesus Christ...*"

Hannah went cold all over. What the hell? And how'd Mary know
about Hector and Hannah?

Hannah said: "If I can track down my sister for bus fare, I'll maybe go
home to Ann Arbor and file the papers. Of course, there will perhaps be
trouble about the baby"—Hannah half-smiled and held up a hand as
Mary looked about to speak—"but I know what you're going to say:
There'll probably be no trouble about the baby on the custody front. Just
perhaps in securing financial support from Richard."

"I wouldn't have said so in so many words," Mary said, "but yes,
that's about the size of it, from where I sit. You'll have no problem with
custody—not from that prick. And Dickie will pay—and I'm not speaking
in the sense of alimony or child support. If you leave Richard alone, it'll
be sheer hell for him. Probably same as kill him. Men like him—like my
husband—can't be alone, not even for a minute. Not and maintain any
equilibrium. It's just not within their power. Loneliness fucking eats them
alive. Back in 'fifty-nine, after some of the bad things in Spain, I tried to
put some distance between Papa and me—just to save myself. Papa said I
was doing it to drive him to suicide. He couldn't stand to be without his
woman that much. Just like Dickie, I suspect."

Mary snorted and lifted her cup. "And he's *truly* dangerous." Mary
smiled, like the idea was just coming to her: "I'll buy you that bus ticket
back to Michigan myself, sweetie, just to get you safely away from both of
them. Get you away tonight. Right now."

Hannah sipped her tea. "Hector's not dangerous." She looked at her
own bruised hand; she wondered what Hector's lip looked like now.

Mary looked grave: "You haven't heard the rumors about Hector and
his last wife's death?"

Over the rim of her raised teacup, Mary studied Hannah's face. Mary
said, "I forget sometimes that you're *so* young. You don't know people yet,
really. You don't know how this world works. Honey, Hector's still sus-
pected by many of having *caused* his fourth wife's apparent drug overdose. Many people believe Hector *murdered* his wife."

Hannah was reeling now. This void looming under her—she could hear her pulse in her ears.

Mary bit her lip: She almost felt sorry for Hannah now; felt a little bad for the terrible expression she'd put on Hannah's face. Well, the job was done, at least. She'd nipped that potential love affair in the bud, and good.

The widow moved to console Hannah as the young woman's chin began to tremble; as Hannah's shoulders quaked. Hannah was sobbing into the hollow of Mary's crepey neck.

Stroking Hannah's back, Mary said, "We'll get you on that bus home to your family tonight, sweetie, I promise you that, Daughter. Then in a few weeks, when things are calmer, once Richard and Hector are behind you, then you and me can start writing my biography. Fuck Richard Paulson. Fuck Hector Lassiter, am I not right, Daughter?"

Hannah was still weighing fleeing Idaho by Greyhound. The stuff Mary had said about Hector—it couldn't *possibly* be true. Hannah thought about it, then dialed Harry Jordan, her private investigator. The man answered on the third ring. He said he hadn't gotten anything of interest on Richard yet, but he *did* have some juicy dirt on Hector Lassiter.

As he shared that intelligence, Hannah got the sense it was drawn from the same magazine articles she had read in the local library. She felt a little taken.

And there was nothing, so far, about any suspicion of Hector having murdered his fourth wife.

But then the private investigator told her something just about as bad: "This Lassiter is shacked up in his room right now with a woman named Patricia Stihlbourne. Dark . . . pretty. Some kind of scholar. She was all over him in the hallway on the way to his room. Clearly an item. He's surely the ladies' man they all say . . ."

Hannah hung up the phone, desolate. She wandered, dazed, to the sitting room. Mary was there in her chair, drinking a gimlet and browsing over *The Paris Review*. Hannah said, "I would appreciate that bus ticket home, Mary. I would be very grateful for it."

Even doubtful accusations leave a stain behind them.

—THOMAS FULLER

35.   FRAME

Hector keyed himself back into his room. The place was gloomy—the shades still drawn. The sheets and bedspread were a tangle, but the bed was empty. He called, "Hey there. Still about, Patricia?"

Frowning, he flipped on the lights and pulled back drapes, squinting in the resulting savage light.

Strange: Patricia's clothes—her dress and saucy underthings—were still slung carelessly across the back of a chair.

The bathroom door was closed. There was no sound of the shower running. Hector rapped lightly once with knuckles, said, "Tish, sweetheart? You okay?"

Scowling, he tried the door. The knob turned. The room was dark. He opened the door wider and flipped on the bathroom light.

Patricia was naked in the tub, her eyes wide and empty. Her right arm was outflung—needle marks on her forearm. A hypo and vial rested on the closed toilet lid. The bathtub was filled with water. There were myriad, nearly melted ice cubes floating in the bath water.

Hector was reeling—seeing spots.

Then this gruff voice behind him: "Hands up, then turn around slowly, Lassiter."

Several Ketchum cops crowded the bathroom door, their service weapons pointed at Hector's heart.

The elder, stockiest cop—the leader—said, "We're placing you under arrest."

Hector said it anyway: "On what fucking charge?"

The lead cop said, "That poor bitch's murder. What else?"

BOOK FIVE

For Whom the Bell Tolls

Forget your personal tragedy. We are all bitched from the start.

—ERNEST HEMINGWAY

36.   TILL DEATH

Richard stood at the creek's edge by the Hemingway Memorial, looking at Hem's bust to avoid meeting Creedy's angry gaze.

His phone had been ringing when Richard reached his room at the lodge. It had been Creedy, ordering him out for this *rendezvous*. Wanting to stall, Richard had claimed his rental car had engine troubles.

"Then walk here, Richard," Creedy had said. "But get your ass here."

Richard *had* walked to the memorial . . . trudging along the shoulder of the road, head down and hands in pockets, surveying the sorry wreck his life had become these past few days.

Richard sighed and rested his hand on Hemingway's bronze head.

Creedy shook his own head. "A tragedy for you that it's come to this, Richard. But you failed me, and worse, you tipped my hand to a very dangerous man. Compromised my plans. So your usefulness to me is at an absolute end."

Licking his lips, Richard sighed deeply. He'd misunderstood what Creedy meant. Richard smiled and said, "So I can go?" Jesus, was this booze buzz ever going to subside? Creedy had a wolf's face now. Maybe Hannah was right about taking the cure. . . .

"You're going to go, yes," Creedy said. "Going to go to that place from which there's no coming back. The 'undiscovered' country." Creedy clapped his hands, said, "Boys?"

Three black-clad men slid out from behind the trees, looking like living shadows in the trees' late-afternoon shade. Wild-eyed, Richard began backing into the creek—the only direction of retreat—until his back was pressed to the Hemingway monument. Richard said, "This isn't funny anymore, Donovan."

"No, funny is the last thing this is," Creedy said. "You're a loose end and a sloppy drunk, Richard. So there's only one thing to be done with you. Don't struggle and we'll make this go quickly." Creedy smiled meanly: "Just close your eyes, *Dick*; think of Papa."

"You *can't* do this," Richard said, his chin trembling. He felt something wet and warm on his thigh and realized this time he had indeed pissed himself. *Jesus.* "You'll be found out, Creedy," he said. "Please, listen to me. *Please!*"

Richard remembered then, saw a slim chance: "My wife knows about you, Creedy! She knows because this crime writer she's mooning after, this Lassiter, knows too! If *they* know, others may, too. Killing me won't solve *anything.*"

Creedy shook his head; curled his lip. "You're some sorry piece of work, Professor. Now I have to kill your wife and child, too! What a shit you are, Richard. Goddamn you for making me do this to them." He waved at one of the men: "Do it. Make it *hurt* for him now."

Screaming, Richard turned to run up the opposite creek bank, but he caught a fist in the face: a fourth black-clad man had come up behind him. The man grabbed Richard by the scruff of the neck and kicked the backs of Richard's legs, collapsing him. His attacker then drove Richard's face against a slick rock.

Bone cracked and Richard screamed again, cupping his hands to his bloodied face. He felt a deep, unnatural depression in his forehead above his right eye and began to whimper. Then he began to wretch.

The man forced Richard's face into the fast-running stream and held him under, with a foot against the back of Richard's neck, until the scholar's legs stopped their kicking.

Creedy tossed a half-empy bota bag of cheap wine to the man holding Richard under and said, "Put this over his shoulder. Scenario: He was drunk. He fell. He drowned. The end."

Not waiting for the last of it, Creedy stalked back up the trail toward his car hidden in the high weeds on the opposite side of the road.

Jesus, to have to kill a pregnant woman . . .

That was just about the worst and too-pat piece of "irony" life could throw at him in this sorry, messy affair. So, of course, life did just that.

But . . . there was *another* way to look at this. Hector Lassiter and Hannah were lovers, or on the verge of becoming so.

Creedy smiled and thought, *Recontextualize it—change the camera angle, so to speak. This having to kill Hannah Paulson and her baby, it isn't irony. It's symmetry. The fearful kind. Hector Lassiter took Victoria and her baby from you. Now you take Hannah Paulson and her baby from Hector Lassiter. Revenge. Yes, that's the way to look at it. That's the way it truly is.*

Viewed in this new true light, well, Creedy figured he might even *relish* killing Hannah Paulson and her child.

Hell, it might even erase the other memories darkening his mind now—his killing of Patricia Stihlbourne, for one.

With her pretty, chiseled features and long blue-black hair, Patricia reminded Creedy more than a little of his beloved Victoria.

As his men had subdued Patricia in the bathroom of the Hemingway suite—holding her prisoner and covering her mouth as Creedy administered the fatal shots of heroin—Patricia's beseeching eyes all too vividly reminded Creedy of Victoria's terrified expression so many years before. . . .

The coroner will find ink in my veins and blood on my typewriter keys.

—C. Astrid Weber

37.   PLOT HOLES

Hector glanced at Jimmy—the retired Cleveland detective was sizing him up now with cops eyes. He'd been allowed one phone call. Rather than playing roulette with some local-yokel lawyer, Hector had called Hanrahan.

The Ketchum cop—a man of fifty; buzz cut and a big gut—said, "You were seen in the bar at the lodge sharing drinks with this woman twice.

Now she's dead in your bathtub. Looks like there was a struggle. Someone shot her up. Gave her a fatal overdose. LSD, maybe heroin. Maybe both."

Now Hector was seething: leave it to a hack like Creedy to throw a hackneyed twist like *this* one at Hector. And leave it to Creedy to concoct a murder frame along *these* charged lines. *Jesus.*

Several years before, Hector's fourth wife, Maria, had died of a fatal heroin overdose a few days after their toddler daughter, Dolores, succumbed to congenital defects resulting from her mother's hidden addiction.

For years, conspiracy theorists had mounted a whispering campaign against Hector, accusing him of having fatally shot up his own wife in an ice-filled bathtub to fox time-of-death estimates and procure his own alibi.

Clearly Creedy, or rather his minions, believed those stories and had decided to play to the dark rumors.

The cop confirmed Hector's suspicions: "Seems this last wife of yours—"

"Stop there, boyo." Jimmy shook a thick finger at the Idaho flatfoot: "My friend was never even *charged* in that death, let alone arrested. It's like he says, we've been bunked at the Hemingway house a time, now. There's a little colleen there, too, nine months pregnant, whose husband is a literary scholar and an alcoholic. He went missing in Boise. Hec drove over there yesterday afternoon to find and bring the man, a fella name of Richard Paulson, back. He left him there at the lodge this morning to dry out. I expect you can find some people who saw the sot carried in by my friend here. He's been playing good Samaritan. Hec's no killer."

"And who the hell are you?"

"Retired detective. James Butler Hanrahan. You can check me out through the Cleveland Police Department."

The Ketchum cop stuck out his chin. "Well, we've got a dead woman on our hands. We don't get many apparent murders in these parts."

Not since July 1961, anyway, Hector thought.

Jimmy leaned in close to Hector's ear, whispered, "Did you know this dead woman, Hec? I mean know her, and *know* her, in the biblical sense?"

Hector gave Jimmy this look. Jimmy said, "This is me, Hector. I *know* you. You and the skirts . . ."

"She was alive when I left her in bed," Hector whispered. "And Patricia was no junkie."

"Jaysus," Jimmy said softly. "If you'd just *once* keep it in your god-

damn pants...Well, I'll do what I can with these boyos. Try to point them in the right directions and not let 'em fuck up interpreting the evidence, such as it is."

Jimmy slapped the chief on the back and said, "Let's go look at that poor colleen again. See if maybe something might not have been missed."

Alone again, Hector seethed and fretted: He'd dodged false murder charges in the past. Usually he was getting arrested for being in the wrong place at the wrong time. Perhaps from poking around the edges of something nasty and accidentally making himself a convenient, but fleeting, suspect.

In the past, there had more than once been some pretty young thing to step forward and lie for him—to claim Hector had been in her bed at some crucial hour. But Hannah was pregnant and married. And Hector told himself he'd rather face incarceration than lie and say he'd slept with Mary Hemingway.

He ground his teeth: This time, he might really be in a fix.

And luckless Patricia? She would be another one of *them* now—another one of those dogging Hector's conscience in the years left him.

Two hours passed. Then the top cop swung by the holding cell's door: "You'll be released shortly, Lassiter."

Hector nodded. "Surely won't argue, but what's changed?"

"Seems the dead woman ordered room service a good bit after you say you left," the cop said. "She had an apricot fizz, whatever that is. Bellhop remembers her because she answered the door wrapped in a sheet. That bartender you chewed out in Picabo remembered you, too. Well, he remembered the bawling out you gave him for serving you a cut drink. Factoring those times against the doc's estimate of the girl's death, even with all those ice cubes, well, barring you having a twin, you surely couldn't have done the deed. Sorry to have put you through this trouble."

He looked around the small, dank cell; just a few more minutes and they should be kicking him loose. Across the hallway, a couple of drunks were bunked out in their cells, snoring and cursing in their sleep. Jesus, what a pit....

Hector stood and rubbed the back of his neck. God bless Patricia for being a drinker. And bless his own short temper and that near-row with that miserly barkeep in Picabo. Frustrated by events, Hector had just kept driving in his Bel Air until he saw that particular bar . . .

They were twists Creedy *couldn't* anticipate when plotting his hasty frame against Hector. It was always the little things that bit you in the ass. . . .

The cop jerked his head at the door. "Your Irish friend's out front, waiting for you, Lassiter. Oh, and some FBI fella asked after you, too."

Hector hesitated at the door. "The Fed—he a son of a bitch named Creedy?"

"Nah, Andrew Langley."

Well, that was inevitable after that attack in the Ram. Hector just hoped he wasn't now going to pass from Idaho police custody to some federal lockup for decking a G-Man.

Hector stepped into the dusk; heard crickets. Jimmy had his broadening ass planted on the hood of Hector's car. A black sedan was parked behind the Bel Air. Andy Langley, arms crossed, glaring, sat on the hood of that sled. He had a hell of a shiner. Hector nodded at Jimmy, flashed the Irishman an index finger, then ambled over to Langley.

"Kid," he said, "I'm so sorry. But one of your bent confreres arranged to have a hit-team waiting out front of the Ram for me and that little gal. Now, me being without a gun . . ."

Langley said, "You might have said something. I might have—"

"For all I knew, or even know now, you're in cahoots with this son-of-a-bitching fellow agent of yours," Hector said. "It was a tense thing. I acted on impulse." He hesitated, then said, "You report me up the chain?"

Langley rolled his eyes. "What, report that *and* the loss of my service weapon to the Director? Are you mad? I want my fucking gun back, Lassiter."

"Sure, Andy," Hector said. He strode over to his Chevy; popped the passenger-side door. He slipped his display handkerchief from the pocket of his sports jacket and reached under the seat. "Here you go, son. Again, sorry for that." Turning his back to Jimmy and Hector, Langley holstered his gun.

Hector said, "You haven't asked me who this FBI agent who tried to have me killed is."

Langley half-turned. "I figure it's Donovan Creedy. I was reporting to him about your movements until a couple of days ago. Then I saw Creedy at the lodge, and figured out why I was instructed to stop reporting."

Jimmy said, "You say that like you two—you and Creedy—maybe aren't so tight, lad."

"He's no friend of mine; maybe not of anyone," Langley said. Looking Hector in the eye, Andy added, "Some around the Bureau say he's gone rogue . . . maybe fishing two ponds."

Hector's pale blue eyes narrowed. "And Hoover tolerates that?"

The FBI agent shrugged. "The Director keeps his own counsel. And like I said, he may have connections that trump even Mr. Hoover." Andy showed them his back.

Jimmy passed Hector the keys to the Bel Air. "Next moves, Hector?"

"Well—" He frowned. There was a phone booth next to the police HQ. The pay phone inside the booth was ringing.

Hector and Jimmy exchanged curious looks. Hector had this feeling. He sighed and walked to the pay phone—folded back the door. He lifted the receiver, said, "Hello?"

The voice on the other end of the line was snarling, unhinged sounding. It was Creedy—that didn't surprise Hector at all. But the undertone of mania in Creedy's voice was something new.

"I'm going to kill her, Lassiter," Donovan Creedy said. "I'm going to kill your darling Hannah and there's nothing you can do to stop it now. How's *that* feel?" Creedy broke the connection before Hector could respond.

Hector racked the receiver and ran back to the Bel Air. He called to Jimmy, "Where the hell is Hannah, *right now,* Jim? It's more than urgent."

Jimmy said, "The colleen, she hotfooted for parts unknown, Hector. Seemed distraught, Mary said. Something about things you said . . . things her husband, Richard the sot, said to her. Oh, and that cocksucker professor cuffed her." Jimmy spat and said, "I mean to harm that son of a bitch, next time I see him."

Hector cursed. "Where the hell did Hannah go?"

Jimmy looked grave. "I've tried to get at that, but Mary's not talking, Hector."

Love sees sharply, hatred sees even more sharp, but jealousy sees the sharpest, for it is love and hate at the same time.

—Arab Proverb

38.   WIDOW'S WALK

Hector refused the offer of a nightcap, just as he had refused the offer of a seat. He said, "Where in God's name is she?"

Mary Hemingway sipped her gimlet and scowled. She pulled the throw closer around her; a brisk wind whipped across the exterior deck. "You're not here on behalf of Dickie, are you, Lasso?"

"That asshole? Nah, that cocksucker least of all. I'm here because someone's been following Hannah. And following me. I've learned some things about all of that, Mary. But you really don't want me to elaborate on *some* of that, right? Now someone else has threatened to kill Hannah. So where the hell is she?"

Glaring at him, Mary held up her hands. "Why in hell would I know?"

"Because Ketchum-slash-Sun Valley isn't lousy with cab companies," Hector said. "A Hamilton bought me the morsel that a cab delivered Hannah to your doorstep about forty-five minutes after she fled the lodge. It wasn't deep detective work, learning any of that."

Mary put a cigarette to her lips and waited for Hector to light her up. She said, "A 'Hamilton'? What the fuck are you blathering about, Lasso?" She leaned into the flame of his old Zippo.

His Zippo clicked shut. "A 'Hamilton' is a goddamn ten-dollar bill. Now where is Hannah? Did she go back home to Ann Arbor, Mary?"

"Why do you care? If she's being followed here—and I have to say Hector, and please forgive me for this, but you're sounding a little like Papa did there at his fucking end. I mean, well, you know, you're sounding *très* fucking paranoid—well, as of now, Hannah's not fucking here. So, problem solved, *oui*?"

"*Non*. There's more at stake here than what *you've* set in motion, Mary."

"What are you fucking talking about?" Mary glared at Hector.

He said, "I'm talking about this bargain-basement private eye you've hired to follow the Paulsons and me. I got the sense this guy chasing the Paulsons was a private investigator. He had the look. So I let my fingers do the walking. There's only one licensed shamus in this cow town. I swung by his office earlier today . . . saw him leaving the joint. Harry Jordan— the Paulsons' shadow. No question. You engaged Jordan because you were aiming to keep us 'honest,' I reckon. Figure you were aiming to make sure everyone is who they say they are. You had your sorry paladin snooping around after hidden motives. *That* plan that you've set in motion is the one I'm talking about. This flatfoot with the receding hairline you've had dogging mine and Hannah's footsteps. Seems to me you are the one sorting for bones in animal crackers these days, Mary. You're the one acting like a textbook paranoid."

The widow drew her hand back, preparing to slap him. Hector raised a finger: "*Don't*, honey. You don't hit hard enough to make it hurt, but it *will* close a door between us if you take that shot. You've been caught . . . let it go. We move forward from here."

Mary's chin trembled. She took a deep breath, then sneered: "Look at you, Lasso, mooning after that girl. And her, married and with a child on the way. Papa always said you were a fool for younger women, and I can see now he was right. Of course, when he first said it to me you were twenty years younger. Now the girls just get younger and younger. And deader, too. Like that scholar at the lodge."

Hector flinched. He said, "Hem was right about me and the right women. And by right, I mean the ones I'm attracted to."

"Girls, you mean," Mary said, curling her lip. "Younger women, always. It's almost as if you think youth is something you can catch or steal from them."

Hector shook his head. "Hannah is in real danger. Now, I can make the road trip to Ann Arbor and be wrong, Mary. And I sense—my presumed sorry passions aside—that you really like Hannah. So I'm telling you, straight and true, Hannah's in *dire* danger. There is more stalking the Paulsons than your hired private dick. The same thing threatens you and me. It's my instinct that's so, and my instincts aren't often to be quarreled with. So please save me some time and maybe save Hannah: Where do I find her?"

"Home," Mary said. "She fucking went home to Michigan, just like you said. But we have an agreement still, don't we, Lasso? About manuscripts, I mean. And we have a deadline."

"I have no deadline," Hector said. "And think again: You're talking about Hem's posthuma. So long as Hem remains dead, there's all the time in the world for that."

"But this FBI man—"

Hector shook his head. "This gambit with Paulson and the key, it's stayed Creedy's hand for now."

Mary said, "He's FBI—there's nothing they can't do."

"There's a limit even to Hoover's powers," Hector said. "And I mean to find those limits. First thing for you to do when I leave is have Jimmy change the locks on the document room. Hide the new keys better. And Mary, start mixing all your own drinks, just in case they get to that maid of yours." He was quiet for a time, then said, "What we *really* need is a wild card. Something to stay their hand *forever*. They clearly felt threatened by Hem. If we only knew why. Whatever it was, it could be something we could use to force a more permanent stalemate."

Mary said softly, "Ernest was always shooting his mouth off... dropping bombshells in letters. I suppose it's possible Hoover heard about Papa's long-threatened project...."

Hector looked up sharply. "What do you mean? *What* project?"

"It's something Ernest talked about several times since the early 1940s. It's like that book about you he kept talking up but never wrote. He had this idea for a novel about Hoover."

"Are you *serious*?"

"Papa yammered on about it over a period of years. Claimed to have all kinds of research and 'dark true gen' he said would make it a blockbuster if he could get anyone to publish it. Publish it? Hell, he needed to write it, first."

Hector wet his lips. "Hem even *contemplating* a *novel* about Hoover would be more than enough to scare the hell out of J. Edgar if he got wind."

Mary nodded. "Particularly given its main thesis: that John Hoover is partly Negro."

Holy Jesus. No wonder Hoover was going berserk. "You're sure Hem never started it?"

"Just more talk," Mary said. "Got to a point where all his work was talk."

Hector let that one pass. He smiled and pulled out his notepad and pen. He began scribbling furiously across the pages.

It was too perfect: Hem's shooting his mouth off about some prospective Hoover novel had bought Hem a lifetime's persecution from J. Edgar. Now that same mythical work could pay dividends long past Hem's death. . . .

This idea Hector had would bring a whole new dimension to the concept of Hem's long game.

Mary said, "What are you doing? You're writing *now*?"

"You ever act, Mary? I hope so, because I'm writing you a script."

"What do you mean?"

"You're going to tell me about this Hoover novel again, but hewing to what I write here. We're going to have this conversation again, but this time, in this scenario I'm scripting, Hem wrote the book and *I* have Hem's manuscript and have had it for some time. And we're going to have this conversation in my Bel Air."

"What end does that serve, Lasso?"

"Draws focus to me and off of you, and more specifically, away from Hem's papers until we can secure those better." Hector finished and passed Mary her script. He said, "Can you read my writing okay?"

"Just fine."

"Now we're going to go to my Chevy and do this."

"Why inside your car?"

Hector winked. "Because while I was dealing with the local cops, Creedy bugged my car. Goddamn thing is riddled with microphones."

An hour later, Hector found a ratty bar in downtown Ketchum and hit the phone booth in back. He opened up his address book and found Agent Tilly's number there—one of J. Edgar Hoover's boys Hector had useful dealings with back in the old days, when Hector would occasionally do the Bureau a favor—before he got on Hoover's bad side, as the 1950s wound down.

Edmond Tilly said, "It's been a long time, Hector."

"Too long, pal. I need some information, and fast. Anything you might be able to rustle up on a guy still in the Bureau . . . probably about my age. Guy named Donovan Creedy—he's everything you hate. The darkest dirt you can turn would best serve the cause, buddy."

"Where do I reach you, Hec?"

"I'll call *you*," Hector said. "I've got a lot of ground to cover now, *muy pronto*."

Hector racked the receiver; jogged to his Bel Air. He flipped on the headlights, then burned down the darkened roads toward Michigan.

There is an air of last things, a brooding sense of impending annihilation about so much deconstructive activity in so many of its guises; it is not merely postmodernist but preapocalyptic.

—David Lehman

39.   GRACE UNDER PRESSURE

Grueling time passed on a stifling bus.

Hannah stepped off the Greyhound suffering terrible stomach cramps.

She beelined for the bathroom of the Ann Arbor Greyhound station; her kidneys ached.

There was blood in the toilet bowl afterward, but not much—not enough to worry over, she reassured herself. Not like after Richard. She'd call her doctor when she reached the apartment; she was already bracing for his lecture.

Hannah walked from the bathroom, pale, a hand pressed to her belly. Then she saw the man in the black suit—slicked-back, graying, anthracite hair and an aquiline nose.

She remembered seeing him one or twice around the lodge. Hannah turned and ran to the extent that she could do that. Hannah saw in a mirror the man was following her.

The loft was stale and dusty from being shuttered for six weeks. Sneezing several times, Hannah struggled with a couple of the old, warped windows, propping them open with dowel rods. She turned on the ceiling fans, sneezing again at the dust they kicked up. She watched the dust motes spiraling in the shafts of late afternoon sunlight and thought about cleaning, then thought better of it.

Never confuse movement for action, Papa had more than once lectured one or another of the younger women in his life. Why leave Richard a clean apartment? Better to pack for her move.

Hannah's sister Aggie, who never approved of Richard, had several times offered Hannah and her unborn baby a deal on an upstairs apartment in a rental property that she and her husband owned on South State Street, in the midst of the University of Michigan campus. Perhaps the offer still stood. Hannah was also promised a teaching assistant post in introductory literature, so there would be some money to augment whatever, if anything, she extracted from Richard. All in all, it didn't shape up to be a hand-to-mouth existence for Hannah and her baby.

Then she saw the man from the bus station, standing down there in his black suit, leaning against a phone booth and smoking a cigarette, staring up at her framed in her window.

Donovan Creedy smiled and called up, "Why don't you let me come up there and we'll talk, Hannah. I want to talk to you about Mrs. Hemingway. About this writer you've been hanging with—this Lassiter." He waited, licked his lips. Mrs. Paulson was a lucky one: Creedy's cab had blown a tire. That cost Creedy a precious ten minutes as he tried to wave down another cab to continue pursuit of Hannah.

Wild-eyed, Hannah shook her head. "I'm calling the police," she shouted down at Creedy.

Then it hit her.

The pain dropped Hannah like blows to both kidneys.

She squealed and was driven to her knees, clutching her belly. She gasped over and over, frantic to catch her breath.

Just as the pain eased, another wave came that was much worse.

A moment's peace.

Two more sharp pains.

And another.

Twice, Hannah vomited. She struggled up to look over the windowsill. The man was still there, staring up at her, but scowling now. She cried, "Please—I need help. Call me an ambulance, *please*?"

The man standing by the phone booth chewed his lip, then shook his head. "Let me in first."

"Please," Hannah pleaded. "My baby . . . I think I'm . . . something's wrong! Please—help me!"

Creedy thought about it. He looked around; the street was quiet. No pedestrians. Something *was* going wrong with her pregnancy. Well, that was a fortuitous twist, wasn't it?

Creedy smiled a last time at Hannah, then turned, thrusting his hands in his overcoat pockets. He began walking, thinking perhaps to look for a good bookstore to browse through.

Gasping, Hannah watched him go, calling after Creedy when she could find the breath. Then she screamed and curled into a ball, rolling on the floor in agony, cursing herself and wishing Richard in hell. What had she been thinking—she who was so committed to fitness and the health of her own body? Months of careful dieting. Months spent walking on eggshells.

Nearly a year of risked madness sans medication to carry her baby to term.

All of it scuttled and made meaningless by six reckless, indefensible weeks without seeing her obstetrician, who must surely think her patient was dead or fully deranged to absent herself for so long. Six long weeks wasted trailing behind Richard Paulson through Papa's old haunts preparatory to Sun Valley: Piggott, Arkansas; Kansas City; and Billings, Montana. Six long weeks in which something could—in which something obviously did—go wrong inside her.

The cord to the phone was just in reach. She pulled on it, and the base and the receiver slid off the edge of the table, banging Hannah on the head.

Hyperventilating, she dragged the receiver over by its cord and dialed.

A dead line.

Hannah instantly made a bitter, intuitive leap: Richard, knowing they would be gone for some time, had skimped and not paid the phone bill. Presumably, he had always intended for Hannah to give birth in Idaho. Richard had merely been paying lip service to his wife's stated desire to have her baby born in Michigan, the birth overseen by her own doctors, with her sister and brother present. Still, there should have been phone company warnings, written threats and testy collection calls before service was terminated.

And where was Richard now—now, in this single moment when she truly needed him? Probably dining drunk in some café while wifey screamed and bled her way through labor.

Well, she *had* given Richard the boot. She saw now that she had insisted on moving to the bar for their last violent exchange because some part of her knew she was going to push Richard into a corner and throw all she had at him until he swung back—literally lashed out—with witnesses. More for her divorce attorney to use against him . . . along with whatever that Idaho PI might turn up.

Hannah clicked the receiver button several more times, her hand shaking.

Nothing.

Hannah pounded on the wall with the dead receiver to alert the neighbors, then remembered that they—two students from Alabama—would be gone, bugged out like so many others in this college town that emptied between semesters.

The stench of the vomit on her clothes made Hannah sick again—hurting dry heaves now, green with stingy bile. She struggled onto her knees and tried to straighten up. Instant agony. She doubled over again, unable to catch her breath. Hannah screamed for help between catches of shortened breath, thinking that it was late and that there wouldn't be foot traffic through campus at this hour.

The pain eased. She thought of that man outside who refused to help her: Who was he? Why wouldn't he get her help?

She tried to stand now, and that got things started again. Hannah fell down, hard, her heart racing, trying once more to catch her breath between racking dry heaves. She could feel the blood vessels in her eyes rupture with each bout of sickness. She felt herself slipping away.

Then, later, she glanced at the wall clock.

She'd been on the floor for two hours. She must have blacked out a time or two.

I'll crawl, she thought. *I'll crawl right down the steps and out onto the street.* She tried to roll over onto all fours and it felt like someone had a knife in her belly. She rolled onto her back, squealing in pain.

She called for help several more times.

Through the open windows that were now letting in a too-chilly breeze, Hannah could hear passing cars. She was propped up between an old bureau and Richard's bookcase full of paperback critical studies of Papa's work, as well as dog-eared, heavily annotated copies of Papa's novels. Hannah began pulling books from the bookcase, tossing them hard over her shoulder through the closest open window. It was a short distance from the window to the sidewalk to the street. With any luck, she might bounce a book off a passing car's windshield—anger someone enough to call the police.

The pain was getting bad again, almost constant. Hannah called for help several more times, lobbing books out the window between piercing contractions.

And the pain, which was always right there now, changed. She knew that it was truly beginning, and now there was no longer time to hope for a miraculous discovery; no time to waste wishing for rescue.

Hannah knew she would have to prepare some things now.

Squealing at the pain that came with the movement, Hannah manhandled a drawer from the bureau and emptied it of the neatly folded bedsheets and blankets inside. She tucked a blanket back into the drawer with shaking hands and positioned one of the sheets under herself. She pulled the laces from her hiking boots and laid them out next to her.

Panting, Hannah paused to throw a few more books out the window, continuing to scream for someone to help her, hearing her voice dim and grow hoarse with each unanswered cry for help.

She emptied a plastic wastebasket of the pages of Richard's sundry, aborted manuscripts so she would have a container for the afterbirth, then she struggled out of her shorts and underwear, bunching them up with a few of the sheets behind her back. She groped around over her head and found a pair of nail scissors on top of the bureau. She cut her nails short since she had no gloves to wear; no water to wash in. There was also no possibility of boiling the scissors to sterilize them; instead, she ran the cutting edges over the blue flame of a Zippo lighter she had found next to the scissors.

The lighter gave Hannah a new idea: Somewhere out there was a grassy median, its thin strip of grass grown brown and combustible from a spring drought. She might burn down the block, but at least she would draw emergency services. Hannah found the fattest book she could—a paperback copy of Richard's single published novel . . . a work of fiction that sank without notice—and set its first thirty or so pages on fire. She pitched this out the window, followed by flaming copies of various scholars' books and several volumes of *The Review*. A first edition of the hardback book on Papa's Paris years that Richard had authored—now something of a minor collectible simply because it was about Papa—followed them out.

Hannah felt the baby coming now, her convulsing body giving way to it, and now she knew for the first time with certainty what was ahead. Her legs began to shake as she realized what she must face alone, and she was cowed and left desolated by the hopeless, bloody prospect of what she had to try.

No:

What she must do.

What she must do for herself and for her baby.

One thing about fighting, Papa said, *the only thing that counts if you fight, is that you must win. Everything else is shit.*

Shivering, she put her back to the wall—her discarded, vomit- and bile-stained clothes and the sheets providing scant padding—and planted her feet flat on the floor, her naked legs spread wide.

Something else Papa was said to have said, perhaps apocryphal, suddenly occurred to Hannah. Asked what the shortest short story he had ever written was, Papa cited a mock classified ad: *For Sale: A pair of baby shoes. Never used.*

Hannah tried hard to control her breathing, and to shut out the pain in her belly that was so much worse than she instinctively knew it should be.

She stared between her legs, her whole body bathed in sweat and quivering now. She raggedly called out for help when she remembered to, tossing another book or two out the window while she waited to see the crown of her baby's emerging head.

Many times over the course of ten or twelve minutes she feared she would pass out from the pain. She really couldn't take it anymore, and she fleetingly wished she had a gun.

No, she lashed out at herself. *That's the one thing I would never do. Ever.*

No matter how bad it ever gets.

No matter how bad it ever gets. I will not *do* that.

And then, when she truly knew she could take no more of it, even though it still hurt her terribly, the pain changed in a way that was like a new beginning—something she suddenly felt for the first time was finite, and therefore endurable.

And then she saw it: something bloody emerging from between her legs. She pushed with unfamiliar but already exhausted and trembling muscles to help it, her hips slipping a bit across the wooden floor that was wet through the sheet with her sweat and the broken water from her womb and with her own blood.

She wrapped her trembling, tired arms around her thighs, instinctively pulling them back to shorten the birth canal.

It was suddenly visible: the bloodied, red, wizened skin of her baby squeezing loose from between her sweaty, trembling, blood-stained thighs.

But something was terribly wrong. What Hannah was seeing emerge from within herself was not her baby's tiny, malleable head, but rather its bloodied little ass.

She screamed.

Being here, like this, trying to deliver her own baby was nightmare enough. By rights, her husband should be walking seven times around the house sunwise or gathering rowan berries for her to squeeze to ease her agony. She shouldn't have to do this by herself; shouldn't have to face it alone.

But she was alone, and now she could see that her baby was in breech— an almost certain death sentence for mother and child . . . for *minny* and *bairn* . . . killed during *lighter*.

All that and now this, she thought, and cursed herself for it: *Thinking*

*in goddamn country song titles while your baby dies inside you. What
the hell is wrong with you?*

Hannah raged at the crush of it all—certain that she was well and truly
and finally, fatally, doomed.

Gasping, Hannah tried to remember what her baby's upside-down
position meant, and what might be done to give them both some slim chance
for survival.

Even with a doctor present, Hannah knew that a vaginal breech birth
was typically treacherous. More often than not, it was necessary to execute a cesarean section—a procedure Hannah couldn't possibly perform
on herself even if she were equipped and trained to do it.

There was another option: She could make more room for her emerging baby by severing the tissue between her own vagina and anus. Even if
she had a knife, Hannah doubted she could cut into herself like that. And
now her baby's body was in the way.

It would be easier to naturally deliver a breech vaginally if this baby
were not Hannah's first, but only a little.

And it didn't matter:

The fact was this was Hannah's first baby and she was alone and
wrung out and her baby was inside her backwards. She and her baby were
likely going to die bloody, protracted deaths.

If the baby were only turned the right way, its head positioned correctly to ease through the birth canal, Hannah thought she just might
possibly be able to do it on her own as she had always heard so many
others for so many millennia had done it.

But her baby was being born backwards.

Her baby's tiny, frail legs were pressed up tight against its little smashed
face. Possibly—quite probably—the umbilical cord's position was wrong,
too.

There was every chance the cord was wrapped around her baby's
fragile neck.

Her maybe already dead baby's neck.

Dead.

Death:

The undiscovered country Papa seemed impelled almost from birth
to explore. Hannah felt differently: certainly better to travel hopefully in

this instance, than to arrive. Papa courted death with half-reticent ardor. Hannah wasn't similarly enamored. She was terrified to die alone and in agony with her tiny dead baby half in, half out of its mother.

And Jesus God and Mary, to have to hurt so much at the end.

Perhaps it's already dead and has been for some time.

Hannah became steadily, freshly nauseous, and now distraught at the thought of her baby dead inside of her.

Sure. Of course it is dead.

Everything up to now has presaged that. I've done every single thing wrong that I could and everything up to now has been pointing to and preparing me for this—my baby being dead.

Now it is all a thing of odds and dumb luck, Hannah told herself. *Of small, pliable heads and big-enough pelvic girdles—far bigger than fellow-Scot Catherine Barkley's, or that of the Indian woman in Papa's story whose cowardly husband cut his own throat in an upper bunk rather than hear his wife's agonized screams as she gave birth.*

Hannah thought about these discomforting things, simultaneously saying choppy prayers and half-remembering procedures browsed over in manuals.

She still hoarsely screamed for help now and then—her voice little more than a ragged whisper.

She kept reminding herself to breathe and push, to push quickly and efficiently to help her little baby through its strangling passage wrong ways down the birth canal. Get it out to breathe and to live—time the pushing to the wracking arcs of pain that came with malevolent, mathematical precision.

And now, instinctively, Hannah wedged her hand inside herself: She felt the skin she once thought of cutting tear, and knew it would cost her later—this inadvertent but, God-willing, *helpful* episiotomy.

Hannah shoved her hand up under her baby's buttocks, cupped under its tiny thighs, and eased it out through her convulsing, grasping, mutilated vagina, simultaneously pressing down on her uterus with her other hand, easing her baby out of her own body.

That's it
that's it
that's it.

It went on like this for how long Hannah couldn't say, her screaming without any voice left, yet all the while so gently and carefully urging her baby's frail body from inside its terrified, wrung-out mother.

And now it remained only to get her maybe-dead baby's head out—the most dangerous maneuver of the whole, hopeless, foredoomed proposition.

Mary Hemingway had at least been granted the good grace to be unconscious throughout the worst of her own abortive ordeal in Wyoming.

Hannah was forced to face her death alone and with open eyes, and she was left bitter and horrified at the prospect of it.

There would come a time, in just a moment or two, when she would know whether her baby's head could pass through its mother's battered pelvic girdle.

If it could not, Hannah could take the last bloody step to try and save herself: She could wedge her hand deep into her own vagina and crush her baby's skull, so that she could free her dead child from her body.

The abortive maneuver could save Hannah, or it could simply hasten her own fatal hemorrhaging.

Please, dear dear God, don't make me have to decide. Sweet Jesus, don't make me have to—because I won't do it, and then we will both certainly die.

Please father.

Please please father.

Let it all be okay.

Please—I don't want to hurt anymore, and I don't want my baby to hurt.

And then, suddenly, it was done.

Once again, crying and screaming for help, Hannah pushed the chubby cord aside and sloughed the thin membrane of mucous from her baby's face—her daughter's face—tipping her feet up higher than her little head to clear the mucous. She tapped her tiny wrinkled feet, and then Hannah heard her baby's throaty, angry cry, and Hannah wiped her baby's face and body with the sheets and placed her daughter carefully on the blanket in the drawer.

Only a little ways left to go now, Hannah consoled herself, proud of herself for having come so far, but still terrified at the prospect of not being found in time. Perhaps lying here for days while her baby froze from the cold through the open window and mommy maybe lay dead and decomposing (for Hannah was bleeding terribly now).

Hannah groaned for help again, tossing a last bloodied, burning book out the window, thinking she heard sirens wailing in the distance. She tossed the soiled sheets, slick with her own blood, halfway out the window.

And then she remembered the important thing that she had forgotten.

The thing that could kill their baby girl—the little girl whom Hannah had already begun in her mind to call Bridget—if she did not move quickly enough.

Her bloodied hands shaking, Hannah tied one of the shoelaces taken from her boots around the pale rubbery umbilical cord, several inches from Bridget's navel. Hannah tied the second shoelace a couple of inches closer to herself. Setting her jaw, afraid that something might go wrong, she cut the cord between her and her crying daughter.

It was done, and Bridget was still mewling softly.

Hannah sat back now, gathering herself for the last bloody part of it— her exhausted, bleeding body's expulsion of the afterbirth.

Hannah Paulson lay there, feeling her heartbeat and the soft gush of blood between her legs that echoed its beat. She was sweating profusely, although the wind through the window was chilly and the air smelled of chimney smoke and embers. She covered her baby in the blanket and smoothed the blanket with her bloodied, shaking hand. Reminded by the blood crusted on her hand that she was still bleeding, bleeding far too much, Hannah looked between her legs. She knew instantly that it was a mistake to look when she saw how much blood there was, and her heart immediately pounded harder and black spots buzzed in front of her eyes.

The blood pounded in her ears.

More blood gushed, and pieces of something plopped stringily into the spreading puddle between Hannah's legs. The pounding in her head and ears was deafening, and now there were things screaming in her ears—

sirens like the whole world was on fire; red and blue lights spun crazily across the walls in the room in which she lay dying.

And there was the pounding, louder now; always the pounding—in her ears, between her breasts, and between her blood-soaked thighs.

Widows are divided into two classes—the bereaved and relieved.

—Victor Robinson

40.   AFTER BIRTH

Hannah blinked a few times, looking around through sleep-encrusted eyes.

She saw she was in a hospital.

She glanced to her right and saw a man asleep in the chair by her bed: Hector Lassiter. He had several days' growth of gray-white beard. A tag clipped to the pocket of his sports jacket boasted, i'm a new dad!

Despite her anger at him, Hannah smiled at Hector's presumed subterfuge.

As she awakened in the hospital bed, Hannah first wondered whether her baby daughter was okay, and then, more prosaically, what exactly had resulted in their rescue. She groped around in the dark with her fresh-scrubbed right hand—the hand that wasn't braceleted and riddled with tubes and covered with patches grounding wires to her flesh—and buzzed for a nurse. While she waited, she said, "Hector? Hector, please wake up."

He rubbed his pale blue eyes, smiled, stood, and leaned over the bed and hugged her tightly. "Thank Christ," he whispered in her ear.

"My baby?"

"She's beautiful. And she's better than fine."

Apart from a mild case of jaundice, Hannah's slightly underweight daughter was perfect, she was told, just as Hector had said. As to their rescue, well, it had been helped along by an emergency call from an irate salesman whose expensive toupee had flared after being struck by a smoldering review copy of Rourke and Evans's slender psychological portrait of Papa.

There had also been the flaming blue canopy of the newsstand directly beneath the Paulsons' apartment, and the long, billowing, bloody sheet twisting from the Paulsons' open window.

Hector assured her no charges were being contemplated by local police. "Frankly, they're delighted to be associated with the notoriety generated by 'saving' a photogenic beauty like yourself," Hector said. "Particularly after she successfully executed the breech-birth delivery of her own child. No mean feat, that. Jesus, Hem would have loved you, Hannah. You're a brick. I was in your apartment to fetch a few things for you. I saw the bloody scene. I'm so, so sorry I didn't get here sooner. What you endured . . ."

Hannah squeezed his hand. "You're here now, and that means the world to me. But . . ."

She confronted Hector then with everything Mary had told her about his fourth wife, Maria.

"Stories . . . sick suppositions," Hector said, looking her in the eye. "That said, Maria same as murdered our baby. I *hated* her when I found out."

Hannah swallowed hard. Then she imagined this scene: Richard taking their baby out for a drive. The worse for drink, he'd wrap the car around a tree . . . Richard would walk away unscathed, but their baby would be dead.

She envisioned herself killing Richard for killing their baby. Yes, she could see herself doing that, could see it too vividly.

If Hector had done something to his wife, well, she understood it. She thought about the woman he'd slept with—Patricia, the scholar. What was there to do about *that*? Hannah and Hector weren't lovers, and he was a well-known ladies' man. She sighed and said, "I'm sorry I hit you."

"Hell, I deserved it."

"Not really." She wet her lips, then offered Hector her hand to hold. Brushing his cheek with her other hand, she said, "You *are* going to shave, aren't you?"

Hector half-smiled. "First chance I get."

Two days later, Hannah, through Hector, was declining requests for interviews from local television and print journalists.

She was also mulling an offer from the promoter-husband of one of her nurses to initiate a dialogue with a boot company for her to endorse the efficacy of their shoestrings in assisting emergency deliveries. Hannah had been skeptical, but Hector said, "It's found money, honey. A one-time opportunity. Best take it. For us *fiction* writers, any publicity is good publicity. Or so I tell myself. Hem always believed it so."

A visiting fireman, one of those who found Hannah, told her an inspection of the Paulsons' apartment revealed Hannah's attempts to phone for help were thwarted by an apparent lightning strike that had occurred sometime after the Paulsons' departure. Probably during a final spring thunderstorm that swept across southeastern Michigan, before the drought had taken hold. The paramedic found several circuit breakers had been tripped. The phone's internal components were fused.

Hannah nodded glumly. So much for angry assumptions about absentee, irresponsible fathers-to-be not paying phone bills.

Forty-eight hours after she was admitted, a huge bouquet arrived, but it was not sent by Richard, from whom she had still not heard a word despite Hannah's brother and sister's grudging efforts to reach him. They seemed to have no trouble finding a certain Idaho widow, however: Mary Hemingway's card accompanying the floral arrangement was terse, but riddled with exclamation points that Hannah heard in her head Mary insisting to the florist be included:

Sweetest Hannah:

You're my hero! Papa would be so proud of you! Grace under pressure, *indeed*! *Please* call me as soon as you possibly can (collect of course). All my best to you and Bridget (Oh yes, I emphatically approve of the name!)!
Love, hugs and kisses,

Your old bird,
Mary

There were other revelations.

Hannah was so damaged internally by little Bridget's crude field delivery that doctors were uncertain whether she could conceive again. If she could, the possibility and prudence of carrying another baby to term was doubtful.

Hannah bore the news well when the doctor delivered it. Bridget's conception had been the result of uncharacteristic recklessness on Hannah's part. She had never really envisioned herself a mother; never craved children. But when the prospect was forced upon her, Hannah had determined to do her best. One child was all she could handle, she told herself. Certainly all that she could afford now. But later that evening, she felt differently.

Hector, sitting vigil by her bed, said, "I was an only child. There are worse things to be."

"I don't want her to be lonely."

"Loneliness gave me my voice as a fiction writer," Hector said.

"I don't want her to be lonely."

"There's always adoption," Hector said, stroking Hannah's hair.

Her growing concerns about money finally induced Hannah to sell her story and a single interview to a national newspaper syndicate.

She was also edging closer to attempting to strike a deal with the boot manufacturer to tout their shoelaces. Apart from the money such a sellout would garner, Hannah kidded herself the notoriety might further jumpstart her writing career.

Hannah pressed the button to call for her nurse. She wanted to have Bridget brought to her room—just to marvel over her. It had been less than an hour since she had last breast-fed her daughter (the doctors and nurses had been left shaking their heads at Hannah's insistence she was going to breastfeed her baby). She had done that several times in front of Hector, unashamed.

Nurses confided to her that when he wasn't by her bedside, Hector was often in the nursery, sitting in a rocking chair, holding Bridget.

Days passed: Hannah grew stronger. She was able to hold Hector's arm and roam the halls; to venture down to the cafeteria for meals. Her baby was getting stronger, too.

Hector had promised to pick her up and drive Hannah and her baby home. Hector had insisted he was going to sleep on Hannah and Richard's couch . . . still adamant that he meant to watch over the two of them. Stroking sleeping Bridget's cheek with a big thumb, he had quietly added, "And I can't go home just now. Hoover's surveillance of me now is *biblical*. For the moment, the bastards have lost track of me. I'm savoring the quiet and privacy."

The bedside phone rang a last time an hour before she was to be released from the hospital.

She sensed motion; saw Hector had returned to her room. She said into the phone, "My friend is here. Can you tell him what you told me? *I*—I can't think now."

Dazed, Hannah passed the phone receiver to Hector, who arched an eyebrow as he raised the phone to his ear.

She said, "Richard is dead."

Writing is a solitary occupation. Family, friends, and society are the natural enemies of the writer. He must be alone, uninterrupted, and slightly savage if he is to sustain and complete an undertaking.

—Jessamyn West

41.   ALONE TOGETHER

Richard's death "by misadventure" had done the divorce court's work, but Hannah nevertheless initiated the steps necessary to revert to her maiden name, as well as to have the surname "MacArthur" assigned to her daughter.

The Idaho detectives requested copies of the photographs of the man that Hannah, and eventually Richard, came to believe was following them around Idaho. Hannah said to Hector, "The film I took—the police may want it."

Hector, still trying to decide how to tell Hannah all he knew about that, said, "I'll mail 'em the glossies if you insist. But I already know who that fella is."

"Who?"

"A private detective. At least what passes for that sorry-ass trade in Idaho. He's a bottom-feeder. *All* private eyes are. Forget what you've seen in movies or read in books. They're hired scum."

"Hired by whom?"

Hector shrugged, not prepared to tell her it was Mary. "That I couldn't find out, and not for lack of trying." As a dodge, he held up his hand, still a bit bruised from beating on Creedy. "The shamus's name is Harry Jordan."

Hannah's blood-pressure spiked; she heard ringing in her ears . . . saw spots. *Oh my God, what have I done?* And did Hector know she had hired this Jordan to follow him, and was kindly lying? If he did, it was all over. . . . Desolation. How could he ever forgive her?

Hector's blue eyes narrowed. He said, "Christ, kid, you okay? Should I get the doctor?"

Hannah shook her head, feeling sick to her stomach, wondering how much her stupid inspiration had maybe cost her with this man. She said, "No, just a little dizzy. It's passing."

She bit her tongue until it hurt. *God*, what an *idiot* she was! After all, Jordan was the *only* private eye in the local yellow pages. She'd gone and hired the very Idaho flatfoot who somebody else had hired to follow Richard and her. The deal was cut over the phone, and she paid by wire. *Brilliant.*

If she'd just seen him, face-to-face . . .

Jordan must have had a good laugh at her expense. Well, she'd sever that relationship, now. Never call Jordan back; never make contact. Maybe later, if there was some kind of governing authority over private detectives, she'd file a complaint about Jordan's deplorable ethics.

She'd keep what she'd done from Hector; chances were he'd never find out she had also hired Jordan. If he did, and then learned she'd hired him to snoop around after Hector as well as Richard? *Catastrophe.*

As the Idaho police pressed ahead, there was also the matter of the Paulson "estate."

The late Mr. Paulson's first wife was dead, and the second and third Mrs. Paulsons had remarried. Hannah and Bridget would likely split any inheritance—if there was indeed anything to be had—with Richard's estranged son.

Presuming Richard hadn't disinherited his namesake in some yet-to-be-found will.

That was also presuming Richard hadn't died intestate, and if not, that he had revised his will after marrying Hannah.

Early prospects weren't reassuring: Richard had made no funeral arrangements—never purchased any burial plots, and his other, living ex-wives expressed little concern to Hannah regarding what was to be done with Richard Paulson's body.

In the course of the next two weeks, Hannah spoke twice to Mary: Once when the elder widow called to express her condolences to Hannah; once more when she offered Hannah two plane tickets and a bedroom in her Ketchum home so they could commence Hannah's authorized biography of Mary.

Hector tried again to dissuade her from writing the book. Hannah dug in her heels. Hector said, "If you're going to pursue this goddamn thing, you're going to need someone watching you. I mean, until this other dark stuff is sorted out."

Thirteen days later, Hannah was wrapping up the last of the tedious logistics necessary to close out the lingering paper trails of Richard Paulson's life. Hannah arranged to buy a single plot in the Ketchum Cemetery. Richard was to be cremated and buried in an annex several dozens of yards distant from Papa's "place of rest."

Because there was only an urn to bury, Richard's internment came cheaply. They dug the professor's grave with posthole diggers.

Surprised by her own single-minded attachment, Hannah nursed and cradled and cooed to her baby, putting her down rarely and reluctantly— only when Bridget slept, and she had the time to work on her own stories and to resume a milder form of her prepregnancy exercise regimen.

Physical exertion sometimes made Hannah tired enough to sleep without dreams of Richard and strangely still bodies of water, but mostly it made her feel thin: A farewell to swollen fingers and ankles, morning sickness, backaches, overactive kidneys, ugly smocks, and elastic waistbands.

Always at the back of her mind was the question of Papa and his death—this prospect of contributing to his legend and the fabric of Hem's literary legacy with her own book that might reshape the way the world regarded Hemingway.

She thought of things Richard had said when building his case against Mary... things Hannah had drawn out from Hector in unguarded moments.

In her mind, a visualization of the crime scene stubbornly took root:

An entryway peppered with the brains, blood, teeth, and powder-burned bone shards of America's greatest writer.

But no true inquest.

Closed autopsy reports.

No paraffin tests performed on Mary's aged hands.

Mary, alone in the house with Hem at the time of the shooting.

The remains, apart from the corpse, were quickly cleaned up by friends and burned. The expunging of any evidence of the death was so swift and thorough that Papa's sister, Sunny, marveled that she could find none of the carnage that had stained the foyer just hours before her arrival.

The weapon was destroyed before it could become a morbid souvenir.

That woman and that sad crazy old man, alone together in that concrete bunker.

As the rain drifted from a downpour to drizzle, Hannah dialed Mary's number.

The elder widow eventually said, "So, when do we get down to it?"

"Right away," Hannah said. "I'm leaving tomorrow."

[Hemingway] is seriously ill, both physically and mentally, and at one time doctors were considering giving him electro-shock therapy.

—CONFIDENTIAL MEMO TO J. EDGAR HOOVER

CREEDY—New York, 1960

The sedatives were having no effect. They had Hemingway in restraints. He was straining against those, screaming at Mary, "Get me out of here, Pickle, please! You have to get me out of here! Don't let them do this to me!"

The doctor said, "Perhaps we should go outside, Mrs. Hemingway."

"No," Hemingway snarled. "This is *my* decision. *My life.* Mary, don't let them do this to me. It'll destroy me!" Wild-eyed, Hemingway looked from Mary to his doctor and back to his wife. "Pickle, please get me away from here." Creedy knew that one of Papa's sons had been given electroshock therapy. So Hemingway *knew* too well what it did to the brain. And with all Hemingway's concussions, there might be no coming back.

Then, over his doctor's shoulder, Hemingway saw him . . . standing there skinny and grinning, wearing a doctor's coat. Hemingway snarled, "Creedy! You cocksucker! *You're* behind this." He said to Mary, "That man! He's fucking FBI! His name is Donovan Creedy—I've told you about him before, Mary, remember? He's one of Hoover's fucking storm troopers!"

Creedy shivered a little—this wonderful tingle coursing through him to have Hemingway recognize him here, now. *Delicious* that Hemingway now knew who was behind his undoing . . . his imminent destruction at the hands of these doctors.

"You see the level of paranoia, don't you Mrs. Hemingway? Now, if you'll sign this . . ."

Hemingway screamed over and over. "Creedy, please, no!"

He felt the rubber bit being forced into his mouth so he wouldn't crack his teeth.

This flash of white . . . pain and straining.

From far away, in what he thought might be a dream, the old man heard Creedy say, "No. Again. And again after that."

There was another crackle and white flash; the old man felt his brain explode.

***

"Only one marriage I regret. I remember after I got that marriage license I went across from the license bureau to a bar for a drink. The bartender said, 'What will you have, sir?' And I said, 'A glass of hemlock.'"

—Ernest Hemingway

42.   THE TRUE GEN

Traced in pink ink on her map, Hannah and Hector's cross-country itinerary resembled nothing so much as a horizontal lightning bolt, or the EKG readings of a terminally arrhythmic heart patient.

Hector was Hannah's self-described wheelman. He'd bought a baby bed with aluminum hooks that fastened to the backseat of his blue-and-white Bel Air.

Hannah and Hector zigzagged north and south. All the while, they continually moved westward on Mary's nickel, carefully interrogating the usual suspects, whose names routinely recurred in a bookcase-worth of miscellaneous biographies and memoirs spread across the longer, if not better, span of too many tumultuous, bloody decades.

Inquiries and interviews, en route to Idaho.

The old woman lit another cigarette with her shaking hand as Hannah unbuttoned her blouse and situated Bridget. The usual baby-bird, open-mouthed, head-thrashing side-to-side commotion ensued until Bridget was secured at Hannah's right breast. Hannah's scribbled-over notebook lay open by the wire recorder.

Hector sat across the room, smoking a cigarette, watching Hannah and Bridget, too aware of this silly smile on his face.

"It was never about death infatuation," the old woman said. "Never,

ever about that. Not for any of them. They were both sick as hell. So many sicknesses. Daddy was suffering from diabetes and paralyzing headaches. He had high-blood pressure. Poor, poor Ernest...."

The great man's sister shook her head slowly. "I read a book once listing all of the injuries he sustained in his life. It was set in little tiny type that made me reach for my glasses, but it filled three pages. Imagine that—three pages." The elderly woman shook her head. "Life had become utter hell for him, and he died on his own terms. Please, dear, leave it at that."

Hannah made an overseas phone call as Hector swabbed her daughter dry following her bath. The receiver was tucked between Hannah's shoulder as she scribbled notes.

Hector rested the little girl on the foot of the bed and began to dress the baby.

Hem's Cuban doctor wrapped up:

"More and more, there after the plane crashes and the many sicknesses that resulted from same, Papa was tired and through and not a damned bit happy about it. I was his doctor during all of his time in Cuba, and I am amazed—amazed, you hear me—that he survived into the 1960s. One of his so-called 'biographers' should give him credit for his incredible feat of sheer willpower embodied by his living past the middle 1950s. Do you understand what I say? Me? I would not have lasted so long. And perhaps not you either. But Papa endured."

Hannah thanked the old Cuban physician for his time, watching Hector playing with Bridget as the old doctor broke the connection at his end. There was a pause, then a distinct, second click of a connection being broken.

Ice down Hannah's back. She hung up and said, "Hector, I think this phone is tapped."

Hector frowned and handed Bridget to Hannah. He sat down with the phone and called his answering service ... jotted down some notes.

Hannah looked at his notes to see what kind of calls the crime writer was receiving: Mary Hemingway, many times ... Alfred Hitchcock ... Sam Ford ... Bud Fiske, the gadfly noir poet. A man named Tilly ...

Hector said, "Thanks, Suzie," and hung up, but kept the phone to his ear—heard that second click. Hector frowned. He hung up the phone. "Someone's tapped it sure enough. I'm thinking FBI. Only Hoover, or someone like him, could set something up like this with this kind of speed." He smiled sadly. "Suppose it's the price you pay for hanging with me, here forward." Rueful, he said, "I think I'm Hoover's new hobby." He smiled, said, "That's okay, 'cause he's mine, too."

Hannah suffered a night of tangled dreams—feverish vignettes that unreeled like some poorly cranked, badly edited, and sometimes-silent film punctuated by restlessly shifting points of view.

The worst was something more akin to a memory:

Hannah's father, Malcolm MacArthur, a large, burly, muscled man with thinning gray hair and a hoary beard, loomed over his smaller, blond daughter. He tore at her flannel nightgown. Malcolm reeked of the black, single-malt whisky he had emptied from the bottle left discarded on the nightstand by his daughter's bed.

As she struggled to escape him, Malcolm wrapped his hands around Hannah's shoulders, forcing her back onto her bed. Malcolm tried to wedge his tongue between his daughter's lips, supporting himself with one big hand while the other fumbled with his souvenir Nazi belt buckle.

Hannah shut her eyes tight against the broken glass that fell in her face as she smashed the heavy Loch Dhu bottle against her father's forehead. Regretting her attack, she clumsily tried to brush the blood from the terrible cut above her father's left eye as, roaring, he staggered back from her bed. Hannah's gown and hand were slick with her father's blood.

She stared at the blood for what must have been a very long time, for her father was now gone, and she found herself on another couch, but this time sitting with a kindly old constable.

The nice old man had come to tell her that her father—who stormed out of the house drunk and angry and bleeding—was reported by another motorist to have been recklessly driving his lorry in wet-falling snow around Lochleven Side.

The other driver saw Hannah's father's plunge to his death when he missed a hairpin turn above Caolasnacon. Although visibility was generally good, there were no skid marks found in the truck's snowy wake—no sign at all of any attempt to brake.

Evidence pointed to suicide, the old lawman confided carefully. Indications, he said, were that Malcolm MacArthur had deliberately driven his truck over the cliff.

The old man squeezed Hannah's hand and raised his eyebrows. "Was yer father drumly—*depressed*—when he left? Upset over anything? Lassie, can ye think of any reason, any reason at all, yer papa would want to hurt himself?"

Hannah shrugged and said, "No sir, nothing at all."

Hannah felt someone gently shaking her then. She realized she was in her hotel bed, bathed in sweat. Hector wrapped an arm around Hannah's shoulders and stroked her damp blond hair behind her ears with his big and callused hand.

Hannah blinked a few times, her eyes adjusting to the dark. She saw the connecting door between their hotel rooms was open. Hector said, "You were screaming...dreaming. A very nasty nightmare, I mean." Hector was sitting on the edge of the bed, hugging her. He had on a pair of boxers. Hannah hugged him back, feeling scars on his naked back.

Very aware of her sweat-slicked fingers on his skin, he said, "You have nightmares like this often, honey?"

"Pretty often, aye." She was still shaking, holding tightly to him, but stroking his back.

"Me too," Hector said, stroking her back as well. "Helps a bit if I write a little just before I go to bed. Gives my subconscious something else to gnaw on overnight."

"I'll try that," Hannah said. "At least I didn't wake Bridget. I'm sorry I woke *you*. I suppose when Bridget is weaned, I'll get back on the medications."

"Like hell." Hector nodded at his portable typewriter. "*There's* your medicine; that's your shrink."

Hector moved out of their embrace. His hand traced her damp cheek. "Must have been a pretty intense nightmare," he said. "You're just soaked."

She nodded. Hector was aware of her looking at him...realized he was nearly naked. "I'll go and fetch a robe," he said.

Her hand on his bare shoulder, stroking it. "No, it's okay."

"Well, you should get back to sleep, darling. It's one A.M. Still plenty of time to rest up."

Her hand was still on his shoulder . . . her fingers trailed downward, her nails dragging down through his graying chest hair. Hannah said, "Hector, I've been watching you with Bridget. I've been thinking a lot about us. About what we could be. You're a very good man."

"You're a beautiful liar," Hector said. "It would probably be a mistake. And Christ, I'm just an old guy. Hell, I don't even buy green bananas anymore."

"You're not old to me. I think you're maybe the finest, most vital man I've ever met." Hannah pulled him toward her. Hector's resistance was token.

She appraised him again, smiling: He was still fit; still had his muscle tone. As her fingers traced the lines around his mouth, Hannah said, "And I am *such* a goner for dimples."

"It's a mistake," Hector said again.

"A mistake we'll make together, aye? That way there'll be no blame to be placed later."

Hannah kissed him, taking charge. "Wasn't that fine, Hector?"

She slipped her wet nightgown over her head and cast it to the floor. She felt his fingers stroking the aching nipples of her milk-swollen breasts . . . then his mouth there, suckling. Hannah's fingers wrapped around his neck and back, drawing Hector down with her onto the damp sheets.

A clique of celebrity-minded hero worshippers surround Hemingway wherever he goes.... To them, Hemingway is a man of genius whose fame will be remembered with Tolstoy.

—CONFIDENTIAL MEMO TO J. EDGAR HOOVER

CREEDY—New York, 1961

He was back in the clinic—in Creedy's hands again. Another round of electroshock that robbed the old man of concentration, robbed him of emotional control and memory . . . robbed him of words.

The old man had managed one last bit of prose, though—a crudely scrawled sign he insisted be posted on his door: FORMER WRITER. Creedy heard Mary tell a doctor the sign broke her heart.

Hemingway lay in his bed, crying. Creedy, dressed in a white lab coat, crouched down next to the bed. His young partner stood with his back to the door, guarding it.

Creedy said, "I told you years ago, one day you'd end up back in the States, and I'd have you to myself."

Hemingway struggled to focus his eyes: "Creedy?"

"That's right, *Papa*. My young friend over there is George Abbott. He's Bureau. I'm not, anymore. Another thing you took from me, in a way. That revelation you shared with me in Africa . . . well, that soured the Bureau for me. How's it feel, Hemingway? To lose everything? After the Bay of Pigs fiasco, you know you can never go back to Cuba. Your house, your boat, your writings there . . . all your books and possessions—they're Castro's now. But I've taken more than that from you. I'm the one who saw the juice was put to you. Wrecked your mind. Stole the words from you. I just wanted you to know, it's me who got the last laugh, *Papa*."

Creedy leaned in closer with a wicked smile. "And when the world learns the state you're in now, that you're quite insane, well, all those 'great novels' of yours won't matter for shit. Me, on the other hand? They'll be reading my novels long after the worms are done with you."

I don't know much about creative writing programs. But they're not telling the truth if they don't teach, one, that writing is hard work, and, two, that you have to give up a great deal of life, your personal life, to be a writer.

—Doris Lessing

43. ROAD WORK

Sitting in the diner after, scribbling away in a notebook, Hector looked up as a skinny shadow fell across his page.

Donovan Creedy.

"There goes the neighborhood," Hector said. He'd been wondering how long it would take Donovan Creedy to come straight at him.

Hector sat back in the booth, smiling and winking. "Take a load off, Creedy."

Pushing his coffee aside, Hector picked up his notebook and pen. He capped the latter and shoved it into the pocket of his sports jacket. The notebook he placed on the seat beside him. "I've read some more of your *thrillers* since our last confab, Creedy. Well, two or three more—all I had the belly for. They're shitty. And with all the politics you've freighted in there, suckers are going to date worse than Dos Passos' stuff did. People reading potboilers don't much cotton to being lectured to. Why are you here? Since you hounded Hem into his grave, you need a new project? Am I the lucky son of a bitch?"

"The Director is concerned some materials that Hemingway may have possessed might have been passed to you. I'm here on instruction from Mr. Hoover to give you the chance to voluntarily turn over those materials, if you have them, and he will pull back on your surveillance. You've seen these past few days how it can be for you, going forward. I'm giving you a chance to dodge that. Not my own choice, of course."

"That's mighty *white* of Edgar," Hector said. He smiled when he saw Creedy's reaction to that simple statement.

Hector said, "Frankly, I'm rubbed the wrong way by all this. After all

I've done for the Bureau, informally, but importantly, over the years? Well, this is a stick in the eye. And I still mean to harm you at some point, Creedy. For Patricia. Figure it was you Hannah saw from her window just before she and her baby almost died. Figure you were there to kill her, like you vowed to. And you did help kill Hem, in a thousand different ways. I've been thinking more, too, about this plot I foiled of yours to fob off all this bogus stuff as Hem's. Thinking of ways to maybe return the favor. Tell me, that pro-Castro piece of crap you snuck in: That *had* to be your work, didn't it? I mean, the falsity of the sex scenes alone was a tipper."

Creedy said, "What happened to that manuscript, Lassiter?"

Hector winked. "Destroyed. Try that again, and I swear I'll do you and your boss damage with *another* Hemingway manuscript." He shook his head. "Just can't believe old J. Edgar would turn on me like this after so many fires I hauled his fat and overtaxed ass out of."

Creedy scoffed: "Any services you rendered the Bureau were voided by your activities in Nashville in 1958. The Director is still furious at what you did there. Me, too. You and your lamentable white man's burden driving you to do all *that . . . Jesus*. Bad as Hemingway."

"What do you mean?"

"Hemingway and his adventuring in that uprising in the Dominican Republic in 1947. And then his last Africa trip. Time I spent chasing his ass around the bush in 1954 cost me operational success in a more important objective. I was *this* close to killing Jomo Kenyatta in prison. I'd have changed history, single-handedly. But chasing Hemingway, I lost my chance. Now Kenyatta's president of Kenya, and the white man has most probably lost the whole of Eastern Africa. Worse, the uprisings over there are stirring up the uppity coloreds back *here*. I could have stopped all that—headed it off."

Hector shook his head. "You're certifiable. Tell me, where's Hem's suitcase? Where are my other writings?"

"Safely hidden. Like this manuscript Mr. Hoover wants."

"Not all of it safely hidden. You evidently tried to peddle a little of my stuff to some bookseller—half the reason I'm on to you, cocksucker."

Son of a bitch: Creedy *had* done that—tried to sell one of Lassiter's few signed pieces. Creedy had done that during his lean time, before Hoover took Creedy back into the fold. If Hoover ever found out he had done that, and that his attempt to profit on Lassiter's old prose had been what had drawn Hector into the fray . . . Still, Creedy couldn't help himself. He said, "I'll yet destroy Hemingway with my manuscripts. Mark my word."

He struck Hector as reckless enough to try and do just that, independent of Hoover.

Creedy said, "I'll trade you. The suitcase and all its contents for the Hemingway manuscript you hold." He hoped Lassiter would say *no*: Creedy was only extending the offer of trading the suitcase because Hoover had ordered him to do it.

"No. Never." Hector chewed his lip. "*Still*, it *would* be nice to drive somewhere without having some asshole in a black sedan riding my Bel Air's bumper. Be heady to end a phone conversation without that extra click. To get an envelope in the mail that doesn't look to have been steamed open and then resealed. I *do* have something for you. Hang here a couple of minutes, Agent. Need to run to my hotel room and fetch something."

Creedy's car was easy enough for Hector to find: standard Bureau issue.

Afterward, he walked back into the diner and took up his seat across from Donovan Creedy.

Hector tossed the empty sack at the agent, spilling a few remaining white granules onto the table between them.

Frowning, Creedy picked up the empty Domino Sugar bag. "What's this?"

"What's left," Hector said. "The bag's contents are in the gas tank of your jalopy."

The agent looked incredulous: "You poured sugar in my gas tank?"

"All of it. Some bird seed, too. Kid stuff, I know. But effective all the same. Just to make sure you don't follow us when we leave here in a few minutes," Hector said. It was all about buying time—time to get back to Idaho and Mary . . . to take the next step to secure Hem's literary legacy from further tampering by Creedy. He said aloud, "And further to that end . . ."

It was one of his oldest moves, but still effective: Hector slammed his heel down on top of the agent's foot. As Creedy howled and banged his knee into the underside of the table, Hector reached across, grabbed

Creedy around the back of the head, and slammed his face into the tabletop.

Smiling his apology to the ashen-faced diner owner, Hector threw a Hamilton on the table, said to the proprietor, "For your trouble, buddy. When he comes to, he'll likely want some ice for what's left of that nose."

BOOK SIX

How It Was

I am as I am
And not as Papa wishes
Is it my fault
That I am so?

—FROM A SONG BY MARY HEMINGWAY

44.   COLLABORATORS

Upon seeing Mary again, Hannah was seized by the notion Papa's wife might be capable of drinking Papa under the table if he still lived.

Hannah had been with Mary for less than an hour, and the elder widow was already draining her fourth cocktail.

Mary's lemon-tinted hair was scraped back this morning, and the hairdo revealed large, just-short-of-comical ears. She looked badly hung-over, and a bit thinner than she had the last time Hannah had seen her: the eyes sunken into deep-set orbits. The high, sinisterly slashing cheekbones and jutting chin had grown prominent to no good effect. The arching crow's-feet that nearly latticed Mary's sunken eyes to her big ears were always there now—not just when she smiled her closed-mouth camera smile.

The widows had arrived in Ketchum within an hour of one another. Thinking Mary was perhaps tired from the long journey from her New York penthouse back to Ketchum, Hannah suggested a nap before they started interviews: "We could maybe both have some luck so that just when you wake up, Bridget will be conked out again like she is now." The baby was resting in her travel bed in the next room.

The old widow smiled. "My, she looks just like you—not an iota of Dickie in there. And it's all right if we start right away: I'm not really tired enough to sleep, and I'm eager to get underway. Well, after a drink, I'm eager to start. Tell me you'll please have something this time."

Hannah chewed her lip. She had used the breast pump before coming over out of deference to Mary: Hannah feared breast-feeding in front of the elder widow might spark bad memories of Mary's near-fatal attempt at childbearing. There were three bottles of formula for spot feeding stashed in Mary's refrigerator. Hannah figured she could likely metabolize whatever she drank before Bridget would require a "source" fill-up.

"Och," Hannah said, arching an eyebrow and putting on a pan-loaf accent. "A wee dram. And that's truly all."

"That's my lassie. What's your preferred poison, sweetie?"

"How about a glass of wine? Preferably red."

Mary beamed, reaching for her pack of Kents. "Great. I'll have one, too. I think we'll make it a nice Barolo. Something Papa used to favor." A hovering maid scurried to draw the cork before she was asked.

"I was going to put you up here, but we're still reopening the house and there's some painting to be done," Mary said. "I've got you a room at the Best Western—okay?"

"Fine."

"You're sure?"

"Yes."

"Hector with you?"

"Aye. My wheelman, as he calls himself. I think it's gangster language."

"I'll get him a room, too. As he's working for me as well, right?"

Hannah smiled. "I think Hector's seeing to his own lodging."

"Of course." A smile Hannah couldn't read, but it wasn't a friendly smile.

The maid handed Hannah her glass of wine. "Cheers," Hannah said and raised her glass. Mary ignored her, said: "Papa's old friend Maury said you made it by."

"Yes," Hannah said, her tongue's tip tingling from her first sip of wine in months. Strong stuff—oak, smoke, and cinnamon. Sublime. Hannah hefted her glass of wine. "It's been a while. Wow."

Mary shook loose a cigarette. "He's doing fine? *Maury*, I mean."

"Seems to be. Claims he is working on his own memoirs."

"He told Papa the same thing in 1953."

"I hope he finishes. One good book about a life like his is certainly something to want to see finished, however long it takes to get it right."

"Sure. It's taking me more time than I expected to write mine."

Hannah smiled.

"I frankly need you to be quicker. What with two unofficial biographies on Papa coming—one written by a man who I can already tell hates me—and the bullfighting and edited *Garden* books coming out eventually . . . well, I could easily be eclipsed by all the hullabaloo that will ensue about Papa. I really need to get out there in the forefront, pronto."

"Of course," Hannah said.

"You have Dickie's manuscript—what there is of it?"

"Aye," Hannah said. "The authorities here boxed it and sent it to Michigan with his other things."

"I'm sorry about what happened, by the way. I never would have wished him dead. Not for your sake, or your little girl's. Daughters need daddies. I'm sure you'll find a man to stand that duty. Some handsome young fella."

Hannah smiled.

Mary smiled back. "Are you doing okay? Living with it, I mean?"

Hannah knew that she didn't have to tell Mary a self-destructive husband's death could come as a nearly welcome respite—a blessing in deadly disguise. Hannah shrugged. "I'm fine. In my heart, I know that Richard did it to himself. These things happen. What else is there to say?"

Mary expelled a thin stream of smoke. "Indeed." A strange smile—a rare one showing teeth. "Do you speak any Spanish, Daughter?"

"Just French. A good bit of Gaelic."

"*Sic transit hijo de puta.*"

Hannah frowned. "What does that mean?"

"He will be missed," Mary said, smiling crookedly. "There is another good one, too: *Dame acá, coño que a los mios los mato yo!*"

Hannah frowned. "What does that one mean?"

"Give it to me, damn it, I kill my own!"

Hannah stared at her hands. "Oh," she said . . . suddenly a bit afraid.

Mary shrugged and drew on her cigarette. "Before we leave this sad subject, is there much there? Much you can use? Of Dickie's manuscript, I mean."

Hannah shook off a chill. "Maybe. There are about two hundred handwritten pages. Nearly all of your early biography is set in first draft. Most of the 1940s, after you met and married Papa, are there, too. The

1950s are laid out in note form. Richard's structure for the book seems pretty sound as outlined. His and my prose styles vary a good deal, however. I'll have to rewrite extensively."

"Honey, it's always like that," Mary commiserated. "God, the rewriting I had to do on Papa's last stuff—I can't tell you."

Hannah shivered again.

Mary groaned. "Gawd, what I had to do to prepare *A Moveable Feast*. I hate to tell you."

"Heavy lifting, huh?" Hannah felt her own jaws tighten and wondered if Mary noticed.

"Had to throw out Papa's sequence for the chapters to make the thing flow the way I wanted. That caused continuity problems that I had to fix. And his titles for the book . . ." Mary rolled her eyes. "My God, how awful those were. His final choice for the thing was *The Eye and the Ear*. Can you imagine that in lieu of *A Moveable Feast*? Truly?"

"No." Hannah couldn't.

"Still . . . it was nothing compared to the work necessary to finish *Islands in the Stream*." The elder widow sighed. "What else? Anything there to indicate Richard had everything he needed to finish?" Hannah met Mary's gaze—the old widow searching her face for any sign of a lie. "I ask," Mary continued, "because Richard made it pretty clear that night before, well, you know, that we were finished. He said he had the perfect ending. I keep racking my brain to remember what I might have said in our last interview that would have given it to him."

Those drunken eyes, searching hers . . . Hannah sipped her wine. "Richard must never have had a chance to write it all down—his first draft simply trails off inconclusively, sometime around mid-1960, I guess."

Mary sighed heavily. She laughed softly to herself. "That's . . . too bad." She shook her head, showing teeth in her smile. "Well, damn. Oh well. Guess I'll just have to keep trying to remember what got said that last night. I have a pretty good memory, you know. Better than average."

Hannah smiled encouragingly. "I'm sure."

Mary said, "Not like Papa's—his may have been photographic. Well, at least until they hit him with the juice."

There's a sucker born every minute ... and two to take him.

—Wilson Mizner

45. SHELL GAME

Creedy stood on a hill overlooking the Topping House, snarling into a radio as he watched it all unfold below him with binoculars. The first truck had rolled out, filled with boxes he presumed to be Hemingway's manuscripts: He'd heard Hector and Mary arrange the move over the phone the previous night—heard through this new handheld listening device that could pierce even concrete walls.

It was a big truck, and Creedy's trailing crew had no trouble picking it up on the road out of Ketchum. Then, about five minutes later, a *second* eighteen-wheeler had rolled up to the Topping House. More loading was undertaken—it was far too much truck for too little job; no way Hemingway could have produced so much paper.

And yet . . .

He *had* to have that truck followed, *too*, didn't he?

Now Creedy was watching the *seventh* truck being loaded, and he was flat out of minions.

Cursing, Creedy ran to his own car and slammed a fist against the dash; no choice, he'd have to follow *this* truck himself.

Clearly it was a game Lassiter was playing—but Creedy had to play along; had to try and get access to those boxes in order to plant the damning materials for Hoover. Creedy *had* to find the right truck.

Through his own binoculars, hidden in a copse of trees, Hector watched Creedy pull off in pursuit of the seventh dummy truck. Each of the rigs was headed off down a different path, paid by Mary to drive empty cardboard boxes several hundred miles to several plats of nowhere.

Satisfied there was no more surveillance, Hector picked up his own radio.

It took Hector and his young poet friend fewer than five minutes to load all of Hem's manuscripts into a black, '65 Pontiac Bonneville convertible.

Hector handed a long thermos to Eskin Fiske and slapped his back. "God's speed, Bud: it's a long way to Cleveland, I know. But Jimmy will keep this stuff safe there, hidden at the Western Reserve until Mary picks the library to safely and permanently catalog and store it all. Give Hanrahan my best."

Bud said, "Can I read this stuff when I get there? I mean, think what I'm hauling..."

Hector slapped his young friend's arm. "Go to town, Bud. Savor the good stuff."

There was some nice irony in all this: Now, with all these authentic documents of Hem's, Photostatted on Hector's nickel and headed to some highbrow library somewhere, well, now all those critics and "scholars" who so plagued Hem during life would become Hem's armor, in a way. Afforded access to all the Hemingway leavings that Mary had, they'd be able to step in and wave a finger at the things Mary might otherwise dare to tamper with—they'd keep the little bitch's hands effectively tied. Hector felt *good*.

The Director said, "You seem to become ineffectual and butterfingered when this Lassiter is in the mix, Agent Creedy. Still, this business of the seven trucks... it *is* almost amusing. *Almost*."

"Let me cancel Lassiter. *Now*. I'd pay you for the privilege, sir."

"No. I've elected not to do that yet. The materials that Hemingway was holding over me—and by extension, the Bureau, for I am the Bureau, after all—those materials are still presumably in Lassiter's hands, but we don't know where. Lassiter has proven himself unexpectedly formidable in thwarting my will. We will wait until we have some opportunity to force the information from Lassiter in a fashion at once elegant and undetectable. We've been patient this long. We have to wait for the tide to turn the Bureau's way, which is to say, *my* way, as it *always* does."

Anyone who conceives of writing as an agreeable stroll towards a middle-class lifestyle will never write anything but crap.

—Derek Raymond

46.   THE WRITER'S CURSE

Hannah finished situating Bridget in her bed in the backseat of the Bel Air, then slid in front with Hector.

She said, "Why didn't you come in?"

"Had another task to see to," Hector said.

Hannah looked back over the seat at her sleeping daughter. She said, "I'm sorry about the baby every morning. Seems two and five are her hungry times."

"I'm sorry for you having to get up at those crazy hours." Hector was dimly aware of Hannah rising from their bed around two the past several mornings to answer her daughter's hunger cries. The five A.M. awakening was just fine with Hector: It was the very hour Hector rose every morning to write. He simply spent that first hour feeding the baby a bottle until she fell asleep.

He'd maintained a second hotel room in which to work in the early mornings. Hannah, more of a night owl and an evening writer, took the spare space over while Hector and Bridget slept.

He steered into the lot of the hotel complex Mary had found for Hannah. It was clean, but unremarkable. Hector had been toying with checking back into the Sun Valley Lodge and sneaking Hannah and Bridget in with him.

Hector looked around the parking lot and saw no green Impala. He carried Bridget, still sleeping, upstairs and waited for Hannah to place the travel bed on the hotel room's second bed. She propped a pillow on either side of the travel bed to keep it from rolling to the floor. She closed the drapes and kicked off her shoes as Hector tucked Bridget in. Over her shoulder, Hannah said, "She should sleep for an hour or two ... plenty of time."

Hector, distracted, toying with the phone—looking for another bug—said, "Time for what, darlin'?" Then he smiled as Hannah's blouse slipped to the floor.

Hector, still trying to catch his breath, said, "Soon as you come to your senses and want to call an end to this new wrinkle in our relationship, darlin', it's important to me that you know that you can do it with no worries about my feelings being hurt."

Hannah licked her lips and scowled, her breasts heaving with her own pants. "Why in God's name would I want this to end? You still think this is wrong, I can tell. But you're not enjoying being with me?"

"Oh, God, *enjoy* isn't the word." He shook his head. "Kid, do you really know how old I am?"

"It's irrelevant," Hannah said. "Let's not talk about this. Or about how long it may or may not last. Can't we just enjoy the moment?"

Hector smiled. "I tend to enjoy my life in retrospect. Never seem able to settle for being satisfied in the moment. Then, later, measured up against some later moment's unsatisfactory 'present,' well, *then* I see how good I had it earlier, and savor what I had or experienced before."

"What a terrible way to live," Hannah said. "That's disturbing... *and* sad."

"You're not the first to say it. I think it's the writer in me. The writer's curse."

"I write, and I don't live like that."

"Guess you're blessed."

Hannah shook her head. "Well, try to live in *this* moment, aye?"

He smiled. "Aye." His fingers trailed down her long back. He stroked her coccyx. "I surely don't deserve you, Hannah."

"I don't want to talk like that, either."

"What do you want to talk about?"

"New Mexico: Tell me about this place where you live now, Hector. I've never seen the desert. It sounds so lonely. Can we visit your house... Bridget and me?"

Hector kissed her then, long and slow. He said, "Just visit?"

Writing is hard work and bad for the health.

—E. B. WHITE

47.   A PURSUIT RACE

Mary phoned to beg off the morning's scheduled interview. She said she might feel better in the afternoon. Mary's voice was slurred and she came off as mildly disoriented. Twice, enigmatically, she called Hannah "Scrooby." Mary must be drunk, Hannah thought, because she should expect for Hannah to know the truth: that Hector was dominating the widow's late morning into early afternoon.

Hannah spent the morning rereading *A Moveable Feast*. She had fallen in love with the book upon first reading. It had immediately become one of the books that had made a difference for Hannah MacArthur, who wanted to be a fiction writer.

She remembered the book as swooningly romantic. A love story of a poor but loving young American couple newly discovering an ancient evocative European city, full of interesting people and places and exquisite art and cuisine and nearly every writer and painter of consequence of the early twentieth century.

This time, while her baby slept softly snoring at her side, Hannah read the book as *Papa* had intended, based on Hector's memory of the original manuscript as he had read it in Cuba in 1959. She read the chapters in the sequence Hem had set them out, and she skipped over the discarded concluding chapter that Mary had restored for publication two years after its author's death. It read as a very different book in that way, and now, knowing more of the biographical details of Papa's life, Hannah read the romantic passages regarding his first marriage as sadly self-delusional or coldly ironic.

The memoir emerged darker and more sardonic than she remembered, and it ended inconclusively with a mean-spirited and not particularly funny broadside at Scott Fitzgerald.

Hannah thought of the book with the title Papa had set forth, and on the whole, decided she preferred Mary's version of the *Feast*. Hannah felt guilty for thinking so. But maybe Hector was wrong about Mary. When it came to nursing Papa's long game, maybe Mary really knew best....

Hannah favored her romantic memory of the book, and regretted re-reading it and ruining that memory.

Mary canceled their afternoon interview, too.

Hannah left Bridget with one of Mary's maids, Renata, who had a three-month-old of her own and had offered to baby-sit on her days off, when Hannah might want to devote full attention to Mary or her manuscript.

Hannah decided to rent a bicycle from a sporting-goods shop.

While the owner slipped into a back room to get more change, Hannah eyed the double-barreled shotgun the proprietor had been cleaning and left leaning against the counter.

She thought about surreptitiously dipping her head down and taking the barrels into her mouth—just to see what it would be like—but Hannah's imagination was strong, and she could conjure up the likely sensations.

And the blue-barrels looked fouler and harder and fatter and worse than the worst thing Hannah had ever taken into her mouth.

The proprietor returned, smiling, and handed Hannah her change and a small, laminated map upon which he'd traced a shortened scenic route for her. From a next-door deli she bought sandwiches and a bottle of spring water, and stashed them in a small knapsack with her notebook and pen.

Hannah stopped early for lunch under some trees several hundred yards before the turnoff into the Sun Valley parking lot.

She tried, fitfully, to get an opening chapter about Mary going in her own words, but found that it just wouldn't come. Richard's plan for the book was chronological. Hannah felt it better to lead with the true events of July 2, whatever they might be, and work back from there.

A big crow landed close by, cocking its head and shifting its gaze from Hannah's face to her sandwich, all the while cawing. Hannah tore off a corner of the ham sandwich and tossed it to the *corbie craw*. The crow picked it up with his black beak and tipped his head back, his oily black throat undulating as he swallowed the wheat bread.

The crow then pecked at the meat and tomato—shaking its head side to side when it tasted honey-mustard. As the crow became more demanding, Hannah set her notebook aside and courted the bird's interest—parceling out small morsels of sandwich and chips. She poured some of the spring water into a little receptacle she made of the sandwich's waxed paper wrapping and set it down next to her. The big black bird ponderously hopped closer, watching Hannah with one black eye as it took the water in swift dips—its fast-moving black beak opening and closing repeatedly with each savored sip.

When others of his kind came to claim a share of his discovery, the first bird cawed once angrily and shook out its black feathers. Hannah dubbed him Wilson as the black bird took wing.

Finicky bastard.

Back on the bike.

Although Hannah couldn't face her dead husband's grave yet, she felt unaccountably compelled to visit the scene of the professor's death.

Hannah pedaled farther up the gradual slope of Sun Valley Road, aware now of a pair of other bicyclists distantly trailing her.

She passed the Sun Valley complex and the Dollar roads to the down-sloping, worn-through-weeds path to Trail Creek and the Hemingway Memorial—a simple bronze bust mounted on a stone pillar, set into a rock squatting in the center of the creek.

Hannah, suddenly shaking and short of breath, found no trace of blood on the half-wet rocks in the stream on either side of the memorial. A small tree had fallen across Trail Creek, affording treacherous access to the tiny island of the stone memorial, and Hannah thought that per-haps Richard, drunk, had tried to catwalk across the wet log and lost his balance. Again, there was no sign of an accident—but of course one couldn't chalk-outline a creek bed. And time had passed.

Spooked, Hannah wiped damped palms down her jeans and climbed back on her bike, grateful the road sloped back down toward Sun Valley, and strangely comforted by the brisk wind across her wind-burned face; glad for the fast, long, downhill glide back into town.

She looked back over her shoulder to glance at the setting sun, and saw the man.

Richard's old stalker was trailing her on a bike: tall, thin. No sports jacket—a windbreaker, khaki shorts, and tennis shoes. His bony legs were sunburned. So were his cheeks. Same widow's peak . . . same glasses, but now adorned with clip-on shades. Harry Jordan—the two-faced private eye.

Instinctively, impulsively, Hannah slammed on the brakes, skidding to one side and nearly upending her bike.

Jordan nearly collided with her, veering to one side and leaning down, into the wind, pedaling furiously. Hannah pointed the front wheel of her bike downhill and set off in pursuit. The man's long bony legs were cranking. Hannah saw him crouch low, limiting his wind resistance. She did the same, leaning down low over the handlebars, pedaling furiously, the muscles in her thighs burning.

They shot past the lodge, on the downhill run now, past grazing horses, down into town: intersections; cross traffic was picking up.

And there was a semi, closing fast.

The private eye made a suicidal push of the pedals and narrowly cleared the grill of the truck—its air horn blaring and eighteen wheels squealing.

Hannah veered, hit the brakes, and jumped a curb. She felt the center of gravity shift as the back tire of her bike rose.

Hannah threw herself to the right, trying to lay the bike down before she would go over the handlebars. She rolled across the pavement, bike bouncing behind her. Some pedestrian stooped to stop her before she smacked the brick wall of a pub.

Bumps. Bruises.

Blood and aching bones.

The doctor found her elbow wasn't broken, but still "worrisome." He made it clear—she was to follow-up with him. Hannah promised to follow his advice to the letter.

Revenge has no more quenching effect on emotions than salt water on thirst.

—WALTER WECKLER

48.   WRATH

"I thought you'd still be at Mary's."

He wasn't to be distracted. Hector said, "Mary's maid called her to say you'd been injured."

Hector checked Hannah's bandages. "All this from a bike accident? I don't buy that. What really happened, Hannah?"

"I really wrecked a bike." Hannah was nursing Bridget. Repositioning her daughter, Hannah winced. Because she was nursing, she'd had to refuse pain medication for her scrapes and bruises . . . still driven to forgo anything she might lactate.

"Tell me everything," Hector said.

She did that, watching the rage that her story stoked inside Hector. Hannah was unsettled by the focused anger she could see building inside him. Hector didn't get red-faced or visibly angry, but his pale blue eyes narrowed . . . his voice grew cold. She'd never seen such concentrated hatred. He said once, "Harry Jordan. Well . . . You'll be okay here, for a time. I'm going out and *end* this."

Hannah said, "Where are you going?"

"Better you don't know. Please, trust me on this."

"Let's call the police. I'll file a report."

"Those bastards have already failed the mission: trust me on that. Trust me on the rest, too. Rest up, then I'll buy you girls dinner when I get back."

He left quickly then. She heard him try the door from the outside, making sure it was locked. Then she heard his voice through the door: "Put that chain on the door, too, when you're next up, Hannah."

———

They were on the deck of the Topping House. Buzzards wheeled overhead. Deer drank from the river.

Mary said, "I will not be fucking lectured by you, Lasso."

"This isn't a lecture, Mary," Hector said. "This is a reading of the riot act before I get down to stopping this business on my terms. I can't believe after our last talk that you still paid to have that son of a bitch follow us around town here. Christ, Mary—you're like a distaff J. Edgar Hoover. I thought we were allies."

"And you're a fucking pathetic mess, Lasso. Look at you, a man your age, sleeping with that young girl. You're old enough to be her child's great-grandfather. And she's a distraction from this other—our campaign against Hoover."

"You nearly made that little baby an orphan having your private eye chase her down that road on that bike."

"Things got out of control. It wasn't ever my intention to see Hannah hurt. I was just keeping everyone … honest. Making sure I didn't get burned by anyone with hidden motives. Not again. That asshole, Harry, he just lost control. Went too far."

"Oh, for Christ's sake," Hector said. "Please. I'm giving you notice now, Mary: My next stop is to see Harry Jordan, your private eye. One way or another, your business relationship with that son of a bitch is over, starting right now. If you hire another to replace him, I'm going to take it very badly and very personally. I'll come back here looking for satisfaction."

"Are you fucking threatening me, Hector? *Nobody* threatens me. Not anymore."

"Threats are cheap, Mary. I don't waste time with threats. I serve it up cold."

Mary pursed her lips; her chin jutting. "Oh, fine, goddamn it. Just fine. Now just forget about that chickenshit private detective and mix yourself a strong delicious drink and set your ass down and let's get to work on my book."

"Don't want your booze, and I have a promise to keep first."

"Forget Harry."

"Not in my nature."

Hector wondered if Mary had called to warn Harry Jordan that he was on his way over.

Harry wasn't answering his door, despite the fact his green Impala was still parked outside his hotel room. Hector knocked again, called, "Harry, open the goddamn door. It'll go easier for you that way than the other."

Hector pounded the door again, looking around while he waited. He saw two faint footprints—partial, bloody footprints on the pavement on either side of his own feet.

Hector carefully moved his feet, and frowning, cupped his hands to the glass of the front window to better see inside the hotel room.

A body was on the floor. The face had been pulped—frenzied overkill. A bloodied baseball bat lay on the floor next to the body. The dead man had a brown widow's peak... wore a blood-streaked nylon windbreaker familiar to Hector. Sure looked like what was left of Jordan....

Hector suddenly wished he hadn't stormed around in front of Hannah and Mary, issuing threats and promising violence against the dead man.

This familiar voice, all authority, behind him: "Turn around slowly, Mr. Lassiter. You're under arrest." What, *again*?

Hector did as he was told: Three local cops had guns aimed at his torso. Hector said, "What's up, boys?"

The too-familiar lead cop: "You're under arrest on suspicion of murdering that man in there."

Hector cursed softly. Donovan-fucking-Creedy: As a writer and a nemesis, he was a fucking one-trick pony. He said aloud, "For Christ's sake, not again...."

Some people walk in the rain, others just get wet.

—Roger Miller

49.   BOTTOMS UP

Hector sat across from the chief of police. The top cop passed Hector his Pall Malls and Zippo. The cop got out his own pack of Lucky Strikes, then handed Hector a frosty bottle of Coca-Cola. Hector looked at the last and shrugged. He said, "No rye?"

"Not for this talk," Chief Randy Paul said.

Creedy stood behind the one-way glass window, willing Hector to take a sip from that bottle of Coke he'd arranged for him in lieu of coffee or water.

"Let's go over it again," Chief Paul said.

"I'd just gotten there," Hector said. "Dust the damned doorknob, *both* knobs . . . I never even touched the son of a bitch. Hell, I don't think I touched the glass peeking through the window to see that body there. Jesus, Chief, look at my clothes—do I look like I beat a man to death with a baseball bat? I'd be covered in blood spray if I had done that. There's not even blood on my shoes' soles."

Well, Creedy had to give Hector *that* one: Creedy'd brought along a change of clothes and showered before leaving the crime scene. He'd been bathed in Jordan's blood.

It was a crazy constellation of circumstances that had led to Lassiter's arrest at the scene. Mary Hemingway's low-rent private eye had been following Richard Paulson, and actually witnessed the scholar's murder. Not realizing the forces he was dealing with, Harry Jordan had been dumb enough to try and shake down Donovan Creedy—to blackmail him for the murder he had witnessed.

Creedy knew Hector was spoiling to get at Jordan. So Creedy had decided to really take it to Jordan—make it look like a rage killing. Then he had dropped some of Lassiter's carefully preserved Pall Mall butts around the crime scene.

Hector showing up at the dead man's room, just minutes after Creedy had fled the scene and called the cops, fingering Hector, had been a delicious fluke . . . the kind of coincidence that would get you mocked if you used it in a thriller.

Staring at the tainted soft drink, Creedy whispered, "Drink the fucking cola, Lassiter. . . ."

Once he did that, Lassiter would confess to the Baby Lindbergh killing if the question was put to him.

Hector ground out his cigarette and began to fidget with the cola bottle. Creedy leaned in, crossing his fingers. Hector started to raise the bottle to his mouth, then shook his head and said to some question, "That's a *fucking lie*. I was *never* in the goddamn room. I couldn't have done this—again, I'm telling you, just call Mary Hemingway, she'll back me up on this."

The interrogation room's door opened. Some uniformed stooge leaned into his chief's ear. The top cop cut out for about two minutes.

Hector tried to make small talk with one of the flunky cops . . . tried to argue the case against himself with this young buzz-cut kid with a badge. Creedy figured Lassiter must really be sweating it if he was turning to this young idiot for help.

Shaking his head, Hector picked up the Coke bottle and raised it to his mouth again. Creedy licked his own lips.

Hector hesitated as the door opened again. "Okay, Lassiter, some new information has come to light."

The crime writer put down the unsampled Coke. The cop went to shake out another Lucky Strike and bumped the bottle with the back of his hand, spilling the cola across the table. Scooting back his chair to protect his slacks, Hector said, "What the hell?"

"Clumsy of me," the cop said. "So sorry."

Creedy said "Fuck!"

The chief said, "Us falsely arresting you is becoming a bad habit, Lassiter. Sorry."

Hector nodded. "It's not a habit you'll keep, brother. I mean to get out of this town, *forever*, and soon."

Chief Paul handed Hector his wallet and car keys. "Mary Hemingway made it clear you were with her when that bastard took his beating, just like you said she would. And that left no time to kill him and then clean up. Still, something hinky about you and all this. More funny? Mary asked me about a Fed named Donovan Creedy—wanted to know if he was on the scene here."

Hector nodded slowly. Thank God for Mary somehow showing some sand, even in her cups. "And *was* Creedy here? Maybe on the other side of that one-way glass?"

The cop shrugged. "Mrs. Hemingway said if this Creedy *was* around, I absolutely shouldn't let you drink anything."

Hector smiled thinly. Again Mary was surprising him. He said, "I *see.* Now I owe *you* a drink, buddy."

Creedy stabbed two fingers into the chief's chest. "You fucking rube! You *had* him! All those cigarette stubs of his. You saw his Pall Malls scattered around the scene. Those alone—"

The top cop grabbed Creedy's fingers and bent them back until Creedy winced and said, "Stop that. . . . Please."

Smiling, the old cop said, "You watch too much TV, G-Man. Probably a third of the men in town smoke PMs. Other two-thirds are smoking Camels or my beloved Lucky Strikes. Now get out of here, you dirty son of a bitch, before I start doing my job you're laughin' at me for. My gut tells me I should arrest *you* for that man's murder, 'cause I swear to Christ I make you as the killer. Maybe also of that poor girl we found in Lassiter's tub a time back."

Literature is a luxury; fiction is a necessity.

—G. K. CHESTERTON

50.   PREPARATIONS

Hector let himself into their room. Hannah rose from the typewriter and said, "I've been worried."

He kissed her hard.

Smiling, Hannah said, "What's that for?"

"Just good to see you."

"What's been happening? You're late."

Hector went for the kind lie: "Just errands. Baby asleep?"

"Probably for another hour."

He smiled, toyed with the top button of her blouse. "Spare a few minutes from your writing?"

"Aye." She looked at her bandages. This smile: "Still a bit stiff, though. Achy. May need your help undressing."

"Entirely my pleasure," he said.

Bridget was still asleep; Hannah was lingering in bed with Hector. The phone rang: Mary calling to set up their next day's interview.

"Time we get back at it, eh, Hannah? How are you feeling, by the way? Okay after the accident?"

"Feeling much better," Hannah said.

Mary changed the subject again: "I have an idea for the dustjacket art for our book! It's a montage of old photos of me, but painted. Just have to find the right painter." The cover concept struck Hannah as daft, but designing book jackets seemed to be a task Mary took real delight in.

A second call came five minutes later. This one was for Hector. He slid from her arms and began to dress. He said, "My parcel has finally arrived. Going to run out and get it."

Hannah said, "Parcel? What's in it?"

"Something for your interview tomorrow," Hector said. "Old memento from Hem, or really, from Pauline Hemingway, his second wife. Something I've been holding on to for a long time and a very special occasion. May loosen tongues. I'll fetch it now. Shouldn't take long." It wasn't as devious as Creedy's mystery brew, but Hector wagered it might have roughly the same effect.

That night, Hannah again lay in bed with Hector, sprawled half atop him, waiting for their hearts to settle. She said, "I was reading more about you at the library today. This article by this guy, Bud Fiske."

"About half accurate," Hector said. "The usual thing: People, even real good friends like Bud, too often confusing me with my characters. Happens to me all the time." He waved a hand, trying to brush it all away. "It's getting old. Persona killed Hem. I really believe that."

Hannah nodded slowly, then kissed his chest. "The novel you're writing now isn't going to help any of that."

"Too late to reinvent myself now, Hannah. Too late, leastways, under *that* byline. You've gotta dance with the muse who made you. Once they brand you, that is."

He remembered then, and slid from the bed. He slipped his Colt under the pillow and climbed back in bed with her. Hannah said, "You're not serious, are you?"

"I sleep that way all the time. Until the past few weeks, anyway. Out of deference to you, and out of trust in you, I stopped. Figure dicey as things are around us now . . ."

Hannah half-smiled, still skeptical. "You *really* always sleep with a gun under your pillow?"

"Really. Always."

"What have your other women had to say about you doing that?"

"Some of my other women are what got me started doing that."

Murder is born of love, and love attains the greatest intensity in murder.

—OCTAVE MIRBEAU

51. DEATH IN THE MORNING

When she arrived at the Topping House, Hannah found Mary sipping a drink that reeked of cocktail. It was 10 A.M.

"You're at it early," Hannah observed.

"It's noon somewhere." Mary frowned, then smiled her closed-mouth smile. "In New York, say. Figure my liver is still on Eastern Standard Time."

"Aha." Hannah shrugged off her coat, pointedly exposing her bandaged hands and arms.

The old woman held up her drink, letting it catch the morning light. "My latest craze," Mary said. "One ounce of sloe gin, an ounce of brandy, one-quarter lemon juice, and half of an egg white, served in a chilled cocktail glass. Here, taste—it's yummy."

Hannah was careful to sample from the opposite side of the glass from which Mary was drinking and took the smallest sip—just enough to get the taste of it. She hated the drink and made a face.

"*Yuck.* What's that called?"

" 'Kiss the Boys Good-Bye.' Want one?"

"Sorry. I'm back on the feeding detail." Bridget cooed in her still-bustier mother's arms. The maid took the baby from Hannah and bustled out of the room.

Hector entered then, holding his mysterious parcel. He leaned down and kissed Mary on both cheeks. He said, "Thanks for yesterday. And enough with the musical comedy drinks, *Pickle*. I have a big surprise for you. Something from the wicked old days."

Mary beamed mischievously. Hector held up his parcel, then pulled out a pocketknife and cut the twine binding it. He pulled loose the brown paper wrappers, opened the box, and pulled out more packing material . . .

soft foam. He said, "My housekeeper, Carmelita, maybe overdid the packing of this." Finally, he pulled out the bottle.

Hannah, frowning, said, "What's that?"

Mary, smiling, said, "Oh, I think I know. Aren't you the wicked one, Lasso?"

Hannah said, "What is that?"

"Absinthe," Hector said. He pulled out another smaller parcel. "Drip spoons and glasses," he said. "Trust you have some sugar cubes around, Mary?"

Another wicked smile. "You can trust, Lasso."

Hannah said, "I thought absinthe was illegal."

"Very," Hector said. "And for a long time. Back in 1935, in the Keys, an old painter brought three bottles of absinthe to a party at Hem's. This is the last of those bottles. After Hem and me had our falling out in 'thirty-seven, Pauline brought the last bottle to me. Said to hold on to it, thinking the three of us would share it once she had patched things up with Papa . . . taken him back from Martha. Once Hem and me had made up. All of that didn't happen like that."

Hannah wrinkled her nose. "Still safe to drink?"

Hector shrugged. "Hard to imagine it being more damaging than it was in its prime."

He winked at Mary. He said, "*In vino veritas*, yes? Warm the belly and loosen the tongue? You game, Pickle?"

Mary winked. "Set 'em up, Lasso."

Hector smiled and began preparing the absinthe.

"I'll pass on this," Hannah said.

"Absolutely," Hector agreed. "Bridget's too young to make her an absinthe fiend just yet."

Hannah was a bit dubious about Hector's strategy to get Mary drunk on absinthe: The widow Hemingway was already in the alcohol fog zone. Mary smiled drunkenly at her. "So, where do we start, Daughter?"

"At the end," Hannah said, smiling. "I told you: Richard has the rest covered."

"But you might think to ask something that he didn't." Mary smiled and accepted her first glass of absinthe. Hector seemed determined to nurse his.

"I've read your draft of your memoir," Hannah said. What a slog *that* had been. . . . Pressing ahead, she said, "I honestly can't think of anything else to ask about those years before summer 1961."

"Fine," Mary said grouchily. "Fire away, MacDuff." She took another drink of absinthe. She said, "You know, it's the first time I've had this. I could learn to love this. Jesus, it's got kick."

"Like a fucking mule," Hector said. "But when it's gone, it's *gone*."

Hannah said, "What did you mean about 'not depriving a man access to his possessions?' I mean, when you locked up all of Papa's guns, then left the keys to their hiding place in plain sight? What were you really thinking?"

Mary smacked her lips and sipped some more of her forbidden drink. "I know what you meant. Christ, Daughter: You go right at it, don't you? *Jesus*."

"What did you mean? About the keys, I mean."

"I meant what I said and I said what I meant."

Hannah shook her head. "I truly believe this is the most important thing left for us to talk about, Mary." Hannah moved closer, looking into the old woman's eyes and shaking her head sadly. "You know as well as I do that you have been vilified for that statement by everyone who loved your husband. By those who feel you somehow failed Papa—"

Pure venom from the widow now: "Ernest failed *me*. And he failed himself, the big weak cocksucker. He failed the concern." Mary's face was red.

Hannah held her ground. She sighed deeply. "Mary, I'm not telling you anything you haven't heard or read about yourself before," Hannah said, soldiering on. "The faithful aren't kindly disposed toward you, not at all."

Hector reached over and shook Mary's knee playfully. "Painting you as a sympathetic character is a tall order, Mary, you have to admit that. At least it's so when it comes to Hem's most passionate readers and scholars. You'll probably see the strongest attack against you made next year, when this professor from Columbia publishes his biography of Papa. I've heard his treatment of you in the book is acid. This is your chance to cut your critics off at their knees. You can neutralize them with candor, I think. Tell them why you locked up the guns, then deliberately left the keys in easy reach. Be frank and pull no punches."

The widow seemed to think about that. She chewed her lip. Hector watched her. He knew the look: casing angles; weighing gambits.

Hannah crouched down and squeezed Mary's hands. "This is about your legacy, you know. Your long game. You have to fight, and fight to win. The rest," Hannah said, stroking Mary's hair with her bandaged hand, "the rest doesn't matter."

Mary was fuming, her already prim mouth a blood-red gash now. She batted away Hannah's hand. "How long am I going to be forced to deal with this fucking, horse's-ass question? You're almost as bad as your use-less fucking drunken husband, pressing me on this fucking, tired old blather. How fucking dare you? Remember, you're working for me, missy." Mary held up her empty glass. "I'm empty, Lasso."

Hector handed her his barely touched glass and set about making two more.

Hannah kept her voice even: "It's the only question that matters, Mary—the one that stands between you and historical revilement, or re-spect. And you certainly do know that. It's the only question that matters, and the only one you've never satisfactorily answered. It's the question your critics will be asking long after we're all dust. Don't leave the critics and scholars this one to speculate and play games with. Not if you value your reputation. Not if you care anything about the judgment of history. That's the long game we both play to win, now. The hands of history are on our shoulders this morning."

Hannah was very aware of Hector watching her . . . measuring her strategies and angles of attack. She sensed he was taking a wary new mea-sure of her. He was so Old World in some ways.

Mary scowled. "I thought you were on my side, Daughter."

Hannah winked. "I am. I'm doing my job—the one you recruited me for. I'm doing what Papa, or Martha, or more importantly, what you, as a professional journalist, would do: I'm trying for the story as it *truly* hap-pened. In the end, that's the only thing that counts for writers like us, aye? Damn the consequences and the window dressing. Tell it how it was, just like you're titling your memoir. But you must dare to go even further than before—far out past the points you've ever gone before now, as Papa did at his best. And you must go still further—far beyond where Ernest ever dared go. Your own book doesn't tell the whole story. You weren't ready to share it when you wrote that draft. The whole, bloody world wasn't ready when it happened. But I wager you are ready now. You've proven yourself a thousand times over, and you stand above reproach. You've nothing to apologize for."

The absinthe had Mary now—Hector had seen it in the eyes of a few others, here and there. He winked at Hannah—their agreed-upon signal to really move in.

Hannah scooted closer, crossing her arms on Mary's lap, looking up into her eyes, besieging Mary to talk. "You stood by Papa and caught hell from him for your trouble. You stayed with him through his alcoholism and his depressions and his selfish brutalities and his sicknesses and stayed on through his decline into madness. You stuck by Papa to his bitter, bloody end, and when he was gone, you nursed his reputation back from the abyss of his self-destruction. You restored and secured Papa's greatness with your version of *Feast*. Don't you know that you're so far above and beyond reproach, Mary? Don't shy away from it anymore: Tell me why, Mary. Why did you leave the keys out where you knew Papa could easily find them?" Hannah waited a beat. She pressed down harder on Mary's bony legs. "Why did you leave them where you knew that Papa would find those keys?"

Mary drained her drink and dragged her sleeve across her tight little mouth. Her eyes were red-rimmed. "It was his time—long past his time. I owed it to him."

Hannah said softly, "How do you mean that, Mary?"

"I failed Ernest so many months before—that awful Friday morning in April when I found him sitting there with the shotgun and the shells. I shouldn't have gotten in his way. It would have been kinder to Papa to let him get the job done then and there. But instead I talked to him. Soothed and stalled him. He kept muttering over and over, 'Today is Friday.' I talked over him. Delayed and distracted him until George—Dr. Saviers— arrived. Then we overpowered Papa and sent him off to the shrinks— those fucking ghouls. I agreed to all their idiot treatments and those horrid electroshocks. It would have been kinder, in the end, if I had let Papa be that cruel April morning. Let Papa get the job done quickly and relatively painlessly when he was still capable of doing it for himself." Mary looked up, startled, as Hector placed a big hand on her shoulder and squeezed. He handed her another absinthe.

Hannah's skin tingled: *When he was still capable of doing it for himself.* Hannah sat up straighter. "Papa would truly have shot himself that morning, you think? Before the Mayo Clinic and the electroshock therapy?"

"Yes," Mary said, her eyes wet now. "Oh, yes. He was ready. It was his time. In stalling him till he could be subdued, all I did was cheat Ernest of escape, and consign him to a few more hellish months that destroyed what little was left of the man. He had every right to hate me at the end. And I waged my wars with him in letters and notes sent to him, bursting with ultimatums and indictments, just as his mother did. Those letters did neither of us any good."

Mary searched Hannah's face. The old widow's eyes were full of tears, and something had changed in them. "Just as bad as your old man. Badger, badger until you break me down. Just like your old man!" She took another deep drink of the absinthe . . . her eyes going farther and farther away.

Then Mary began singing softly:

Soy como soy,
Y no como Papa quiere
Qué culpa tengo yo
De ser así?

Hannah pressed: "What happened to Papa?"

It seemed that Mary was a long way away now, living in some bad memory. "I tell you, Daughter, Papa was clearly sick before that April morning. Sick, and so terribly tortured. He had been for years. All those awful injuries when the planes went down just piled up on him and destroyed him. The internal injuries and the terrible headaches. God knows how many concussions that poor old head of his sustained. When the second plane went down, there was a hole in his skull all the way down to his brain, and the stupid quacks were pouring gin in the hole and letting Papa drink while they worked on him. Papa was pissing blood and scraps of kidney for days.

"He was never the same after that," Mary said, shaking her head. "He'd have these terrible dreams and he'd wake up screaming and I couldn't convince him that he was truly awake and back safe with me. Papa said he couldn't tell his dreams from what was real anymore, and I said, 'They're still only dreams, darling, and so what can it really matter?' He sneered and said that I was a bloody fool."

Now Mary slipped into an imitation of her late-husband's voice, remembering some long-ago tirade, reciting it as if she were some rickety recorder: "'Dreams are as real as any real thing that happens to you when you're living within them,' he said. 'Dreams make you sweat and they make you short of breath as though you're really living it all. Dreamers are overtaxed and given heart attacks and routinely die in their sleep because of the exertions they make in their dreams. We pull muscles from using them in our dreams and wake up with cramps. Hell, dreaming of loving can make the young and even some of the old—a lucky few—actually come . . . or haven't you ever had a wet dream? Most of my own best little deaths have come in my sleep. Dreams, good or bad, are as real as the realest thing that ever happened to you when you're alive and moving within their country. And anyway, these aren't dreams I am having, they're bloody fucking nightmares.'"

Hannah remembered the bad summer of her own crack-up, when she had been wracked by the same horrible condition: swamped by dreams so real and detailed and mundane—dreams too-accurately mocking the dismal, mundane rhythm of her day-to-day existence. They left Hannah helpless to distinguish her waking from her sleeping hours. Even now, there were events in her life that Hannah couldn't be sure were real or imagined.

Mary sighed. "Ernest's ability to discern what was real around him became fuzzier. It got to be that just a simple thing like television did wicked things to his poor beleaguered brain: I was enjoying a presentation of *MacBeth* when I suddenly realized that Papa was not absorbed in, but rather terrified, by the program. Papa was quite insane—but not crazy, and that's the worst way of all to be." Mary kneaded her knuckles. "I'm coming to know that, on my own."

When he was capable of doing it for himself.

Hannah couldn't escape Papa's last wife's observation. Mary's phrasing of Papa's earlier, failed suicide attempt still resonated. Hannah said:

"July second, 1961: When you came down the stairs, Papa wasn't dead yet as you have always said before, was he Mary?" As she asked the question, Hannah extended her hand. Hannah held her breath. Mary, with a shaking hand, reached out and squeezed Hannah's hand.

Hector was smoking a Pall Mall and watching Hannah, his pale blue eyes narrowed.

"No." The old woman sobbed. "No, God forgive me, he wasn't. He wasn't dead yet."

"What was Papa doing when you found him downstairs, Mary?"

"He was sitting in the foyer with his gun—clutching his unloaded shotgun again and rocking back and forth. He was sobbing, and his hands were shaking so badly that he couldn't slip the shells into the breech. He couldn't even load his own damned gun anymore because his hands were shaking so badly. He kept dropping the shells. He couldn't chamber them, no matter how hard he tried."

Hannah took a deep breath. "What did you do?"

Mary squeezed Hannah's hand harder. "I talked to him, like a fool again. Just talked, talked, talked. Talked about *nothing*. Dithered on about seeing Paris together again. And Africa, and Spain. Talked of new places neither of us had seen, but might try: Alaska or Australia or Scotland or Wales."

Hannah winced at the mention of her homeland. "What did Papa say?"

"He smiled sadly, wiping his tears with his swollen, shaking knuckles, then he reached into his shirt pocket and handed me a note he had written for me.

"I read it over twice, crying, and squeezing his trembling hand as I read it. There was little left for him to say that he hadn't written out for me. I understood how miserable he was. I knew he was through and that it was cruel to keep him alive simply for the sake of keeping him alive."

Mary smoothed Hannah's hair, and Hannah rested her face on the old woman's lap. "I'm so sorry for you," Hannah said. "Such a burden to carry."

Mary smiled and stroked Hannah's blond hair. "God shapes the back for the burden, sweetie, don't you see?" Mary cupped Hannah's trembling chin. "It had to be that way—you understand, don't you? How it was cruel to deny Papa what he wanted? You see how it was?"

Hannah hesitated, then went with it: "I see."

"We both knew it was over," Mary continued, "but Papa couldn't kill himself, *himself*—you see? He said he wasn't capable, anymore. He said he needed me. He needed me to help him. So it really wasn't my fault, do you see? You see how it wasn't my fault, don't you, Daughter? Please . . . you have to see how it wasn't my fault that Papa died. He asked me to. He really did it himself after all, when you look at it in a certain light. You see that, don't you?" She looked from Hannah to Hector. "It wasn't *my* fault."

Hannah heard her own voice cracking. "So you . . . helped Papa? Is that how it was?"

Mary was sobbing and shaking now, her slight, sloped shoulders heaving and her breath coming in ragged gasps. Mary slumped over, still holding tightly to Hannah. Hannah felt Mary's tears, wet against the back of her own neck. "Did you help Papa, Mary?"

"Yes, yes. Yes, I did."

"Tell me how it was . . . please . . ."

"You don't blame me?"

"I swear to you—I don't blame you. It wasn't your fault. It wasn't anyone's fault but Papa's own. Maybe not even his fault. You were good to help him if that is what you did." Hannah felt her own body beginning to shake. "I just . . . I need to know exactly how it was. I need to know what happened, so we need never talk about it again."

The widow nodded. "He . . . he just begged me to help. I tried to argue, and he kept pleading—his sad, empty brown eyes besieging me. And I put the shells in the gun and handed it back to him. He hugged me and kissed me and tried to use it, but Papa's hands were shaking so badly he could hardly hold the gun. His arms seemed too weak to support it. Papa put the gun's butt against the floor and pushed his poor forehead to the barrels, but then couldn't reach the triggers with his trembling, striving fingers. He tried to use his foot—to use his toes. But he couldn't balance and nearly fell down. Finally, shaking and crying, he handed the gun back to me and fell back against the wall, crying. He whispered hoarsely: 'You have to help me, Kitten. Please? Please, darling? Won't you?'"

Mary sobbed again, and Hannah felt the old widow's nails digging into her shoulder. "Jesus, I didn't want to."

"It's okay. *Really*, Mary. You're not to blame. One way or another, you always lose them."

Mary nodded and smoothed Hannah's hair back.

"What happened next, Mary?"

Mary hung her head. "He handed me the gun. Ernest crossed himself, and he began to pray out loud—'Hail Mary, full of grace'—and I put the barrel to his forehead, and still praying, Ernest smiled. His sweet brown eyes crossed as he looked up at the barrel pressed between his eyebrows, and he said, "Holy Mary . . . at the hour of my death, I am sorry my love, but now, oh now my blessed Kitten . . .'"

Mary shuddered in Hannah's arms. The old woman, her cracking voice muffled against Hannah's shoulder, said:

"And I killed him."

Hannah held the old woman close. Hannah looked up at Hector—he turned, unable to face her, not wanting her to see his expression. His back to Hannah, Hector just shook his head.

The old widow sniffled several times. "There was a blinding white splash that turned pink, and a red splash across the oak paneling. Papa's headless body fell back, tumbling over, the awful mess of what was left of his head pumping and spraying blood on the walls and tile. Papa's red robe was covered with his blood, as was mine, and I dropped the shotgun, screaming, and tried to stop his body from falling. Tried to save him being hurt anymore—and the blood was pumping terribly from his neck and what was left of his chin as I grabbed the front of his robe and tried to stop him collapsing. I screamed and screamed and screamed and screamed, but Papa was still dead and I had killed him."

The nonsensical phrase that post–World War II Papa had become strangely fond of echoed in Hector's head:

How do you like it now, gentlemen?

Mary smiled and wiped her eyes.

Hannah scooted back, knuckles brushing her eyes dry. She could see it too vividly—the blood and all the bits of brain.

Mary said to Hannah, "What will you do with all of this?"

"I don't know."

"I'm so tired of carrying it alone."

"That time is over, Mary."

"If . . . if you decide, Daughter, that you do want to tell this story, will you please wait until . . ." The old woman smiled hopefully at Hannah. "Yes?"

Hannah nodded. "Yes."

Mary looked up at Hector. "And you, Lasso?"

Hector shook his head; Hannah searched for a word to describe his expression. . . . The writer in her settled on *ineffable*.

Hector said, "Hem was my *friend*. It's not my story to tell. Not a story I'm sure should *ever* be told. Old friend once said, 'When legend becomes fact, print the legend.'" He hesitated. "You said Hem had written you a note, Mary . . . an actual suicide note. What became of it? What did Hem write?"

"I hardly remember now," Mary said. "Not after everything that morning . . ." She was quiet; then her voice became strange. "There was the other thing, too. I ran to the phone to call for help—to change from my bloody clothes. I left the letter there on the table. When I came back, it was missing. I never found it again."

Hector narrowed his eyes. "Missing? Where the hell could it go?"

Mary's voice grew strange: "When I came back, there was a footprint on the floor by Papa's body, and the front door was unlocked."

"A footprint?" Hector searched Mary's face, trying to decide if this was all some kind of lie.

"Yes . . . a bloody footprint . . . from a man's shoe, I think."

Hector said, "You're claiming someone else was in here with you that morning? Maybe saw all this?"

"Or the aftermath," Mary said. "It's not a *claim*. It's the gospel truth. And it's had me in fear ever since."

Walking to his Bel Air in a soft rain, Hannah took Hector's hand. "For you, most of all, that had to be *very* hard to hear."

Hector took a deep breath and let it out slowly, staring at a black Ford parked across the street. A man sat inside, smoking a cigarette. The profile was different now with the broken nose, but Hector was sure it was Donovan Creedy in the car.

Savoring the smell of the mountain rain, glad to be out of that crazy concrete house, Hector said, "I'm not sure I believe Mary about that. About her shooting Hem like that. I've been an author for a very long time, Hannah. I know a book pitch when I hear one. I think Mary might have been trying something out on us. Scribner isn't pleased with what they've seen of her planned memoir. But if she could take this crazy tale—this story about 'mercy' shooting Hem herself—and go to Knopf, say, or to Simon and Schuster?"

"You think that's all a lie?"

"Or maybe an exaggeration. Maybe it really happened as she says. Maybe not. Fact is, we may never know for sure."

He got the Chevy in gear and started driving back toward the Sun Valley complex. "I'm dropping you at the hotel—there's something I need to finish. Need some time alone to think, darlin'. Time to plot..."

Hannah smiled uncertainly, searching his face. "Plot a story?"

Hector nodded. "Of a sort."

If we could read the secret history of our enemies, we should find in each man's life sorrow and suffering enough to disarm all hostility.

—HENRY WADSWORTH LONGFELLOW

52.   LAST MOVES—1966

Hector stood by the window, looking down on the pedestrians bustling along Broadway in the rain. Mary and the publisher were chatting, following their handshake agreement.

Mary rose, said, "You coming, Lasso?"

"I'll catch up with you in a few minutes," Hector said. "We have some business to discuss about *my* new novel now."

Mary nodded and smiled her close-mouthed smile. A little tipsy after all the rye, she picked up her purse and tottered out the door to wait on Hector.

His publisher offered Hector whisky—top-shelf stuff now that the Widow Hemingway had departed.

"Have to thank you again, Hector. This is *huge* for us. Imagine what this will do when it becomes public. Can't imagine how Scribner is letting this one get away. Now, if I can just keep a lid on it until we're ready to release the book..."

Hector sipped his whisky, said, "I think your bigger problem is getting the ending you think you're buying with this memoir of Mary's. My advice to you is to write the contract closely. Otherwise, that ending might change on you."

"What do you mean? Why on earth would Mary recant, Hector?"

"Because she has every reason to," Hector said. "You know, there's no statute of limitations on murder."

Creedy walked briskly through the windswept streets of Greenwich Village, head down against the Alberta clipper that stung his eyes and made his ears burn. He'd gotten the call earlier in the morning. Marcus Shawn, his publisher at Silver Medallion, said that after years of courting the man, Shawn had finally persuaded a legendary figure in the industry to guest edit a few titles for Medallion's fall release schedule. It was, Marcus said, a tremendous coup for a paperback-only imprint.

Best of all, Marcus said the unnamed guest editor had singled out Creedy's newest, *Hell's Own Vixen*, as the likely lead title for this new sub-imprint to debut in September.

Creedy was beside himself with joy. After so many years alone at his typewriter, the tide was finally turning.

Now, practically jogging through the Village to the offices of Silver Medallion, Creedy wondered who this legendary editor might be. Maybe this next book would be the one that would finally vault him to hardcover publication. Maybe, in time, he and his new editor would gain legendary status as one of the great publishing partnerships. Like—well, yes, like Hemingway and Maxwell Perkins.

When he reached the Medallion building—well, brownstone—Marcus vigorously pumped Creedy's hand. "I'm excited, Donso. I hope you're excited, too!"

Grinning, Creedy said, "I am! Who is this editor?"

"My surprise for you, Donnie. He's right through that door."

Heart pounding, Donovan knocked once, then opened the door to his new editor's office. The lights were off in the office, and the only illumination came through the room's single window—a harsh shaft of winter sunlight. The man was standing in the window, his back to Creedy. The light through the window made the man a tall, slender silhouette.

Not sure how to begin, Creedy said, "It's me . . . Donovan Creedy."

A baritone voice, vaguely familiar, said, "Your novel has promise, Donovan. I see the possibilities in what's there now. But it's like freeing the statue from the stone. I won't lie to you—it's going to be hard work. Terrifically hard work for us both. But if you'll meet me halfway, I think we can make a real novel of what you've got there."

"Of . . . of course," Creedy said, trying to sound polite . . . not too resistant to the editing process. "But it can't be *that* much work."

Hell, Creedy thought his latest to be near perfect . . . mature . . . complex . . . gripping.

"Almost a total rewrite is required," the man said, shaking his head. "What's there now is meretricious, fatuous, and derivative. There's hardly any characterization, and it has no pace. The dialogue is wooden. The sex scenes are wince-inducing. And the book has no second act. But these things we can fix, with hard work and some creativity."

The man stepped from the light in the window and sat down on the corner of the desk, smiling.

Hector Lassiter said, "So what about it, Creedy? You man enough to write a real book under my editorial direction?"

Creedy snarled and slammed the door behind him. Through the door, Hector could hear Creedy hurling obscenities at Marcus Shawn.

Smiling, Hector lit a cigarette with his old Zippo, then followed Creedy out into the reception area. Creedy slammed the door behind him, still cursing as he stormed down the hallway.

Shawn shook his head and said, "Damn, that didn't go well. What the hell happened, Hector?"

Hector smiled and planted his butt on the corner of the receptionist's desk. He winked and smiled at the buxom redhead, flipping through her Rolodex. "Oh, Don will come around, Marcus, no sweat there. He's just playing the artiste. Suspect Don's never really faced an editor who truly cares. Cruel to be kind, you know? This was just the rough wooing."

He found Creedy's address and pulled it loose from the chrome rings. He winked again at the receptionist and said. "You're very sweet; I *promise* to bring this back, darlin'."

Donovan Creedy keyed himself into his Georgetown apartment. It was raining and frigid and they were predicting an ice storm for the District of Columbia . . . possible power outages from fallen limbs and lines.

Surveying his options following Lassiter's treachery, Creedy was racing a deadline on a revision of a long-languishing, unfinished novel for a new prospective publisher. It had been conceived to be Creedy's big book—a historical thriller on the Bay of Pigs as only Creedy could tell it. Only now did he feel he truly had the reach to deliver the novel he envisioned. He planned to get a big fire going, then settle into his leather writing chair with his pipe, some good bourbon, and a notepad, and think about something that might punch up the back end of the book a tad. He'd put a little Wagner on the stereo and . . .

He paused, standing in the front room of his place.

He sniffed. Funny how the mind works—he could already scent that fire.

Creedy reached his study and flipped on the light. There was a man sitting in his writing chair, helping himself to Donovan's liquor and work-in-progress. This big crackling fire was already going . . .

Hector tossed the manuscript pages aside and picked up the long-barreled Peacemaker from his lap. He pointed the Colt at Creedy's right eye.

"I knew you wouldn't have the stones to submit to a real editor," Hector said. "Alas. But I see you've tried to address a few of my concerns. Well, anyway, take a load off, Agent Creedy. I've come to reclaim some property."

Creedy was actually frightened . . . trying to figure out how Lassiter got in . . . and got in *safely*. So much for all the security his money could buy. Creedy said, "What 'property'?"

"Hem's suicide note, for starters. There at the end, *you* were always watching Hem. Always there. You were in Idaho that morning, weren't you? Followed Hem all the way from the Mayo Clinic and back to Ketchum, I'd wager. When Mary bolted from his body, you crept into that crazy house . . . stole Hem's last letter. I've come for it, and don't try to feed me some lie. Even you couldn't destroy a document like that one."

Creedy surprised him: "You're right . . . I *couldn't*. When I read it, it was very strange what happened. I finally came to like the son of a bitch, a little." This funny smile: "Hem really was a magnificent bastard, wasn't he?"

"Yeah," Hector said. "The best. The letter—I want it *now*. Otherwise I'm going to start with your fingers." He hefted his gun. "I brought *a lot* of bullets, and these old walls are thick."

Creedy crossed to his desk. He saw now there was something there in the fireplace—reel-to-reel tapes crackled amidst the logs. Hector said, "Your Topping House collection."

Hector followed Creedy to his desk. He said, "If you pull a gun, Creedy . . ."

The agent tossed a yellowed piece of paper to Hector. It was worn at the folds . . . as if it had been read many times. Hector opened it just enough to confirm Hem's distorted but recognizable, downward-sloping hand. He slipped it into the pocket of his sports jacket. "Thanks for this, Creedy. Now, just two more things: Hem's suitcase. Fetch it now or I'll blow holes through your kneecaps."

Creedy stared at the big old Colt, then decided to comply. This was a mere plot reversal, nothing more. It was a chess move, Creedy figured. Not the match.

Standing at the door, hefting Hem's long-lost valise, Hector said, "Now, that *last* thing: that morning, July second, 1961. What did you see? Did Mary *really* shoot Hem?"

Creedy shrugged. "The window was covered with dew. The rising sun cast a glare on the window glass. Honestly? I saw more of my own re-flection than anything that happened inside that damned house. I just don't know."

Hector thought Creedy was telling the truth . . . and really, deep down, did he truly want to know? The prospect Hem shot himself wasn't much more comforting than the notion Mary might have done the deed at his request. He said:

"There's one more thing you can tell me. Victoria ... did she really kill herself?"

Creedy searched Hector's blue eyes. Hector looked resolved. Creedy figured if he told Hector the truth he'd get himself shot.

He'd come to Victoria, vengeful, angry out of his mind. They'd argued, and he had strangled her. Creedy had meant to subdue her, to scare her. But he'd choked her to death before he realized what he was doing.

He put her head in the oven and turned up the gas to make it look like a suicide.

Still searching Hector's eyes, he said, "I think she killed herself because of all the things that went wrong in her life. I blame *you*."

Hector considered that ... then strode over and drove the butt of his Colt into Creedy's temple.

Hector sat in a booth alone in the back of the Italian restaurant. The freezing rain was lashing the windows, and the trees lining the streets of Georgetown looked like glass sculptures. He took another sip of red wine and pulled the letter from his pocket. He read it five times:

Poor dearest Pickle:

There is no surprise in this.
I'm awfully sorry for the mess.
The body's been dying for some time (from the moment, really, that second plane went down at Butiaba), and the rest has raced in pursuit these past months. It has all finally gone to pieces and I am beat to the wide beyond promise of recuperation or recovery.
Now it's over and you can get on with your life.
I've spent my mornings since the last war working at four books I can't finish. And all of these last, unfruitful years spent rummaging through the *remise* of my memory for likely material has only stirred up old ghosts and guilts. Untenable regrets that all of the bottles of giant killer I am now denied and all of the last bits of love that you might still muster towards me cannot palliate.
A writer who can no longer write can no longer live.

The books I can't bring to term have only underscored the sad fact we both have known for too long: I can't pull out of this one by simply enduring and sweating it out as I have so many times in the past. I have come to accept that I am now one for whom there'll be no *belle époque*.

It's bad now, darling, worse than it has ever been. I could wait and waste time hoping for a change, but hope is such a taunting, bloody moveable feast and I would probably be left worse off and maybe unable to act when I later truly knew change was not to be.

I've just lain awake for hours in that dark time you well know is worst for me—hours spent thinking about it all and weighing the bloody, unsatisfactory options. Awake or asleep (and it's harder to discern the difference with all the pills and disrupted memory from the shock treatments) it is all a horrible bloody fucking nightmare from which there is no awakening. All things toil to weariness and a man cannot (satisfactorily) utter it—not deprived of his instrument.

So this: Self-indictment and self-contempt, contrition and release, self-administered at the tug of a trigger.

Please try to make the boys see how it had to be this way.

I'm truly sorry again, sweetheart, for all the mess.

Love always,

Ernest

P.S. Kitten, destroy this note before calling anyone.

Hector read it over a last time. He'd decided to honor Hem's wishes—the last thing he could do for his oldest friend.

He scooted the ashtray closer and got out the Zippo given to him by Hem so many decades before.

Hector flipped the Zippo open with one hand and set fire to the corner of Hem's note.

The letter curled to charred ash. Hector looked at the suitcase … thought about reading a few pieces of Hem's or his own over another glass of wine, but the restaurant was closing down early for the ice storm.

Sighing, Hector slipped on his overcoat, buttoned it over his scarf, and slid out the door into the eye-stinging storm. He walked about twenty yards when the young tough stepped from a door and shoved a gun into his throat. "Your wallet," the kid said. "And the bag."

Hector said, "Whoa there, son. You do not—"

Another young tough snuck up behind Hector—hit him in the back of the head with a bar of soap shoved into a sock. The blow sent Hector sprawling to the sidewalk.

Hector came to ten minutes later. He wretched once and looked around at the icy, empty streets: His wallet lay at his feet, less the money inside.

Hem's suitcase was missing. Hector struggled to his feet, cursing.

Donovan Creedy drove through Silver Spring, trying to outrun the storm, stealing glances at the precious old suitcase on the passenger seat next to him.

The cure for crime is not the electric chair, but the high chair.

—J. Edgar Hoover

CREEDY—Los Angeles, 1969

The first time it happened, Creedy was running surveillance on the Watts Writers Workshop headquarters. The Workshop was a creative writing group for young black writers that had been founded by screenwriter Bud Schulberg after the disaster of the Watts riots. Another gambit gone awry: Creedy and his fellows had finessed racial tensions to a fever pitch. The hope had been the riots would go on a good bit longer . . . require more military and civilian intervention. With luck, the whole lot might have been annihilated. Schulberg was ex-OSS . . . among the first to the concentration camps. A bleeding heart. Cocksucker.

Creedy had watched actor Yaphet Kotto leave the Workshop HQ—marveling the actor could both be a Negro *and* a Jew. Creedy saw some members of the Watts Prophets, joking with one another.

The Bureau had deeply penetrated the Workshop, salting the group and much of its literary output with radical "Kill Whitey!" sentiments as an excuse to crush the Workshop under the boot heel of COINTELPRO.

A bit later, Creedy was paying off his informant, Darthard Perry, behind a Watts record store. Creedy had identified Perry as his best candidate to destroy the Workshop. Creedy had just finished with Perry when he saw Hector Lassiter in a window reflection, smiling at him.

Startled, Creedy turned, searching for Lassiter's face, but saw only black faces looking back at him. He shrugged it off that time: After all, Hector Lassiter was famously two years' dead—shot to death in 1967 by a junkie journalist come to interview the dying crime writer at his home in New Mexico.

But then Creedy thought he saw Lassiter again in Georgetown, and once more in New York City at a signing for Creedy's latest thriller.

That last time, as Creedy autographed books, Lassiter seemed to be standing at the back of the line, smiling mockingly at Creedy for several minutes.

After that last episode, Creedy almost began believing in ghosts.

Then, a month later, he received a letter that chilled him:

So, Donovan, you're Russian by birth, and I hear connections with your Red motherland linger via Cuba. And there's the matter of your mother's affair with that Jewish fella from Odessa—a coupling that produced you. They say the child is the father to the man. In your case, I'd swap out "man" for "monster." Rest assured, I'm going to pass this intelligence on to your D.C. superiors at the proper moment—the *precise* instant that it will do you the most damage. Wait for it, cocksucker.

—HL

Creedy had been so unnerved by that note, he'd gone straight to Hoover...eventually talked the Director into ordering exhumation of Hector Lassiter's body to confirm his death.

The night before the body was to be dug up, someone else had allegedly broken into the grave and stolen Lassiter's head—some prank attributed to Yale's Skull and Bones Society.

What was left of the body—along with the remains of Lassiter's daughter—had been briskly moved to some other, unmarked grave before Creedy or Hoover could intercede.

Hoover's reaction to all that had been predictably self-centered: "Stands to reason Skull and Bones *would* do that with Lassiter's head, Mr. Creedy. They're closely knit to the CIA, and when those bastards heard *I* was interested in exhuming Lassiter? Well, they *had* to do something like this. Best to just let it go, Agent Creedy."

But Donovan Creedy *couldn't* let it go. He still harbored these *fears....*

Creedy kept seeing Hector Lassiter everywhere he looked.

Hoover said, "Maybe you need a leave of absence, Mr. Creedy. Perhaps those chemicals Lassiter slipped you all those years ago are having a residual effect of some kind."

That thought horrified Creedy—he couldn't countenance the loss of his own faculties.

He snarled back at Hoover, "I'm fucking *fine.*"

BOOK SEVEN

Winner Take Nothing

Justice is incidental to law and order.

—J. Edgar Hoover

53. ENDGAME—Washington, D.C., May 2, 1972

Andrew Langley looked up from his lobster bisque and nearly choked. He stammered, daubed at his chin with a napkin, then managed, "You're supposed to be dead."

"I am dead," the man said. "Keep thinking of me that way. But I've brought you something." The man tossed the file on the table next to Langley's boilermaker.

"I've been watching your career with interest, Andy. You've come up in Hoover's world. I think what's in there can take you over the top. You have an old agent in the Bureau named Donovan Creedy. I know you know the fella, but you don't know this: Since the 1920s, Creedy's been a loose cannon—running some crazy schemes against writers and artists for Hoover. It's threatening to become an issue for the Bureau—to go wide. The folder will explain it all. Creedy would make a useful scapegoat if the public ever learns. He's also got some troubling ties to Fidel...stuff I don't think Hoover knows."

The man lit up a cigarette with an old Zippo. He smiled through smoke, said to the FBI agent, "You feds *do* still execute your traitors, don't you, Andrew?"

The FBI man shook his head. "Afraid not. Not anymore."

The man nodded, thought about it. This wink and a wicked smile: "You know, I think I have a *better* option for you. Some nice and fearful symmetry in this one."

———

J. Edgar Hoover sat in the booth, fidgeting with the white linen napkin, looking around the restaurant. The diners looked back; everyone knew his face. Not just in this town, but *everywhere*.

His hands were damp; he rarely went anywhere without security, but knowing what could be done with taps and mikes and lip-readers, the Director couldn't risk anything less than being here alone, just as the man who arranged the rendezvous had insisted.

The Director stared at the capital dome in the distance; the sun burned across its ivory surface—so white it hurt his eyes.

He'd come so far from so little.

Now this man, goddamn him, was threatening all that, just as the other, Hemingway, had.

This motion; a long shadow falling across him.

The well-dressed man slid into the booth, smiling.

Hoover searched the pale blue eyes, said, "You're remarkably fit for a dead man. I congratulate you on your ruse. You even fooled *me*."

"Fooling you, and those like you, was a major objective," the man said. "You made 1966 and 'sixty-seven a living hell for me, just as you intended. I needed breathing room. Time to savor what's left of life. And time to *dig*. Hem savored reading his own obituaries; I enjoyed writing mine."

Hoover grunted. "What do you propose to end this stalemate?"

"Your resignation," the man said. "It's in all the papers that Nixon wants it, too. It's well past time you packed it in. It's forty-eight years, to the month, since you were put in charge of the Bureau. Too long for any man, even a good one, which you certainly *aren't*, to hold so much power, hombre. Christ knows you've abused that power terribly."

The man threw a parcel on the table between them. "There you go, Director. All the documents I've found these past years, plus odds and ends from Hem. Taken together, it's incontrovertible. But you'll note those are all copies."

"This isn't what we agreed to," Hoover said, his face growing red. "Where are the originals, goddamn you?"

"I've been reading the local papers. I've come to enjoy the work of these two young, enterprising reporters. This stuff on Watergate they've been doing fascinates me. So, I've given *them* the documents. Expect you'll make the *Post*'s morning edition. It's a hell of a revelation. Particularly after the Bureau's actions related to the Ku Klux Klan...to the Watts Writers Workshop."

The man stood, preparing to leave.

The Director stared up at him; spittle on his chin: "What? No asking for money to stop this? What do *you* get from this?"

The man smiled at Hoover, shrugged. "Satisfaction, I guess. I mean, seeing your face like this after so many years bumping up against your minions and machinations? Well, it does my heart good. That, and maybe getting a big piece back for an old friend you and your goon squad put in the ground."

He left the FBI director sitting there, desolate and sputtering... Hoover's fat bulldog face red with fury.

The man swung into the vintage Chevy. His one-eyed chauffeur said, "I put the top up; looks like a storm coming."

"A big one," the man said, smiling. "Gonna be worse for some than others."

Rolling past the Washington Monument, his driver said, "He bought it?"

"Pretty sure."

"What are you *really* going to do with those documents?"

"Hold on to them. Wait and see how Hoover jumps. I'll bide my time."

"This was probably crazy...."

The man waved a hand; shook out a Pall Mall. "Time will tell. Let's try and be patient." Age had finally given the man some of that—some *patience*.

The young poet asked, "Where to now?"

The click of a Zippo closing. "Not sure yet, Bud. Let's just keep driving...."

From the A.P. wire, May 3, 1972:

J. EDGAR HOOVER DEAD

Legendary Bureau chief dies of massive heart attack

Andrew Langley watched Creedy in the padded room through the one-way glass.

It *was* the perfect solution in terms of making Creedy's other masters squirm: Creedy as a corpse would allay fears. A mentally unbalanced Creedy, on the other hand? Donovan Creedy rendered a drooling loon deprived of any self-control or will? That would give his CIA handlers and some others cold sweats.

They were just fitting the rubber bit in Creedy's mouth, preparing to administer the juice.

The young doctor fidgeted. He was in a fix, sure enough: The organizations he'd belonged to in college were, well, sure, they were *lavender*.

But this FBI honcho had told him they could make his dubious school affiliations appear *Red*—cost him his position at the hospital. Maybe nullify his very medical license.

Still, he had to try: He said to the man, Langley, "*Seven* consecutive courses of ECT at this level? That could destroy Mr. Creedy's higher brain function."

Langley smiled sadly and patted the young doctor's shoulder. "A chance *you'll* just have to take."

BOOK EIGHT

In Our Time

I know that ghosts *have* wandered on earth. Be with me always—take any form—drive me mad! only *do* not leave me with this abyss, where I cannot find you!

—Emily Brontë

54.   R.I.P.

Hannah and Bridget left Ketchum and returned with Hector to his home in New Mexico.

Hannah MacArthur-Lassiter spent a year writing Mary's story on the nights her own writing was difficult.

Usually these nights came when the milk wouldn't come, and her breasts ached. Worrying about its failure to come—the milk or the words—only made things worse.

Gradually, however, the manuscript took shape and Bridget was weaned.

Hannah had completed her manuscript and locked it away in a succession of safe-deposit boxes.

Years later, single again, Hannah read the posthumous books as they continued to appear: A collection of Papa's Toronto journalism and *The Dangerous Summer* and the edited, bowdlerized *The Garden of Eden*. Gutted as the latter was, it sparked pride in Hannah—Papa was trying for something new and fresh and far beyond anything he or anyone else had done before or even tried, and she found herself goaded on by her master's example.

Over the course of many years, she continued to correspond with Mary, the flow eventually slowing to a trickle . . . exchanging phone calls on birthdays and holidays.

Hannah was weighing an offer to teach in Glasgow—everything in her said, *Go.*

In November 1986, six weeks before she was to leave for Scotland,

Hannah was sitting in a lounge at Ohio State University with her research assistant, Chris Lyon. He was just a few years older than Hannah's daughter, and a former student of Hannah's. When Chris was an undergraduate, and a student of Hannah's, following a long night with her class in a campus bar—a night of drinking and discussing the works of Hemingway and Hector Lassiter—Hannah, the worse for wine, had taken Chris to her bed, and he remained her occasional lover. Chris insisted on writing material that was closer to crime fiction than the novels Hannah thought he should be writing. Because of his proclivities, and his enthusiasm for Hector's work, she had recruited Chris to help her assemble a collection of Hector's neglected short fiction.

Hannah and Chris were sitting in the lounge together, sipping coffee and debating story sequences, when someone mentioned offhandedly that Mary Hemingway had "finally" died.

"Let the games begin," the English literature professor said with a grin.

Hannah shook her head, alone with her terrible wisdom.

If you reveal your secrets to the wind you should not blame the wind for revealing them to the trees.

—Kahlil Gibran

55.   THE BURDEN

They buried the old woman in a plot several incongruous feet from her famous husband's right hand, nested between twin evergreen trees.

Mary Welsh, the middling journalist from Leech Lake, Minnesota, selected for herself a twin memorial marker to the one denoting her Nobel-awarded husband's grave. Mary was the only one of his wives who would ever be buried with Papa and with his last name.

At their feet lay the grave of a Basque shepherd; the Hemingways were flanked by the graves of dead local chums.

Pointing at the big flat marker, Bridget said, "Where's Dad's? Is it like these?"

"No, not like these." Hannah took her daughter's hand.

In a corner of the Ketchum Cemetery where nobody but the groundskeeper would likely venture, Hannah found the small sunken plot of ground that had been dug with posthole diggers—looking like some half-assed, underfunded core sample from which some strange weed was beginning to sprout. Hannah hoicked it, hoping it wasn't poisonous.

A small marker stood crookedly over the tiny hole. It read in part:

Here lies Richard Paulson
"Much wisdom is much grief . . ."

Seeing it for the first time, set in stone, Hannah regretted the spiteful epitaph she had chosen for the dead professor whose book she had midwifed. Then she remembered the one she had first proposed, half-facetiously—the one that almost made the marker salesman hang up on her: *"He drank anything too thin to eat . . . now he's dead as Phlebas."*

Back at the hotel, Bridget sat on the bed, sifting through the pages of her mother's manuscript that Hannah had sentimentally packed for her last trip to Ketchum.

Bridget restacked the pages and lifted the pile that weighed so heavily in her hands. She bit her lip. "Is this all true, Mother?"

"As it was told to me, yes, every word."

"What the hell are you going to do with the thing, Mom?"

Hannah honestly felt as she had once told Richard: The revelation that Papa was shot by a henpecking wife would mutilate the myth. Papa's greatness would be compromised by the tabloid madness triggered by Mary's confession to murdering her internationally beloved husband.

But this revelation, which Hannah now had within her power to reveal, was something else again. How would the world regard an Ernest Hemingway who was a casualty of a mercy killing? What was it Hector had said so long ago? *Print the legend?*

Would euthanasia at the hands of a poorly chosen wife threaten Papa's place in the canon? Certainly it would be so for those critics and scholars who still clung to the "code" interpretation of Papa's work.

Euthanasia was inconsistent with stoical, laconic men who could be destroyed, but not defeated. Begging your wife to blow your head off would almost certainly be regarded as cowardly by *those* Papa aficionados. Maybe more cowardly than blowing out your own brains.

Asked for his opinion again when they were alone after Mary's revelation, Hector had said, "May be best to let the people have their myth, Hannah. That's my vote. Whether Mary did it or not, Hem would have gotten around to it eventually anyway. He'd have found a way. He rightly wanted to die."

Sometimes Hannah wondered if, in the end, Mary had indeed conned them. What better revenge for a spiteful widow than to assume responsibility for her famous husband's last decisive act? In essence, Mary's claim robbed Papa of the last thing that was truly his own.

Had Mary imagined—or worse, faked—her Hemingway's mercy killing?

Had Mary's demented confession been an absinthe-stoked scam?

Hannah truly hoped so.

Even so, it was a hell of a story—a sleazy tell-all upon which to build a tabloid career.

But how to follow the thing up?

Perhaps an exposé alleging a drunken, murderous Scott Fitzgerald had faked his own death and burned down Highland Hospital in a murder-nine-women-to-slay-Zelda gambit?

Maybe a breathless account of Virginia Woolf's murder by drowning at the hand of cousin (and retrospective Jack the Ripper suspect) James Kenneth Stephen?

Or maybe something *worse*: Make a case that it wasn't Papa dead under Mary's bedroom that July morning in 1961. He faked his death and is risen—let the rickety Papa sightings commence.

Hell, Hannah knew another fiction writer of similar vintage who had done just that, bless his dark heart.

It would be a dirty, if *lucrative*, career.

Lightning flashed through half-closed blinds. A gusty wind lashed rain against the glass.

The eternal quandary loomed: publish or perish?

Hannah said, "I've never been able to decide, Bridget. So I'm leaving this for you. You take care of it. Keep it . . . destroy it . . . use it. I leave it in your hands."

Bridget nodded. Then she said, "Did you ever finish that novel you started with Hector's help?" Hannah shook her head again, unable to look her daughter in the eye.

We dance round in a ring and suppose,
But the Secret sits in the middle and knows.

—ROBERT FROST

56.   NIGHT TRAIN—Winter 2010

That night, the rain still falling following her mother's funeral, Bridget MacArthur dreamed about Papa:

The red-jacketed porter stowed Bridget's big bags and the small valise containing her mother's manuscript of Mary's tale that crescendoed with the real story—how it truly was—that morning of July 2, 1961.

Her compartment was small, but roomy enough for Bridget to stretch out her legs during the long journey on the night train from Paris to Switzerland.

Bridget took a long last look at the small valise, then checked her watch: thirty minutes until scheduled departure.

She wandered out under the Gare de Lyon's glass dome, through which she could faintly see the fast-moving storm clouds, nearly invisible in the gathering dusk. Occasionally she glanced back at the men and women empty-handedly boarding and vacating the Paris-Lausanne Express.

Roaming amid the newsstands and snack carts, Bridget bought a couple of magazines and a bottle of Evian. As she sipped her bottled water, she peered up at the smartly dressed diners in the Train Bleu restaurant. The pigeons that flew in under the glass canopy with the trains foraged around her feet. She crumbled up some bread from her sandwich bun and sprinkled it at her feet for the birds.

Bridget watched the diners in the Train Bleu, and wondered if the two of them would ever have the money to eat there.

She heard the last call to board and dashed back to her train car, taking the steps two at a time. The porter quickly moved aside to make room for her as she vaulted up and past him. Bridget held her breath as she turned sideways, squeezing by the other riders negotiating the narrow vestibule.

She closed her eyes as she entered her lonely compartment, raising her head to the level where she guessed the shelf was, upon which the porter had placed the valise containing the manuscript.

Bridget opened her eyes and saw that the valise was missing.

A contented sigh . . .

She sat down, curling her legs up under herself, and stared at the empty space where she had left the bag.

Bridget smiled, hugging herself and imagining how pleased Papa would be when he met her train in the morning and heard what she had done.

Do you suppose you could ask Edgar's boys to stop stepping on my heels? They think I am an enemy alien. It's getting tiresome.

—JOHN STEINBECK, WRITING TO ATTORNEY
GENERAL FRANCIS BIDDLE IN 1942

ACKNOWLEDGMENTS

Print the Legend is a work of fiction, but like *Head Games* and *Toros & Torsos*, it is constructed upon a foundation of unsettling historical fact and cold-eyed supposition, nearly all of which is based on official documents and public records.

Countless nonfiction books were consulted during the composition of this novel, but most useful was Michael Reynolds's multivolume biography of Hem, including *The Young Hemingway*; *Hemingway: The Paris Years*; *Hemingway: The Homecoming*; *Hemingway: The 1930s*, and *Hemingway: The Final Years*.

Want to *really* know Hem? Seek out Reynolds's books—they are *definitive*.

I'm indebted to my wife, Debbie, and our daughters, Madeleine and Yeats, for their love and support, and for making room for the writing. It truly wouldn't be possible without them.

Grateful thanks to my editor, John Schoenfelder, for his belief, dedication, unstinting hard work, inspiration, and for invoking the name of E. Howard Hunt. Thanks also to David Rotstein, Naomi Shulman, and Sarah Melnyk.

Continuing thanks to Svetlana Pironko and Michael O'Brien, who set me on this path.

Thanks also to Madeira James for all her great work on my Web site, and to Recorded Books' Tom Stechschulte, the "voice" of Hector Lassiter.

I'm also indebted to all the independent bookshops and mystery specialty stores and booksellers who have taken the Hector Lassiter series to their hearts and urged the novels on their customers, as well as librarians who've recommended the books to their patrons.

Finally, much gratitude to Valerie Hemingway, and especially to the late George Plimpton, for sharing their personal Ernest Hemingway memories with me.

When *The Garden of Eden* was finally released as a painfully bowdlerized novel, a pacer racetrack's promotional scheme brought several celebrities through my Ohio hometown. Most attending reporters beelined to fashion designer Oleg Cassini and billiard player Steve Mizerak. I, alone, gravitated to Plimpton, spending much time discussing *The Garden of Eden*, its ties to Hemingway's short story "The Sea Change," the art of interviewing, and all manner of Hemingway anecdotes from Hem's one true interviewer.

Only in retrospect do we see the moments that most matter: for me, that was one.

I interviewed Valerie Hemingway upon the release of her own memoir, *Running with the Bulls: My Years with the Hemingways* (Ballantine Books, 2004) and her memories and insights into Mary Hemingway's personality were invaluable.

For those who doubt aspects of this story as regards Hoover-era FBI harassment of novelists and poets, the most cursory of Google searches will reveal acres of information on J. Edgar Hoover's insane and contemptible campaign to stalk and cow pivotal twentieth-century American authors and performing artists.

For a more detailed account of the FBI's surveillance of many of the twentieth century's greatest novelists, poets, and painters, see Herbert Mitgang's *Dangerous Dossiers: Exposing the Secret War Against America's Greatest Authors* (Donald L. Fine, 1988).

Those around Hem at the time believed he was paranoid or deluded when he insisted he was under constant FBI surveillance. Now we know that the FBI was not only *always* dogging Hem's steps, but Hoover's agents followed him straight into the Mayo Clinic and are reported to have consulted with Ernest Hemingway's physicians.

As has been ruefully noted by pivotal Hemingway biographers, "even paranoids have real enemies."